NIGHTMARES
OF
nature

HarperCollins*Publishers*

Acknowledgements

For Samantha

HarperCollins*Publishers*
77-85 Fulham Palace Road
London W6 8JB
United Kingdom

© Richard Matthews 1995

ISBN 0 00 220015 5

Colour reproduction by
Radstock Repro, Bath
Printed in Great Britain by
Butler & Tanner Ltd, Frome
and London

The subject of this book necessitated in-depth research of a wealth of topics and animals from all corners of the globe. Few people can claim to be equally knowledgeable about subjects as disparate as the behaviour of great white sharks, the chemical composition of bee venom or the psychology of human fear. I certainly do not. In researching the material I have relied heavily on help from others and have drawn upon the experiences and knowledge of a great number of people, some of whom have spent a life-time studying animals that I know very little about. To them all I am indebted. In particular I would like to thank; Isaac Marks for his guidance on human fears and phobias; Brock Fenton, Les Hall, Gareth Jones and Ewe Schmidt for their help with bats; Paul Rodriguez and Nicola Bradbaer for bees; Stephen Herrero and Steve and Marilyn French helped with brown bears; Carmen Arocha-Pinango for caterpillars; Robert Hartwick for box jellyfish; Gary Ferguson for chameleons; Jonathon Hutton and Grahame Webb for crocodiles; Trooper Walsh for Komodo dragons: Ramon Sukumar and Cynthia Moss for their help on elephants; Harold Cogger for sea snakes; Zakaria Benlasfar, Goyffon and Tim Benton for scorpions; Gonzalo Moya-Borja and Martin Hall for screw worms; Romulus Whitaker, Harry Green, Mark O'Shea, and Bill Lamar for helping with snakes; David Warrell for information on snake bites; Bernard Stone for ticks; Ullas Karanth for his knowledge of tigers; Kim Holland for tiger sharks; Hendryk Okarma for wolves: John McCosker, Mike DeGruy and Peter Scoones for help with sharks and marine animals in general.

During our travels around the world our task was made infinitely easier by a great many people who often went out of their way to advise us and ease the innumerable problems we encountered. They include; in Australia Lee Moyes and Graham Lean; in Brazil Fatima Resende; in Colombia Camillo Arroyo; in Costa Rica Mamood Sassa; in France Parc Zoologique de Paris; in India Jane Saberwhal and Dattaraja; in Kenya Willie Roberts, Joseph Tibong and Viewfinders; in New Caledonia Pascale Joannot; in Tanzania Mr. B.T. Mugongo; in Thailand Tina Fresco; in the UK Ian Dean-Netscher; in the USA Paula Kelly and Keith Turner; in Venezuela Julio Garcia, and Dan Freeman; and in Zambia Jo Pope.

A number of people kindly gave permission for us to film reconstructions of dramatic encounters that they had had with dangerous animals. Our research into those incidents and the subsequent filming of them often brought back painful memories for those concerned. To them I owe much indeed for their experiences have added life to the text and the films and have provided us with another insight into the lives of animals. In Florida Diane Hooper helped with the shipwreck and shark encounter incident. In Venezuela Bill Lamar relived his encounter with an anaconda. In Australia Valerie Plumwood permitted us to write about and reconstruct her almost fatal encounter with a crocodile and Janine Dean relived her encounter with a huntsman spider. In Wyoming, Barbara Moore helped in the reconstruction of her encounter with a grizzly bear. Alan Root talked about his near fatal experience with a hippopotamus in Kenya. In Tunisia the Tagyoussi family allowed us to film their daily life in the oasis they share with scorpions. And in Brazil the Buritos family relived their nightmare with vampire bats.

This book was written whilst we were filming five documentary programmes for the BBC and National Geographic Television. However, neither would have been produced without the assistance of a production team of dedicated and talented individuals who have worked alongside me over the last two years. Their names and those of the other main behind-the-scenes contributors are listed at the end of the book. I am indebted to my producers, Mary Colwell, Martin Hughes-Games and Adrian Warren who helped sift through mountains of research and devised the story lines for the television programmes which I have used as a backbone for the chapters. Mary Colwell helped write the chapter on creepy crawlies and her sound advice on how the book could be structured was invaluable. The basis of all good films and books is good research and for this we had a team who assiduously tracked down information from the flimsiest of sources. Mary Singh of the National Geographic Society, and Clare Brook and Hilary Jeffkins helped in the early stages of our research. Tim Martins' enthusiasm for all things reptilian was infectious; to him I am particularly indebted for his work on the chapters about cold-blooded creatures and the night and for his eye-catching pictures which enhance the book. Jan Castles' knowledge of the underwater world was invaluable and her attention to detail and stubbornness even under my most scathing questioning frequently steered me from pitfalls. Peter France made general cooments on the text and gave us insight into the historic aspects of dangerous animals. Honor Peters was given the task of collating the information and correcting my grammar and helped me meet the tight deadlines set by our publishers.

It often comes as a surprise to many to learn how long natural history television programmes take to make. In this instance, the series was produced under the most hectic of schedules, and yet it still took eighteen months to complete. However, planning for the series began three years before production started. As an independent producer it was a worrying time during which I never knew for certain whether my efforts would ever be rewarded. I am greatly indebted to my agents Ron Devillier and Joan Lanigan for their faith in my ideas and abilities and for helping with all the negotiations which eventually led to the series being produced.

National Geographic expressed an early interest in "Nightmares of Nature"; without their commitment the series would never have been produced. In particular I would like to thank Tim Kelly, Tom Simon, Michael Rosenfeld, Cathy Mc Connell and Pam Hogan for their support of what must have seemed a high-risk and expensive venture. Television series are today only possible with the cooperation and financial support of a number of co-producers. In the BBC Natural History Unit I found a kindred spirit in Alastair Fothergill who instantly recognised the freshness of our ideas. Together with Mark Reynolds of BBC Enterprises Alastair's commitment to the series permitted those ideas to become celluloid reality.

The impact of this book owes much to the fabulous pictures which grace the pages. Although I am a keen stills photographer the scope of the book far exceeded the subjects I have photographed. In compiling the book we have drawn from the work of many talented photographers from around the world and to them all I owe thanks. Roger Sapsford and Mark Reynolds at Fuji went out of their way to see that we always had enough cine and stills stock, and Chris Elworthy at Canon UK helped with stills equipment.

When I was very young I was fortunate to travel to many exotic lands with my parents. It gave me a fascination of places, people and animals around the world – an interest that has influenced my career ever since. This book is, in a way, a culmination of all those years travelling and many years in natural history film-making. It has been a life frequently of intense pressure and hard work, yet it is the most rewarding of careers and one which I would not change in a million years. It has given me the opportunity of meeting some extraordinarily gifted and fascinating people in far flung places and has provided me with many unforgettable moments whilst watching and filming wild animals. Fifteen years ago I was fortunate to get a job as a researcher with the renowned Natural History Unit of the BBC in Bristol which gave me a solid grounding in film production. However, my career took a dramatic turn when ten years ago I left the BBC, turned freelance and took up camerawork. That move was only made possible by the support of my elder brother, David Matthews whose generous financial assistance and enthusiasm for all my ideas, however risky, made it possible for me to purchase my own camera equipment and invest in my own films.

From the very start of my freelance career Samantha has been by my side. Her love of the wild and concern for all living things has been a beacon of light in the most testing of times. Her presence has not merely been a support but also an inspiration.

Producing this book alongside the television series was only made possible by the hard work and expertise of a dedicated team of people from my publishers, Harper Collins. Jennifer Fry researched and displayed the illustrations with flair and professionalism, whilst Myles Archibald not only added intelligibility to the text, but also steered the project through from concept to final publication. To all and everyone I am grateful.

Richard Matthews, Bristol, July, 1995

Contents

Foreword

The idea for Nightmares of Nature came to me in 1990, on a filming trip to Western Australia. Australia boasts some of the most unusual and fascinating wildlife on Earth. It also harbours some of the world's most dangerous and venomous animals; among them funnel-web spiders, taipans, salt-water crocodiles, box jellyfish and great white sharks. I began to wonder if these much maligned creatures lived up to their lurid reputations.

I had a feeling that most of it was hype – I frequently film potentially lethal animals, but hazardous encounters are rare. This is because my job as a cameraman depends on my knowing my subject as intimately as possible. By learning about individual animals I become able to judge their moods and behaviour, which helps me to predict what they are likely to do next. It's this knowledge that enables me to film my subjects unobtrusively, sometimes in very close proximity, without exposing myself to unnecessary danger. It is ignorance that puts us at risk.

Because sensational stories sell well, a great deal of what is published and transmitted is very biased. In Nightmares of Nature I undertook from the outset to produce a series of films and a book that, as far as possible, described the dangerous and venomous animals of the world without bias. In attempting to present a realistic picture, I have not shied away from pinpointing those animals that are truly dangerous. Some people may feel that this can only be detrimental to the reputation of an animal, but I believe that a realistic view can only be achieved by presenting the facts as openhandedly as possible. Media sensationalism, and the playing down by conservationists of the threat posed by some creatures, add to the swarm of myths surrounding nightmare animals. The truth is that although there are many lethally equipped creatures, very few actively seek to injure man. Our main concern should not be about those few animals that are lethal, but about those that indirectly cause illness and death by spreading disease organisms such as malaria. In fact, it is animals that irritate us by their continual biting and stinging which have the greatest impact on our day to day lives.

The series and the book are related, the information presented in the latter being an expansion of the ideas in the films. It is hoped that, although neither can claim to be definitive, one will complement the other, and lead to a better understanding of the natural world for viewers and readers. I have divided the subject of nightmarish animals into six chapters. The first chapter deals with the psychology of fear, and the way we perceive animals. The subsequent five chapters deal with different groups of animals. 'Maneaters' deals with the large land animals; "The Deep" looks at animals of fresh and salt water; "In Cold Blood" delves into the lives of reptiles and amphibians; "Squirm" looks at creepy crawlies; and "A Cry in the Dark" uncovers the secret lives of nocturnal animals. Each chapter opens with a nightmare scenario – a true-life encounter with a dangerous animal. It then goes on to explore other animals in the group, and the weapons, behaviour, or physical traits which endow them with nightmare qualities.

Some animals, such as birds, have been omitted because we did not feel that they warranted a programme to themselves, and the fears that they engender are similar to those elicited by animals already included. It was also beyond the scope of the television series and this book to cover all the dangerous and venomous animals of the world. Wherever possible we have tried to concentrate on the most important, or unfamiliar and thus intrinsically nightmarish examples.

Although a lot of my knowledge has come from first hand experience, I am indebted to the scientists, naturalists and field researchers around the world who have shared their knowledge with me. Without their cooperation, wildlife films would be impoverished. In compiling the information for this book, we have had to rely on a variety of sources – personal experiences, published information, scientific journals and people's interpretation of animal behaviour. Sometimes the only information available on an animal is dubious, or biased. While first-world countries can afford to carry out in-depth scientific research, in third-world countries, struggling against poverty, disease or war, gathering statistics is understandably low on government agendas. Yet it is often in these poorer countries that many of the worlds most venomous and dangerous animals live.

A problem which we had to grapple with in the series was to try to identify the "most dangerous" animals. We have had to make a distinction between the most venomous, in terms of the toxicity of their poison, and those which actually injure or kill the most people – the two not always being the same animal. After taking advice from many sources, (sometimes conflicting), we have decided to classify the most dangerous animals as ones that, for whatever reason, kill the most people, regardless of distribution, behaviour or the toxicity of their venoms.

Finally, in order to simplify the text, I have tried to stick to common names when describing animals. However, for those who want more information, scientific names have been included in a comprehensive index at the back of the book.

Basic Instinct

Why are we afraid of certain animals? Fear inclines us to be cautious, which would have been essential in the survival of our forebears and is, perhaps surprisingly, still essential today. Humans evolved alongside the great carnivores and developed a healthy respect for them. Their superior physical attributes – power, weapons and speed – meant they could easily run down, capture and kill humans. To survive, our ancestors had to rely on superior intelligence, combined with a degree of caution acquired at an early stage in life.

Man is born prepared to fear the unusual. This natural caution was, and still is, shaped by experience – it was obviously beneficial to learn to distinguish between animals that were dangerous and those that were not. An infant, crawling away from the security of its cave-dwelling parents and the warmth of the fire, was more likely to come into contact with wild animals. It was important for human babies, in their helpless state, to avoid things which could be dangerous. It is therefore at this stage that we are most prone to developing strong fears of unusual objects and animals.

All animals need to be afraid to stay alive. Freedom from fear is, from a survival point of view, a bad thing. Fear is a response to a perceived danger, and if we no longer felt it as we approached the cliff edge or the motorway pile-up, we would all have shorter lives.

Although fear is an experience we all have and can recognise, it is not easy to define. One solution is simply to say that fear is what we feel when we are afraid – but this does not take us very far! Fear can

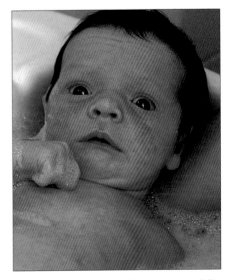

Fear is an intrinsic emotion (*above*), but can be overcome (*left*)

cover a range of emotions from mild unease to blind panic. Also, because we are dealing with something as subjective as an emotion, it is hard to understand it objectively: your emotions may be quite different from mine when faced with a charging rhino.

Perhaps the most obvious starting point is with the effects fear has which we can observe. This is where Darwin began:

> The frightened man first stands like a statue, motionless and breathless...the heart beats quickly and violently...the skin instantly becomes pale...the hairs also on the skin stand erect and the superficial muscles shiver...in connection with the disturbed action of the heart, the breathing is hurried...the mouth becomes dry...one of the best marked symptoms is the trembling of all the muscles of the body and this is often first seen in the lips

Most of the physical changes we associate with fear are generated by adrenaline, a hormone secreted by the adrenal gland. If we are given an injection of adrenaline, the sympathetic nervous system reacts and we sweat, our heart rate increases, our pupils dilate and our hair stands on end. We exhibit all the physical symptoms of fear but we do not necessarily feel afraid. So the state of physiological arousal alone is not sufficient to induce the emotion of fear.

The quotation from Darwin which sparked off so much discussion of the relationship between physical and mental states raises another essential question: what is the origin of our fear? For Darwin, as for so many ethologists today, the origins of human emotions lie in our animal ancestry. Fear has a survival value, not only in making us avoid dangers, but in preparing us to cope with them. Darwin pointed out that the increased pulse rate and breathing make the animal better able to fight or to flee; the thinly scattered hairs stand erect over a human's body through the action of the same minute muscles as those which make an animal bristle and so appear larger and more terrifying to its enemies. Fear equips us to cope with danger. If we want to understand it better, we should look carefully at the animals with whom we have a shared evolutionary history.

At this point we need to deal with an approach to the natural world that many biologists today think of as a major folly: anthropomorphism. This simply means attributing human emotions and motivations to animals. Scientists who work in the field of animal psychology and behaviour watch each other like hawks for any sign of this misdemeanour and do not hesitate to scream loudly when they come across it. It was a common mistake among field naturalists of the 19th century, and is common today in children's books and a certain genre of natural history television film. Because serious zoologists always get into a lather about it, we need to get it into perspective. If an animal runs away from danger, is it reasonable to say that it is afraid? We know that the physiological responses are the same in humans as in other animals, and that they tend to be attributable to infusions of adrenaline into the bloodstream. So, although we can never be sure that an animal feels fear in the same conscious way as we do, it seems reasonable to say that an animal which shows the same physiological symptoms as ours in the face of danger is afraid.

Humans have refined and developed fear in subtle ways that arise from our twisted psychologies. A phobia is a fear which is out of all proportion to the actual danger, and cannot be reasoned away. Phobias have been reported since the time of Hippocrates, but were not recognised as disorders in their own right until the

It is difficult to prove that spiny pocket mice show the same emotions as humans, even when about to be swallowed by a tropical kingsnake

end of the 19th century. It seems to have taken the professionals a surprisingly long time to recognise something that most of us come across from time to time. Perhaps they were loath to label as a disorder something which affects everybody to a small degree.

Amongst the most common phobias are those involving insects, snakes, diseases and animals in general. A survey of fears conducted in America in the early 1980s produced some surprising results: here in the apparently violent and crime ridden culture of the United States, the fear of being mugged didn't feature. People were more afraid of speaking in front of an audience than anything else, and this was twice as terrifying to them as insects and bugs.

In this book we shall be dealing with our fear of animals – not only with seemingly unreasonable phobias, but with the very reasonable anxieties many of us have towards creatures that we think can harm us – whether we are right or not.

We all fear the novel situation, the unusual, the new experience. It may be exhilarating, but it is definitely scary. As infants we need first to recognise our parents, for this brings security and comfort. This is as true in humans as it is in many other animals. Lion cubs first learn to recognise their mothers. As a result, they react with great alarm to the presence of a male, and for a very good reason. A male strange to the pride will try to kill the cubs, in order to bring the mother more rapidly back into oestrus, so that he can mate with her. Whilst filming lions in the Serengeti we captured on film a distressing infanticide. Early one morning we came across three young cubs with their mother out in the open. Three strange lionesses suddenly appeared over the hill, and on seeing the mother, immediately gave chase. As she fled, they approached the cubs, which we thought they were going to harm. Instead they merely sniffed them, before running off after the mother. The cubs themselves appeared completely unafraid of the new lionesses – presumably they looked very similar to their mother. In the wake of the lionesses came a beautiful large maned lion. On seeing him, the cubs cowered down with what, to us, looked like utter terror on their faces. It was a justified reaction, for the male discovered their hiding place and killed all three cubs. Within days the mother was back in oestrus and ready to mate again.

Human fear of animals is usually reported as having existed since childhood. Even at birth human infants startle readily to any novel stimulus. Between the ages of six and twelve months, an infant learns to recognise its parents, and having done so, begins to develop a fear of strangers.

Newborn infants do not fear snakes and only begin to show the first signs of fear at the age of two. From then on they become more and more cautious, with their fear increasing up to the age of six. Fear of animals tends to occur at about the same age but it seems that the fear of snakes may be partly built-in in humans. In other words we have a preparedness for it. Despite the rarity of poisonous snakes in Britain, one third of British children fear them. It is well known that writhing or jerky movements frighten monkeys and humans, and this might be the basis for the fear of snakes.

Children find animals far more frightening if they are moving rapidly toward the child in a jerky way, or if they loom above the child. Young toddlers can handle live animals fearlessly until they see the animals stalking or rushing towards them – this is likely to immediately frighten them.

Fears arise in children for little or no apparent reason, and die down just as mysteriously, without further contact with the phobic situations. By the age of six, fear of the dark and of imaginary creatures has superseded fear of animals. Thereafter children seem resistant to acquiring new phobias of animals. Their fears diminish very rapidly between nine and eleven, though a persistent anxiety about spiders, snakes, mice and bats is common among adults.

Older people seem to be resistant to acquiring fear of animals. Whilst fear in young children appears unexpectedly, often for no obvious reason, animal phobias that start for the first time in adolescence or adult life are rare and usually associated with trauma such as a dog bite.

The degree of panic when confronted by the feared animal can be intense, particularly if the animal moves. The fluttering of a bird's wings, the scuttling

Some animals that look terrifying are totally harmless. Parson's Chameleon

of spiders, or the silent swooping of a bat can produce panic, sweating, trembling and terror. Only a minority of phobics believe that the animal will actually hurt them. For the rest, the fear is the more intense because of its irrationality. A woman who was afraid of butterflies and moths, and had to leave buses or trains if she came across one, said that she was not worried by earwigs, furry caterpillars or spiders and that she would rather face a boxful of black widow spiders than one large English moth.

Practically any animal may be involved in a phobia. The most common fears are of birds and feathers. When a phobia develops, the sufferer can be completely disabled by it. A spider-phobic woman was so terrified at finding a spider in her house that she ran screaming to a neighbour and spent two hours trembling at her side; another found herself on top of a refrigerator with no idea how she got there; yet another flung herself into the sea because she saw a spider in a boat. She was a non-swimmer. A country woman was unable to walk past any pond that contained frogs, or even look at their pictures in books, and an archaeologist afraid of locusts had to stop going on digs in countries where locusts were common.

Nobody would think it unusual or a sign of psychological disturbance to admit to a fear of man-eating tigers, charging rhinos or spitting cobras. So a degree of fear when faced by animals that can harm us is prudent and reasonable. What we often find difficult is to know what to fear, and how much fear is appropriate. A greater understanding would help to reduce the fear, perhaps even permitting us to rationally take the right evasive action, or dispelling our fear altogether.

In this modern age, we are increasingly dependent upon television, radio and the written word to keep us informed about the outside world. However, sensational stories and headlines increase audience and readership figures, and generate income. It is hardly surprising therefore that many stories are designed to play on our natural fears, and misinform us about the facts. It is hoped that the chapters in this book will help dispel much of the hype about the worlds' most dangerous and venomous animals.

Left Many people are scared of 'creepy crawlies', especially large species. Stag beetles
Above Seemingly benign creatures can have a nasty side. This wide mouthed frog is swallowing a mouse

We shall be dealing with fears, phobias and facts. Often it happens that the animals we most fear are not dangerous to us unless we force them to be so. In most situations the confrontation is accidental, or the human victim, at least, has a limited but free choice of action; the animal often has none. By a greater understanding of potentially dangerous animals, we may learn to observe them and even to live alongside them, without harm. On the other hand, the animals we are most afraid of are often not the most dangerous; we should be more aware than we are of unfamiliar risks.

The following chapters will hopefully enlarge our understanding and increase our awareness and enjoyment of the wilder areas of the world, to which television has introduced us, and cheaper transport is increasingly allowing us access.

Maneaters

The railway carriage tilted strangely to one side as it stood in the deserted siding of Kima station, 250 miles inland from Mombasa, Kenya. The line had only recently been constructed and the siding had not settled well. The two men who lay inside on the night of 6th June, 1900 slept soundly, one in the bunk bed over the table and the other stretched out on the sloping floor of the carriage, his feet towards the sliding door. Ryall, the Superintendent of Police, had offered him the lower bunk but he had said he was happy enough on the bare wooden boards while Ryall took the first watch outside. The man-eater had recently killed nearby. He would come back. The men were ready.

Ryall peered into the shadows along the gleaming lines. The East African night is never dark, never silent. But he knew the sounds and the darkness held no terror for him. Even when two bright and steady glow-worms appeared in the bushes, like eyes steadily gazing at him, he was not afraid. He knew them for what they were – or thought he did.

As the night wore on Ryall felt more secure. No point in waking the others. The lion could be miles away. Let them sleep on; they would be more alert for the hunt in the morning. He crept quietly into the carriage and closed the door, sliding it gently and silently on its brass runners leaving a gap to allow the night air to refresh them as they slept. He crawled into the lower bunk.

Left A lion strangling a wildebeest
Above The carriage swayed slightly...

Ryall was deeply asleep when a soft paw slowly reached into the gap and, just as silently, pushed the door open. As the lion shifted his weight into the carriage it swayed slightly, the door slid back, snapped shut and the three men were trapped inside with the man-eater they had come to kill. The lion went straight for the lower bunk and seized Ryall, standing on his sleeping companion who woke with a scream. The man in the upper bunk leapt onto the lion's back as the only way to reach the door but, as he tugged at it, he realised with horror that the terrified railway workers were holding it shut from the outside.

His panic gave him strength and he managed to squeeze an arm and then a foot, and finally his body past the sliding door which the men immediately tied shut with their turbans, terror-stricken at the noises from inside. There was a brief pause and then a great crash. Splinters of wood and broken glass showered everywhere as the window burst and the lion leapt through holding Ryall's body in its jaws, and vanished into the night.

Fragments of Ryall's body were found in the bush about a quarter of a mile away and taken to Nairobi for burial. The Tsavo Man-eaters brought to a halt the construction of the railway line from Uganda to the Indian Ocean and had the distinction of being mentioned in the Houses of Parliament by the British Prime Minister. They were finally killed by an engineer assigned to the construction of the bridge over the Tsavo river, Lt. Col. J.H. Patterson, who wrote a lively account of the episode and concludes that the lions deserved their mention by Lord Salisbury:

> Well had the two man-eaters earned all this fame: they had devoured between them no less than 28 Indian workers, in addition to scores of unfortunate African natives of whom no official record was kept.

The story of the Tsavo Man-eaters, etched deep into the soul of East Africa, was one which I read with wide-eyed wonder as a child. The incident happened almost a century ago yet it remains one of the most famous in history, and it neatly illustrates the feelings that man-eating engenders. Man-eating is generally aberrant behaviour exhibited only occasionally by the big carnivores. The incidents cause such terror, and elicit such primeval reactions of horror and revulsion that even isolated cases are reported with a morbid fascination that gives them an importance far in excess of reality.

Our fear of the large land predators is quite understandable. They can see, hear and smell better than us, and they can run much faster. Of all the carnivores, the big cats are the most perfectly adapted for a life as a predator – they are either stealthy ambush hunters or swift runners, powerful creatures with lightning quick reflexes, lethal teeth and razor sharp claws.

Because the larger predators are so much more powerful than human beings they have become the focus of religious cults which acknowledge their superhuman strength and attempt to placate or appease them. Even in our modern societies they are the stuff of which myths, legends and bar-room stories are made. We all meet these dangers at an early age through *Peter Pan*, *Goldilocks* and *Little Red Riding Hood*, and they satisfy the same emotional need as *Crocodile Dundee*. The problem is of course, that although we are reassured by our heroes coming out on top, we are left with entrenched attitudes to the animals that are overcome. Our fears of predators are often misguided, and though they may be justified, they are rarely based on accurate knowledge of the creatures we fear.

People who have lived alongside lions for generations have, quite understandably, a very different attitude and more balanced approach to the dangers posed by big carnivores. The Masai have long shared the same land with lions and respect them as fearsome adversaries. It is a respect based on experience, as Masai warriors have for centuries hunted lions as a way of showing their bravery and courage. Without doubt, lions can distinguish between Masai and a European. On the African plains the tall dark figures of the Masai morans, or warriors, are

The number of attacks by lions, even in captivity, has probably been exaggerated

DÉVORÉ PAR UN LION

unmistakable, and lions recognise them and respond accordingly. Lions will generally avoid humans when given the chance, but their response to Masai is exaggerated and dramatic. The very sound of distant cowbells is enough to send a lion slinking into hiding knowing, from past experience, that Masai are heading towards him with their cattle.

Most species of animal have learned to maintain a safe distance between themselves and potential danger: the so called 'flight distance'. The point at which an animal runs away may vary from place to place, or be dependent on what carnivore is approaching. Antelopes may run from hunting dogs when they are on the horizon, and yet allow lions to approach as close as 100 meters before fleeing. Their response is geared to the potential danger; hunting dogs can catch an antelope that remains within 200 meters of them, whilst lions need to stalk to within 30 meters or so to be a real threat. So long as an intruder stays beyond the flight distance, the animal will watch but take no action. A closer approach and it will retreat or fight back. We need to remember this when stepping suddenly out of a car to confront an animal unaware of our approach. Even the lion will naturally avoid humans if its 'flight distance' is not breached. People have been killed because they jumped suddenly out of a vehicle, hoping to get a close-up photograph, when the only response the lion could make at that distance was hostile.

I almost made a similar, fatal mistake when I saw my first wild lions at the age of eight. A lioness had just caught an antelope in Nairobi National Park in Kenya, and I was watching from the safety of our car, only 15 meters away. The next moment I opened the car door and jumped out; apparently I was off to save the

Lions can kill animals much larger than themselves, especially when hunting in prides

A lion in its natural habitat

antelope. Fortunately my mother managed to grab hold of me and pull me back inside the car before the lioness had time to react. After many years of observing and filming lions I now know a lot more about these magnificent cats. Today my actions are tempered by their moods and behaviour, behaviour which I need to try to understand and interpret if I am to film them without endangering myself or disturbing my subjects.

The Masai have, over many years, come to understand lions and the danger they pose to them and their cattle. If we are to understand the big predators and how they are likely to behave, we too need to learn more about our subjects; to become students of behaviour.

Although all the big cats are potentially dangerous to man, man-eating is common in only two, the lion and the tiger. Lions are probably the best known of all the big cats. Once they were widely distributed from the Cape of Good Hope to the Mediterranean, as far west as Greece and as far east as India, where today only a few remain in the Gir Forest. They were hunted out of North and South Africa by the end of the 19th century, and the big game hunters have greatly reduced numbers all over the continent since that time. They still manage to thrive in the

savanna and plains habitats, feeding grounds for the larger herbivores, where they are the most numerous large carnivore, next to the spotted hyena.

The lion is the largest African carnivore, adult males weighing around 260 kg and females 170 kg. With a head and body length of 2.5 meters and standing over 1.2 meters at the shoulder the lion is 2 feet longer, a foot taller and three times the weight of a Great Dane, interestingly called the 'lion dog' of Africa. To cap it all, the lion can reach speeds of over 50 kph in short dashes, when it attacks – almost as fast as a greyhound.

The size of a lion was really brought home to me when, a few years ago, I was making a film on them in the Serengeti and decided to use two stuffed lions for a sequence on territoriality. The two polystyrene-filled animals duly arrived from England. I had filmed lions many times, even at close range, but they were always in their natural environment and curiously never looked impressively large. For the first time I now had a chance to stand side by side with a lion. I was stunned. They were enormous. What was more, these young males had no manes and were not yet fully grown. We had nowhere safe to keep the stuffed lions and so left them standing in the house overnight. The following morning there was a scream from the living room and the next moment a colleague bolted past to the safety of her room. It was only then I remembered that I had not told anyone in the house that

I had put the lions in the lounge. For my sleepy friend, the sight of a lion filling the lounge must have been terrifying. We left the lions there for a number of weeks and, even though everyone now knew about them, they never failed to startle anyone who absentmindedly opened the door to the lounge.

A single lioness is quite capable of killing an animal three times its

Above A lion's size can only be appreciated when you are up close – in this case to a stuffed animal with a false mane

Left People in vehicles can now get very close to lions in the wild – here seen mating

Overleaf Two lions fighting and showing their two major weapons – teeth and claws

A lioness intent on her prey

weight. Adult males, with their huge manes and bulky bodies, are designed to defend the pride from rival males. Being slower and more easily spotted by prey they usually leave the hunting to the lionesses.

Like other cats, lions can accelerate very quickly and run fast, but they are not long distance runners and can only keep up this speed for one or two hundred meters. Almost all their prey animals can run faster and for longer, so the lion has to get close by stalking or ambushing.

Lions find their prey by either seeing them or hearing them, and smell probably seldom plays an important role. When hunting, the lioness watches intently, rarely taking her eyes off her prey as she moves cautiously closer. Whilst hunting she is alert but never aggressive, for she is simply trying to catch her lunch. She is an expert at moving stealthily when her victim is not looking. She creeps forward, and then freezes, using every scrap of cover she can find. She will try to get within 20 or 30 meters before breaking from cover. She usually misses – only one in five hunts ends in a kill.

Lions are more successful when hunting at night, so most hunts occur just after dark or just before the sun rises. Like other cats, they have unusually large eyes for their skull size. Their eyes are designed for night hunting. The familiar eyeshine of cats occurs when light in the eye which has "missed" the retina, and gone undetected, is reflected back onto it by a special mirror-like layer, the tapetum. In this way, the maximum available light is detected. Together with the large number of light sensitive cells or rods in the retina, and the comparatively large size of the pupil, this allows the cat to operate quite effectively under conditions that we would consider pitch black.

Lions are also more successful hunters when hunting together, and this they commonly do. But contrary to popular opinion, they do not hunt cooperatively in the true sense of the word. All the lions stalk independently, yet they watch one another and clearly pay attention to what their companions are doing. Interestingly, lions have distinctive black markings on the backs of their ears which is thought to perhaps help hunting lions to keep track of each other.

Eventually one lioness will get close enough to make a rush at an animal. In the ensuing confusion an animal fleeing from one lion may run towards another and get caught. By hunting together lions are twice as likely to be successful as solitary hunters. Some early explorers and white hunters suggested that lions stampede prey towards other lions waiting in ambush, sometimes even roaring to increase the mayhem. This seems very unlikely and certainly has not been reported by any lion researchers. Lions roar to communicate with one another and so it is no surprise to find that prey take little notice of this and certainly do not stampede. Another myth is that lions hunt taking wind direction into account. In the Serengeti, at least, this does not seem to be so and lions are as likely to hunt downwind as upwind.

Lions usually catch their prey by seizing the rump or shoulders with their claws and pulling the animal off balance. The lioness then quickly bites and holds it either by the throat or the muzzle, preventing it from breathing. In a very few cases they break the neck of the animal. Cats have been described as the perfect killing machine – and some are able to tackle prey many times their own weight.

Although lions have been recorded as eating almost any available animal, including grass mice, lizards, tortoises and quails, they normally catch large to medium sized animals like buffalo, zebra, antelope and warthog. They are powerful enough, however, to bring down young elephant, bull giraffes, rhinoceroses and even 4000 kg adult hippopotami.

Big though the lion is, it is not the biggest of the cats – the tiger is. The largest tiger is the Siberian, Amur or Manchurian species – which can weigh around 350 kg and be almost twice as long as a Great Dane. The Indian or Bengal tiger is slightly smaller, weighing up to 270 kg. The strength of the tiger is immense. One individual dragged an adult gaur (a type of wild ox) 12 meters, which 13 men could not move an inch.

Mouth to mouth suffocation

The image of the tiger has a unique mysticism. Because tigers are not only beautifully formed and powerful, but elusive and secretive, they have inspired awe for thousands of years. In India, tigers and humans have lived in close proximity for centuries and occasionally killed each other. Despite the fact that the tiger kills many people, it is respected as well as feared.

Although tigers do occasionally socialise at kills, they are generally solitary animals. Designed to live in dense cover, they never evolved the social system of lions. So while male lions only hunt occasionally, male tigers do so as a matter of course. Tigers usually rest in dense cover during the day and hunt at night. A stalking tiger uses maximum cover for concealment. Slowly approaching its prey from behind, it places each foot carefully on the ground and pauses before advancing the other. Like the lion, it must approach to within 20 meters if the final dash is to be successful. It covers that distance in a few bounds and often the

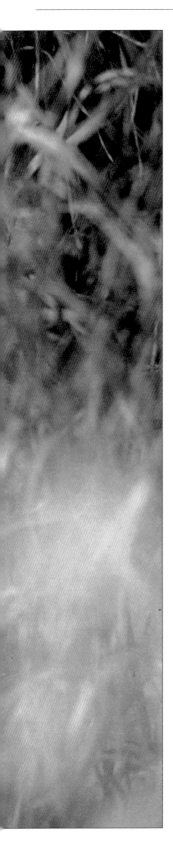

momentum of the attack will carry the prey off its feet. The tiger does not usually launch itself into the air or spring on its prey from a distance; when it seizes the animal by the throat, back, or neck, its hind feet are on the ground.

The tiger uses two methods of killing, either biting the back of the neck which severs the spinal cord, or biting the throat to suffocate the animal. The skull of a tiger is specially foreshortened to give extra shearing leverage to the powerful jaws. If the kill is made in the open the tiger usually drags it into dense cover to feed.

A tiger will eat whatever it can catch, but the bulk of its diet is from the larger ungulates in the 50-100 kg range. Tigers will occasionally take very large prey such as rhino and elephant calves, water buffalo, moose, wapiti and gaur.

Tigers have been responsible for killing more humans than any other big cat. An observer of the depredations of Indian tigers has remarked that "at one time in parts of India at the beginning of the 19th century man-eaters were so prevalent that it seemed to be a question of whether man or tiger would survive". Villages were protected by encircling fires and the villagers only went abroad in large bands, beating drums and accompanied by armed men. The fear was justified. In the 1930s, tigers were estimated to be killing between 1000 and 1600 people every year. The most notorious man-eater, the Champawat tigress, killed 436 people. Although these figures are today regarded with some scepticism, what is undisputed is that there are tigers that have and do prey extensively, and occasionally exclusively, on people. Man-eating tigers seldom venture into villages, but attack and kill people who venture into their domain during the day.

It is rare for a tiger to become a man-eater, but when it does the effect on the communities around can be devastating. Markets and religious festivals are cancelled so that people will not have to travel. Cattle are not taken to pasture, crops are not harvested, even firewood is not collected. Because tigers are great travellers, victims may be taken up to twenty miles apart and there is no way of knowing when or where the next kill will be made. Fear spreads. One solitary man-eater can bring village life to a standstill over a wide area.

Tahawar Ali Khan, a Pakistani hunter and naturalist, who is called in to deal with man-eaters today, has given an evocative account of the experience of being close to one in the jungle:

> Time seems to stand still and all the human senses become intensely concentrated. The nervous tension becomes unbearable. Every inch of ground has to be probed and re-probed by anxious and suspicious eyes; every sound has to be listened for, analysed and explained; and every step has to be taken in the knowledge that a wrong one can be your last. Always expect the unexpected, otherwise you are liable to lose your life.

Once there were around 40,000 tigers on the Indian subcontinent. Today the population has been drastically reduced by hunting, poaching and the depredation of the forests and grasslands they inhabit. Now less than 4000 wild tigers remain in the wild in India, and possibly less than 6000 in the entire world. The chances of coming across this magnificent beast outside a protected area are remote. Those that do live in parks will almost always slink away into the undergrowth before you even have a chance to see them.

There is one area of the world, however, in which tigers seem to be especially

Tigers can be very difficult to see until you are too close

dangerous – the mangrove jungles of the Sundarbans, in the Bay of Bengal. Here, in the vast tidal forests at the mouths of the great rivers Ganges and Brahmaputra, there live today some 600 tigers – the largest single population anywhere in the world. The forests cover an area of nearly 10,000 square kilometres, over half of which lie in Bangladesh, and the remainder in India. The Sundarbans, or 'beautiful forest' is notorious for its man-eaters. Both Bangladesh and India have set aside areas here specially for the tiger, where there are no settlements. But people still penetrate its forests, tidal creeks and rivers to collect wood and honey, to catch fish and prawns. Even the fishermen are not safe.

One night in May 1969, Nagar Ali was cooking supper on his boat and chatting to a fellow fisherman, Malek Molla. He looked up from his cooking pot when he heard a splash. His friend had disappeared. He flashed his torch around the boat, sweeping the waters, and its beam fell on a tiger standing on the bank. It held Malek Molla's body in its jaws, like a cat with a fish. It slipped quietly into the jungle. The half-eaten body was found next morning. Back in the 17th century a French traveller in India, Francois Bernier had described the Sundarban tigers swimming out to the boats to take fishermen. The practice lives on. In all it is thought that around 60 people are killed by tigers in the Sundarbans every year.

Nobody has yet satisfactorily explained why so many of the tigers of the Sundarbans become man-eaters. One suggestion is that the drinking of the saline water in this delta region makes the tiger irritable by damaging its liver and kidney. This is supported by the fact that the man-eating problem peaks in May when the salinity of the water is at its highest. The peak of killing in May could be put down to the fact that it is then that the honey collectors roam the forests in small bands in search of combs.

Certainly the problem in the Sundarbans is partly an economic one. The per capita income here is less than half the state average and in the struggle for survival some 4000 fishermen, 500 honey collectors and 500 wood cutters enter the region. Those with official permission were once given fire crackers to scare off the tigers. Now more sophisticated methods are used. Since tigers normally attack from behind rather than face to face, cheap masks representing human faces have been provided for the forest workers to wear on the back of their heads. This has been dramatically successful. In 1987 thousands of workers began taking these face masks with them to wear when they went to fish, collect honey or cut wood in the Sundarbans. In two and a half years, only one man wearing a mask has been killed by a tiger and he was attacked from the side on the lower half of his body. This success, say the local people, cannot last. The tiger is too clever to be deceived for long.

So other methods are being tried – for instance, a life sized clay model of a worker is dressed in used clothing and soaked with urine to provide a genuine human scent. It is then left in an area where man-eating tigers have been active, with a galvanised wire around its neck attached to a 12 volt battery, energised to 300 volts. When the tiger attacks it gets a shock, but a fuse immediately blows and there is no danger of it being electrocuted. So far about a dozen man-eaters have been shocked, and the hope is that the lesson learned by this aversion therapy will spread to other tigers in the Sundarbans. In the meantime, pigs are bred for release into the tiger reserve to ensure they are well fed, and fresh water tanks are being dug in the forest with the hope of keeping the tigers in better humour.

Tales of man-eating form a large part of the literature of adventure and a wide variety of opinion exists on the subject. A white hunter, James Sutherland, wrote in 1912 that:

Above The full power of a tiger can only be seen when it is out in the open

Right The world's most notorious man-eating tigers are found in the Sundarbans. The local fishermen now wear masks on the back of their heads to trick the animals into thinking they are being watched, as most tigers like to attack from behind (*far right*) and catch their prey unawares

People living in the perfect safety of their homes in a Western country
have no conception of the insecurity that is felt by blacks in their kraals
in the interior of Africa. The cause of this feeling of insecurity is chiefly
the man-eating lion and no other animal of the forest inspires such terror
into the black man's heart. In villages far in the heart of the pori, where
the white man is never seen, not hundreds but thousands of Africans are
annually eaten by these monsters.

Humans do not form part of the natural prey of most carnivores. Even renowned
man-eating tigers and lions seldom live solely on humans and supplement their
diet with normal prey. The great land predators, in particular the big cats, have
evolved alongside man. Despite their superior size, power and agility, over
thousands of years they have come to fear man as the dominant predator. The
American biologist George Schaller discovered that when lions attack humans they
did not assume an aggressive facial expression, but instead a bared-tooth,
defensive one, demonstrating an element of fear.

The great cats generally shun man, often going out of their way to avoid conflict.
However, throughout history there have been records of big cats killing man. Perhaps
the most notorious big cat that ever lived was the man-eating leopard of
Rudyaprayag, which between 1918 and 1926 killed 125 people in the Garhwal Hills
of India. When man-eaters lose their fear of man they become extremely cunning in
their search for human victims. This leopard was just such an animal, but it was also
extremely lucky – truly a cat of nine lives. It survived poisons, a barrage of bullets,
trip guns and even a spring trap which snapped shut but closed on the cats leg at the
very place where there was a tooth missing in the trap. The leopard escaped.

In comparison to tigers and lions, however, leopards rarely kill people, and
the jaguars and pumas of the Americas do so even less. The cheetah and the snow
leopard have never been known to kill people. Of the two most notorious big cat
man-eaters it is generally thought that the lion is bolder. Unlike the tiger it will
hunt man at night, even coming into his villages and huts to do so. But this very
boldness can also be turned against it, for it makes the man-eating lion very much
easier to kill than the tiger.

So why do big cats sometimes lose their fear of man and become man-eaters?
A cat may become a man-eater if there is a shortage of prey. This is more likely to
affect the lion and tiger than the jaguar and leopard, for they need
a regular supply of medium to large prey animals. Man-eating lions are often old
and disabled animals with broken or worn down canine teeth.

The man-eater may not always be disabled, however. The Tsavo man-eaters
were healthy specimens in their prime of life. Man-eating is also said to be more
prevalent during wars, as the big cats acquire a taste for the flesh of the dead and
injured, and prey on people who are forced into the wilds.

One question is whether the cubs of a man-eater become man-eaters
themselves. Latest research into the predator-prey relationships of the Bengal Tiger
suggests that this may well occur. Cubs learn from their mothers what to hunt, and
what to fear. I have watched lion cubs slink away frightened at the first distant
sounds of cows bells. Their mothers knew from experience that Masai were
bringing cattle to the waterhole they were lying beside, and their cubs had learnt
that this sound was a signal to move on.

A tigress that has overcome its fear of man and actively hunts him could well
pass on the experience to her cubs. It is much less likely that the taste of human
flesh is addictive. 'Once a man-eater always a man-eater' is certainly not

necessarily true either, for there are records of man-eaters reverting to feeding on their normal prey when it became readily available again.

Man-eating among the great cats is surprisingly rare. Sadly, on the strength of a few killings, they have gained a bloodthirsty reputation, and for generations have been hunted by this puny yet aggressive creature called man. Their habitats and their food supplies have been destroyed. Rarely do they retaliate. Man is in good supply and is the least fleet-footed source of protein, but the great cats prefer, on the most part, to leave man alone.

The great cats are impressive creatures – the most efficient predators on earth. With their razor sharp claws, dagger like teeth and immensely powerful bodies it is easy to see why we so fear them. But the cuddly, bumbling, amiable bear, which joined us in our childhood daydreams in a search for honey pots rarely figures in our nightmares.

The relationship between bears and men stretches right back to the time of Stone Age man. In preparing to kill these immensely powerful carnivores, people developed ceremonial dances and songs that deified the bear and helped assure the success of the hunt. With time bears came to be held in awe around the world as gods.

Why do big cats become man-eaters?

Bears, with their human-like features, came to be accepted as having a special relationship with man and were frequently referred to as brothers, grandfathers or grandmothers by the North American Indians. The Modoc Indians of California believed that they were descended from the union of a grizzly bear with the daughter of the Great Spirit. There are stories all around Europe and the Middle East of young girls being abducted by bears and producing offspring that were sometimes human and sometimes half-human.

Around the world the bear is frequently seen as a symbol of life and death, for it appears to die in winter when it hibernates and is reborn again in the spring when it wakes up. However, the bear came to be seen as a creature of brute strength and savagery by Europeans and the pioneers of modern America. It was shot or chained, and baited in fights with vicious dogs and trained to perform in degrading and often cruel circuses.

The negative image of the bear started to change at the beginning of this century, when in 1902 the American President Theodore Roosevelt refused to shoot a black bear chained to a tree. The incident fired the public's imagination and the friendly and lovable toy teddy bear was born. During World War Two, the bear's image was further improved when 'Smokey the Bear' was used in a poster campaign to help prevent forest fires.

In all there are eight species of bear around the world, and although they are usually peaceful animals that try to avoid conflict, if wounded or threatened they can be formidable adversaries. The epitome of the cuddly bear and perhaps the most loved animal in the world is the giant panda which has been adopted as a symbol of wildlife conservation. Once, they roamed over much of eastern China, but today there are only 700 pandas left in the wild in a few fragmented forests on the eastern edge of the Tibetan plateau. Weighing up to 160 kg, the giant panda eats bamboo almost exclusively, though it will also scavenge for meat and catch rodents and fish. The giant panda is a peaceful creature but has on occasions attacked people, inflicting serious injuries with its large canines and long claws.

Even the smallest bear in the world, the sloth bear, is held in great respect in its home forests of India and South East Asia. Although shy and not considered normally dangerous, this bear is unpredictable and often panics if accidentally encountered. Consequently it is one of the few animals with a reputation for charging without provocation and can inflict severe wounds with its long claws and powerful jaws. However, like most bears, the ferocious reputation of the sloth bear is probably highly exaggerated.

Of all the bears, four species are of any significant danger to man; the Asiatic and American black bears, the brown or grizzly bear, and the polar bear.

The polar bear is the most northerly species and one of the biggest of all bears. The largest ever recorded was an adult male which measured 3.5 meters (12 feet) long and weighed 1002 kg (2210 lbs), but an average adult male usually weighs 500 kg to 600 kg (1100 to 1320 lbs).

Sometimes called the sea bear, it is normally found near the edge of sea ice and open water. At home in the icy Arctic waters, the polar bear is an excellent swimmer quite capable of swimming 95 km (60 miles) without a rest.

Above Bears are revered by many cultures in North America. Kwakiutl Indian carved house post, NW America

Below The teddy bear craze was originally started by Theodore 'Teddy' Roosevelt, who never lived down the association

Westminster Gazette.]
John Bull and his real Teddy Bear

Left Grizzly bears are inquisitive animals

Polar bears are rarely seen close to man, but garbage dumps in the high Arctic can be rich feeding grounds

On land it can outrun a reindeer over a short distance. Unusually for a bear, it has excellent eyesight and hearing, at least as good as a human's. But it is its sense of smell which is quite incredible. Polar bears can detect a dead seal more than 32 kms (20 miles) away.

The polar bear is a carnivore, a solitary nomad that lives on the vast expanses of offshore polar ice, so it rarely comes into contact with people. Despite a reputation for ferocity the polar bear remains one of the world's most popular animals.

The only place in the world where large numbers can be seen close to human settlement is at the tiny town of Churchill, on the west coast of Canada's Hudson Bay. About 40 miles inland is the largest known denning area for polar bears in the world. Here the bears dig summer dens into the permafrost which serve as ice boxes to keep them cool in the summer. About 800 people live in Churchill and have learned to live with the dangers of having polar bears wandering down the

streets of the town. They have a Polar Bear Alert Programme, designed to protect people from bears, and bears from people. They do this by maintaining a 24 hour watch, especially over the town dump and areas where the bears are likely to wander in search of a meal. If one is spotted it is immediately tranquillised and removed to an area called the 'Polar Bear Jail'. Occasionally they have accommodation problems as the jail only holds 22 bears, but when it gets full a helicopter is called and the bears are airlifted out. The average catch is 36 bears each year, but they have managed to handle 86. The inhabitants of Churchill have managed to evolve a *modus vivendi* with their magnificent and awe inspiring neighbours which has made the town world famous as a centre for observing polar bears. Churchill must be the only place where armed motor patrols and parents accompany children on Halloween trick-or-treat night.

But the bear that is most famous for its encounters with humans, and challenged the settlers in their long march to the West of America in the mid-19th century, is the grizzly or brown bear.

The brown bear vies for title of biggest of the bears with the polar bear. Perhaps the largest of all are the brown bears found along the coast of Southern Alaska, and the nearby islands of Kodiak and Admiralty. These bears weigh on average 780 kg (1700 lbs) and a Kodiak bear might weigh as much as 820 kg (1800 lbs).

The brown bear has a reputation for being one of the most dangerous animals in North America, and this may certainly be true if one disregards venomous insects, domestic animals like dogs, disease-carrying rodents and snakes. Normally brown bears will try to avoid people, but if startled when accompanied by young or feeding on a kill they can be extremely dangerous.

The name 'grizzly' is not a reflection on the animals' character, but a reference to the long hairs on its back and shoulders, which are often frosted with white, giving the bear a grizzled appearance. The name can be confusing because it refers to the inland race of the brown bear of North America, while the ones which live on the coast are called 'Alaskan brownies'. A line arbitrarily drawn approximately 120 km (75 miles) inland from the coastline divides the two bears – any brown bear east is a 'grizzly' whilst those on the seaward side are 'Alaskan brown bears'. How far the locals are aware that bears crossing the line should change their names has not been researched.

The brown bear has one of the greatest distributions of any mammal. Once they roamed as they pleased, over the North American continent from the sea coast to the mountain ranges, from Mexico to Canada. In California alone there were 10,000 grizzlies and the total population in America may have exceeded 100,000. Now the only grizzly to be found outside a zoo in California is on the state flag. The total population of the lower United States has been estimated at less than 1,000. Hunting grizzlies was an act of heroism for Native Americans, like joining a war party or taking a scalp, and for the early white settlers, a sign of true grit, as this recollection shows:

If you kill your bear, its a triumph worth enjoying; if you get killed there yourself, some of the newspapers will give you a friendly notice; if you get crippled for life you carry about you a patent of courage which may be useful in case you go into politics...besides, it has its affect upon the ladies. A 'clawed' man is very much admired all over the world.

It must have taken courage to face an enraged Grizzly with the primitive fire power available to hunters in the mid-19th century. They are immense, have good hearing and a keen sense of smell; they can run fast enough to catch elk and bighorn sheep on mountain slopes and their jaws are powerful enough to crack open the leg bones to get at the marrow.

People came increasingly into contact with bears with the development of the national parks in North America. At that time the bears were encouraged to feed on the refuse from the park hotels as this attracted them down from the mountains to places easily viewed by tourists. Soon the American public came to view both black and brown bears as tame animals which could be treated as household pets. This familiarity understandably led to problems, yet the number of injuries and deaths caused by the bears remained remarkably low. Concern for people's safety grew, and eventually the rubbish dumps were closed, and feeding the bears was discouraged. Closing the dumps, however, created a new problem for there were now lots of bears which had lost their fear of people, and fatalities and injuries rose sharply. The most recent idea is to create feeding centres for the brown bears in the back country, to lure them away from human habitations, but this suggestion remains controversial at the moment.

Today the Wilderness movement, which is growing in strength in America, encourages people to hike off into the wilds. Those who forsake the comfort and security of their homes for the challenges of the backcountry surely have a duty to know something about the animals whose seclusion they are disturbing? Sadly, they are often equipped with just about everything but knowledge and understanding.

A comprehensive study of bear attacks has provided recommendations on how to cope with sudden

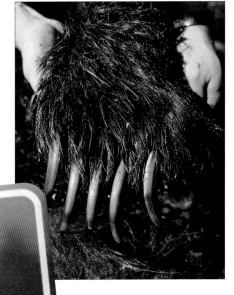

Above The size of a bear's paw, and the length of its claws, shows how dangerous it could be

Left The increasing popularity of visiting wilderness areas can result in unwanted bear/human interactions

Far left Despite their cuddly image, grizzly bears are dangerous animals and should be treated with the utmost

Bear Country

All Bears Are Dangerous
Bears Enter This Campground
Keep A Clean Camp
Use Extreme Caution

encounters. The first rule is to avoid bears whenever possible, giving them ample warning of your presence. Some people ring bells, blow whistles or sing. Bears prefer, on the whole, to avoid people, so being noisy reduces your chances of meeting one.

You might well, on the other hand, be in the wilderness to observe what you can of the wildlife, and so plunging through the bush like a drunken banshee may defeat the purpose. A more discrete approach could bring you up against a grizzly, and what you must do then depends on the circumstances. It is now that it really pays to understand bear behaviour.

Interestingly bears often treat people as if they were other bears. Threat displays and direct eye contact are part of a bear's repertoire of behaviour upon encountering another bear, so it is important not to stare at the bear as it can be interpreted as an aggressive action. If the bear feels threatened it may charge, so do not shout or make aggressive or sudden movements. The bear may rear up on its hind legs, but this is probably merely to get a better view – in North America bears do not attack from this position. You may be able to move slowly away without alarming it. If the bear should drop onto all fours and begin running and circling to get downwind, it is trying to scent the intruder. A bear about to charge will lay its ears back. If that happens you are in serious trouble. A grizzly is surprisingly quick and agile and can run at 48 km (30 miles) an hour or 14 meters (44 feet) per second – that is faster than an Olympic sprinter, so there is no point in trying to outrun the bear. If you decide to climb a tree its a good idea to start before the bear charges as even adult Grizzlies can climb up to about 5 meters (16 feet) from the ground. Some people have managed to escape by dropping an object such as a camera or rucksack to distract the bear while they find a tree to climb; others by dropping to the ground and playing dead. Barbara Moore, a ranger in Yellowstone National Park, had an almost fatal encounter with a grizzly:

> On an August day in 1984, my late husband, Bob, and I were hiking in an area in the park that I was previewing for a scheduled nature walk the next day. We were wandering through some Larch Pole Pine and, as we came to the edge of the trees we saw a dead bison about 100 yards away. Now when you see a dead animal in grizzly country one of the cardinal rules is that you do not approach it. So we stayed at the edge of the trees looking at the carcass through binoculars. Suddenly Bob yelled, "Barb, Barb, look out". I turned around just in time to see a sow bear charging towards me, followed closely by her two little cubs. What do you do in a situation like that? Fortunately I had had some training and I knew that I should not run, and that it was best to face the bear as charges are often bluffs. However this bear completed the charge and grabbed me by my left thigh. The next thing I remember was that I was on the ground and the sow was on my back. I could feel her teeth or her claws, though I could not tell what she was doing. I was yelling at the time but very quickly realised that my best hope was to stay still – to play dead. Almost immediately the bear left me and ran to my husband who was crouched behind a small broken down tree. The sow bit him in the knee and then came charging back to me. I had not moved. I was face down where she had left me. She rolled me over onto my back but I used my momentum to carry on rolling until I was face down again.

Black bears are less dangerous than grizzlies, but should still be treated with respect. They can kill a fully grown deer

Three times she did this, and three times I rolled back onto my face. It seemed to take a long time, but probably only lasted seconds. And all the time I do not think I drew a breath. Then the bear and her cubs left and we never saw them again. It all happened so incredibly quickly, but what was really horrifying about the attack, and its a lasting image, was seeing her coming at me, her head getting larger and larger. I think that if I had not had some training I would have responded as a lot of people do and struggled. One of the things that is very typical of grizzlies with young cubs is that they are much more likely to be defensive than aggressive, and as long as I was struggling she would have continued to maul me. Once I became quiet, I think she no longer perceived me as a threat.

Though her husband's injuries were slight, Barbara's were more serious, with a lacerated thigh, a fairly severe head wound and multiple puncture and claw marks. Fortunately, however, they were still able to hike out to the road a mile away to get help. Barbara's knowledge of bears may have saved her life.

Playing dead with grizzlies may be the correct tactic, but with American black bears it could prove fatal, for some black bears have been known to attack people with the sole intention of eating them. For black bears the best defence could well be a good offence. There are several reports of people being able to subdue or kill a black bear armed only with a rock or a pocket knife. Any sort of aggressive defence against a black bear is worth trying as a last resort. There is one catch – make sure that the attacking animal is a black bear and not a brown one! One way to tell the difference is that brown bears, unlike black bears, have very long claws that are easily visible even when the bear is walking.

Black bears are common in the national parks and, unlike grizzly bears, are considered harmless. Statistics, however, show that people should be more respectful of black bears than they are. From 1960 to 1980 more than 500 people were injured by black bears in America. Most of the injuries happened in the parks, usually when the bears were searching for food in the dumps of the camping grounds or begging from tourists. They have become so habituated to contact with people that some will stand on their hind legs and even 'dance' for titbits. People take incredible liberties with this cuddly looking, yet powerful animal. Some shake hands with the bears, and in one documented case a father placed his child on a bear's back to get a winsome snapshot. An even more potentially horrific incident was set up by the couple who smeared their child's face with jam to get a snap of the bear licking it off.

For those foolish enough to try such pranks it is worth remembering that the black bear can bite through a tree trunk thicker than a man's arm, and kill a fully grown deer with a bite to the neck. They are dangerous and they can kill. They can also run and climb well, so the chances of getting away from an attacking black bear are slim. Most attacks are attempts to get at food and the recommendation is to hand over whatever the bear seems to be after.

The black bears of Asia are slightly larger and generally more carnivorous than their American counterparts. Wherever they occur, these bears are troublesome to humans, often mauling and even killing people. In Japan, two or three people are killed each year, and a further 20 or so injured by these bears. June is the worst month attacks as people venture into the forests to collect wild bamboo shoots, a delicacy which the bears also adore.

Even though there are now many records around the world of bear attacks on humans, it would be wrong to think of this as normal, everyday behaviour. Attacks are usually a response to sudden confrontation – they are defensive, rather than aggressive. Except in very rare instances, bears do not stalk, seek out, and kill people in order to eat them.

Our misconceptions of carnivores are epitomised not only by our views of bears but also of wolves. In ancient times the wolf had a better image than today. The Greeks associated it with the gods Apollo and Zeus; the founders of Rome, Romulus and Remus, were suckled by a she-wolf and thus saved from starvation. By the time the Old Testament was written however, it had already become the ravenous creature that destroyed flocks, so savage in its disposition that should it live with the lamb, this would signify that good had finally prevailed over evil, and the rule of God had begun! In the New Testament it symbolised the abuse of power, and that association stayed with it throughout the Middle Ages, when monks who stole land, tax gatherers who pocketed funds and the rich barons who oppressed the peasantry were all 'wolves'. The wolf had become accepted as the embodiment of evil.

The wolf's reputation as a man-killer is completely unfounded

Once wolves roamed over most of the Northern Hemisphere above 30 degrees north. They were all over western Europe from Portugal to Finland, east through the Balkans across the Near and Middle East and south into Arabia. They were in Afghanistan and northern India, throughout Russia, north into Siberia and across into China and the islands of Japan. On the American continent they reached from Mexico City to Greenland. The wolf was so prevalent then that measures had to be taken to keep it from our door. Today they have been exterminated in the British Isles and most of Europe. There are still wolves in Mexico, Alaska and Canada and about a thousand are still at liberty in northern Minnesota. The size of the populations in China and Russia are unknown.

Wolves range in size from about 22 kg (28 lbs) for an adult Arabian wolf to 50 kg (110 lbs) for a large timber wolf. The largest wolf on record was shot in Alaska and weighed 79.5 kg (174 lbs). They are agile creatures with tremendous stamina: the Tundra wolves have been seen to run five or six miles behind caribou before accelerating to attack. They can smell prey a couple of miles away.

Larger prey is attacked by several wolves, which inflict massive damage to the hips by slashing with their teeth until the stride is broken and the animal falls or comes to a halt. When it has taken its death stand, one or two wolves may keep harassing it – one holding it by the nose while the other attacks from behind – and the rest play or sit panting, apparently taking little interest until the prey finally falls. Then they all rush to feed. The wolf's mouth is elongated to accommodate 42 teeth. The long canines seize the prey, the premolars shear and tear the flesh, the incisors strip shreds of meat from the bones which the molars then crush with a power of up to 105 kg/cm² (1500 lbs/in) – twice that of the German Shepherd.

Although the wolf inspires fear, attacks on people are very rare. In fact, there

are no undisputed cases on record. It seems quite likely that our present image of
the wolf as a killer arose almost 600 years ago, when the Black Death spread
across Europe. It was a time when many people died and many remained
unburied. Wolves were common then and probably scavenged the remains of the
dead. This habit almost certainly led to tales of wolves killing people. The most
harrowing stories are all from the distant past: in the Scotland of James VI in the
16th century the threats to travellers from marauding wolves were said to have
been so great that special houses called 'spittals' were erected by the highways so
that travellers could take shelter at night. In Russia, in 1875, 161 persons were said
to have fallen victim to wolves; yet that report was only made in 1890. The wolves
of North America have the reputation of being less aggressive to humans and
when a newspaper in Ontario offered a reward of $100 for proof of an
unprovoked attack, the reward went uncollected.

Wolves may acquire a taste for human flesh by scavenging human corpses but
the opportunities to do so are fewer in the frozen north than in the tropics. They
may be frenzied by rabies, and attack; but there are only unsupported anecdotes
to tell that they do so. In fact, the rejection of the black reputation of folklore
combined with a growing scepticism towards the man-eating tales have resulted
in a rehabilitation of the wolf. In Sweden, Poland, Germany and Portugal,
conservation centres have been set up to encourage a growth in the remnant
populations there. In the United States, where wolves have been protected since
1873 under the Endangered Species Act, wolves are drifting south in small
numbers across the Canadian border. Today in a somewhat controversial plan they
are being reintroduced into Yellowstone National Park, where the tee shirts, coffee
mugs, key rings and baseball bats on sale bear the image of the wolf.

It is worth remembering that it is man who has bred the domestic dog from
the wild wolf, to become fierce and dangerous. In America alone domestic dogs
cause more than two million bites, and on average 9-12 deaths every year.

Today's wolf is projected as noble, righteous and benevolent and its
reintroduction is seen by campaigners as a symbolic atonement for past sins against
it, and the declaration that humankind is willing to share the planet with other
forms of life. The wolf has come a long way since the days of Red Riding Hood.

Our perceptions of animals are often stereotyped. We think of the large land
predators as being meat-eaters equipped with fearsome teeth and razor-sharp
claws, whose superior power and acute senses make them a threat to our lives.
Yet there are other animals on the land which are, in fact, just as dangerous,
perhaps even more so.

Without weapons to protect ourselves we are extremely vulnerable, and can
be easily injured by other animals, however harmless they may at first appear. This
point was vividly brought home to me not so long ago when I visited a friend in
Kenya who had a tame male Thompson's gazelle. Tommies, as they are known,
are small, cute antelopes about two feet high and 25 kg (60 lbs) in weight. They
are the Bambies of Africa; the animals one often sees cheetah chasing in films of
the East African plains. I had just closed the door of my car when the Tommy
sauntered over towards me in a very purposeful way. His head was held low and
his small dagger-like horns gleamed in the light. Instinctively I knew he was up to
no good. This was his patch and he saw me as a threat to his dominance here. The
next moment I found myself running around the car chased by a highly aggressive
animal with horns pointing menacingly forward. There was no way I was going to

A grey wolf at a kill

joust with him, and with a wild leap I vaulted onto the roof of the car, my heart pounding. Had he caught up with me, this small antelope could have inflicted quite serious injuries.

In the wild, male Tommies do battle with each other over territory and females, clashing their heads together and sparring with their rapier horns. Occasionally males die in these fights.

There is, you might think, no other animal with so fearsome a reputation as the tiger, and yet it shares the continent of India with a creature which, despite its reputation for intelligence, remarkable memory and gentleness kills three times as many people each year: the elephant.

Between 200 and 250 people are killed by elephants every year in India. To understand why elephants are so dangerous we need to look into the history of man's relationship with this, the largest of land animals. It has been a unique relationship, one perhaps unsurpassed by any other animal, including the dog or the cow. Man has worshiped the elephant as the incarnation of a god, used them in war, offered them as ambassadors of peace, kept them as beasts of burden, but also slaughtered them for their meat and ivory. And man and his crops have been trampled by the elephant.

Domesticated 4000 years ago, the Asian elephant was first used in agriculture and in warfare. They were, however, of limited use in war and in 326 BC Alexander the Great exposed their vulnerability when his horse-based cavalry was confronted by the massed war elephants of King Poros, ruler of the Punjab. Alexander's army were terrified at their first sight of elephants, but Alexander rallied his men and cunningly outflanked and encircled his opponents. His archers then shot the mahouts, while other men hacked at the elephants with scythes and spears. The enraged animals became uncontrollable and trampled friend and foe alike. Despite this defeat there was no denying the splendour of war elephants and it became essential for any ruler in India to maintain an elephant stable, if only as a matter of prestige.

With the invention of gunpowder, the effectiveness of the elephant in battle was further reduced. Tame elephants were of little use against rapid-firing guns, and wild ones were more efficiently slaughtered by them. Ivory has been coveted by man for thousands of years, but while tuskers were in demand on the battle field, their safety was assured. When elephants were no longer captured for the army, they were killed for their tusks. The population of wild animals was further reduced by the hunting of elephant for 'sport' which was introduced by the British at the end of the 17th century. In Asia, an estimated 100,000 elephants have been either captured or killed during the last two centuries.

Today the elephant is protected. In Asia it still plays a part in ceremonies, guarding the temples and carrying tourists around the wildlife sanctuaries. There is still a force of over 5000 domestic elephants in Burma which is vital to the logging industry there. There was a bitter reminder that the elephant can still play its part in 20th century warfare when the Americans bombed elephants in Vietnam to prevent their being used by the Vietcong.

Why should the elephant be the most feared animal of the jungle? It is, after all, a herbivore and not a carnivore, so why is it so aggressive towards people? We travelled to the Nilgiri Hills in the Western Ghatts of India to film and find out more about the elephant problem.

The forests of southern India harbour one of the largest remaining populations of Asian elephants – between 5000 and 6000 individuals. Not surprisingly, the south

Top Elephants are highly social animals – tending to their young for many years – but in areas where they are common they can totally destroy fields of crops overnight *(left)*. In India, they have been used in agriculture and ceremonies for centuries *(above)*

has some of the worst problems with elephants in the country. But it is here too that the worship of the elephant is most prolific. During the third and fourth centuries there arose in India a powerful symbol for the veneration of elephants – Ganesh, the elephant-headed god of the Hindus. Originally Ganesh was seen as the 'creator of obstacles', for the wild elephant was a threat to man and crops over most of the subcontinent. But today Ganesh is revered as 'the remover of obstacles' – a complete reversal of the old image, which can possibly be attributed to the elimination of elephants in the wild and their increasing significance in armies.

One of the most inflammatory interactions of elephants with man is when they raid farms. Crop raiding can be traced back thousands of years, probably even to the beginning of agriculture. In southern India there is a definite yearly pattern to raiding. Elephant herds of females and calves are a particular nuisance when the crops of finger millet, maize or sorghum ripen in January and again towards the end of the year. The bulls, however, are the most persistent raiders, and will venture onto the farms even in the dry months of February to April in search of perennial crops like banana, jack fruit and mango.

Crop raiding not only endangers the lives of people, it is also dangerous for the elephants, for they face a barrage of hostility from the landowners – they have fire balls thrown at them, they are electrocuted with live wire fences and they are shot. Why do elephants bother to raid farms when faced with such risks? Contrary to popular belief, they do not simply raid crops because there is insufficient food or habitat left for them. There is a connection between raiding and the natural wanderings of the herds but, more importantly, the crops provide elephants with the best quality food. Cultivated paddy and finger millet plants are higher in protein, calcium and sodium than the wild grasses. In a single night a bull elephant can easily eat 200 kg (440 lbs) or more of fresh cereal – almost enough nourishment to see him through the entire day. So the lush farms are not only an irresistible temptation, they also allow an elephant to spend more time resting during the remainder of the day.

Bull elephants spend almost fifty nights a year raiding crops – six times more than the family groups. For males the extra risk is worth taking, for well nourished bulls have an advantage over bulls which have eaten the less nutritious wild foods. Such an advantage may well help a bull mate with more females and sire more young. Its perhaps for this reason that the bulls are the most persistent crop raiders.

Although many people are killed or injured by crop raiding elephants, even the most friendly and docile of domesticated male elephants can become unpredictable and dangerous when in musth. Musth, a Sanskrit word meaning drunk, has been known in Asian elephants since ancient times. Charles Darwin wrote in *The Descent of Man* that "no animal in the world is so dangerous as an elephant in musth".

A bull is in musth once or twice a year for a period of a few days to two or three months. In this state they have been known to kill handlers at circuses and zoos, and even mahouts with whom they have been on close terms for many years. During musth the bull's testosterone level shoots up to as much as 60 times the normal. The temporal glands on each side of his head ooze a copious dark, oily secretion. His penis becomes engorged, protruding and dribbles urine. At this stage, some mahouts try to calm a captive bull's fury by feeding him tobacco, hashish or opium balls. Slowly the violence and restlessness subsides, the flow from the temporal gland diminishes, the penis relaxes, and the whole physical and mental state of the animal returns to normal. The elephant is once more the peaceable,

When in musth, bull elephants can be unpredictable and aggresive

loyal and friendly companion of the mahout – until the next time.

The duration of the musth seems to be determined by the bull's health and age; the older a bull is or the better his condition, the longer the duration of the musth. Mahouts have traditionally taken advantage of this to help control bulls which have become aggressive and troublesome in musth. By reducing the amount of food an elephant is given when the first signs of musth appear, the mahout can reduce the condition of the bull and hence lower the intensity and duration of the musth.

Musth has been known in Asian elephants since ancient times, yet only recently was it recognised in African elephants. In both species it has a very special role in their lives. Not only does it increase the testosterone level in the elephant, but it also changes the physiology and behaviour of the animal. A bull in musth becomes more aggressive towards other bulls and actively searches for oestrous females among the herds. Though it is not necessary for a bull to be in musth to mate, it does greatly increase his chances of doing so. Females prefer males in musth and sometimes go to great lengths to prevent being mated by less potent males.

It is not surprising then that captive chained bulls become irritable and uncontrollable when in musth. Wild bulls, on the other hand, usually do not bother people, for they are busy courting females. Today the image of the 'rogue' wild bull still persists, simply because male elephants are responsible for killing more people than females.

Much research has gone into the relationship between man and the Asian elephant, but it seems highly likely that the African elephant causes even more problems, if only because there are so many more of them. In most instances, crop raiding and musth possibly account for many of the deaths or injuries to people, but sometimes the incidents occur as the simple result of a close encounter with an elephant. One of the amazing things about elephants is just how quiet a ten foot high, five tonne adult can be in the densest of vegetation. It is therefore quite understandable that people frequently stumble upon elephants by accident when walking along forest trails. In India, there is one cardinal rule which should never be broken when walking in the jungle – do not take your dog with you. Granted, the dog will almost certainly see the elephant before you, easily scamper out of its way and obediently return to its owner, barking excitedly. However, the full wrath of the elephant will now be directed straight to the place where you are hiding, silent and terrified. Craig Sanderlock, a Canadian ethologist whose wife was researching the relationship between people and elephants, ignored this advice. He had arrived two months earlier in the Nilgiri Hills. On the 26th December his naked body was found battered and bruised, only 200 meters from his house on the forest edge. The broken bushes, trampled ground and torn clothing said it all. He had gone for a short walk with his dog into the forest and had stumbled upon an elephant, a tuskless male known for his aggression. The dog was almost certainly the first to spot the old bull, concealed behind bushes on which the elephant had been browsing all morning. Yapping, the dog must have scampered back through the undergrowth straight to his master. It seems that Craig tried to distract the elephant by undressing and leaving some of his clothes behind, but he did not stand a chance. The enraged bull grabbed him with his trunk and thrashed him against the bushes and ground, shredding the rest of his clothes and leaving his body broken and naked.

Throughout history elephants have killed man and trampled his crops. Today there are less than 60,000 wild elephants left in Asia, only a tenth of the number of African elephants. Both species are on the endangered list. Despite this sad decline, the latest research into the Indian elephant suggests that we now have no choice but to cull elephants, especially notorious males, that consistently kill people or raid crops. Such a recommendation is never taken lightly, but in the case of the Indian elephant it has special significance for here is an animal that has shared with us an unprecedented relationship. For the Indian elephant to survive drastic measures are required; the problem of rampaging elephants will simply get worse as they are confined to smaller and smaller areas.

An animal's looks and its public image can be deceptive. One of the most cuddly looking, almost comical creatures, adored by the public, is reputed to be one of Africa's biggest man-killers; the hippopotamus.

The lives of river and lakeside people in Africa have long been influenced by these massive, lumbering animals. Their shape is homely and unthreatening. They are short-legged and barrel-like, with the reassuring qualities of a domestic sow, though they are undeniably bulky: the males, which are larger than the females, reach 165 cm (5 ft) in height and over 4000 kg (8800lbs) in weight. They look clumsy on land and seldom travel at a greater speed than a jaunty trot, but are capable of up to 30 kph (18 mph) in a very short burst – faster than a human!

Hippos may live alone or in groups of one or two hundred, usually composed of females and their calves. They spend most of the day resting in the water but come out to feed at night, often wandering many miles in their search for good pasture. Hippos usually stay submerged for only two or three minutes, but can stay under water for as long as 30 minutes. Adult males hold territories which contain a narrow strip of water and the adjacent land. Holding a territory is absolutely essential, for without one a bull will not find a mate. Bulls are extremely aggressive towards all other hippos, even youngsters. The incisors and canines of hippos are tusk-like and grow continuously; the lower canines may reach 70 cm in length (over 2 feet), half of which extend above the gum. Hippos can open their mouths extremely wide and do so to help settle contests in which they clash jaws with rivals. In serious fights they drive the huge lower canines deep into the opponent's haunches or shoulders, inflicting terrible wounds.

I once had a narrow escape from a hippo. Ten years ago I was on my first assignment as a cameraman, and the pressure was on to produce the goods. I was working with my companion and colleague Samantha Purdy looking for big cats along the banks of the Mara River in Kenya. Early one morning we came across an adult hippo walking across the plains. It was moving very slowly and appeared in some distress. Huge red gash marks cut deeply across its back and flanks –

The cuddly-looking hippopotamus has an impressive array of tusks which makes its reputation as Africa's biggest man-killer more understandable

probably the result of a fight with another hippo or even an attack by lions. Keen to get a film sequence we followed the hippo into a forest and filmed the wounds. I soon realised that, apart from a few rather gory shots, this was likely to be a very lethargic sequence which was destined for the cutting room floor. I needed something more dramatic, more dynamic. By now the hippo had quietly lain down and looked like a smooth boulder in dappled sunlight. Had it been a lion I would never have dreamed of doing what I did next. To Samantha's utter astonishment, I slid out of the four-wheel drive Suzuki and, camera in hand, proceeded to stalk closer. I knew this was a dangerous, and in retrospect, foolhardy thing to do, but I was looking for the ultimate shot. I knew something about hippos and had reckoned on having to move rapidly sooner or later, so I did not lie on the ground, but instead crouched, ready to spring aside. It was now that my inexperience as a cameraman was revealed. I had chosen an ultra-wide angle lens, which is brilliant as an effects lens, and can create dramatic tension in a composition. The only problem is one has to get very close to the subject for it to appear anything bigger than a speck on film. Cautiously I crept along the ground, closer and closer to the wild, injured hippo. I knew I was now far too close, but I was intently watching the animal, scrutinising it for any tell tale signs that would make me flee. When I was only 10 feet from the hippo, it opened its mouth wide a few times showing its huge tusks – a threat gape warning me not to approach. Then it stood up – the full grown, nervous and wounded hippo towered over me. I stayed crouched, ready to react instantly. But this was the shot – all the hippo had to do was sit down and I would have the most amazing low angle view of the animal doing so. It never did. The next moment it charged. All I remember is diving to the side behind a small tree which I knew was there. As I did so my camera was torn from my grasp and the hippo shot past, inches away, and then stopped, wondering perhaps where the crazy cameraman had gone. It was just a few feet away, and I could have reached out and touched it. In front of the hippo was the vehicle and Samantha. With a lunge the hippo attacked the car, a tusk slicing straight through the metal of the bonnet. Then it turned and ran off into the forest leaving behind an ashen woman and a more respectful cameraman. I never did get the shot.

Because much of the social activity of hippos takes place in the water or at night, they have not been extensively studied. The research that has been done suggests that hippos kill more people in Africa than lions, elephants and buffaloes combined. It seems that they are particularly dangerous during the dry season when confined to narrow waterways and drying pools. This is also the time when the males are especially aggressive, for they are on the lookout for oestrous females. Hippo attacks can occur both in and out of the water. Attacks in water are often the result of people getting too close to territorial males or herds of females with young. The aggressive or panicking animals will charge and attack small boats, upturning them and slashing out at the bodies of the people that spill into the water. On land however, hippos spread out to feed over a large area and rarely attack people unless provoked. Most incidents here are of people walking along hippo trails. The trails provide easy pathways through thick bush, but can be dangerous should one accidentally chance upon a hippo. A startled hippo will charge along the paths in its rush to get back to the safety of the river, brushing aside or trampling anyone in its way. In the past the hippo undoubtedly came into conflict with man simply because it was so widespread, and lived along waterways

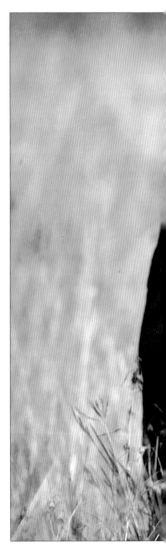

frequented by man. Hippos used to occur throughout Africa south of the Sahara, in any areas with suitable rivers or lakes. Today the hippo, like the elephant, occupies only a fraction of its former range and is largely confined to central and eastern Africa.

It is very difficult to verify many of the stories that surround the reputations of wild animals. Very few records are kept of human casualties in the remote areas of third world countries. Yet these are the very places most likely to still have reasonable populations of large wild carnivores and herbivores, and consequently more conflicts with people.

The most experienced of the old hands in Africa will often say that the most dangerous animal on the continent is the African buffalo. These views frequently have their origins in big game hunting. Many stories recount incidents of wounded buffalo, said to be especially dangerous and extremely cunning, often doubling back or hiding in wait for their pursuers. In the folk lore of the white hunter, death

African buffalos are particularly dangerous when they are alone or wounded

from buffalo attack can be particularly gruesome. Men have been trapped, it is said, in low trees by an enraged buffalo, which then rasped the flesh from their legs with a file-like tongue. Buffalo do have rough tongues, but it is likely that most of the anecdotal information circulating about buffalo attacks has its origin in campfire yarns.

The buffalo certainly has the size and weight to be dangerous. The males can stand 170 cm (5 feet) at the shoulders and weigh 900 kg (1980 lbs). But it is their horns that are especially impressive. The horns are very distinctive and are different in each individual, some curving upwards and others backwards. Both sexes have horns, but those of the male are especially massive and joined together by a large heavy shield, or boss, covering the top of the head. The horns of the African buffalo are amongst the largest of any animal, and those of a male can have a spread of over 3 meters. They are the animals' chief weapon and are used in defence against lions or, for that matter, people.

The African buffalo is reminiscent of the ancient cattle, the aurochs – powerful and deadly fighters easily capable of running at speeds of over 50 kph (30 mph). It has good eyesight, an excellent sense of smell and exceptional hearing. Buffaloes are generally peaceful creatures, most living in herds sometimes numbering many hundred individuals. Very old bulls usually leave the herd to live out the rest of their lives alone or in the company of a few other old males.

When buffalo are in herds they rarely present a threat. If disturbed they will all turn to face the intruder and, heads raised, will approach en masse before stopping and watching intently. Such a display can be a frightening and humbling experience as I can affirm. In reality the animals are merely trying to find out more about you, and almost always turn tail and lumber off together.

It is a different story with solitary or wounded buffalo. These animals really are dangerous, especially when accidentally disturbed whilst quietly resting in long grass or thick bush during the day. Old buffalo are often partially blind, and rheumatic and so, perhaps understandably, cantankerous. They are reputed to stalk humans and attack without reason. An aggressive bull may warn you by grunting, tossing his head and goring the ground before charging. But because many incidents occur at close range, you may never see the bull that charges you. The charge is of such force that, in one incident reported in Uganda, a charging buffalo which missed its target broke its own neck against a tree trunk. There are many records of buffaloes tossing lions into the air and goring them to death. Every now and again tourists foolish enough to take an unofficial stroll through wild Africa are killed by buffalo, split open from their groin to sternum with a single sweep of its horns. Despite these odd incidents, the bad reputation of the buffalo is one largely perpetuated by stories. Researchers studying them today view them much the same as the local African people do – from a distance with respect and caution.

Around the world the large herbivores deserve respect if only because their huge bulk makes them formidable – respect they often do not get. In North America bison are considered to be the most dangerous animals in Yellowstone National Park – even more dangerous than grizzly bears. In common with other herbivores, all injuries are caused by people getting too close to the animals. Whilst visitors are advised to stay a safe 100 meters away from a one tonne bison, they often approach to within 1 meter! Each year two or three people are seriously gored by bison in this park. Occasionally they are killed.

Bison were once amongst the most numerous mammals on earth. On the great plains of North America alone there were estimated to have been perhaps 50 million bison, only a few hundred years ago. Today, there are just 100,000 or so left. A similar decline has occurred to the rhinoceros. Once rhinos were widespread and numbered hundreds of thousands. Today you are lucky to see one, as all five species are threatened with extinction.

The cause of their decline has been poaching. The rhino has a front horn which, in the black rhino of Africa, can grow up to 130 cm (over 4 feet) and which is literally worth its weight in gold. The horn is cherished in the Far East as an aphrodisiac and in many Arab countries as a dagger handle. Made up of hair, the horn, in reality, has no know properties of use in love making, except perhaps as a stimulating itching powder! The idea of rhinos being champion lovers may stem from their habit of copulating for an hour or more. But, if the truth were known, the male rhino certainly does not give the appearance of being an expert at the job. He finds even mounting his partner awkward and, once on top, he is forced to shuffle along on his hind legs as his partner wanders around. Frequently he falls off in an ungainly belly flop fashion. He is not quite the casanova his horny reputation would let you believe.

Of all the species of rhino, the black rhino has the reputation for being the most pugnacious and easily aroused, which is in complete contrast to the placid temperament of the other African species, the white rhino. The black rhinoceros is about as tall as an African buffalo, but twice as heavy, the male growing to 1400 kg (3000 lbs). Rhinos have poor eyesight and rely on their acute sense of hearing and smell to detect intruders. In Africa rhinos also have a built-in alarm system – oxpeckers. These garrulous birds are often associated with rhinos and feed on the ticks and other parasites in the animals' hide. The oxpeckers are highly adapted for a life riding the backs of animals, and can often be heard noisily quarrelling with other oxpeckers that dare come close to their host. As far as they are concerned, the animal they are perched on is their territory and worth protecting. Oxpeckers are always alert and their alarm calls warn the rhino of the approach of any predator, including man.

Rhino horn is a much sought after aphrodisiac

Contrary to popular opinion, rhinos are extremely agile and are able to run at 50 kph (30 mph) and nimbly turn within their own body length. Although their reputation is probably exaggerated, black rhinos, especially, are unpredictable and will charge vehicles or people on the least provocation. Human scent alone can cause panic. When preparing to charge the rhino utters a screaming groan with its upper lip curled, its eyes rolling and tail raised. The charges are almost always simply threatening behaviour but should be taken seriously. Usually, however,

The white rhino – white is derived from the Afrikaans for wide, which describes the shape of its mouth. It is a much less aggressive animal than the black rhino

they will rush harmlessly off in the opposite direction before spinning around and galloping back for another look. Today with rhinos so rare, any threat they may once have posed to human life is now largely academic.

Of the large predators that inhabit the land, there is one, above all others, that should be treated with respect, perhaps even fear. Like a rhino it is armour-plated and it grows to be as heavy as an African buffalo. It can remain hidden in knee-deep water for an hour and then strike with blinding speed. Its jaws are powerful enough to crush the leg of a buffalo yet sensitive enough to gently cradle an egg without breaking it. It is arguably the most efficient predator on earth and it kills more people than any other large animal. It is the crocodile. Few people ever escape a crocodile attack. Val Plumwood was one of the lucky ones. In 1985 Val Plumwood visited Kakadu in the Northern Territory of Australia. Being the end of the dry season, the weather was hot and muggy with the expectation of the 'big wet' that would soon unleash torrential rain across the parched landscape. Kakadu is a magical place and Val took a canoe out to paddle around the lagoons. Although this part of Australia is renowned for its large salt-water crocodiles, canoeing in local selected lagoons was not fraught with danger and something that many people did. On the second day Val decided to spend the whole day exploring the lagoons and swamps a little further from the ranger station.

> I'd spent a pleasant time observing the birds and had reached a point in the paper bark swamp where I could not go any further because the channel was petering out and it was getting shallower and shallower. I had not realised that I'd followed a back water of the Alligator River and had come to the banks of the river itself. I'm told that this is a very

highly populated crocodile area – I should not have gone anywhere near it but I did not know that it was a potentially dangerous site. I decided to come home and started back the way I'd come. I had not gone more than five minutes down the stream when I came around a bend and I saw what appeared to be a stick. Something about the stick drew my attention – it suddenly seemed to develop eyes and then I got closer to it and realised that it was in fact a crocodile. I did not initially feel particularly alarmed by this because I'd seen crocodiles before and they'd always moved out of the way. So I did not see any reason to be particularly concerned about it – it only looked like a very small crocodile. Anyway my canoe was moving along fairly swiftly and I was getting closer to it quickly. I do not recall taking any evasive action, but it seemed that in no time at all my canoe and the crocodile were adjacent to one another.

It was an encounter that Val would always remember. The crocodile suddenly started to bash the canoe.

I was taken aback to put it mildly. This was completely outside what I'd been led to expect would happen as I was told people are rarely attacked in boats. So the unbelievable was happening – this crocodile was actually attacking my canoe. What was I going to do?

Val paddled for shore and leapt for a low branch of a paper bark tree.

The speed with which it moved seemed almost incredible. It seemed like almost the instant I leapt into the tree it leapt out of the water. I did not even get my foot onto the branch. I just had this vision of a huge splash of water and an incredible gaping jaw, and then it had me around between the legs, right between the legs. Then I was in the water and my feeling was one of disbelief – it could not be happening – this was a bad dream. In that incredible split second I had the thought that I was

The number of people visiting wilderness areas has put more people at risk

going to die and that no one would know how I died. I was rolled under the water – the experience is hard to describe – I guess very few people have lived to tell the story. I was just enveloped by an incredible boiling blackness. Fear, incredible fear – I felt totally helpless.

Fortunately for Val the water was shallow and the crocodile was unable to drown her.

I came up. I could not believe it. My head and shoulders were above the water. I did not notice any pain. It did not register until much later. I was conscious that it had me between the legs – one of its teeth had dug in about a centimetre behind the vagina – the tooth mark went right through the coccyx. Apart from that it just had its teeth right between my legs. I imagined that if I did survive I would be mutilated, but actually that has not turned out to be the case.

Inexplicably, after rolling her underwater for a second time the crocodile let her go. But as she tried to climb out of the water it attacked again dragging her underwater and rolling her a third time. Then it let her go again.

Salt water crocodiles have been implicated in many man-eating incidents

I was able to climb up the bank and I stood up – I could not believe it – by this time I was completely incredulous to be alive and had an incredible feeling at first of elation – I could not believe I was still here. I did not know how long my luck would last so I started to try to runaway, but I only took a few steps when I realised there was something badly wrong with my leg – my leg was not functioning at all. But I did not stop to look – I just remember thinking at the time, "It's broken my leg." As I stumbled down the creek I was calling out and crying. I reached the edge of the swamp that I crossed with the canoe – the ranger station lay on the other side of that."

By now it was dark and Greg Miles, a ranger at the station, was becoming

concerned that Val had not returned. He checked on the mooring – the canoe was still missing. On the other side of the swamp, Val heard the noise of a motorbike and saw a faint light flicker through the trees.

Five hours after the attack Val Plumwood was found alive by the rangers. But why was she attacked? The local rangers think that the crocodile was acting aggressively in a territorial way. It was almost certainly a small specimen less than 10 feet long, possibly a young male that had been chased away from the Alligator River by larger territorial males. Territorial aggression between male crocodiles is common and they frequently inflict deep wounds and even kill one another. The animal that attacked Val Plumwood may have mistaken the canoe bearing down on it for a large aggressive crocodile and attacked in self defence.

Another theory is that the crocodile was particularly cantankerous and it was just an unlucky incident with an usually aggressive animal. Val Plumwood survived probably because the crocodile was not in a feeding mode and the water was shallow. All over the world, crocodiles use water as a hiding place from which to launch an attack, and as a way of quickly dispatching prey, by drowning. In this way they are able to tackle some of the largest land animals.

The crocodiles and alligators are close relatives of the dinosaurs. They dominated life on our planet between 245 and 65 million years ago, and they are still around. They must be doing something right.

Crocodiles have been venerated by humans for thousands of years. In Egypt they were even embalmed after death and kept in the tombs of kings. A famous African 'white-hunter' once wrote: "It is strange there should be a common enemy to man and beast, but it is so, in the hideous monster, the crocodile. It can be aptly described as a loathsome beast, unloved and feared by all". In areas where crocodiles live the tourist industry has not been slow to exploit this universal fear and to arrange trips to 'crocodile country' for those with a taste for a cheap thrill. Warning signs with a dramatic crocodile head logo are regularly stolen and taken home as souvenirs of bravery by visitors to Australia where the worldwide success of the film *Crocodile Dundee* has given a boost to the outback.

Crocodiles and alligators are closely related and the differences between them subtle – but there is one obvious way of telling them apart. Both have a large fourth tooth in the lower jaw. The crocodile has a notch in its upper jaw to accommodate this tooth so that, when its mouth is closed you can see the tooth. The alligator has no notch so when its mouth is closed the tooth cannot be seen.

Crocodiles were once thought of as being lethargic hulks that spent most of their lives basking in the sun. Today we know them to be remarkable predators with fascinating life styles. They have an excellent sense of smell, keen eyesight, good hearing and their brain is more complex than that of any other reptile.

They are unusual amongst reptiles in showing parental care, the mother and sometimes the father guarding the nests and the hatchlings. The eggs take two to three months to incubate and the female remains near the nest to ward off would-be predators, like monitor lizards. During this time she is particularly aggressive and will not even leave the nest to eat. When the young are ready to hatch they make piping noises from inside the egg. The sound is loud enough to be heard above ground. It is a signal for the mother to start excavating the nest to help the young to the surface. Once she has uncovered the hatchlings she carefully picks them up in her massive jaws and allows them to wriggle into a pouch in the bottom of her mouth. Once they have all been collected she carries them down to the water where she releases them. For the next six to eight weeks she will guard the youngsters defending them against other crocodiles and predators in general.

Interestingly the success of the crocodile can partly be attributed to its habit of basking. By lying in the sun they conserve energy, and this helps them to survive when food is scarce. The adults of the largest species routinely capture and drown animals even heavier than themselves. Yet they can also feed opportunistically on prey as small as frogs. So successful are they as predators that they have undergone few changes over the last 60 million years.

Above Despite their fearsome appearance, crocodiles and alligators are very good at looking after their young

All species of crocodile have the reputation of killing people. It is something that they have been doing since man first evolved. At the famous archaeological site at Olduvai Gorge in Tanzania, a hominid skull has been found punctured by the tooth marks of a large crocodile. There are, in all, twenty one species of crocodile, of which seven are recorded as having, at some time, attacked humans. Of these, only two do so with such regularity that they can reasonably be called 'man-eaters'. They are the Nile crocodile and the Indo Pacific crocodile.

The Nile crocodile has the reputation of being the biggest killer on the African continent – over 1000 people are said to fall victim to them every year. It is, to start with, far more widely distributed than the other man-killers – the lion, leopard, buffalo and elephant, and it is far more abundant than all of them put together. Nile crocodiles thrive in rivers, swamps, estuaries, and lakes, where millions of people all over Africa live, work, and play daily. These people transport themselves in small boats, canoes or rafts on the crocodile – infested waters and sometimes even wade across wide shallow rivers. As populations increase and areas are developed, these waters are increasingly used for recreation, and the domain of the crocodile is further invaded. In its waters, the Nile crocodile is in competition with predatory fish and sharks, monitor lizards, three other species of crocodile, and hippopotami; on land it has to defend territory and offspring against a range of threats from mongooses to elephants – including humans.

They are amongst the largest of crocodiles. The adults can weigh up to 1000 kilos (2200 lbs) and grow to 6.5 meters (21 feet) in length. They are big and look ponderous but have a hunting technique second to none. They are cryptically coloured, so that as they lie motionless in the water with only their eyes and nostrils above the surface they are all but invisible. They are masters of camouflage and will conceal themselves further by lying next to a stand of reeds, under the overhanging branches of trees, or close to other floating objects. In this ambush situation they can breathe, smell, see and hear without being seen. Sometimes they will see a potential victim when they are drifting some distance from the shore. They will then submerge and approach closer and closer, keeping the victim under observation until the distance is right for attack.

Often crocodiles take up this position on the approach of cars or tourist buses. People who get out, spread themselves along the edge of the water and complain that the animals they have paid to see are not around had better watch out. The Nile crocodile is not only agile – it can move faster than a man both in and out of the water. A submerged crocodile can explode from the water like a Polaris missile and its final lunge can carry it 10 meters (30 feet) up the beach. The powerful tail drives it out of the water and the hind legs curl under it to give a thrust when it hits the sand. Often the crocodile seems to vault straight out of the water. Such is the power of its jaws that it needs only to get a grip on any part of its prey to be able to drag the victim back into the water and drown it.

Crocodiles can even hurl themselves vertically out of the water and many a relaxed fisherman has been taken from what seemed to be a position of safety five feet above the surface. Nesting weaver birds high in the reeds can be flipped into the water with a flick of the tail to be snapped up.

Contrary to popular belief, there is no safety from crocodiles in either noise or numbers. Most human victims have been in groups, fording rivers, washing clothes or bathing, and making a great deal of noise at the time. Crocodiles are attracted by disturbance in the water and such behaviour may draw them to the scene if merely for curiosity's sake.

The jaws of a crocodile are immensely powerful and close with huge force. Once the victim has been seized, it has little chance of escape but the crocodile is unable to chew it to pieces. Its 66 teeth are used for holding or crushing the prey. It cannot move its jaws sideways and so has to reduce the size of a victim by violently shaking it to pieces. The crocodile then simply tosses back its head and gulps down its food.

If the prey is large the crocodile will grab the animal in its mouth and spin to tear bite-sized chunks off. This technique, however, would be useless if the victim were also to spin with the crocodile. So Nile crocodiles sometimes hunt cooperatively and take it in turns to spin and feed, or hold the prey for others.

The Nile crocodile is not the largest of crocodiles. The Indo Pacific crocodile of South-east Asia and Australia is the largest reptile in the world. Adult males grow to an average 4.5 meters (14.5 feet) and weigh around 500 kg (1100 lbs). Specimens over 7 meters (23 feet) have been recorded.

The Indo Pacific crocodile is also called the saltwater or estuarine crocodile, but this is something of a misnomer, because it is not exclusively marine or estuarine, though it has been found far out to sea with both turtle and shark in its stomach.

When a few years ago I was filming in Western Australia, we visited the Prince Regent, a river which runs deep into the heart of an area known as The Kimberleys. The river is infamous for a fatal crocodile attack on an American woman in 1987. We motored up the river in a small rubber dinghy and went ashore looking for fish eagle nests. After clambering high above the river we turned and looked back through binoculars at the dingy far below. To our amazement there, in amongst the weeds, right next to the boat was a large salt water crocodile. It had presumably swum over to the boat to take a closer look, perhaps out of mere curiosity. Yet when we returned to the boat half an hour later there was not a trace of the animal. Had we not seen it for ourselves, none of us would have guessed that a large crocodile now lurked in those dark waters, perhaps only a few meters away. For me it was an enlightening experience.

The Indo Pacific crocodile was responsible for the most gruesome incident involving man-eating ever recorded. On the night of 19th February 1945 Japanese troops were trying to escape from the island of Ramree, off the coast of Burma, to the mainland 18 miles away. The channel was a mire swamp, overgrown with mangrove. Sitting in a marine launch which had been grounded in the channel was the naturalist Bruce Wright, a member of the British forces who had trapped the Japanese on the island. He wrote of what then happened:

> That night was the most horrible that any member of the M.L. [marine launch] crews ever experienced. The scattered rifle shots in the pitch black swamp punctured by the screams of wounded men crushed in the jaws of huge reptiles and the blurred worrying sound of the spinning crocodiles made a cacophony of hell that has rarely been duplicated on earth. At dawn the vultures arrived to clean up what the crocodiles had left...Of about 1000 Japanese soldiers that entered the swamps of Ramree, only about 20 were found alive.

The many attacks from Indo Pacific crocodiles that occur each year in remote parts of South-east Asia and the Pacific go unrecorded, but the crocodile has recently been under a glare of publicity in Australia. After being extensively hunted there to satisfy an insatiable world demand for skins to make handbags and shoes, the crocodile was first given legal protection in Western Australia in 1971. Other states followed, but in Queensland in 1975 a fatal attack was reported just a year after the crocodile had been given protection. The victim was an Aborigine and it took place in the Gulf of Carpentaria. It was put down as a freak occurrence, perhaps a visiting animal from Papua New Guinea.

Ten years later the attack on Val Plumwood was extensively reported, and when, before the year was out, a mother of three waded out into a north Queensland river to cool herself during a Christmas party and was taken, the slaughter began. Within the first few months of 1986 about 10% of the known crocodiles on the East coast had been killed. The public antipathy to them was fed by the death, in February, of a young deckhand on a fishing trawler, and again in September when a Queensland visitor went to sleep on the banks of the McArthur river after a drinking session. Only his shirt was seen the next morning and his torso was recovered from the stomach of a 4.5 meter crocodile two days later. Despite the public outcry there have been only 12 fatal attacks in Australia in the last 20 years.

So the crocodile in Australia has again become the target of public hatred and fear. It raises in the most powerful way the question of how far Australians can be prepared to share their land with the majestic survivors of the reptilian era who have preceded their occupation of the continent by 200 million years.

The conflict between advancing civilisation and the crocodylia is even more sharply thrown into relief by the alligator attacks in Florida. These increased from the late 1960s to the mid 1970s and rarely failed to make newspaper headlines. This was a period of phenomenal growth in the human population which spread out into the developments adjacent to wetland areas. During this period, about 5000 complaints a year were received by the Florida Game and Fresh Water Fish Commission, citing alligators as a threat to life and property. A programme of harvesting alligators against which complaints had been laid was started, and

Right A land animal in water is at the mercy of any passing crocodile. Nile crocodile pursues a young wildebeest

about 2000 alligators were removed each year. Florida is by far the worst affected state in America, and since 1948 there have been 180 attacks on humans, with thirteen fatalities in the last twenty years.

Now the number of fatalities has been reduced though each year brings its record of unprovoked attacks. Where alligators live close to humans without fear they cease to run away, and there are areas in which they are regularly fed by humans. But increased familiarity can lead to unpredictable attacks and a common warning notice reads: I BITE THE HAND THAT FEEDS ME.

There is no doubt that the fear inspired by alligators and crocodiles is an ingredient in the popularity of tours to the areas where they live. To allow visitors to experience this without putting themselves into danger, a code of safety measures has been worked out: Do not fish within 3 meters of the waters edge; do not let dogs or children paddle in the shallows; if travelling in a boat, keep your bottom on the seat, and don't hang over the edge; and do not walk around at night without a torch.

The public's hysterical reaction to crocodile attacks is on a par with those of sharks and tigers, and is perhaps a reflection on the often gruesome nature of the injuries sustained by the victims. For this reason attacks by the large carnivores receive far more publicity and achieve far greater notoriety than the attacks of animals like snakes and insects, even though the latter cause far more human deaths.

In the Gambia in West Africa people used to, until recently, live in surprising harmony with the Nile crocodile, and even actively encourage them to stay near the village. The people looked upon the crocodiles as sacred animals and protectors of the village. During the dry season, the pools in which the crocodiles lived shrunk, and the crocodiles were forced to aestivate in burrows which they dug in the banks. When the rains returned, the crocodiles emerged and lay along the banks within feet of women and children washing and swimming. The women would occasionally audaciously lay their clothing to dry on the backs of the ten foot crocodiles basking in the sun. Why did they take such risks? The people regularly fed the crocodiles fish and felt safe in the knowledge that the crocodiles were well fed and so unlikely to attack. For them these awesome predators were the guardians of the village, and not man-eaters. Today the only pools where this continues are maintained for the benefit of tourists, who pay to feed and stroke the crocs.

There are, among the predators, those so saddled with a fear-inspiring image that they have been hunted to the point of extinction. It has, for many centuries and across many cultures, been thought of as a virtuous and courageous act to kill them, even though they present no real threat to humans. Some of these animals, like the wolf, are on the road to rehabilitation, though their existing image lies deep in the human psyche and is hard to eradicate. Others – like the crocodile – which are dangerous, attack humans who are ignorant of their capability to inflict devastating injuries. Finally, there are the those, like the big cats, who are properly feared for their evident superiority to us as efficient hunting animals, but which, for the most part, would prefer to keep out of our way. As the opportunities increase, through easier travel, to come close to all of these creatures, the most secure defence we can have against harm is an awareness and understanding of the nature of the large animals that share the planet with us.

Above Crocodiles tear prey into more manageable chunks. A Nile crocodile feeding on a Thomson's Gazelle.

Right Man is encroaching on the alligator's habitat

The Deep

The oceans are among the most exciting places on earth and their many moods are a source of endless fascination. They can be serene and tranquil; yet they can also be violent and awesome. They can be crystal clear and inviting or dark and sinister. I was introduced to the Indian Ocean at the age of two and, like many a child, it was love at first sight. When I was nine we went on holiday to Hawaii. Strolling along a breakwater I was mesmerised by turquoise waters so clear that it appeared that I could reach down and touch the bottom. It was a thrilling sight whose lure I could not resist. Leaping off the parapet I plummeted straight to the bottom fifteen feet down. I had been deceived by the inviting crystal waters – I had not yet learned to swim in the deep end and it was much deeper than it looked. Fortunately my elder brother was at hand to dive in and fish me out.

Even the most placid sea should never be underestimated, but a violent sea is a most terrifying place as the following account relates. The family involved had to contend not only with the forces of the ocean itself, but also with some of its most nightmarish inhabitants...

On the night of the 2nd of July 1974 Diane Horne and her husband Ed set off in a motor boat from Carrabelle, Florida, to cross the Gulf of Mexico to Tampa St Petersberg three hundred miles away. Diane was pregnant at the time, and aboard the Richardson 43 footer were all five of their children – Diana (14), Gerald (12), Billy (10), Melissa (4), and three year-old Tex. Gerald had just had kidney surgery and his fever was again high. After consulting their doctor back in Texas, the Hornes decided to sail that night to try to get Gerald to hospital in Tampa as soon as possible. The conditions for the trip looked auspicious. The weather bureau predicted a dry night with calm seas, and the overnight trip would mean that they would arrive at the unfamiliar harbour of Tampa in the light of the next morning. For 25 years Diane has tried to forget what happened on that night. This is her story:

Left and above The true size and power of a great white shark can sometimes match the mythical creatures that inhabit the deep

It was very beautiful, very uneventful for the first few hours (on the boat). We sat around and watched the sunset, laughed and talked about the things we'd do over the next few days. I was putting the kids to bed. Gerald had called to me and I went in to check on him. When I felt him I realised he had fever and I gave him medicine. I had to get up on the bunk to do that. When I stepped down off the bunk I felt water on the

The Horne family shortly before they departed on their ill-fated trip. Left to right: Gerald, Billy, Diana, Melissa, Tex, and Mr and Mrs Horne

floor. I started walking around and wherever I walked throughout the boat it was wet. It was just wet everywhere.

Whilst Diane had been reading to the children in bed the conditions outside had deteriorated dramatically. The storm seemed to come up from nowhere.
"You know there is water in this floor, I don't know where from," Diane hollered to Ed. "Well there's lots up here. Go check the bilge pump, maybe something has gotten in the strainer or something," Ed replied. Diane checked the bilge pump but everything looked sound and in order. It was around ten o'clock in the evening and by now huge waves were crashing clean over the boat. With the boat shipping water Ed suggested they all put on lifejackets.

It was hard for me to believe that anything like that could be happening. The kids put their lifejackets on and then one of them said, 'Mother you need a life jacket. You're the one who can't swim.' And so I put mine on. I still didn't feel it was that severe. I just didn't believe it. These were things that don't happen to you in life.

As conditions worsened the family went upstairs. Downstairs the washer or something came adrift and crashed around, letting in more water. The Hornes tried to radio for assistance. A fishing boat and the coastguard heard but thought that it was a prank, and did not take it seriously. In the mountainous waves, their boat began to break up. The superstructure crashed down, showering glass everywhere.

Above We saw a dorsal fin...

I had at one point stuck my hand through the glass to get at the radio. I remember getting shocked by the radio. I had to break out the glass more. We really weren't that cut up as I would have thought we would have been. There was a cut on Tex's leg, but we really didn't see it because it was dark. We don't know how that occurred.

Only now did someone answer their mayday calls – but Diane cannot remember any details. The Hornes clung on to the front railing of the boat and for a while tried to signal with a huge flashlight before it finally went out in the water. Suddenly the railing broke and they were flung into the water.

When we were all in the water it was like a huge relief because we weren't having to hang on and be tossed about. We were going up and down like in a giant wave pool. Now everything was going to be fine.

The Hornes roped themselves together, lacing a line through their lifejackets so that they could all slide back and forth along the rope. Two or three times they spread out so that they could all just lie back and float in the water.

We were just out there it seemed like forever. And then it began getting light and we knew we would be rescued. We saw a dorsal fin but

The bull shark is one of the species that may have attacked the Horne family

thought it was a dolphin. We were talking about it, and thought it was Flipper and how dolphins lead people to safety. Well into the day we saw a plane, and we were screaming and hollering. We saw it twice. We never saw a boat ever, never even saw the fishing boat approaching us. With the glare of the sun, and the salt and everything I think we couldn't see that well at that point, or we were just tired. Or maybe our eyes were sunburned. I don't really know. We were all together. Then all of a sudden the boat was there and the sharks hit at the same time. I was pushed way out of the water and then went down again – my feet must have been on the back of one because I was raised up by one. I hollered, 'Billy come over this way' and he said, 'I can't swim.' That's when I saw his arm and I just grabbed him. His life jacket was ripped apart. I think the shark maybe hit Billy and then went right under me and that's when I felt myself going up and then back down.

That shark grazed her leg and left a tooth-like scale embedded in her skin. The people in one of the rescue aircraft reported seeing masses of sharks circling all around the family in the water. Diane held Billy in her right arm trying to hide his wound with his jacket and prevent the terribly severed arm from falling off. In her other arm she held Tex who had by now lost consciousness from cold. Gerald and Diane tried to keep Tex's head above water. By now a coastguard helicopter had joined in the rescue operation and dropped a paramedic into the water to help them.

I remember it being very difficult to get up onto the boat and it was also extremely painful. I remember the man on the boat trying to give Tex mouth to mouth resuscitation. Billy was laying in a bunk. We flew to Tyndalls Airforce base in Panama City. When they took us to the hospital in the ambulance I began asking 'How are my babies? Where are my babies?' And no one would tell me. They wouldn't tell me anything. So I knew. When we got into the emergency room there was a doctor there who said, 'You're not going to like it.' And I said 'I know they are dead.' He said 'Yes they are.' And I said, 'Both of them?' And he said 'Yes both of them. They had arrived dead'. Tex never regained consciousness. They said it was because of the temperature of the water, the exposure – he was very small. He was three. Maybe Billy died from loss of blood or exposure and shock.

The terrifying experiences of that night have understandably had a profound effect on Diane and her attitude to the sea and sharks:

There is not a night that I have laid my head on the pillow that I haven't thought of this. These twenty years there is not one night I have not

Tiger sharks are one of the few sharks
responsible for man-eating – but they will
also readily turn cannibals

away, helpless and insignificant dots in their vastness. We traditionally divide the worlds oceans into four: the Pacific, Atlantic, Indian and Arctic. But if you look at a globe of the world from the South Pole, you can see they are connected – enormous branches of one vast system, that together with inland waters, cover over 70% of the surface of the earth. They are powerful, unpredictable and relatively unknown. In fact the open oceans are the least known habitat on earth. It is a mysterious environment in which even the commonplace can appear unfamiliar and frightening.

When we enter this alien environment we put ourselves at an immediate disadvantage. We cannot breathe without artificial aid. Our senses of hearing and sight are impaired, which makes us even more apprehensive of the dangers that we imagine surround us. It also makes us slow to become aware of any threat. Even when we suddenly recognise danger, we cannot move swiftly enough to get away. We are physically outclassed and outmanoeuvred by the creatures that surround us. We flounder helplessly while they move effortlessly around us. If we are to overcome our fears of the oceans we need to learn more about this environment, and the strange creatures that inhabit it.

It is in the shallows of the ocean, not its depths, that Man has most to fear, for this is the region inhabited by most marine life, and is also the zone where people spend most of their time. The greatest and most widespread fear for people who venture into the shallow seas is of shark attack. People are afraid of being bitten, maimed or scarred by animals, and have an even more deep-seated fear of being eaten. The astonishing success of the film *Jaws*, which suddenly and unexpectedly grossed more than any previous movie in the history of Hollywood, shows that it touched some deep, and almost universal, human anxiety. Its setting in a sunny resort where families swam from a popular beach increased the horror. Because of the intensity and widespread nature of our reaction to the possibility of shark attack, it is important that we try to understand more about the reality that lies behind this nightmare. Are sharks really the threat they are purported to be, or are our fears misdirected?

Sharks are among the most efficient predators on earth. A sign of their efficiency is that their basic design has changed little in the course of 200 million years of evolution. This design blueprint has been adapted to such a great range of different life-styles that very few sharks actually fit our stereotyped image of the one in *Jaws*. For a start, more than half of the 350 or so species of shark are less than one meter (3 feet) in length. Many are inconspicuous fish, which feed on crustaceans or shellfish. The biggest, the whale shark, 12.65 meters (41.5 feet) long, and basking shark, 12.3 meters (40.3 feet) long, are not voracious predators but gentle giants that feed placidly on plankton. The smallest shark is a mere 150mm (6 inches) long, the spiny pygmy shark.

Other sharks have adopted a parasitic lifestyle. The cookie cutter shark, which reaches a length of 50 cm, lives in the depths of the ocean, and swims each night to the surface where it waits for whales, sharks and other large fish. They are thought to be lured towards the cookie cutter by the bright green light which it emits from its belly. The small shark clamps on to its prey with its sharp teeth and

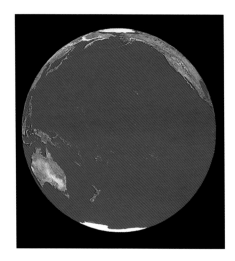

Above The shark's kingdom covers over 70% of the earth's surface

Right Cookie cutter sharks bite disc-shaped mouthfuls of flesh off other sea animals

Above and right The whale shark is
the largest fish in the sea, but eats
only plankton

powerful jaws, and twists until it has gouged out a circle of flesh, leaving a round scar, 5 cm in diameter, that looks like a cookie. This shark was only discovered when an explanation was sought for the strange circular marks found on the rubber casings of the sonar domes of submarines.

Some sharks are fearsome, however. We are probably fortunate that *Carcharodon megalodon* became extinct long before humans evolved and took to the high seas. Our only evidence of the existence of this giant shark are its fossil teeth, first discovered on the ocean floor at a depth of over 2000 fathoms (3600 meters, approx 12,000 feet) in 1873. These spectacular teeth are up to 13 cm (5 inches) long, implying that *megalodon* is likely to have been upwards of 15 meters (49 feet) long which makes it the biggest predator that ever existed on earth with the sole exception of the sperm whale. Even the much-feared great white shark only reaches a maximum of 9 meters (30 feet) in length, a midget by comparison. *Megalodon* existed as recently as 15 million years ago and it is interesting to speculate that it just might turn up again one day like the coelacanth, which had been declared extinct for 70 million years but was rediscovered in 1938, caught in the nets of a South African trawler.

It would be wrong to imagine that all big sharks are either extinct, sift plankton, or survive without posing a potential risk to humans. It is the fast, streamlined sharks which are the basis of our nightmare image of sharks. These include reef sharks, blue sharks and great whites. These sharks are indeed active hunters, using speed, an impressive array of senses, and an equally impressive set of teeth to hunt fish in the shallow seas and open oceans. Prey are impaled on the pointed teeth of the lower jaw, and those of the upper jaw are used to saw away a section of flesh. The serrated edges of the teeth of species such as the great white, tiger and bull shark help with this process. The teeth, while sharp, are also brittle and are constantly breaking off. New teeth are created all the time to compensate for this, and rotate into position from the inside of the jaw as they are needed. As a result, five or more rows of teeth may be present in the mouth at any one time, folded back into the jaw tissue.

However, despite this terrifying arsenal, very few sharks ever bite people. The explanation lies in their behaviour; like a large dog, although they may be capable of biting a human, they may not be inclined to do so. Our reluctance to accept this fact may

The tooth of the extinct *Carcharodon megalodon* in comparison to that of a great white shark

be because much of our knowledge about the large sharks, particularly great white sharks, has come from studying and filming them by baiting. The sharks are lured into view with a cocktail of blood and fish oil, and their behaviour at the feeding site is observed. Naturally, their behaviour is almost exclusively related to feeding. Many of the spectacular pictures and film taken of sharks show them at these sites. No wonder we see them as voracious predators – mindless, automatic killing machines.

Modern research is turning these prejudices upside-down, with increasing evidence of their complex behaviour. Even large sharks prove to be very wary of new objects and unfamiliar food, and are therefore reluctant to bite something without careful investigation. Very few are confident enough to tackle as large and strange a prey as a human. The reef sharks commonly encountered by divers and snorkellers rarely grow more than 3 meters (10 feet) long and are almost always shy and nervous of people, posing no threat. Sharks have a relatively larger brain than that of many birds and some mammals. They are not automatons – they can learn and in captivity have been trained to press levers to obtain food as quickly as laboratory rats. So sharks are gradually becoming recognised as complex, intelligent animals – a far cry from our preconceived image of cold, robotic killers. Contrary to popular opinion, sharks also show themselves to be individuals, each behaving in its own peculiar way.

Attacks on humans do occasionally occur, however, and are enough to fuel our worst fears. Of the 350 species of shark, only 32 have ever been implicated in attacks on humans. Of these the most dangerous are the bull shark, the great hammerhead, the tiger shark and the most famous of all – the great white shark or white pointer.

The bull shark is unusual in that it frequents fresh water in the mouths of rivers, and is never far from land. It therefore has the dubious reputation of being the only shark which has attacked people who have not even entered the sea. It is found in the rivers and shallow seas of most tropical and temperate areas of the world including the Americas, Africa and Asia, but is absent from Australia and the Mediterranean region. It lives far inland in some rivers, reaching up the Atchafalaya river in Louisiana as far as 160 miles from its mouth, and has been recorded up the Zambezi river system in Africa, 695 miles from the sea. It also lives in the Amazon, Ganges, Tigris and Euphrates rivers as well as in inland waters such as Lake Nicaragua. Many of these rivers and lakes are murky and shallow, and people entering them to fish, collect water or wash, present an easy target for a bull shark. Because it shares these shallow-water habitats with humans it is likely that encounters with bull sharks are relatively common. Very little is known about this shark, however, and many attacks are probably wrongly blamed on other shark species, or even on crocodiles.

The bull shark was responsible for the most infamous series of shark attacks ever to occur in the United States. They took place along the New Jersey coast in July 1916 and, although the British and French armies were at the time attacking German positions in France, the shark attacks made front page news and roused the whole country. Only four people were killed and one seriously

Below Blue shark – another man-eating shark

injured. War was declared on the sharks and hundreds of people took to their boats with nets, guns, dynamite and spears against the common enemy. Many sharks were killed, each one being identified as the culprit – until the next attack.

The story concludes with the capture of an 2.5 meter (8.5 foot) great white shark which was found to have in its stomach "the shinbone of a boy and what appeared to be part of a human rib". But the great white, as we shall see, is an oceanic species rarely found in such waters. The uncredited monster of the New Jersey coast was almost certainly a bull shark.

While the bull shark is found in rivers and estuaries, the hammerhead is a shark of both the more open ocean and the shoreline. Its sinister reputation is largely due to its strange appearance, with an eye on each tip of the hammer-like extensions to its head. This unusual design brings many advantages to the hammerhead, although we still do not fully understand its entire function. The hammer almost certainly provides a larger surface for information gathering through the shark's sensitive skin sensors, and may also give enhanced stereoscopic vision. Other researchers have suggested that it acts as a rudder, making the shark more manoeuvrable. Hammerheads commonly grow to between 3 and 6 meters (9 to 20 feet) long.

There are four species of hammerhead and only one, the great hammerhead, has ever been implicated in attacks on humans. In some parts of the world, hammerheads are a major tourist attraction for divers. The only problem is in getting close enough – even these large predators are wary and shy of unfamiliar objects and sounds. In the Galapagos Islands and Cocos Island of the eastern Pacific, divers swim out into the open ocean to attempt to take photographs of hundreds of hammerheads passing in formation. As the diver approaches, the column gently curves, keeping a safe distance from the bizarre intruder – and nobody yet knows where these sharks are headed, nor why they go there.

One of the most infamous of sharks is the tiger shark. It is a shark that I clearly remember hearing about as a boy, when we lived in Aden and in East Africa – it is the most feared shark in these waters, and one whose jaws I could readily identify. Their teeth are unusual, being sharply notched on one side, looking rather like cockscombs, and they have a very broad head that is almost square when seen from above. They are not called 'tigers' because of their particular ferocity or tendency to kill humans. The younger specimens have stripes on their backs which fade with maturity. They are found in all tropical and semi-tropical seas around the world. Tiger sharks are amongst the largest of sharks – an average specimen is 4 meters (13 feet) long. The largest specimens recorded were caught in Australian waters and measured 5.5 meters (18 feet) long.

Tiger sharks are indiscriminate feeders and this may well explain why they have been involved in attacks on humans. Amongst the objects found in their stomachs are boat cushions, rats, tin cans, turtles, the head of a crocodile, driftwood, seals, the hind leg of a sheep, conch shells, horseshoe crabs, a tom-tom,

Above Sand tiger shark

Overleaf The reason for shoaling behaviour in hammerhead sharks is unknown

an unopened tin of salmon, a coil of copper wire, nuts and bolts, lobsters and lumps of coal. It is a bizarre diet for any animal but highlights their habit of being opportunistic feeders, taking advantage of whatever food is available. They are often found near the mouths of rivers or discharge pipes where lots of refuse is found. Consequently they may be less wary of unfamiliar objects than other species of shark and may therefore more readily bite humans – or scavenge their remains.

Most famously, a tiger shark caught on April 18th 1935 in New South Wales, Australia, vomited up a human arm which had a piece of rope tied round the wrist and a tattoo of two boxers. The arm was identified from fingerprints as having belonged to one James Smith, a 'billiard marker' from Gladsville, near Sydney. It had been cut – not bitten – off. James Smith was never found but the court ruled on the case of the 'Shark Arm Murder' that a single limb could not be legally considered a murder victim. As there was no body there had been no murder. As far as the law was concerned, James Smith was still alive, even though his arm had joined the bizarre catalogue of contents of the stomachs of the 'dustbin of the sea'.

Many sharks have the apparently uncanny ability to congregate at seasonal food bonanzas and tiger sharks in particular seem to exploit unusual prey. At Raine Island off north-east Australia they gather in the shallows as green sea turtles land in large numbers to lay their eggs in the sand. As the tired females pull themselves back to the sea at dawn, the sharks are waiting to ambush them. At French Frigate Shoals in the Hawaiian Island chain, tiger sharks prey on fledgling Laysan albatrosses which are learning to fly during the months of June to December each year. Albatrosses are heavy birds and require a considerable run up to get airborne. The technique takes some practice to perfect. As the inexperienced albatrosses rest on the water surface, they are attacked from the least expected angle – tiger sharks which have carefully stalked them drag them under the water and consume their unusual meal.

Tiger sharks also attack people on the main Hawaiian islands. Over the last 36 years, shark attacks have been carefully documented. In many cases the identity of the shark was not recorded but it seems likely that tigers are the main culprits. They seem to feed in shallow water mainly after sundown and may also congregate around outflow pipes and river mouths where refuse collects and the water is murky. A reasonably alert bather can still avoid them because they are cautious and methodical in approaching potential prey, circling slowly before attacking and usually beginning with a small sampling bite. Surfers may be more at risk as they are often in the water at dawn and dusk and go out deeper where the sharks may be more common. Every year bite marks in surf boards are displayed for the tabloid press.

A spate of attacks in recent years has led to vociferous claims that the rate of attack is on the increase and that, therefore, the population of tiger sharks must be increasing. Various theories have been put forward for this increase; sea turtles have been protected in Hawaii for several years and their population has increased, it is said, so consequently the number of sharks that feed on them has also increased. Others say that the sharks are losing their fear of humans.

The supposed fact that tiger shark attack is on the increase is far from universally accepted, however, and is the subject of hot debate. The truth is that there is no firm evidence of a meaningful increase in shark attacks. The statistics can probably be explained by the simple fact that more and more people are using the seas of Hawaii and that reporting is much more thorough. In fact, tiger sharks may well be learning to avoid people. In the public perception, however, one shark attack is one too many, and people are less prepared to accept the tiny risks that they involve than far greater risks of any other kind. The current debate about tiger sharks in Hawaii may say more about our psychological need to fear sharks than it does about the sharks themselves. Nevertheless, they are labelled by many in Hawaii as an increasing problem, which may have detrimental effects on the tourist industry. This industry relies on the thousands of swimmers and surfers visiting the most famous holiday beaches in the world each year. Now, the first formal studies to document the sharks' movements and behaviour may start to throw some light on the animal behind the debate.

The great white shark was the star of the film *Jaws*, and consequently it is the most famous shark of all. It accounts for a third of the human fatalities in which the attacking species has been identified, even though it is most active in cooler waters where fewer people swim. It is also known as the white or the blue pointer in different parts of the world. Its colour is in fact a light or dark grey, with a whitish underside that can have a rusty tinge. The distinguishing feature is a small head that comes to a sharp point in front. The longest specimen to be reliably

Top Sharks often attack surfers and their surfboards

Left A sea lion that has had a lucky escape from a shark

measured was 9 meters (29.5 feet) and weighed more than 4.5 tonnes. Their average length is 4 meters (13 feet).

The great white shark is found in all the oceans of the world and occurs in deep water as well as inshore areas. However, it is most commonly encountered in deeper water, particularly close to its food source. So it is usually only seen by divers and boats operating in areas away from shore.

Although the great white is known as a man killer it has no particular taste for humans. But its sheer size and weight, combined with the energy and speed of its attack makes it particularly dangerous. Even an initial exploratory bite can cut a man in half. In 1970 it was discovered that the great white, unusually for sharks, is warm-blooded, and can maintain a body temperature higher than the surrounding cold waters. Its muscles work more efficiently than those of most sharks which helps it to rapidly work up to attacking speed. It needs to eat voraciously and is the most active of hunters, often thrusting its head above the waves to see what may be on reefs and beaches.

Although they are found all over the world, great whites have learned, like tiger sharks, to exploit seasonal food. Around the Farallon Islands off the Californian coast there is an area known as the red triangle. Here, northern elephant seals and Californian sea lions come to breed every year, and the sharks move in to feed on the pups and youngsters. Some researchers say that the attacks on humans are simply a case of mistaken identity on the part of this specialist hunter of marine mammals; a swimmer lying on a surfboard can look remarkably like a seal from below. Certainly most great whites will release a human after the first bite, but that is often all that it takes to kill its victim.

The image of the great white as a man-eater is big business and continues to sell magazines and films. The photographs used to reinforce this image are not always what they seem. A common illustration is the great pointed head of the shark attacking the bars of a cage in an apparent attempt to seize the diver inside. The truth behind this image is a good illustration of the way we bend the facts to feed our fears. Sharks have an extraordinary ability to sense electric fields in the water. When a great white shark is attracted to a diver's cage by blood and oil in the water, it circles before coming in to seize the bait which has been suspended just in front of the cage. As it lunges for the bait it closes its eyes to protect them and relies for the last few meters on its electromagnetic sense. The metal bars of the cage create a galvanic field around them which is stronger than that of the bait, and the shark therefore bites the more attractive object automatically – not in an attempt to get at the diver. This makes for a great but misleading picture.

There are some areas of the world in which the great white shark may well be declining today through persecution and sport-fishing, all stimulated by the negative image we have created. As it reproduces very slowly it will take many years for the shark populations to recover even if we decide to stop persecuting them.

For all the hype relating to great whites, we know very little about them. We have just found out that they act as individuals and are very wary, first tasting unusual foods before feeding. At a feeding site there is a definite hierarchy, the larger individuals being given first bite. What we do know is minuscule compared to what we don't know. How do they reproduce; how long do they live; how far do individuals range, and how many are left in the ocean?

Like any other carnivore, a shark needs to locate prey, and to help them find food they have an impressive array of senses. They can detect a trace of fish flesh so faint that it represents only one in ten billion parts of sea water. When a hungry shark detects the minutest trace of particles signalling food, it faces into the current and heads for the source. Once it gets close to the source it has several senses which help it pinpoint the potential meal. Sharks have two systems for picking up the vibrations caused by movement or sound in the water. One system uses special sensory cells which detect pressure variations through canals that open to the water, via pores in the skin of the shark's head and body. The other is through the ears which are situated on top of its head. Used together, they give an accurate fix on the slightest movements of prey and allow the shark to home in rapidly.

Sharks also possess a remarkable sense which enables them to locate their prey even if they cannot see or hear. Small pores in the skin of their nose, just in front of the mouth, lead to specialised sense organs that can detect the weak electrical currents generated by the muscles of animals. This allows them to trace shoals of fish in the open sea, and enables bottom-feeding sharks to detect prey such as flounders which have buried themselves in the sand. They also have good vision, allowing them to distinguish moving objects from their backgrounds, and their night vision is enhanced by a mirror-like layer behind the retina of the eye which bounces back the available light and increases the visual stimulus (it is a similar system that causes eyeshine in cats and enables them to see in the dark.) On a bright day these mirrors cloud over with black granules to prevent them being dazzled – the chilling black eye of a shark has its own built-in sunglasses.

Even from inside the protection of a shark cage, great white sharks can look very menacing

However much we may try to understand, and even admire sharks, the fact remains that they are most famous for eating people, and it is an inescapable fact that shark attacks do take place. The extent and frequency of attacks are wildly exaggerated – worldwide about 100 attacks take place every year, and only around 50 of these result in the death of the victim. Your chances of dying from a shark attack are about 300 million to one, far less likely than being struck by lightning. Your chances of being eaten by a shark are even less. Almost no victims of shark attack are actually consumed. Most fatalities are due to the victim drowning, or from blood-loss or shock. It is sobering to think that an estimated 580 people die every year from drowning in England and Wales alone. 306 Australians drown every year, but only one is killed by a shark. In fact no sharks should really be called 'man-eaters' although a few may deserve the name of man-biters. Sharks have a discerning palate, and for the most part seem to be wary of unfamiliar items in their diet.

Perhaps it is the intensity of shark attack together with the horrifying mutilation which often results that causes such widespread public anxiety, usually fed by colourful press reporting. A story of a single shark attack will beat countless car accidents for headline news. It is often the infrequency and unpredictability of shark attacks which gives them so great an impact. If we could come to understand the circumstances in which shark attacks take place, we would be better psychologically prepared for them and better able to avoid them. The figures on shark attacks allow us to make a few tentative moves towards this, but statistics can deceive and may say more about human than shark behaviour.

Most shark attacks occur when the water temperature is above 20 degrees, in shallow water, less than 1.5 metres deep, and they are less frequent at noon than at 11am or 3pm. These facts may simply reflect the weather conditions, and depth of water, but more particularly, the time and conditions when most people prefer to go for a swim – for instance, people tend to get out of the water to have lunch, hence the dip in attacks around noon. More men are attacked than women – in fact 31 times as many; this may simply be because men tend to put themselves more at risk by swimming alone and further out. More English speakers are recorded as being attacked than others; sharks do not feel particularly aggressive towards the English language – it is just that the International Shark Attack File from which most statistics are drawn was compiled by the United States Navy and the Smithsonian Institute and the incidents reported tend to be from English-speaking countries.

More helpful than the statistics is the information we now have on the pattern of behaviour involved in shark attacks, as such knowledge may help us to understand the signals which a shark may be giving, and in this way avoid injury. Shark attack seems to relate to one of two different shark behaviours, one where the shark is feeding and the second where it is defending a territory.

In a feeding attack, a hungry shark will first tend to circle its prey, gradually increasing its swimming speed. It then cuts across the circle and nudges or bumps the prey to gain information about it and decide whether it is suitable food. Many shark injuries are of this type, as the shark's skin has many sharp denticles which can cause severe abrasions (it used to be used as sandpaper). Next, the shark may decide to feed. It swings back its head to bring up the mouth, projects its upper teeth forward, and bites the victim. The force of the bite can be seven tons per square inch, and the victim may be thrown well clear of the water. The violence of the attack makes it terrifying, but although it causes extensive injuries, a victim who remains conscious has a surprisingly good chance of survival. There are many cases of sharks being fought off after a single bite, or simply not returning to the victim. The main cause of death from such attacks is blood-loss. In a third stage of a feeding attack, other sharks move in a feeding frenzy. The sea boils, blood spouts and the sharks attack each other and everything that moves, leaving little chance of escape.

The second form of shark attack is linked to its defence of a territory, and has so far been reported from only one species, the grey reef shark. This shark, which can reach as much as 2.5 meters long, in found on reefs and lagoons off the east coast of Africa, SE Asia, Australia, and throughout the Pacific. Like the bull shark, it is known to spend extended periods of time of the floor of the ocean. In the Pacific, these sharks appear to have territories which they defend against other sharks. A diver who strays into the territory is seen as a challenge and the shark warns the human to move away by swimming in a very distinctive way; it arches its spine, points its pectoral fins downward and waggles its head from side to side. If the diver recognises this warning, as another shark would do, and leaves the area, an attack will be avoided. If not, the shark will attack what it perceives to be an intruder in its territory. The attack is lightning swift, the shark lunging at the diver, biting rapidly and then just as quickly swimming away.

A friend and colleague of mine, Mike DeGruy had a near-fatal encounter with a grey reef shark. Mike is a professional wildlife cameraman and producer, specialising in underwater films. He started out as a marine biologist, and in 1987 was in Enewetak Atoll in the Marshall Islands in the Pacific, as manager of a marine laboratory for the University of Hawaii. Enewetak is south-west of Hawaii, in the middle of nowhere; it's one of the largest atolls in the world, with a lagoon 20 miles wide. Mike's job entailed diving around the lagoon to familiarise himself with it, so that he could support and advise scientists who came to do research there.

Mike and his buddy Phil Light were diving on a pinnacle which rose from the sandy lagoon floor 200 feet below. The pinnacle was a column of coral, covered in marine organisms – an oasis of life in the open waters – and was out of sight of land, about eight or nine miles into the lagoon. It had probably never been dived before. Measuring 300 metres across, it came to within 40 feet of the surface. Leaving their small boat at one end of the pinnacle, they dived in and started swimming towards the other end. Mike was particularly interested that day in the grey reef sharks. He had been involved in a project on these sharks and so was very familiar with them.

> I saw two or three, you know, coming very close to me, but as usual no
> problem. Swim by, watching, nice and slow, every now and then they'd
> twitch a bit and swim off. I was taking pictures and I was very
> impressed with the pictures I was getting.

The sharks were about 2 meters (5 to 6 feet) long; a typical grey reef shark is relatively small, stout, sturdy-looking, powerful and beautiful. They are easy to recognise – the trailing edge of the caudal fin and the underside of the pectorals fins are black, and the shark is grey on top, and whitish underneath.

The sharks filled the viewfinder of Mike's camera. Although they appeared more curious than usual, Mike was unconcerned – they were very common in the lagoon, and on previous days he had seen hundreds of them. After a while, the sharks disappeared and Mike went on diving. As they reached the edge of the pinnacle, where it dropped off from 12 meters (40 feet) to 60 meters (200 feet), another grey reef shark appeared, well out in blue water. It was about two meters (six feet) long, and had adopted the threat posture – arching its back, raising its nose, lowering its

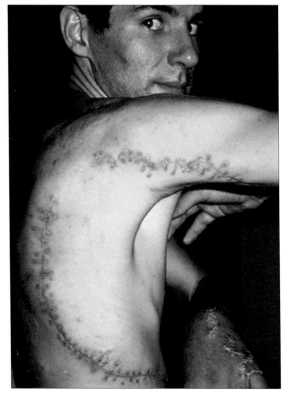

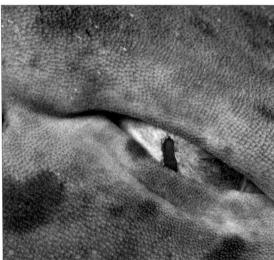

Top Chain mail can be a useful defence against smaller sharks, but only a full understanding of sharks behaviour, or luck, can save a person from a full attack from a larger shark *(left)*. It is not only the shark's teeth that should be avoided *(above)*; sharks skin can cause very nasty wounds if brushed against – it used to be used as sandpaper pectoral fins and swimming in a strange pattern, tail down, looking very awkward. Mike had studied and elicited this behaviour from grey reef sharks with an eminent marine biologist, Don Nelson, in Enewetak, so it was familiar to him.

> We'd been trying to figure out what the posture is. It is analogous to the rattling of a rattlesnake. It is a threat posture, and if you do certain things while they're posturing – bam, they'll snap out of that posture and attack every time. It's not a good thing to see if you're an unprotected diver, or if you don't know what you're doing, because you're on the verge of big trouble. These are not big animals, but they are very powerful animals and lightening-fast. As I'm sure you know, when you're underwater and something wants to move fast, a human is a joke by comparison. We're like running through molasses while these are lightning bolts flying around us.

Although the grey reef shark is not considered a man-killer, it is powerful enough to take a human's head off.

> All of the time we had been studying this, in no circumstance did an attack ever occur when the animal was more then ten feet away. This one was twenty feet away. The other thing that was unique about this situation was that generally, they had to be where I was and I would have to be where the shark was, to get an attack. In other words, the shark would have to be backed up against the reef and somewhat cornered.

Unsure why the shark was posturing, but aware he could be in danger, Mike eased back.

> The best thing you can do in this situation is stop moving and do everything you can to look like a rock and that is what I did.

As Mike watched the shark, he noticed that it had a row of teeth marks behind its dorsal fin – it appeared to be a serious injury.

> The more I watched the scars and the animal, suddenly I started to think, 'Wait a minute, this isn't a posture, that thing is injured.' And so I raised my stills camera with a strobe and took a picture, which is probably one of the stupidest things I've ever done, because the moment the strobe flashed, bam, the shark broke posture, and before the mirror could even return into its normal position, so that I could see through the viewfinder again, I noticed that the shark was half-way there – screaming towards me. And so I just pushed the camera out in front of me. It looked like slow motion. It was astonishing the way this unfolded, because I remember so clearly watching the shark with its mouth closed coming towards me. And right as it got there it opened its mouth, its head almost went flat, and it turned it to the side and just pushed the camera out of the way. The camera moved to the left of my body, which naturally presented my elbow, and this vertical wall of mouth just closed right on top of my elbow.
>
> As soon as I started feeling pressure then there was normal speed again; the slow motion was all over. It [the shark] grabbed the top of my arm and started shaking like crazy. In disbelief I thought, "This never

As more research is carried out, it is becoming clear that some sharks are territorial. A grey reef shark in s-posture is warning an intruder to leave or it will attack

happens, this can't be happening", as I was looking at this thing right on my elbow, six inches from my nose, biting and ripping into my arm. I could feel the teeth going 'pop, pop, pop'. Then it was right in there, and it just started shaking. So I was beating on top of its head, doing whatever I could, and it just shook and removed the top of my arm. Then it did what appeared to be a back loop and came up at me from the bottom and I kicked at it and luckily it grabbed one of my fins. Same thing. Shook, tore out a chunk of rubber from my fin. Swam over to my diving partner, who had a shark bully – a heavy gauge aluminium shaft with a bunch of barbs sticking out at the end like big nails. And he was prodding this thing at the shark trying to keep it off of him.

Luckily, Phil wasn't injured as badly as Mike, although the shark raked his left hand with its teeth before swimming away. For months, Mike had been experimenting on what concentrations and types of blood attracted sharks. The experiments had shown that the first shark would be attracted within a minute, and within five minutes there would be 50, 60 or 70 sharks swimming around, going mad – and here he was, 60 feet down, with a gaping hole in his arm. He swam to the surface and used his left hand to clamp off jets of blood spurting from the holes in his right arm. At first he couldn't see the boat or land – the sea was rough and choppy. Fortunately he went up on a wave at the same time as the boat did and, taking a compass bearing on it, he rolled over onto his back and headed towards it, swimming with one fin and no arms!

I think that the thing that saved my life was that I was one hundred per cent convinced I was going to die. No way what I going to make it out of this.

Mike knew that when there is a fair amount of blood in the water, sharks don't waste time before feeding. They have to do that – they're opportunists, as well as predators – they're not going to pass up a meal when there is no risk of injury to themselves.

I knew this was going to happen and so I wasn't afraid. I thought 'It's over. I'm dead.' As simple as that. And I started wondering 'Now what's it going to feel like. Are they going to grab my legs first or my back?' Not to be morbid, but these are the sort of thoughts that I was having because there was no way I was getting out of this. I knew too much about that area locally and I also knew too much about that shark.

Everyone says sharks are unpredictable – Mike thinks differently.

They are very predictable. Just because we don't' know a whole lot about them doesn't mean they are unpredictable, it just means that we are ignorant. I learnt a whole lot about this shark. I learnt that it isn't as predictable in the sense that you have to be six feet away from it to elicit an attack. I wouldn't have thought that the strobe would have made it attack, also.

On the surface, Mike rolled over to look into the water, but couldn't see a thing because of the blood. He realised that even if he could have seen something, there was nothing he could have done.

The boat was about a hundred yards away, a pretty good hike. It took me twenty-five minutes to swim back to the boat, and on the way back I was thinking, 'Why am I not being eaten?' It occurred to me that the reason I was not being eaten was because Phil (perhaps) was.

Eventually Mike reached the boat to find that Phil was already on board. "Even as I was being pulled into the boat, I thought they were going to grab me. I couldn't believe that I was going to get out of that."

None of the other sharks came anywhere near Mike, and to this day he can't explain why. He had eleven operations on his arm over the next eighteen months, two skin grafts and a tendon transfer. The surgeons had to wire all the tendons of the fingers in his right hand to one tendon from this wrist, which was once part of his grip. The tendon that once closed his hand now opens it and Mike has had to learn how to control the electrical impulses leading to it. Although he

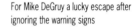

For Mike DeGruy a lucky escape after ignoring the warning signs

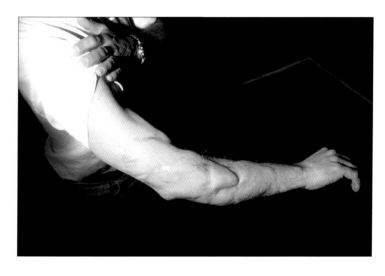

has recovered most of the movement of his right hand, it will never be the same again.

Mike has since been on a lecture tour, advising divers about grey reef sharks. In his opinion, it is most important to recognise the behaviour of the shark. It is important not to put yourself in their path – always give them an open escape route. If a diver meets a posturing grey reef shark, the best advise Mike has is: "Do absolutely nothing. Don't try and swim away. Anything you do at that stage could trigger an attack. The best thing you can do is to blend in with the reef. Ninety nine times out of a hundred they will posture for a while and then back off – because that is the whole point of it. They are telling you to back off. It is a warning. If you do anything, they may misinterpret it as a threat to them, and they will retaliate. But they don't want to – they wouldn't have this posture if their immediate reaction was to bite you."

No one knows if grey reef sharks display to other sharks, but is seems highly likely. Why else would they evolve such a posture, if not to deter predators, like tiger sharks, or intimidate rival grey reef sharks? One thing is certain – they didn't evolve the posture to intimidate humans. It seems likely that humans are simply large enough to be threatening to the grey reef sharks, and hence elicit a threat display, or even an attack.

Mike is one of the world's most experienced divers, with an excellent knowledge of sharks. Even he made a mistake – he was unaware of what the shark had been trying to tell him. It is a mistake he will not make again. What else do we still have to learn about shark behaviour?

Although sharks do sometimes attack humans, these incidents are insignificant when compared with human attacks on sharks. We kill up to one million of them every year in commercial fishing. Often only the prized fins are sliced off, and the rest of the shark is thrown back to starve or drown in the sea. In some popular resorts, gill nets are set to prevent sharks from approaching too close to the beaches and many sharks become entangled and die. Accidental catches by commercial fisheries add millions to the toll, and the annual total is currently estimated as 100 million. Sharks kill about 50 people a year, so the balance is skewed heavily in our favour – for every person killed by a shark, humans kill around 2,000,000 sharks. The cold facts of this astronomical imbalance need to be more widely known.

The universal fear of sharks, which we have done so much to exploit, is a driving force behind the 'sport' of shark fishing, and it has become traditional for the victorious fisherman to pose with his victim for a celebratory snap to amaze his friends. There are healthy signs that the general approval of this behaviour may be cooling. When a charter fishing boat harpooned a 4 metre long tiger shark off Miami in 1992, the fishermen sailed triumphantly into port expecting a hero's welcome. The shark turned out to be a female containing 50 unborn pups and the crowd was unsympathetic. The fishermen even had threatening phone calls.

Sharks have been swimming around the world's oceans for 200 million years; people have been bathing in the sea for recreation for a far shorter period. Remember, when you go swimming in the sea you are entering the world of the shark; would you just as casually go for a stroll through a strangers house, uninvited? We should accept that shark attacks are the result of one animal (us) invading another animal's (the shark's) domain. Contrary to what we may be led to believe, the vast majority of encounters between man and shark end badly for the shark. When men fish for sharks they stay at the end of a rod and reel or simply hang a mesh net to entrap it. On the rare occasions when they venture into the sea, as divers in search of sharks, they can equip themselves with a battery of offensive weapons, such as spears and billy hooks, or even explosive powerheads and CO_2 cartridges that can literally blow up the shark. Man is the most aggressive animal in the sea as well as on land. A large tiger shark weighs 50 times more than a man. If sharks were as aggressive, it would not be safe to enter the sea and our coasts would be red with blood. It's a sobering thought.

There is an alternative way to relate to sharks that makes the fearful reactions of the western world seem rather idiotic. In many cultures where people live close to the sea, complex mythologies have built up around sharks which cast them in a very different light. In places as diverse as Hawaii and Alaska, there have been shark gods, but it is in Polynesia that the tradition is perhaps still strongest.

In the Solomon Islands, grey reef sharks have traditionally been worshipped as harbouring the spirits of dead ancestors. The islands were visited in the 1870s by explorers and marine biologists who were the first outsiders to witness the ceremonies surrounding this exceptional form of shark worship. The sad end to this story is that this first visit opened the floodgates to tourism and the islanders realised that money could be made by exhibiting their ceremonies. This was the beginning of the end for the shark gods. These days, only the oldest members of the village maintain the original shark ancestor worship. The younger villagers have abandoned these beliefs and a much more modern life-style exists. The older men shake their heads and warn of the dangers of losing their shark friends.

Ever since humans started travelling the oceans, legends have sprung up about the fabulous monsters that inhabit their shadowy depths. Many of these stories had an element of truth, as they were often based on glimpses of extraordinary animals at sea, or dead animals, whole or in fragments, that had been washed up on shore. Unfamiliarity with these marine creatures lent them an added glamour and mystery. Exaggerated reports seasoned with a liberal pinch of imagination transformed these morsels into a menagerie of wonderful beasts. From Norway came tales of the Kraken, a sea monster reputed to be over a mile in circumference. From all the oceans of the world came sightings of sea serpents that plucked men out of the rigging, or twined their huge coils around ships and dragged them to their doom.

There are indeed snakes in the oceans, and many of them thrive not only in coastal waters, but also on the high seas. The yellow-bellied sea snake lives its whole life at sea, and may be the most widespread and numerous snake in the world, out-numbering any terrestrial snake. Sea snakes rarely exceed two meters in length, and could not be candidates for even the most inflated of yarns. They also occur in their greatest numbers in the warm waters of the Indo Pacific Oceans, whereas the most colourful tales of giant serpents are from the Atlantic Ocean, where sea snakes are unknown. The only snake which could be the basis of sea snake legends is the African python, which can reach lengths of 6 meters and has been known to swim between islands in the Indian Ocean in search of

The sea has held many mythical beasts

food. An attempt to pull one aboard ship could well have given support to the sea
serpent yarns, but it seems unlikely that such a familiar animal could have been
the source of such widespread tales. There is evidence for the possible true
identity of the Kraken and sea serpent in the accounts that follow.

In the late 18th century a Dutch ship was becalmed off the coast of West
Africa, so the captain decided to put the time to good use by cleaning the hull.
Sailors were lowered on planks over the ship's side to begin the work. Suddenly,
two huge arms appeared out of the calm water and wrapped themselves round
two men, hauling them off the planks and into the sea, never to be seen again. A
third arm reached up and caught a man who was in the rigging, but he held fast as
his shipmates hacked off the arm and set him free. From its size and thickness, the
ship's captain, Jean-Magnus Dens, estimated that the whole arm must have been
30 or 40 feet long. In the 1790s, part of another giant arm was found in the mouth
of a whale that had been harpooned. It was 35 feet long with two rows of suckers,
and had been broken off at both ends, so the original arm must have been longer
still. The fact that this arm was found in the mouth of a whale is a clue to the true
identity of these legendary sea monsters. Scientists have shown that sperm whales
dive down to depths of 3 kilometres or more in search of their primary prey, the
giant squid. It seems likely that the fabled monsters of the deep were, in fact, giant
squid that live at these depths.

The giant squid is the largest marine mollusc, a relative of snails and slugs,
and can have tentacles up to 28 metres in length, far longer than any snake. These
tentacles are snake-like, especially if broken off, although the suckers along their
underside give them away. The only enemy of the giant squid are a few species of
whale, for which the underside of a
ship may easily be mistaken, and this
might account for the aggression

Although the suckers of the giant
Humbolt squid are lined with razor-
sharp teeth, they are rarely large
enough to cause much damage

which has been reported by those who have seen the huge tentacles. Squid feed on fish and crustaceans, and it may be that the giant squid enter shallower water in pursuit of their prey, and thus encounter ships and humans.

The ocean depths have been called 'inner space' to compare them with the outer space that lies between the stars. Inner space is that part of our planet which lies below the sunlit surface layer of the seas. It is the least known environment on the planet. Scuba divers explore only the first 70 meters or so of the oceans and light itself hardly penetrates below 200m. Beneath this is a vast world of perpetual darkness reaching down to nearly 11km in the deepest ocean trench. The depths of the sea were first penetrated by man on 23rd January, 1960, when Dr. Jacques Piccard and Lieutenant D. Walsh of the U.S. Navy took the bathyscope *Trieste* down to a depth of 10,000 meters (35,802 feet) in the Mariana Trench in the Pacific. This is the world's deepest, extending further below sea level than Mt. Everest extends above. They described the bottom as a "waste of snuff-coloured ooze". Here the pressures are enormous and only highly specialised life forms can exist.

The tales of giant squid probably exaggerate the size and ferocity of a creature which we know little about. Similarly, tales about, and the very name of the killer whale are a distortion of facts. Because they hunt in packs like wolves, and feed on marine animals, it was long thought that killer whales, or orcas (after their scientific name *Orcinus orca*), would actively hunt humans in the water, mistaking them for the seals, sea lions or other pinnipeds. This idea was given support by some inaccurate reporting. In 1911, when Captain Scott's expedition was preparing for the last attempt to reach the South Pole, some husky dogs were tethered on floating ice. The expedition's photographer, Herbert Ponting, was with them when eight killer whales began to bump the ice from below. Although they left without doing any harm, the story was repeated, and the dogs were left out so that the episode could be portrayed as an attempt by the whales to attack a human. The United States Navy's recommendations for the Antarctic warned that orcas would "attack humans at every opportunity" and the manual for naval divers put the killer whale as among the most dangerous of animal hazards. One U.S. scientist was quoted as saying that "like man, they are one of the few animals that will kill for sport".

The killer whale's reputation for attacking people standing on ice floes seems to derive from one incident on Scott's expedition to the Antarctic, when killer whales were seen breaking up floes to get at huskies (*above*).

Only in the 1960s was the myth of the killer whale as a bloodthirsty man-hunter challenged. Extensive research failed to uncover a single record of an orca attacking a boat or a person. The increasing use of them in oceanaria showed them to be gentle, intelligent and playful animals. They are the largest members of the dolphin family and are highly developed, sociable animals living in tightly knit groups of up to 50, and communicating with each other through a range of complex sounds. Orcas are fascinating, responsive and approachable, and the name 'killer whale' is a record, not of their nature but of human misconception.

During the making of Sir David Attenborough's *The Trials of Life* series cameramen Mike DeGruy and Paul Atkins were commissioned to film a sequence on orcas feeding on seals on the Patagonian coast of Argentina. For years these whales had been under close observation by scientists. During the seals' calving season, the whales move to this coast and hunt the seal pups. The beach here is gently shelving, but there is a deep channel at one point which the whales use to

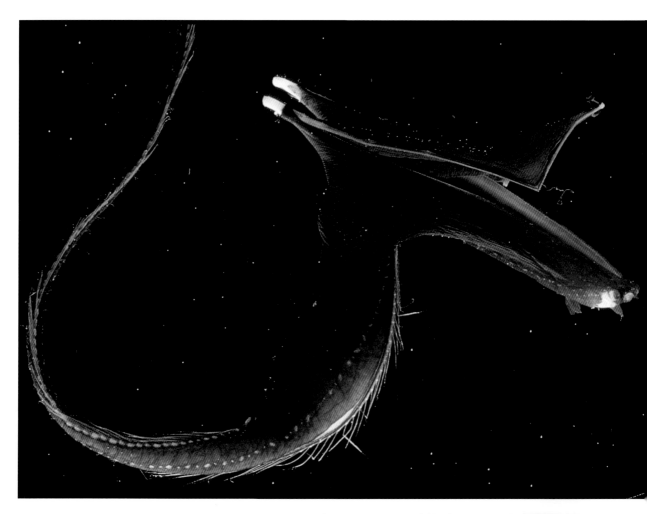

True nightmares from the deep
Left Hatchet fish
Above Deep sea gulper
Right Stargazer fish

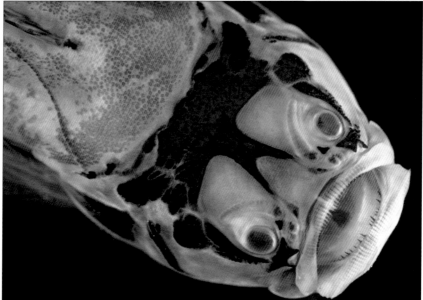

Killer whales have certainly developed interesting ways of capturing their prey – in Patagonia they 'surf' up the beach to grab unsuspecting seals and penguins

get right up next to the beach. After three weeks of filming the whales from the beach, it became obvious that the whales could tell adult seals from pups. Mike and Paul wanted to get shots of the whales catching the seals underwater. But dare they enter the sea? This they did and the whales came charging inshore, sweeping within feet of the camermen to attack the seals in the surf. It was a remarkable display of courage from the cameramen, but also it showed that their knowledge of the whales had been born out. The whales could tell the difference between man and seal, and had no interest in hunting man.

Deep sea submersibles, and trawlers using deep nets have brought us examples of the creatures which really inhabit the depths of the ocean. What these creatures lack in size, they make up for in appearance! Among the inhabitants of this world is the hatchet fish, which grows to only 3 inches (7.5 cm) in length. It has grotesque protruding eyes and luminous patches inside its mouth, which may be used to attract prey. Gulper eels have a luminous tip to their long tapering bodies, and a huge stomach, as well as formidable teeth. Rat trap fish have huge distendable jaws projecting below their bodies and a glowing red light just below the eye. When

brought to the surface in trawl nets or by deep ocean probes, these animals appear monstrous to our eyes, but they are simply adapted to life in a very different environment to our own, or even that of fish living near the surface of the oceans.

The ocean depths and the vast plain of the ocean floors are a desert in comparison with the teeming life of the surface. The total absence of light means that there are none of the myriad tiny plants which harness the Sun's energy and form the basis of life in the shallows. Food is therefore scarce, and deep-sea animals must either scavenge, feeding on the rain of detritus which floats down from the surface far above, or develop unusual methods such as luminous lures for attracting living prey. Once food is discovered found, it makes sense to eat the whole prey rather than take just a few bites – after all, who knows when the next meal might turn up? So distendable jaws enable the prey to be engulfed and swallowed whole.

There are also creatures in inland waters whose jaws are specially adapted to make them more effective feeders. The most famous of these are the piranhas of South America. Anthropologist Harald Schultz, who knew South America very well and was known as 'Indian Schultz' related this whimsical and not entirely believable piranha story: "As my father was just 15 years old, he fled before attacking Indians in a small fragile canoe. The boat tipped over and he swam away but, as he climbed out of the water he was just a skeleton; that could never happen to him again." Schultz senior had fallen victim to what has been described as 'the fiercest of all fishes of the Neotropical region (south and central America)', which has the reputation of never attacking alone, but setting on anything that moves in the water with such ferocity that they can strip a horse to the bone in minutes.

Surprisingly there is no authenticated case of anybody ever having been attacked and killed by piranhas. They are a very diverse group of South American fish, with very varied feeding habits, none of which includes humans in their diet. They do have sharp teeth and strong jaws, but tend to use them to munch fruit or seeds or to steal bites out of the fins and scales of other fish which then grow back, providing a renewable food source, allowing many species to live together.

The only species which can be considered at all dangerous – and only in the low water season when food is scarce – is the red-bellied piranha. Designed to feed by taking small bites of flesh, the red-belly has very sharp teeth, firmly anchored in the jaw to form a saw-like cutting edge, and a blunt face. Many piranhas, contrary to the public image, are solitary, but the red-belly often hunts in groups, particularly when the water is low. As they become concentrated in the shrinking lakes on the flood plains, they search for any suitable prey, selecting the

Although piranhas possess very
dangerous looking teeth, there are no
authenticated cases of anybody ever
being killed by them

most vulnerable such as diseased or injured animals. While their usual prey is other fish, often quite small, they may attack a floundering or swimming mammal at this time, scouts first biting the prey, and then the others suddenly joining in a feeding frenzy like sharks, each grabbing a bite and then darting away.

Local people avoid swimming in muddy lakes at such times, and the ones who are bitten are usually those who fish for piranha. There appear to be no authenticated records of anyone being reduced to a skeleton in minutes. A cameraman was once asked to film a piranha feeding frenzy. Try as he might he could not find anywhere to film this in the wild, so decided to rig the sequence by filming a dead capybara with piranha. The resulting scene looked gory and was cut to accentuate the action. He had his sequence, but the truth had been distorted and the myth of the piranha enhanced.

Another fish in the Amazon with a reputation to match that of the piranha, is the candiru. Found in Venezuela, 'the candiru' is actually a group of fish which belong to a family of catfish. Most are very small, usually less than 3 cm (one inch) long, and some are slim and needle-like. They are mostly parasitic, and live on the flesh of large fish, feeding on mucus and blood. The species which cause nightmares enter the gill chambers of larger fish, where they suck the blood or take bites out of their gills. The story that makes our hair stand on end is that this fish can home in on a urinating man or woman, and swim up the stream of urine and into the body, where it lodges itself in the penis or urethra, and cannot be extracted because of its backward pointing barbs. This story is widespread, and local people confirm that, for once, it is a hair-raising tale actually based on truth. The candiru has also been found in other body orifices, and menstruating women traditionally avoid bathing in places where they are common.

Many dangers tend to be exaggerated, but there is a very real menace in the shallow beach waters of the river basins of South America, in the shape of the stingray. These relatives of saltwater stingrays can reach over a meter in diameter and weigh up to 30 kg (66 lbs). Like sharks, all rays have skeletons that are made of cartilage rather than bone. Because they are bottom feeders and do not need to pursue agile prey at high speeds, they have not developed the superb tail of the shark but have only a vestigial, long thin extension which, in stingrays, has one or two barbed spines half way along it. This serrated barb-like sting ensures that the victim receives not only venom, but a severe wound. The sting response is only used in defence, when the stingray cannot escape from danger, and is triggered whenever pressure is felt on the body. It easily penetrates rubber boots and can even be driven some distance into wood.

As stingrays bury themselves in the sand along river banks by day most accidents occur when they are stepped on. The pain is extreme and can last up to ten days. It is often accompanied by cramp, and the victim may take up to five months to recover completely. Recommended local treatments are rubbing tobacco juice on the wound, or urinating over it. The last prescription is said to be fully potent only when the opposite sex is called on, but for this there is no independent medical evidence.

According to popular imagination the stingrays of the oceans are included among the perils of the deep. The barbs of saltwater stingrays can grow to the size of a breadknife, and can slash through wet suits and tear deep gashes into flesh. About two thirds of stingray species have venomous spines that can cause ulceration of the wounds, but the poison is not powerful enough to be life-threatening. The chief danger from encountering a stingray is the likelihood of infection in the wounds, especially if the barb breaks off and becomes lodged in the flesh.

Actually, marine stingrays rarely cause any injury. Like their freshwater cousins, they bury themselves in the sand, but in water too deep for them to be accidentally stepped on by paddling humans. Most injuries are caused by divers or snorkellers coming across them accidentally or by people actually harassing them. But not all encounters end badly. The stingrays of Grand Cayman island in the Caribbean have become famous for providing one of the strangest underwater phenomena ever recorded. About a hundred of them, ranging in size from ten inches to five feet across regularly come together to feed in shallow waters, from 3 to 12 feet deep, so that boats can anchor and snorkellers stand in the water and play with them. They are so tame that divers can hand-feed them, hug and stroke them and swim with them for indefinite periods. In spite of their terrifying appearance – the wide flapping body and long armed tail – these stingrays have been described by a visiting journalist as "the friendliest, happiest stingrays I had ever encountered" and the place of encounter has been named 'Stingray City'. The anthropomorphism of all this may be reprehensible to scientists, but it certainly provides a unique experience for the tourists.

Southern Stingrays

Humans have a fascination with danger, and love taking controlled risks. Human interaction with dangerous and possibly unpredictable animals is a source of enjoyment for many people. Eventually, the animals involved may become accustomed to the attention, like the stingrays of 'Stingray City'. Another inhabitant of warmer seas that is capable of being tamed is the moray eel, which can grow 3 metres (about 10 feet) long, with a body as thick as a man's thigh, and has ferocious teeth. Divers in Australian waters have won their confidence with titbits of food so that they can be stroked and handled with apparent ease. There are now underwater feeding sessions, with the colourful morays as part of the tourist trip along the Great Barrier Reef. But this is conditioned behaviour and it would be as unwise to stroke a strange moray, as it is to pat an unknown guard dog.

Morays are shy animals which spend most of their time in a hole or crevice, which provides them with protection, from where they can scan the surroundings for a possible meal. Any large animal which comes too close is likely to be perceived as a threat, and the moray will rapidly retreat into its hole, or bite in defence when there is no other option. Their teeth are designed for grasping prey that is too big to be swallowed whole. They lock onto the body of a fish, and then the eel ties itself into a knot with a tight muscular contraction that travels up from the tail, arriving at the head with such force that the jaws are wrenched away to one side, carrying with them a huge hunk of flesh. Bites on humans can be deep and tearing. Although the moray has no venom apparatus, these bites almost always become infected. Morays outside the tourist venues should be treated with caution.

An equally ferocious biter which is even more feared is the barracuda. It too has a large mouth filled with long and fearsomely pointed teeth. The reputation of the barracuda is partly based on this appearance, and partly on its terrifying bursts of speed which are alarming in so large a fish. A 1.2 meter (3.9 feet) barracuda can produce a maximum swimming power of 0.6 kw, which is six times as fast as a similar sized bull shark. They use this ability in hunting, when they will hang

almost motionless for long periods, waiting for a prey to swim within reach, and then suddenly dart forward to seize it. Like the moray eel, they feed by tearing off huge hunks of flesh from prey which is too large to be swallowed whole.

Large solitary barracuda will often follow divers around, which is unnerving, but is probably only in the hope that the diver will disturb a suitable prey. There are no substantiated reports of unprovoked attacks by barracuda. Most incidents involve the taking of speared fish which attract the barracuda and result in fishermen being bitten.

In the South Pacific, barracudas are far more feared than sharks. The shark is sometimes a god – the barracuda always a devil. They are terrifying in the water because they move at explosive speed against a shoal, tearing to right and left to kill and maim fish which they then return to feed on at leisure.

There is a cliched scene in Hollywood's underwater

Above and right Moray eels are very territorial and can inflect a nasty bite if aggravated

Opposite Sharpfin barracuda

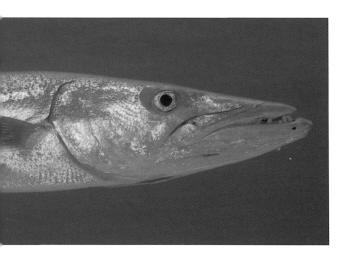

Above Barracuda do have a good array of teeth

nightmare epics in which the heroine, swimming at ease along the tropical reef, extends a shapely ankle into an open corrugated shell which then swiftly and silently closes, holding the victim powerless as the tide rises and the waters lap over her head. Only then does the hero appear, knife between his teeth, to dive and free her from the dreaded clutches of the giant clam.

They are big enough to do it: the real giant clams, *Tridacna gigas* and *Tridacna derasa,* can grow to over a metre across and weigh more than 260 kg (572 lbs). A French naturalist tested the strength of one by hanging buckets of water to the shell, and found that he needed a pull of nearly 900 kg (1980 lbs) to draw it open. So if they caught your ankle, they could certainly hang onto it. But it takes several minutes for a giant clam to close its shell fully, so you would have to be patient as well as suicidal to keep your foot in there long enough to get caught.

There is another, much smaller marine fish, found in Polynesia, which occasionally and without intention can cause physical damage. It is the 'Living Javelin' – the needlefish, or garfish. These fish have very long pointed bodies, and elongated jaws with large pointed teeth. They patrol just below the sea surface, feeding on small fish and crustaceans. Although they are in no way aggressive to humans, they can be a danger because of their habit of suddenly leaping clear of the water, possibly as a way of avoiding predators, and may become impaled in anything or anybody which happens to be in their path.

In parts of Polynesia men go out fishing at night in canoes, and attract flying fish by lighting palm frond torches. The fish are lured to the surface by the light, and often behind them come the needlefish, which can leap out of the water suddenly and cause injury. There have been several cases of fishermen being killed as a result of injuries caused by needlefish. When populations of needlefish reach numbers that are judged to be dangerous, torch fishing is called off for the season.

Because so much that we come across in the sea is unfamiliar, we can occasionally do ourselves damage through our own ignorance. One hazard of the marine environment that does not exist on land is from the stinging cells or cnidae of jellyfish, hydroids, anemones and corals – all members of the group Cnidaria. These devices can only function in water, and so have not evolved in the land animals that are more familiar to us. The translucent globes of jellyfish that drift by our boats, and the tempting jewel-like anemones we see when snorkelling along a bank of reef can give an unexpected and painful sting.

These stings are, of course, all accidental. They were not designed to hurt humans but to protect the fragile organisms and help them obtain food. The majority of these animals are carnivorous, feeding on a range of food from microscopic plankton to larger fish and crustaceans. Such large prey has to be quickly disabled before it can do any damage to the unprotected and soft bodies of the predators. A jellyfish, for example, which can deliver agonising and sometimes lethal stings, is composed of at least 95% water. While most anemones and corals are sessile – that is, fixed and unmoving – in their adult form, the majority of jellyfish are free-swimming as adults and are most likely to be encountered accidentally.

Their stinging cells – the feature of greatest interest and importance to us – represent one of the most extraordinary weapon systems in the animal kingdom. Those of jellyfish are called nematocysts, and come in several types. They consist of a bladder, within which lies coiled a long hollow thread. On stimulation, the thread is shot out at great speed, turns itself inside out, and either sticks to the victim or exposes barbs which embed themselves in the prey. Sometimes they also release toxins. These poisons are complex proteins, some of which affect the heart and circulation and others of which act on the brain and nervous system. Different nematocysts

are specialised for different functions, either poisoning or adhering to the prey, or transferring it to the jellyfish's mouth.

The firing of the nematocysts can be triggered by 'tasting' certain chemicals in the sea water, or by touching a small hair-like trigger on each cell. This is the mechanism that causes swimmers to be stung when accidentally brushing against the tentacles. Once fired, a nematocyst cannot be recoiled, but must be replaced, and this takes about two days. While nearly all jellyfish can sting, we only feel the effects of those in which the barbed threads can penetrate our skin and where the toxins are strong enough to affect us.

Our fear of the monsters of the deep – sharks, sting rays, giant squid – are much

Top Some jellyfish can grow very large. Almost all can sting, but most are not deadly to man
Above Each stinging cell is very small, but the number and density can result in a large injection of venom

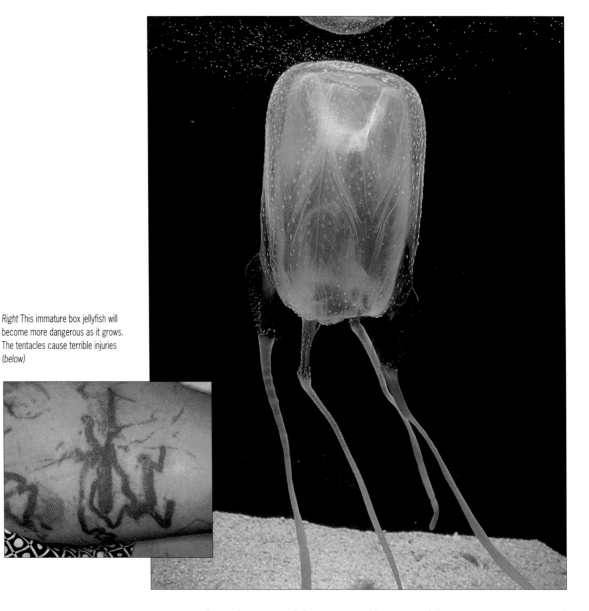

Right This immature box jellyfish will become more dangerous as it grows. The tentacles cause terrible injuries (*below*)

exaggerated, yet the potential dangers posed by some of the venomous creatures of the sea have been overlooked. In Australia, for example, the most feared marine threat is the great white shark but in fact, the real peril comes not from four and a half tons of shark but from half a pound of jelly.

About 60 people in the tropical inshore waters of Australia have been killed by the box jellyfish since the 1880s. That exceeds the combined total of people taken in the same region by sharks and crocodiles. No other jellyfish is capable of directly killing healthy people, but the box jellyfish has by far the greatest combined length of tentacles, and therefore the most stinging capsules, and its venom is many times more toxic than that of other jellyfish. It is the most advanced jellyfish known, with the most highly developed nervous system, and can move faster in the water than a person can wade, trailing its tentacles as much as three metres behind it. Along these tentacles the stinging nematocysts are arranged in bands with their tips just reaching the surface. They are astonishingly closely packed: more than 1000 venom-injecting threads can be fired from an area about the size of a pinhead. Unlike a snake or spider bite, the venom in a jellyfish sting is therefore injected in multiple tiny doses over a wide area of skin so the venom is absorbed rapidly and symptoms start to develop almost immediately.

A person stung by a box jelly suffers mounting waves of pain that cause them to tear at the tentacles, and thrash about in agony. This increases the stinging, and also the rate of absorption of the venom into the bloodstream. Wheals like whiplash marks, up to 0.5 cm wide appear in a cross-barred pattern wherever a tentacle has made contact. About six hours later these start to blister, and within a day skin death may begin. If the lesions are untreated, there may be deep, long lasting ulcers and permanent scarring. But in a major envenomation death can occur in less than five minutes.

The Portuguese man of war jellyfish is more famous than the box jelly, but far less dangerous. It is possible that the deaths caused by the box jelly in Australia were attributed to the Portuguese man of war before the box jelly was discovered, giving it a reputation it did not deserve.

This is not a true jellyfish but a colony of their close relatives, hydroids, with tentacles that can trail up to 200 feet. This wide sweep increases the range of the colony's food gathering but also makes it far more likely to entangle a swimmer. As in true jellyfish, the stinging cells contain a venom which is a complex mixture of enzymes, containing cardiotoxins and neurotoxins similar to that of snakes. Usually the amount received by swimmers is enough only to cause painful weals and muscular pain.

The Portuguese man o'war may be less dangerous than originally thought

The man of war has an unlikely predator in the shape of a tiny sea slug, or nudibranch, which gulps a bubble of air and floats on the ocean surface looking for the jellyfish. The slug feeds on the man of war, ingesting the stinging cells intact. These are then carried through the slug's digestive system and out onto the feathery cerata on the slug's back. Here the undischarged cells are ready to be used as a formidable second-hand defence system by the tiny slug. Even more remarkably, the sea slug can choose the nematocysts it wants, and only deploys the most virulent on its back for protection. A sting from this tiny slug can be much worse than that of the Portuguese man of war itself.

The great majority of jellyfish have stings that are not painful to humans. Some have lost their power to sting altogether. In the inland salt lakes of the Republic of Palau in the West Pacific, there are jellyfish which have evolved an unusual

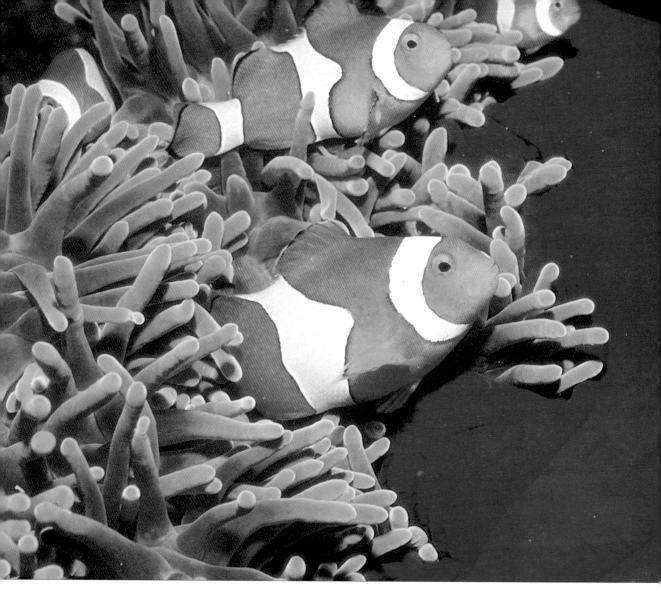

Above and right Clown fish live amongst the tentacles of coral, but are not stung by them.

method of feeding. There is little food in the lakes, and so little need for stinging tentacles to help capture it. So one species of jellyfish which thrive here have turned from hunting to horticulture. They have 'gardens' of algae which live within their tissues, and photosynthesise to produce food. This is a perfect symbiotic relationship in which the jellyfish receive food, and the food-producing algae receive protection. The behaviour of the jellyfish ensures that the algae get plenty of sunlight: as the sun moves overhead the jellyfish follow it by migrating across the surface of the lake, rotating gently to make sure that the algae in their cells receive maximum exposure to the sunlight. At night they dive deep into the nitrogen-rich depths of the lake to provide the nutrients which act as fertiliser for their algae.

While bathing in the seas it is quite possible for us to brush against free-swimming jellyfish. The fixed anemones and corals have to be sought out on the reefs or sea floor, but it is not uncommon for swimmers to touch them, either deliberately, because they are often intriguingly beautiful, or by scraping against them as they project from the surface. Most anemones have stings that are too mild to affect us, but they do operate to catch plankton and other small particles which they sieve from the sea water. Anemones, like the Palau jellies, have organisms which have been specially adapted to live on them, without being stung by their defensive stinging cells. There are several species of shrimp found in association with sea anemones. Here they can hide from predators among the stinging tentacles. When these shrimps first approach the anemone, they are stung like any other prey and they respond by jerking back and walking away, sometimes leaving an appendage or two behind. After a time they will approach again and sit gently on the anemone: they are not stung so long as they remain motionless. They even begin to nibble at the tentacles, eating the mucus and discharged stinging cells. After a while the anemone does not react and it is thought that the shrimp may secrete a special chemical protectant which inhibits the firing of the cells.

Corals also have nematocysts which are effective in repelling some predators. They are still preyed upon by a huge variety of fish, starfish, urchins and other animals, however. Most predators feed on pieces of coral, allowing the colony to grow back, but others have a more drastic effect. The crown of thorns starfish can grow to 60 cm (2 feet) across and is protected by hundreds of needle-sharp spines each enclosed in a sheath, containing venom cells. This starfish grazes on the corals, undeterred by their stinging cells. It can evert its stomach and digest all the living polyps in a patch of coral half its own size every night. Periodic and inexplicable out-breaks in the numbers of these starfish have caused widespread devastation along the great coral reefs of the Indo-Pacific, and the measures taken against them have not been completely effective. One type of coral has the answer: *Pocillopora* harbours tiny crabs, shrimps, and fish which pinch and bite the crown of thorns' tube feet, persuading it to go off and feed elsewhere. After a blanket of crown of thorns has moved across a reef surface the branching colonies of *Pocillopora* are often the only corals left alive.

Whereas the brightly coloured coral polyps may attract us to touch them, there are more dangerous poisonous creatures in the sea which are invisible. Quite often bathers have staggered back

Below Glaucus *is a sea slug that eats jellyfish and then uses the undigested stinging cells to protext itself from attack*

The stonefish *(above)* and the greater weaver *(right)* are both very well camouflaged and are often trod upon by unseeing humans

on shore in excruciating pain without knowing what has stung them. There are two groups of closely-related fish so effectively camouflaged that they can hardly be seen. Stonefish and scorpion-fish have rather squat bodies often blotched with a cryptic pattern of pinks, browns and greens which blend in perfectly with the coral and algae-encrusted rocks among which they live. Sometimes they bury themselves in the mud or sand, leaving only their heads protruding and looking like small lumps of rock. They even have small frilly appendages around their heads to help them merge in with the background.

These fish sit invisibly among the rocks until a small fish or crustacean ventures within range. They then suddenly dart out and seize the prey, sucking it in and swallowing it whole. Because they have adapted to using the technique of ambush to capture their prey, they have sacrificed mobility for camouflage, and are not able easily to escape from their own predators. If attacked, the scorpionfish will dart away at great speed, but can only travel a short distance before settling again; stonefish rarely move at all. Both fish then raise a row of spines along their backs which are so strongly constructed that they can pierce through sandstone –

or, more easily the sole of a shoe. At the base of these spines are venom glands and when pressure is applied to the loose skin that covers the spines, venom flows along a canal to the sharp tips. Any would-be predator is hopefully dissuaded from swallowing this easy-looking meal.

Above The lionfish's spines are very poisonous, but it is a very obvious fish and so easily avoided

   Because these fish normally lie motionless on the sea bottom and are common in shallow waters, they are easily stepped on by bathers or even people paddling along the shore. The venom is an unstable protein which produces an intense narrowing of the blood vessels, so its effect tends to be localised. It contains myotoxins which cause paralysis by preventing nerve impulse conduction in the muscle tissues. Some species of scorpionfish have a fairly mild form, which produces intense swellings and pain – which can be dangerous to a swimmer – but the stonefish venom is far more severe. The stonefish may well be the most poisonous fish in the world. Its venom affects the muscles which control breathing and can cause death by asphyxiation; it also contains a chemical which acts on the involuntary muscles of the heart and can cause death by cardiac arrest. It is ironic that the venom is injected by the victim applying pressure to the spines – the fish

Above Cone shells have such toxic
venom that they can immobilise fish
instantly

has absolutely no control over the process. Talk of 'attacks' by stonefish or
scorpionfish is therefore nonsensical.

In another quirk of natural history, the large headed sea snake, *Astrotia
stokesii* actually feeds on stonefish among other bottom-living fish – and is
completely unaffected by the venom.

There is a close and colourful relative of the scorpionfish which is rather more
active in its pursuit of prey. The lionfish, or firefish hover in the water in large
shoals, their feathery fins raised like fans. They are striped in white, red or brown,
in what seems to be an attempt to be both camouflaged for ambushing prey, and
to give off warning signals to predators – a difficult combination to bring off
successfully. Lionfish drift gently around rocky outcrops and coral heads, and
gradually close in on the small fish on which they feed. There is one particular
species, *Pterois volitans* which has a cunning device to trick its prey. It approaches
a small fish and corners it against the rocks, blocking off the escape with
outspread fins; but there is a small window in the fin, which the cornered fish sees
as the only way of escape. It is thought that as the prey fish darts towards what

looks like an opening, it passes right in front of the lionfish's mouth and is gulped down.

There can be few creatures less likely to inspire fear or populate our nightmares than snails. We are irritated when we see them in our gardens and some of us are delighted when they appear properly sauteed in butter and garlic on our tables. We may feel disgusted by them but we do not, on the whole, feel scared of them. But there is a group of tropical marine snails that are truly fearsome. The 350 to 400 species of cone shells are marine snails that employ a venomous barbed dart to paralyse and capture their prey. There are three different types of cones shells, depending on their food preference: the majority, which prey on worms, the ones which prefer molluscs, including other cone shells, and the most poisonous variety which feed on fish.

For a slow-moving mollusc to catch a fish, it has to be equipped with a weapon that acts rapidly to stop the fish in its tracks before it escapes. The fish-eating cones have a venom which simultaneously attacks different parts of the nervous system and the muscles, immobilising the fish in seconds. The venom is delivered through a hollow dart sculpted from chitin – the same substance that forms the outer skeleton of insects. This is propelled by a hydraulic system, that uses the viscous venom as a hydraulic fluid. When the snout of the snail touches a fish, a muscular bulb at its base contracts sharply, pushing the venom along the proboscis. The pulse of venom forces the dart ahead of it into the prey and the venom is injected under pressure. Fish have been observed to die instantly, without a twitch.

These cone shells are nocturnal feeders, and so are rarely seen during the day, but they come into contact with people for two reasons. Firstly, they are, together with cowries and volutes, among the most popular shells for collectors, and can fetch high prices at shell sales. Secondly, they tend to inhabit the same warm shallow tropical waters that are extensively used by humans for recreation.

People are stung when handling them or standing on them as they lie buried in the sand or mud. There is a common fallacy that to grasp a cone shell by the large end is safe, It is not, as the proboscis is highly extendible and can reach all parts of the shell. Wearing porous gloves or placing the shells in plastic bags is not safe as the cone can pierce both. There are few case histories of humans being stung, but in 1935 a 27 year old male was stung on the palm of the hand, and suffered blurred vision after 20 minutes. His legs were paralysed in 30 minutes and after an hour he lapsed into a coma. He died five hours after the sting. There is as yet no antivenom and the only treatment available is to ease the symptoms. Cone shells are to be avoided.

Very common, and far more visible in tropical and subtropical waters are the sea urchins, that lie like dark pin cushions among the rocks. Their spines easily break off and lodge themselves in the wounds they make, causing infection. Some species have venom on the spines which can be dangerous. The most toxic is the flower urchin *Toxopneustes pileolus* which has densely packed spines in the shape of three-petalled blossoms. These stings can cause collapse from shock, hours of muscular paralysis and respiratory failure. It is much dreaded in Japanese waters where it is said to have killed several divers.

The more common sea urchins are likely to cause little more than infection, and their spines, when lodged in wounds, tend to dissolve within a few days. But they are often seen, frequently cause injury, and should not be handled

The reputation of the octopus, as seen by the highly charged imaginations of writers, has made it a character in many nightmares. The most distinguished author to cash in on its reputation was Victor Hugo, who in his *Toilers of the Sea* had a fisherman wrecked in the Channel Islands, and attacked by a 'devil fish' with double rows of suckers on its giant arms like so many mouths 'devouring you at the same time'. It was excellent stuff for horror novels: "To be eaten alive is more than terrible, but to be drunk alive is unspeakable".

In spite of their evil image, octopuses are rather defenceless – they are simply molluscs without the protection of a shell – and they can only evade their enemies by swimming away or by hiding and ejecting ink to cloud the water.

In the Gilbert and Ellis islands there is a traditional sport involving catching octopuses by biting them between the eyes. The story is told in Sir Arthur Grimble's best seller A *Pattern of Islands*. Occasionally, it seems, the octopuses fight back, and there was a report in early 1986 of two divers who were killed by being held underwater by octopuses 3-4 metres (10-13 feet) long. This is quite possible, because a man weighing 80 kg (176 lbs) could easily be held under by a pull of only about 4 kg (8.8 lbs), which a healthy octopus could exert with one of its tentacles anchored to a reef.

There is one group of octopuses – *Hapalochlaena* – which is far more deadly than anything dreamed up by the most fertile imagination. It is tiny. It can hide away in a can or bottle. It is a dull yellow colour with circles or spots of pale blue on the arms. In fact, it's rather like a pretty toy, and it's called the blue-ringed octopus. If you are bitten by one, the likelihood is that you wouldn't realise it. In fact, you might never realise it, because the venom is so powerful that it causes paralysis and death within hours. The venom glands of the blue-ringed octopus are as large as its brain, and contain enough poison to kill ten men. A medical report on its effects records that a human who has been bitten may find the site relatively painless. If enough venom has been introduced, the victim will notice tingling sensations in the mouth and lips and soon have difficulty in seeing or speaking. Within ten minutes collapse occurs and breathing stops because of paralysis. If mouth to mouth resuscitation is not given, the victim will become unconscious and die from heart failure because of lack of oxygen. The blue rings of this octopus are a clear warning of their dangerous nature – if we would learn to recognise the signs. Before the blue rings develop, the young octopuses rely on giving out ink to cloud the water and escape from danger – just like any other octopus. After the blue rings develop, however, they are apparently such a strong warning of their poisonous nature that predators leave them alone, and they no longer need ink to help them escape from danger; the ink sacs of at least one species shrivel up.

Above The blue-ringed octopus's colouration is a warning that it is an exceedingly dangerous animal. In Australian waters more people die from its bite than from the bite of a shark

Poisons have their own fascination, and people can even give themselves a macabre thrill by tasting them. There is a delicacy in Japan, much sought after by affluent gourmets, called 'fugu'. Only certain restaurants are allowed to serve it, and the ones that have the license often prepare it in many different ways, and serve it up course after course to the enthusiasts who love to eat it. One of the reasons they are excited by fugu is that they experience a slight tingling of the lips and tongue as they eat. This is because the flesh contains slight traces of a deadly toxin which has been removed by the chef. He has to do this with some care because one tenth of a gram is enough to kill.

This poison is produced by a slightly comical creature that blows itself up to scare off its enemies – the pufferfish. There are hundreds of species, and they are spread all over the world in warm and temperate waters. They are very easy to catch with hook and line, so often come into contact with people. It is important to recognise them. The most common group are shaped rather like avocados with teeth. The teeth are unmistakable, being fused together on both jaws with a cleft in the middle so they look as if they have only four very wide teeth rather like a beak. They don't have true separated scales but are covered instead with a bumpy plating rather like a shark's skin. They could be responsible for the prohibition in Deuteronomy against eating fish without scales. The poison is found inside the fish's internal organs, so although the fish can be handled safely, it should never be eaten.

In August 1965 a psychiatric nurse, Philip Cartledge, who was 23, and his girlfriend, Jocelyn Jones, 19, were spending a holiday camping on Long Beach, near Eden in New South Wales. They had been together for a year and were planning to marry. Philip set up the fishing lines and Jocelyn prepared the frying pan to deal with the first catch. Three days later Philip staggered to the highway and was taken by a passing motorist to a doctor in Eden. Before he collapsed he said that the first catch had been a tough skinned fish 15-20 centimetres long with spots on its back. Jocelyn was still on the beach, unable to move. In a few minutes Philip was dead. So was Jocelyn, found by the police on the lonely beach. The post mortem revealed that they had eaten pufferfish.

The most common form of fish poisoning is insidious because it is not associated with any particular species of fish. Tens of thousands of people get ciguatera poisoning every year. Their lips burn and tingle, the hands and feet have pins and needles, hot things seem cold and cold things hot. The vomiting and diarrhoea indicate it's something they ate. The name ciguatera is from the Spanish word for a Caribbean snail but you can pick it up from many fish. It is thought to be caused by poisonous dinoflagellates that live on the reef and are eaten by herbivorous fish. These, in turn, are eaten by the carnivorous fish that are much prized in our kitchens and so the poison is passed on to us. As the blooms of dinoflagellates arise and die out in an area, ciguatera comes and goes. So a particular species of fish may be poisonous at one time and not at another, or perfectly safe in most places and then poisonous in a particular spot.

There is, among the Fiji Islands an annelid sea worm *Eunice viridis*, locally called 'palolo', which lives in crevices and holes in the reefs, and rises to the surface near reef passages with uncanny regularity each year. It usually comes twice, in October and November. The old men know exactly when and where it will rise and they paddle out in canoes before daybreak to wait.

At the first touch of sunlight, the bodies of the worms begin to spiral and twist, and being divided by a series of joints they break up and rise to the surface. Some are green in colour, being filled with green eggs, and the others are yellow, filled with a creamy fluid. On the surface they meet, and the whole sea is a wriggling mass. Shoals of fish come to the place to eat the palolo worms, and they are also caught by the canoers. Wading men fill buckets, baskets and nets. The transparent envelopes that contained the eggs sink to the bottom, the eggs are fertilised by the creamy fluid and they too sink. Then only the milky water is left. Palolo is either fried, tasting like whitebait, or made into a soup which has a greenish colour.

The season of palolo is one of festival. But the locals know to beware. At this time, and for up to two weeks afterwards, their favourite fish dishes, the reef-feeding fish and especially the barracuda, cause those familiar symptoms of the tingling lips, the pins and needles in the hands and feet; and then diarrhoea and vomiting...

So what are the real perils of the sea? Without any doubt, the biggest killer is the sea itself. Most seas are too cold for the human body to survive for long. Even in tropical waters the water temperature is lower than 36.9°C – the body's natural temperature. Since heat always flows from from a hot source to one lower in temperature, the human body will lose heat to the water. If the body temperature drops below 35°C, hypothermia sets in. This leads to a malfunction of organs and cells, loss of consciousness, and ultimately, death.

It is not just temperature that kills. Even some of the most tranquil looking waters hide powerful underwater currents which can sweep a man off his feet in thigh deep water, and carry him helplessly out to sea. No matter how good a swimmer, you are no match for the relentless power of the ocean. The moods of the ocean too can spell danger; at one time being calm and tranquil; at another thunderous and rough with mountainous waves.

There are, as we have seen, numerous sea creatures which have the ability to harm us. Coastal waters, particularly in the tropics, are the home to many often unfamiliar creatures, which frequently cause painful stings. When diving, I find the dazzling array of colourful animals and plants enchanting, and I frequently reach out to caress or inspect something totally new to me. It seems I have a irresistible urge to find out from trial and error which are painful to touch and which are not. It is a temptation which anyone would be best advised to resist because so many of these beautiful creatures are not quite as innocuous as their appearance may lead you to believe. However, one can very quickly pick up enough rudimentary information to make a dive a magical experience.

Of all the creatures in the sea most likely to inflict injury to us, jellyfish are perhaps the most widespread and common. Yet, though they can be extremely painful, very few are lethal to humans. Although statistics are difficult to gather for all the world's oceans, it does appear that there is one group of animals which kill more people in the sea than any other. They are the sea snakes. This statement must be treated with caution, for though seas snakes are amongst the most poisonous of animals, very few species are of any threat to humans.

The most abundant of all snakes spends its whole life in the oceans, and is never seen on land. The venom of the yellow bellied sea snake, which is found throughout the tropical waters of the Indian and Pacific Oceans is many times more poisonous than that of the most deadly of land snakes. However, these snakes usually live offshore in ocean currents where they feed on the many tiny fish sheltering under the debris floating on the water. People hardly ever encounter them, and when they are washed up on shore they are too weak to even return to the water. Despite their potent venom, people are almost never bitten; even when threatened the snakes are shy and reluctant to bite, and their fangs are relatively weak.

Sea snakes are actually land snakes which have returned to the sea. The move was obviously successful because this has occurred at least four times, giving rise to four separate groups of sea snakes. One group, the kraits, feed on fish at sea, but must return to land to lay their eggs, and may spend time digesting their food on land. Others, such as the yellow bellied sea snake, stay in the sea, where they give birth to their young. These emerge in the form of miniature adults, rather than eggs, as in most snakes.

All sea snakes must rise to the water surface to breathe, but they have an oversized lung which stretches down to the base of their tails, which together with an ability to absorb oxygen from water through the skin, allows them to dive to 50 metres and to stay submerged for over two hours. This ability to absorb water brings its problems, because the salt in sea water tends to dissolve in their body fluids. If they were to become as salty as the sea they would die, and so they have

Sea snakes are very venomous, but are very rarely encountered as most of them live far out to sea. *Above*, yellow-bellied sea snake; *left*, banded sea snake

a specialised salivary gland to deal with the problem. It lies just under the tongue sheath, and produces a concentrated brine that it then secretes in the sheath. When the snake sticks its tongue out, the brine is pushed back into the sea.

The venom apparatus of the sea snake is similar to the elapids on land: paired venom glands on each side of the head are linked to its hollow fangs by venom ducts. The fangs of most mature specimens are in the range 2.5-4.5 mm long, which is adequate for penetrating the dermal tissues of prey species and human skin, though not long enough to penetrate a wet suit. The teeth are quite small and not suitable for cutting or tearing, so the sea snake has to swallow its prey whole. They have been seen to swallow eels almost the same size as themselves. *Enhydrina schistosa*, the beaked sea snake, which feeds almost exclusively on catfish, can swallow fish up to twice the diameter of its neck. The poisonous spines of the catfish present no problem during swallowing because, once bitten, the fish is paralysed and in a relaxed state. The spines then fold back as the fish is eaten head first.

It is an unfortunate accident that humans, which have never formed part of the diet of sea snakes, are so susceptible to their venom. Fish tend to be quite resistant to venom, so it has to be strong. It acts on both the heart and the nervous system, rapidly paralysing. When hunting, the sea snake probes nooks and crannies among the rocks with its slender head until it finds one that is occupied. It then curls its body into a loop across the entrance, so the fish cannot escape, and seeks out the trapped prey with its head. Once bitten, the fish relaxes, floats out and can easily be swallowed. The sea snake can control the amount of venom released in a particular bite so that the viscous fluid, which takes time to produce, is not wasted.

The probing head technique has been further developed by another sea snake – *Emydocephalus annulatus*, which spends most of its life with its head in the sands. It lives on fish eggs, and seeks them out by probing the sand with its thin head, its tail waving vertically above it. Because fish eggs can't fight back, the snake has lost most of its teeth as well as its venom.

Sea snakes tend to be timid, and are shy of approaching people. Experienced scientists and divers have been handling them for years without mishap. But the most poisonous species, the beaked sea snake, causes more deaths than all the other species combined. It kills thousands of people every year in South-East Asia. This is mainly because this species inhabits the shallow muddy estuaries, where fishermen often step on them or find them caught up in fishing nets and are bitten as they try to release the fish.

The majority of sea snakes, although venomous, represent no threat to humans. We can share the sea with them without their endangering us, and we have no reason to threaten them. If we enter the underwater world armed with a greater understanding of its creatures we will be better equipped to deal with the dangers that it may conceal.

In Cold Blood

The taipan is widely thought to be the most dangerous snake in the world. It is right up there with the black mamba and the king cobra as a man-killer to be feared and destroyed. But the fear it inspires is out of all proportion to the threat it constitutes. Just where do the real dangers lie in the cold blooded world of reptiles and amphibians? Where does the myth end and reality begin?

We feel at home with warm blooded creatures – they seem to be, like us, responsive, affectionate and above all, emotional. We cherish the warmth of our own emotions – society places a high value on them. A crime of passion is one we can understand. What we cannot forgive is 'cold blooded' murder, because to be cold blooded is to lack affection. Cold blooded creatures are alienated from us by the lack of that quality we most value. They are heartless. They view the world with unwinking eye.

The term 'cold blooded' in relation to reptiles is, in fact, inaccurate. Their blood is not cold – it is as warm as the external environment. We place mammals higher on the evolutionary scale than reptiles, and feel therefore that warm bloodedness such as ours is superior. It certainly keeps us active. The wolf can track its prey for hours; the tiger is ready to leap night or day, but in most environments reptiles need to warm up in the sun to get themselves going. We warm blooded creatures also grow much more quickly than cold blooded ones. It seems puzzling that warm blooded animals have not reclaimed the world from the slower, less active, reptiles, which are more dependent on external heat and conditions. Mammals would seem to be much better suited to surviving on Earth than reptiles, and yet there are more species of reptile alive today than there are mammals.

The reason for this is that maintaining a stable, warm body temperature requires a large amount of energy. An animal or bird needs almost ten times more calories than an equivalent sized reptile, which is why they have to spend so much

Opposite A single meal can keep a fer-de-lance snake satisfied for weeks

The classic image of a snake-man interaction

more time searching for food. From the reptile's point of view, mammals are incredibly wasteful. In contrast, a 'cold blooded' animal does not need to eat high energy foods regularly to maintain its body temperature. As a result they can occupy habitats in which such foods are not available. It is also far more efficient at converting the energy from the food it obtains into bodily tissues for growth or reproduction: the reptiles can convert up to 50% of this energy, compared with only 1.4% for mammals. If global catastrophe overtakes us in the future, the survivors are likely to be the low maintenance 'cold blooded' creatures.

Throughout history man has reacted in an emotional way to snakes. They have been deified and feared, transformed into dragons and sea-serpents, woven into legend and myth, and their powers and size have been wildly exaggerated. Snakes are one of the most hated of all creatures. Studies suggest that one in four

people in the West fear them. Why do we react in such an extraordinary way towards these superbly adapted animals?

Many people hate snakes for the simple reason that they can be venomous, but there is more to our fear than just this. Some people feel nauseated and faint simply looking at a snake, even a perfectly harmless one. It seems extraordinary that even today, when Westerners seem to have less to fear from snakes than ever before, we should still harbour such a dislike for these creatures.

One of the most prevalent reasons for this hate seems to be that people believe that snakes are slimy, even if they have never touched one in their lives. In fact snakes are neither slimy nor dirty; they are dry, clean and often silky smooth, but in our hygienically conscious society their association with dirt and filth is a major reason for our dislike of them.

The long sinuous body of the snake and its habit of rearing up have contributed to its association with sex. In our society sex is still something of a taboo subject, an act to be performed in private, a sinful deed laden with guilt. So sex is often associated with filth, and similar feelings are associated with the snake.

As people are crowded more and more into cities, we are becoming further and further removed from the realm of the snake. Just how many of us have ever encountered a snake in the wild? As package holidays open up the possibility of travel to the remotest areas of the world, the snake has become an animal more feared than seen. It seems that our fear of snakes are caused by a number of factors. Our response to snakes may be the result of subconscious symbolic factors, religious beliefs, or lessons from teachers or parents – "some snakes are venomous so they are best all left alone"! But there may be a more basic reason for our fear, one that is built-in, hard-wired into the evolution of man's behaviour.

An inborn fear exists in our nearest primate relatives. On continental Africa, primates evolved alongside venomous snakes, and have developed a fear response to them. Chimpanzees show instantaneous terror on encountering snakes in the wild, and shriek and hurl sticks at them. In East Africa, vervet monkeys have even developed a specific alarm call to distinguish a snake from their other main predator, the eagle. Further evidence for inherited fear is found in the primates of Madagascar, the lemurs, which have evolved without poisonous snakes, and show no fear of them.

Fear of snakes would have been a useful and reasonable response of early man. As a ground dwelling primate, his natural curiosity would have been balanced by a rapid response reaction to danger. As children, our fear of snakes increases up to the age of six. This early childhood period is a time spent in exploration, in tasting and touching everything. It is our way of finding out more about the things around us. A natural aversion to anything writhing or snake-like in appearance would therefore have been of great survival value to our ground dwelling ancestors.

When people in the West think of snakes they usually think about 'the jungle'. The oppressively hot tropical forests are legendary for their dangerous animals, and of these, snakes are the most feared. Ten years ago, whilst on a filming trip in central Brazil, the boat we were travelling in capsized, and I had to walk through the dense riverine forest in the dead of night. Our single torch, drenched in the river, flickered and died, so we blundered and hacked our way through the tangle of undergrowth on a compass heading. It was one of the most frightening things I have ever done, my imagination conjuring up dangerous animals in every vine that snagged an arm, or twig that crunched underfoot. Four or five times we plunged

waist deep into water as we stumbled into overgrown oxbow lakes in the darkness. In all it took us five hours to tear our way out of those forests. We eventually crawled out exhausted, on all fours, through the surrounding tussock grassland towards the lights of a rescue vehicle which had been sent to look for us. That trek was the most horrendous experience, yet the most memorable thing was that not one of us was injured by a single animal – not even an ant or wasp sting, let alone a bite from an unseen snake.

Forests seem to breed paranoia. Deserts and scrubland actually harbour more poisonous snakes, yet we worry less, perhaps because they are open and light with good visibility. In forests, however, the dark brooding, claustrophobic nature of the environment heightens our fears and our nerves. Here the play of light and shadow, and the movement in this three dimensional world creates an alertness of mind and eye. The great explorer, Colonel Percy Fawcett wrote of a sudden encounter with a large viper whilst walking along a trail in Bolivia:

> All of a sudden, something made me jump sideways and open my legs wide, and between them shot the wicked head and huge body of a striking bushmaster…What amazed me more than anything was the warning of my subconscious mind and the instant muscular response.

Today, equipped with the same responses evolved by our African ancestors, we stay alert and alive in the vanished forests of the world, wherever we may be. Our fear of the hidden dangers of the forests is something which only subsides with time, and with increasing familiarity with the environment.

Nobody knows how many species of snake there are in the world. Well over three thousand different kinds have been reported, but whether or not they are all separate species and how many remain undiscovered are questions for the future. Since there are so many types of snake it seems helpful here to concentrate on the ones which are an actual or potential danger to people. These may be easily divided into the big snakes which can kill mechanically, by squeezing, and the smaller ones which kill chemically, by injecting poison. A number of snakes do have the ability to kill humans, and around the world hundreds of thousands of people are bitten by them every year. Each continent has its shortlist of infamous snakes; in South America there is the anaconda, the fer-de-lance and the bushmaster; in North America, the rattlesnake; in Africa, the mambas and cobras; in Europe, the adder; in Asia, the cobra and king cobra, and in Australia, the taipan. But are these the species which we should really watch out for?

We travelled to the remote rain forests of Costa Rica to film one of Central America's most notorious snakes and the one that so nearly bit Colonel Fawcett – the bushmaster. The bushmaster is a pit viper, a type of viper distinguished from all other vipers by possession of a heat sensitive pit between its nostril and its eye. Not only is it the largest viper in the world, but it is also one of the largest poisonous snakes in the world, stretching to a record 3.6 meters (nearly 12 ft). Only the Indian king cobra, the taipan of Australia and the black mamba of Africa outstrip it. It commonly exceeds 2 meters (6 ft) long and is as thick as a man's arm, but the patterns of colour on its back blend in so perfectly with the leaf litter of the forest floor that it is almost invisible. We found the bushmaster doing what it does best: waiting, coiled in ambush.

Three weeks before it had been gliding along the forest floor when its flickering tongue picked up minute traces of the scent of rodents. Smell is the most

Left Bushmaster snakes are well camouflaged.

important sense for many snakes, but they do not smell through noses like humans. Instead they taste the air by flicking out their forked tongues, and trapping traces of scent particles. These are then identified by the Jacobson's organ, two small cavities on the roof of the mouth into which the two forks of the tongue are inserted. The advantage of having a forked tongue is that it allows the snake to smell in 'stereo', in the same way that two ears tell an animal where a sound is coming from. A few flicks of the tongue enabled the bushmaster to identify the direction in which the scent was strongest and so pinpoint exactly where the rodent had passed by, days before. There was no need to go hunting. Rodents use well defined trails and, one day, a rodent would return along the same trail. The bushmaster has plenty of time. It can sit absolutely motionless, save for the occasional shifting of a coil, for months without food. It sits in total stillness, and then strikes, holds and swallows the prey in a few seconds of lightening activity, before lapsing back into immobility.

Although this is by far the largest viper in the world, the bushmaster maintains its bulk on a frugal diet. Amazingly, only half a dozen spiny mice a year will keep this monstrous snake going. Like other pit vipers, however, it can also kill and eat prey heavier than itself.

The bushmaster's venom is highly toxic, and its fangs are long so that it is quite capable of killing humans. It seldom does so, because it lives only in the depths of undisturbed rain forest in Central America, and the northern half of South America. Even in these forests it is rare, and seldom seen by people. The tribes that live here know of the dangers, remember where different bushmasters have their territories and where they are most likely to be lying in ambush. The only other human contact the bushmaster might have are with people gathering forest products such as timber, rubber and nuts. The odd biologist makes inroads into their territory and, of course, the occasional wildlife film crew. But their impact on the human race has been minimal: in Costa Rica only 10 people have ever been recorded as having been bitten. Five of them died.

The forests of the world harbour some of the most notorious of snakes. The rain forests of west and central Africa are the home of one of the most fearsome of all – the Gaboon viper. Sluggish, massively bodied and superbly camouflaged, this 2 meter (6 ft) snake, the African equivalent of the bushmaster, possesses the longest fangs of any snake. Two inches long, they inject highly toxic venom deep into the prey.

Further east, in the primary forests of South-east Asia and the Phillipines, lives the world's longest venomous snake, the king cobra. Growing to over 5 meters (16.5 ft) this swift moving snake eats other snakes, and is famous as the only one which makes a nest for its eggs. It is also one of the very few snakes which is reputed to chase anyone who ventures too close to its nest.

Despite the world-wide notoriety of these forest-dwelling snakes, they seldom kill people, for the simple reason that they live deep in the forests and are seldom encountered. Far from being a danger to us, the king cobra and bushmaster in particular are becoming increasingly rare. These large charismatic snakes are good indicators of the quality of a forest; like jaguars or leopards they are top predators, and like big cats they are among the first animals to vanish when the forests are damaged by people.

One of our greatest fears in the claustrophobic confines of the forest is of attack from on high. The profusion of plant life that grows all around and above us

The Gaboon viper's colouration is very distinctive

would seem to provide a myriad of perfect ambush sites for a wealth of venomous creatures. So do the forest branches drip with lethal snakes?

As the bushmaster waits patiently on the forest floor, a smaller, more brightly coloured relative might be sitting in the tree above. It may have a ground colour of green, rust, or light blue with a diamond pattern of darker colours, or it may be pure vibrant yellow. It is small, averaging about half a meter in length, and has a row of enlarged scales which protrude like miniature spikes just above its eyes, giving rise to its name – the eyelash viper. Nobody knows what purpose the spikes serve, but they give the snake a very distinctive appearance. Contrary to popular belief, forest branches are not festooned with deadly snakes. The eyelash viper, and the other closely related palm vipers of South and Central America are

Eyelash vipers come in a variety of
vibrant colours. They live in tropical
trees, waiting for an unsuspeting
humming bird to fly past.

also pit vipers, and they pose even less risk to humans than the bushmaster. They are more noteworthy for their diversity of startling colour forms. Nobody knows why the eyelash viper has so many colour forms, which often make brothers and sisters of the same litter look like completely different species. Some colour patterns are cryptic, helping the snake to blend with the mosses and lichens on branches, but others are so bright that some biologists think that they may actually lure birds to their doom: nectar-feeding birds such as hummingbirds that fly in search of flowers may be attracted to the bright colours of the snake. It may also be that the bright colours make the snake so unsnake-like that birds fail to recognise it as a threat. Whatever the reason, the eyelash viper is a successful hunter among the leaves and floral bracts of forest flowers, where it rests and suns itself, waiting to ambush lizards and small birds by day, and bats by night, attracted to nearby flowers. Occasionally it may catch a hummingbird, but more often than not the hummingbird's sharp reflexes and exquisite flight control help it to veer away in a fraction of a second, out of reach of the viper's lunging fangs. Like the bushmaster though, this snake can afford to wait – a single small bird can keep it going for several weeks. To maximise the chances of netting a meal, the eyelash viper, like many tree snakes, has long curved fangs with which to grip prey. Unlike snakes living on the ground, the eyelash viper cannot afford to strike and release prey, since it would never be able to find it again; instead the snake has to hang on grimly during the unfortunate animal's dying struggles.

Although the eyelash viper's venom is not very powerful, because it is an arboreal snake it is more likely to bite people on the chest, face and neck, as they walk through dense vegetation. Bites to these parts of the body are potentially more dangerous than bites to extremities, such as the feet and hands, since venom is more rapidly absorbed. Frightening though this may be, the risk of serious injury is slight: the only report of death from an eyelash viper bite was a man who was bitten on the tongue!

Around the world there are only a handful of really dangerous snakes that live in trees: the shy and elusive green mamba from Africa and Asia, and the rear-fanged boomslang and twig snake which are restricted to Africa. Despite being relatively common, none of these snakes cause many deaths. By far the greatest dangers lurk on the ground.

Our fear of snakes is closely associated with the harm they can do us. The ability of snakes to kill through injecting poison is a most fascinating, even spell-binding adaptation, that is extremely useful to a limbless animal that has to capture and subdue prey capable of biting, kicking, scratching or just running or flying

The hypodermic-like fangs of a red diamond-back rattlesnake

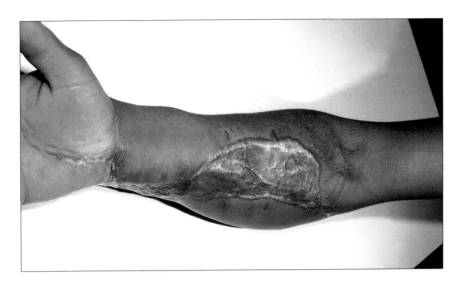

away. Strangely, venom is simply a modification of saliva. If a snake were injected with enough human saliva it would die. Human saliva contains an enzyme for breaking down the starch that we eat. Snake venom is a more concentrated form of saliva, containing a much greater variety of enzymes, each of which specialises in digesting or impairing the function of a different part of the victim's body.

The mixture of chemicals in snake venom may not be lethal, but can cause serious scaring. A 3 month old rattlesnake bite

Producing and storing such a lethal concoction does have its problems: the poisons do not discriminate between the tissues of the snake and the prey, and are potentially dangerous to both. To counter this, some snakes have special proteins that they mix with their own venom to stop them damaging their own bodies. These chemicals inactivate the venom during storage. When the venom is injected into a victim it rapidly becomes diluted by the animals' body fluids, and this separates the inhibitor proteins and allows the venom to start its destruction.

In the less venomous species of snake, the venom's main function is to assist digestion; in the more highly specialised snakes which tackle more dangerous prey, it has the additional role of killing the prey as rapidly as possible. The analysis of venom from different species is very complicated, but most venoms are cocktails containing a number of ingredients, including blood poisons (haematoxins), nerve poisons (neurotoxins), muscle poisons (myotoxins), coagulants and anticoagulants.

The blood poisons cause the disintegration of the tissues and the blood corpuscles, whilst the nerve poisons attack the nervous system and affect the operation of the heart, and the muscles used for breathing. Their action tends to be rapid: symptoms appearing within minutes of a snake bite if large doses are injected. In contrast, the muscle poisons are slow acting and may not destroy the muscle fibres for several days after a bite. The coagulants in the venom cause thrombosis or the clotting of the blood whilst venoms with anticoagulants prevent blood clotting causing the victim to bleed to death.

The majority of snakes have poisons in their saliva, but this in itself does not threaten people, unless the snake also has the means to inject it through the skin. The threat which a snake might present depends on the efficiency of the delivery system of the venom. In other words, it depends on what sort of fangs they have. Fangs are teeth modified for injecting venom: simple fangs are teeth with grooves down the side for venom to flow down, advanced fangs are hollow, more like hypodermic needles than teeth, through which venom can be injected under pressure. Fangs vary between the different groups of snakes. The vast majority of snakes do not have well developed fangs for the simple reason that they have no need for them. Their prey consists of amphibians, insects, snails and other invertebrates. Frogs are the mainstay of many snakes since they are abundant, and easy to catch and digest. Such animals have little chance of fighting off a snake, and once in the snake's mouth they are quickly subdued by the snake's toxic saliva which diffuses through their permeable skins.

But there are exceptions that can catch out even the most experienced herpetologists. The colubrids, the largest group of snakes, is normally considered to contain only harmless species, most of which eat frogs and invertebrates, so have no need for fangs. But a few of these snakes have taken to more challenging prey, such as lizards and birds, which are powerful, fast moving and protected by scales or feathers. To subdue these animals, snakes have had to evolve specially adapted teeth near the back of the upper jaw; hence their name 'back-fanged'. The back-fanged colubrids are an oddity: a handful of dangerous snakes amongst a vast group of harmless ones. In these snakes injecting venom into a victim is an awkward process. The animal has to be manipulated to the rear of the mouth, and the jaws rocked from side to side in order to drive the fangs into the victims; so these snakes never used to be considered to be a danger to people. As more and more types of snakes have come to be kept in captivity it has become clear that some of these back-fanged snakes are far more dangerous than was once assumed.

Two African snakes, the boomslang and the twig snake, are particularly dangerous since they possess potent venoms, and they have unusually long fangs much further forward in the mouth than other back-fanged snakes. Although normally a shy, elusive snake, a frightened boomslang will strike out with its mouth agape permitting its rear fangs to come into contact with the victim. Fortunately the boomslang only secretes a small amount of venom and, because of its relatively inefficient fangs, it has to chew on its victim to allow the poison to penetrate the skin. If knocked away quickly the bite is usually not too severe. But should any venom reach a person's blood the effects are dramatic producing extensive internal bleeding, often leading to death.

On 25th September, 1957 a group of herpetologists were discussing a small live snake which had been sent to the Chicago Natural History Museum for identification. It was known to be African with a characteristic head shape, keeled dorsal (upper) scales and a bright colour pattern. It should have been easy to name but the task was proving to be uncommonly difficult. One of the men, Dr. Karl Schmidt, without thinking, rather carelessly took the snake from his colleague. In hindsight it was a stupid thing to have done for his grip was too far behind the snakes head. Immediately the snake swivelled round and bit him on his left thumb. Only the rear fangs of the snake entered his thumb, one biting down to a full 3 mm. Dr. Schmidt kept a record of what happened next:

> The punctures bled freely and I sucked them vigorously. 4.30-5.30pm strong nausea during trip on suburban train. 5.30-6.30pm strong chill and shaking followed by fever of 101.7°F. Bleeding of mucous membranes in the mouth. 12.20pm A good deal of abdominal pain. A little fitful sleep until 4am.

After breakfast Dr. Schmidt felt so well that he telephoned the Museum to expect him at work the next day. He got up to eat at noon but vomited after lunch and

soon began to have difficulty breathing. This grew worse until his laboured efforts could be heard all over the house. His wife called for help and he was transported to hospital around 3.30pm. He was dead on arrival. The autopsy revealed that he had extensive internal bleeding throughout the body. He had died from respiratory paralysis and cerebral haemorrhages. The snake turned out to be a young boomslang, now known to have venom even more toxic than such notorious snakes as the cobra and the mamba.

A boomslang snake, showing the back-fangs. These are further forward in the mouth than in other back-fanged snakes and can thus cause a very dangerous bite

The more advanced snakes, the vipers and elapids (cobras, mambas, coral snakes and kraits) specialise in eating large, difficult prey: rodents, birds, lizards and other snakes – all animals that have the ability to struggle and fight back, or flee at speed. Consequently these snakes have a more refined way of killing using fangs at the front of the upper jaw with canals in the teeth for conducting venom into the victim. The base of the two hypodermic-like teeth are close to ducts from the venom glands allowing venom to be injected under pressure. This ability to inject venom quickly is important to the snake's survival. A typical strike lasts a few hundredths of a second during which time a full dose of venom can be injected. Because the time of contact is so short the victim has little chance to retaliate against the snake. The fangs of the elapids and seasnakes are all relatively short and immobile.

The black mamba is Africa's most awe-inspiring snake. Growing to almost four meters (13 ft), it is the second largest venomous snake in the world. Like the Boomslang it is shy and elusive and glides off rapidly given half a chance. Black mambas hold the record as the fastest moving of all snakes, being capable of 16 kph (10 mph). On a flat surface a healthy person can easily outrun a mamba, but in the bush the tables are turned. If the black mamba feels threatened it will not hesitate to attack, and is renowned for its rapid and accurate strikes high to the body.

All these front-fanged snakes use venom for hunting and for self defence. The problem with biting in self defence is that it makes the snake vulnerable to counter attack from the irate and frightened victim. It would be safer to ward off enemies from a distance. A few cobras do just that: they spit venom from a distance of up to three meters (9 ft). Their hollow fangs have holes at the front, instead of the tip of the tooth, so venom is squirted forwards when the snake compresses its venom glands. The venom can be projected with considerable accuracy and is usually aimed at the eyes of an attacker. Some rear up to deliver their poison but one, the Mozambique spitting cobra, is able to spit whilst lying concealed, perhaps under a log. Often the unwary victim may not even see the snake before being doused with venom. Any that gets into the eyes must be washed out immediately as the venom is extremely potent and can cause temporary or even permanent blindness. Although venom was developed for capturing and incapacitating prey, spitting is purely a defensive strategy. When hunting these snakes rely on bites to subdue their victims.

I am fascinated by snakes, although I must confess to being far from an expert on them. In all my travels I am always on the look-out for snakes, and at every opportunity I try to find out a little more about these unique creatures. Seldom am I lucky enough to encounter snakes, but my interest in them has led to some interesting experiences. Once when driving across the Serengeti short grass plains, I came across a cobra which was out hunting during the morning. As I drove up to get a closer look the snake suddenly turned and shot under the car. It did not come out the other side! Too late I realised that it had sought refuge in the closest hiding spot – the engine compartment. Only afterwards when I related the story to an old bush hand did I find out that this was what I should have expected. Unfortunately the car was due for a service that day, and I did not want to take it in with a deadly snake under the bonnet. If I had mentioned the problem to the people at the garage the snake would more than likely have been killed. My first problem was to open the bonnet, which entailed feeling under the lid for the catch, not knowing where the snake was – a very unnerving experience. Once the bonnet was open, I found the snake coiled tightly in a corner over the front wheel arch. As I leaned forward to get a better look, stick in hand, a jet of venom shot out and hit me square in the face. Fortunately I wear spectacles, and I was able immediately to wash the little venom that sprayed into my eyes out with water. For two hours I tried to prise the snake out of the engine compartment. Firstly I angled the car into the sun knowing that the snake would have to shift its position as it grew hotter and hotter. This it did, but before I could catch it, it slithered down into the recesses of the engine and draped itself inside the hollow bumper. At one point, gripping a coil and gently pulling whilst desperately looking for the head, the dangerous end, I was suddenly sprayed in the face. The snake had worked its body around and come up unexpectedly to my right whilst I was looking under the car. Had it been a foot longer it would have bitten me. Eventually I was able to pull the snake carefully from the car and release it in one fluid movement, allowing it to glide away across the plains to the safety of a nearby burrow.

The most advanced snakes are the vipers, front-fanged snakes whose long fangs

are hinged back, lying flat along the top of the mouth. When the snake strikes, it opens its mouth wide and the bone to which the fangs are attached rotates and brings them down and forward. In this way the prey is stabbed. This is the most efficient system of venom delivery, as the snake can deposit large quantities of poison deep into the victim's body with immediate effect. Not surprisingly, these are also the most deadly of snakes for humans. One of the most potent of snakes, the Gaboon viper, has fangs two inches in length, a world record.

Some snakes, like the bushmaster and rattlesnake, have a means of detecting prey even in pitch darkness. On each side of the head, between the eye and the nostril, pit vipers have a cavity which is heat sensitive and allows them to locate prey in the dark. Until recently it was thought that this did not operate very accurately and that it was only sensitive at close range. Recent research has shown that the pit receptors are represented spatially in the brain and the snake not only sees an image from its eyes but, superimposed on that, an infra red image from these pits which allows it to strike with great precision. A pit viper such as a rattlesnake can register a change of temperature of a few thousandths of a degree centigrade, allowing it to detect a mouse 30 cms (1 ft) away using body heat alone, or a larger object such as a person several meters away. The large constrictors also have heat sensitive pits; in fact they have a row of small pits along the edge of their mouths, but theirs have less than half the range of the pit vipers' pits.

Snakes never hunt man. It seems on the face of it puzzling, therefore, that they should have developed a capacity to kill an animal so many times bigger than they would ever hunt. We are not and have never have been part of their diet. So why

The spitting cobra can deliver venom with great accuracy from a number of meters away. The venom can cause blindness

Overleaf Pit viper. The two pits on either side of its nose detect infra red, so they can see in the dark

Taipan snakes are not dangerous to each other, but are the most dangerous to man

should they be dangerous to us? The answer lies in the snake's need to rapidly immobilise a prey that can retaliate by biting or scratching, or can run or fly away. The snake can only hold with its mouth and, being cold-blooded, it lacks the stamina for pursuit. So the venom must be powerful enough, and produced in a large enough quantity to disable or kill quickly. The more dangerous or agile the prey, the greater the need for a powerful poison. So the rat-catchers among the snakes are some of the most venomous, and can deliver a powerful toxin through long fangs deep into the victim.

Which are the most venomous of snakes? Australia has the unenviable record as the home of the world's three most venomous land snakes. The taipan ranks third for toxicity, but it has the reputation of being the most dangerous of all Australia's snakes because it is the longest, it can inject the most venom and it bites repeatedly when roused. It also boasts the longest fangs of any Australian snake, and so can deliver massive amounts of venom deep into its victim. Taipans live mainly in north Queensland, where they feed exclusively on mammals – particularly marsupial mice, bandicoots and rats. Their fondness for rats and mice brings them to sugar cane fields or rubbish dumps and into contact with humans. In one of the few recorded cases of someone surviving a taipan bite without antivenin treatment, the bite was through a leather boot and thick sock, and the bitten man's friends gashed him severely at the site with a chisel and forced him to bleed profusely. A four year old boy bitten six times on the upper thigh and buttock in Townsville in 1979 died in ten minutes.

The taipan was so lethal for so long because there was no known antivenin. The story of its development is one of human heroism. In 1950 a young Sydney snake collector, Kevin Budden, found a taipan in a rubbish tip. He seized the 1.9

meter (6.2 ft) snake and took it to his car. As he was stuffing it into a sack it gave him multiple bites on his thumb. Witnesses tried to kill the taipan but Budden stopped them and, before he became paralysed and lost the power of speech, stressed that it must be kept alive and sent to the Commonwealth Serum Laboratories in Melbourne. Kevin died a few hours later, but his instructions were carried out, and the taipan was milked yielding venom from which, two years later, the first taipan antivenin was produced.

The most recent reports from Australia suggest that the number of deaths from snakebite has fallen dramatically. From 1910 to 1926, a total of 198 deaths were recorded; from 1980 onwards, deaths from snakebite have stabilised at one or two a year. The place of the taipan as Australia's most deadly snake has recently been overtaken by the brown snake, whose venom is the second most toxic in the world. On 23rd December, 1991, a group of friends were enjoying drinks on the banks of the Murray River at Berri, South Australia, when one of them spotted a snake swimming in the water. Some of them started to throw rocks at the snake, but one man dived into the water "like Tarzan", swam out to the snake and grabbed it from behind. As he headed back for the bank it turned and bit his hand. After climbing out of the river he tore off its head. Protesting that he was fine, he was taken by ambulance to the nearest doctor's surgery but collapsed and died from cardiac arrest before arrival. The time from the bite to his death was only 35 minutes. He had been bitten by the brown snake.

The most venomous land snake in the world is, fortunately, a shy retiring Australian animal which was thought to be extinct. The naturalist who rediscovered it in 1967 was bitten on the thumb – the only recorded bite of a human by this snake. He was given first aid and flown to hospital where he was given the wrong antivenin because he mistook the snake for a brown snake. He became critically ill, his heart stopping twice, and was lucky to survive. The snake he had discovered was later identified as the inland taipan or fierce snake. A bite from this snake can deliver enough venom to kill a quarter of a million mice! Its venom is more than twice as toxic as that of the taipan. Despite its toxicity and name, the fierce snake is not really much of a threat, as it has retreated inland away from the spread of agriculture and can rarely be seen today.

We naturally think of snakes as having the most potent venom in the world. But this is not so. There are, in the forests of Central and South America, tiny, brightly coloured animals with a capacity to kill far in excess of the most poisonous of snakes – the poison-arrow frogs. These animals are unfrog-like in their habits, for they are active by day, their chirps, peeps and trills contributing to the chorus of sounds in the tropical forests. They are small creatures, varying from about a centimetre to five centimetres in length, and are brilliantly coloured in vivid reds, neon blues, oranges and vibrant greens. Not only are they jewel-like in appearance, they also seek out prominent perches in shafts of sunlight to advertise their presence to mates. Frogs are soft bodied, and lack the strong teeth and claws of mammals. As a result they are much sought after by predators, so such flagrant activity during broad daylight would appear to be suicidal. How do these frogs get away with this outrageous behaviour?

The bright colours serve a purpose – they are a warning that these frogs should be left alone, for they carry a poison in their skin so deadly that the merest trace could prove fatal to a would-be attacker.

The most poisonous species are found in Columbia, and the Choco Indians who live there use the venom from these frogs on the tips of their blowgun darts. The locals scour the forests for these unmistakable frogs and carefully manoeuvre them into hollow bamboo cages, where they are kept alive until needed. To extract the poison, the frogs are gently roasted on spits, making them perspire with a white froth of venom into which the points of the arrows are dipped. These darts remain lethal for a year.

In the late 1970s the forests of western Columbia yielded a new species of frog, with a poison so deadly that it was called *Phyllobates terribilis* – the terrible frog. Its poison is twenty times more potent than any other known frog. So toxic is this new species that a chicken and a dog died simply by coming into contact with the rubber gloves discarded by researchers. Special precautions were obviously needed to deal with these lethal animals. One of these tiny frogs may yield up to 2 grams of poison, a tenth of which is fatal if it enters your bloodstream. However, the poisons are purely a defensive mechanism, and unlike snakes, frogs have no way of actively injecting the venom into another animal. Though they are deadly, the poison dart frogs in reality pose little danger to humans. The poisons cannot be absorbed through contact with skin, but have to enter the body through a cut or abrasion in the skin to be effective. If this does happen even the smallest of doses could prove fatal as no effective antidote is known.

Research into the poison of these frogs has revealed that it is amongst the most potent of naturally occurring toxins. The venom acts rapidly and affects the nerve and muscle cells of the victim causing heart failure. Only the Choco Indians of Columbia use the frogs for poison darts. Elsewhere the technique did not evolve, and the people there came to rely on other hunting methods or poisons, like the less potent curare, which they made from the scrapings of the bark, stems and roots of plants. Outside Columbia the poisons found in other closely related frogs are neither potent nor concentrated enough to make the rapid killing poisons necessary for blowgun hunting.

Rainforest hunters have to bring down their game, birds and monkeys, from the canopy of the forest. A wounded animal can easily escape among the tangled branches so a rapid-acting poison is essential. The hunters move quietly and easily through the forests listening for the tell-tale sounds of their quarry – perhaps the honk of a toucan or the chattering of spider monkeys high above in a fig tree. Silent though they are, the hunters are often spotted and the monkeys will bark in alarm and peer down from the brightness of the canopy into the shadows below. In one fluid movement the hunter draws a poisoned dart from the hundreds he carries in a woven palm canister. He twists a ball of cotton onto the blunt end of the dart and inserts it into his heavy polished black pipe of shan't palm. Carefully he raises the blowgun, takes a deep breath, and aims it at an exposed monkey. With a sudden explosion of air his powerful diaphragm muscles send the dart skywards and up into the monkey's body. Within seconds, the monkey begins to sway on the branch. The poison breaks down its nerve impulses and causes its heart to pound irregularly. Within minutes it is dead and falling to the ground. The hunter has only to wait quietly below.

Surprisingly these most poisonous of frogs can be kept in captivity without much danger to their keeper. The longer they are kept captive the less virulent their venom becomes. After a year it is only half as potent and in time they lose their poisons altogether. Only recently was it discovered why this should be. Apparently the frogs acquire their venoms through their diet. In the wild they eat

Clockwise from top left. The most poisonous frog in the world - Phyllobates terribilis. These are collected and kept in wicker baskets. The poison darts are produced by squeezing the frogs until they begin to perspire poison, which is then smeared on the end of the dart

a variety of small invertebrates that are found in the leaf litter of the forest floor. The poisons that naturally occur in these animals are used and concentrated by the frog in its skin. By eating a variety of toxic invertebrates, the frogs accumulate a variety of different skin toxins. Small millipedes and beetles have been identified as the source for several frog toxins, but the prey animals responsible for the rest have yet to be traced.

With such deadly poisons secreted in their skins you would be forgiven for thinking that these anurans have no enemies. Amazingly even *terribilis* is not immune from predators: one snake is known to feed on them and other poison-dart frogs. The Lyophis snake is a member of the colubrid family, which does not have fangs, so is not dangerous to humans. It is a very beautiful snake with a delicately mottled brown back for camouflage, and a scarlet and black banded underside, which presumably startles enemies that pick it up. This snake hunts by day, its large eyes helping it to pick out the brilliantly coloured but tiny poison-dart frogs. Nobody knows how these snakes manage to neutralise the toxin, or how often they eat poison-dart frogs. It may be that they prefer to eat other frogs, but will resort to venomous frogs if there is no alternative.

No other vertebrate can approach the poison-dart frogs in the extreme toxicity of their venom, but there are other amphibians which have developed intriguing ways of repelling aggressors. In 1981, a party of biologists was camping at the northern end of the Venezuelan Andes when one of them noticed a frog which seemed similar to the poison dart frogs. This anuran was, however, larger and active at night. When they tried to examine one, it gave off a strong stench of sulphur. It was a frog that had never been seen by scientists before. They called it the Venezuelan skunk frog and they were right – it was a poison dart frog. The skunk frog is probably the most primitive of these frogs with a defence mechanism which developed only to the stage of producing a skin secretion foul smelling enough to put off predators, without actually poisoning them.

Unlike snakes, all amphibians have mucous glands in their skins which produce slime and help to keep them moist. In the poison-dart frogs this slime has been developed into a lethal venom, whilst the skunk frog has developed an evil smelling mucus. But these are the extremes of the anuran world. In many the skin is merely foul tasting.

Around the world toads are renowned for producing unpleasant tasting toxins

Poison dart frogs come in all sorts of colours

A cane toad swallowing a mouse

in their warty skins. It is a defensive strategy which has left many a domestic dog retching. The sugar growers of Australia have to put up with one of the most dangerous in the world. When their crops were being threatened by a beetle in the 1930s, news came of a giant toad in Hawaii which had been introduced to the cane fields there from South America to keep down the beetle population. It seemed to be doing well, and soon after a number of toads were brought from Hawaii and released in the cane fields near Cairns. The toads soon showed themselves to be completely ineffective against the Australian beetles – the native frogs did far better. Instead, with no natural enemies down under, they spread rapidly and quickly became pests, destroying honey bees, poultry and pets.

The giant toad grows as big and plump as a dressed chicken. But it would be a mistake to eat one, because the warty lumps on the back of their heads cover huge poison glands. The poison is strong enough to kill snakes, cats and dogs within an hour of swallowing a toad. If people handle them the poison can penetrate the skin through tiny cuts, making the heart race. Cane toads are best avoided.

Most frogs and toads are no threat to people and may even be looked upon

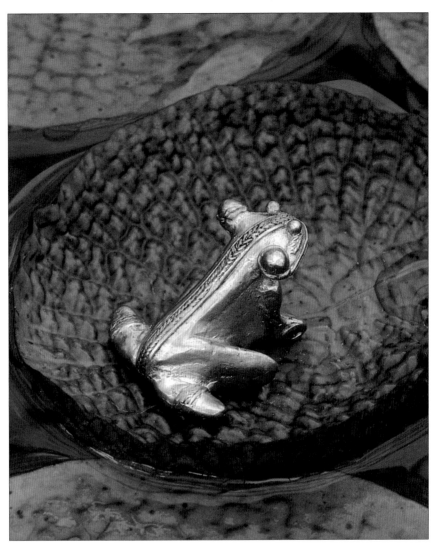

A Colombian gold frog – an unusual species to be revered

with some fondness. With their grasping hands, large blinking eyes and tailless bodies, frogs they are often considered cute in contrast to our opinions of most other cold-blooded animals. Ancient peoples of Central America revered frogs, and fashioned a multitude of ornamental frogs from solid gold. One of the most enchanting tourist attractions in Latin America is the gold museum in San Jose, the capital city of Costa Rica. Its underground display cases glitter with frogs and other intricate gold ornaments. These are surely the crown jewels of the Americas. But frogs are not everyone's cup of tea. Sudden jumping frightens some people, while others cannot bear the sight of their 'slimy' skins.

Contrary to popular opinion the majority of amphibian skins have very little slime at all, they merely look slimy because they have to remain damp so that their owners can breath through them. Larger amphibians, with a comparatively smaller surface area to body size, require a much greater expanse of skin to breath than smaller ones. The world's largest amphibians, the aptly named giant Japanese salamanders which grow to over a meter in length, have great wrinkled folds of skin hanging loosely from their bodies. With tiny eyes set in a spade-like head its a nightmarish creature as hideous and frightening as anything in the natural world.

In contrast to giant salamanders, most lizards look harmless, even friendly, as they dart in and out of the sunlight. Their skins are protected by a mosaic of shining scales. Just like frogs they may look slimy, but in this case it is dry polished scales, rather than moisture, that give lizards their sheen. Some are slender enough to be mistaken for snakes. Indeed they have much in common with snakes, which evolved from burrowing lizards, whose legs became reduced to vestigial bumps over millions of years of underground life. Lizards are the blueprint for a source of terror that runs deep through many human cultures – dragons. The bearded dragon, and the thorny devil of Australia are lizards that look as menacing as their names imply. In mythology the dragon is often portrayed as a large lizard with wings, such as was slain by St. George, or seen in King Arthur's dreams. The name 'dragon' means 'the seeing one', but its supernatural sight is the least remembered of its qualities. The dragon breathes fire, keeps maidens imprisoned in castles and can only be slain by the virtuous. It is the embodiment of evil. So widespread and familiar is the dragon in myth and fairy tale that few of us can look upon a snake or a lizard without a subconscious echo; and the echo is an unsettling one.

The dragon has had a long and successful career as a bankable star in Hollywood films, from *Gertie the Dinosaur*, one of the earliest cartoons made in 1906 through *The Creature from the Black Lagoon* and *The Beast from 20,000 Fathoms*, to the most commercially successful film ever made, *Jurassic Park*, with the multi-million dollar spinoffs such as T-shirts, plastic toys and videos. It seems that the legend of the monster or dragon is more durable than any of its manifestations, for it exists in the human subconscious and crops up from age to age in different shapes around the world. As someone said of the Loch Ness monster, it is not a problem for zoologists as much as for psychologists. In any event, the closest resemblance we see in nature to the dragon of imagination is the lizard.

Lizards, however, are only superficially dragon-like. Although there are about three thousand species (as many as there are snakes) only two are known to be venomous to man – the gila monster in the southern United States and the beaded lizard from western Mexico. They feed on nesting birds, ground squirrels and young rabbits, which their venom helps them to subdue. Being slow movers, they prefer to ambush rather than chase agile prey. Their venom glands, like those of snakes, are modified salivary glands, but in the poisonous lizards these glands are in the lower jaw and are not connected to the teeth. The lizards' teeth are grooved and the poison flows along the grooves from a series of ducts which open into the inside of the lower jaw. As the lizard cannot inject the poison with the efficiency of a snake, it has to chew it into the victim, working the poison into the wound tenaciously until it takes effect. This means that a bite from one of these lizards is not only painful but the lizard itself is very hard to dislodge. The gila monster hangs on like a bulldog and has to be prized away with pliers. The poison acts on the heart and respiratory system and may cause internal haemorrhaging. There are 34 known cases of gila monsters having bitten humans, eight of which were fatal; but the victims who died were either in poor health when bitten or drunk.

In reality few people fear such saurian oddities. In contrast, the harmless chameleons of Africa and Madagascar inspire a terror in local people, as strong as any in the realm of human emotions. The inhabitants of Madagascar, or Malagasy as they are known, have little to fear from the bizarre animals which share their island. The only snakes are non-venomous boas and colubrids, and there are no dangerous

The gila monster has such a powerful bite that it sometimes has to be prised-off with a pair of pliers

big cats on land. Only the crocodiles in the rivers pose a danger. Perhaps people need to fear some animals, or at least these highly superstitious people seem to, since many of the stranger-looking Malagasy creatures have become objects of terror. Of these the chameleon is the most widely and intensely feared.

In its long association with man, the chameleon has gathered around itself an unearthly mythology which is still potent. Its bones were discovered alongside the earliest protohuman remains in Olduvai gorge in Tanzania where there is a belief that the devil made chameleons using parts of other animals – the tail of a monkey, the skin of a crocodile, the tongue of a toad, the horns of a rhinoceros – and sent it into the world to spy on humans for its master. In the Bantu account of the origin of death, the chameleon is the fall guy: at the beginning of time when man was immortal, the chameleon was sent, in answer to a question, with the message that man would live forever. The lizard followed behind with a contrary message that man would die. The chameleon dawdled on the way and the lizard got here first. So death entered the world. In Somalia, people believe that a camel, if bitten by a chameleon, will prove barren; if a pregnant woman touches one, her child will be born dead or retarded – a retarded child is called a 'chameleon'.

The chameleon is certainly an odd creature: it has a somewhat prehistoric appearance, combined with many strange features that set it apart from other animals, for example its independently rotating eyes which are unique in the animal kingdom, and its startling changes of colour. The chameleon is feared by millions of people who live longest it in Madagascar and continental Africa. It can, and does, hurt flies; but it is completely harmless to people. A few species live further to the east, in the Middle East and India; here people pay little attention to chameleons, such is the fickleness of the human race. Almost all our fears are the result of the culture we grow up in.

There are 80 species of chameleons which are all grouped with lizards among the reptiles. They are highly specialised for climbing trees, which is why they have such strange feet for gripping the branches and long prehensile tails, that act like an extra hand for holding onto twigs. The advantage of this is particularly obvious when you see two chameleons mating or fighting in a tree, when their feet are needed for grasping each other, leaving the tail to stop them falling off their perches. The eyes are also well adapted to chameleon lifestyle, since they enable the chameleon to look all around for prey without moving the head – a movement that might alert the prey, or catch the attention of predators. Thanks to its superb camouflage a still chameleon is almost invisible. The eyelids have a vertical slit and the eyes protrude so far that they look as though they have started out of their sockets. They can be moved independently through a wide range – one can even look forward while the other looks back. Any movements the chameleon makes are slow, and with a rocking motion that blends well with the swaying of leaves in the breeze, making it harder for insects to notice the chameleon's approach.

At times the chameleon can sit for hours in ambush, completely motionless apart from the steadily circling telescopic eyes. When they spot an insect the eyes converge, giving very precise three-dimensional vision, and the tongue, which is pointed like a javelin, strikes unerringly. Amazingly the tongue can extend up to one and a half times the length of the chameleon, in a blur. So fast is the action that a chameleon can shoot a five inch tongue out fully in a sixteenth of a second – fast enough to catch a fly before it can take off. The tip of the tongue is club-like and sticky and with it the chameleon can catch prey almost half its weight. Most of

A vibrant coloured chameleon

the tongue is a long sock-like tube of muscle, which is stored gathered up on a tapering bony spike in the chameleon's mouth. When the chameleon wants to fire its tongue it contracts this tube of muscle, but because the bony spike tapers, this contraction causes the tongue to fly off the sharp end of the spike, out of the chameleon's mouth. You can see the mechanism in action if you squeeze a slippery apple pip, making it shoot across the room. This is because it tapers, just like the bony spike on which the chameleon keeps its tongue.

Chameleons vary a lot in size, shape, and colour. One of the largest, the Malagasy giant chameleon (or Oustalet's chameleon) from the forests of Madagascar, grows to over two feet in length. It catches birds, insects and rodents with its tongue which is also over two feet long. The ground dwelling Madagascar stumptail chameleon is the world's smallest, at a little over two inches in length. In most of Madagascar, killing a chameleon is prohibited under the system of taboos known as fady. Drivers will suddenly swerve or stamp on their brakes if they see one crossing the road. They also believe that any injury you inflict on a chameleon will certainly eventually happen to you. Strangely, this fear does not relate to size. The larger chameleons are even considered to bring good luck in a few areas but the dwarf ones are universally feared and are given the names of evil spirits which lie in wait for humans in the leaf litter of the forest floor. Illness or even death will visit anyone who steps on these evil creatures. That such a harmless creature should have retained an evil reputation for so long is an interesting example of how a culture can perpetuate a myth through the careful use of selective memory: when misfortune followed contact with a chameleon, the incident is remembered and talked about; when nothing happened, the contact with the chameleon is forgotten.

The best known of the chameleon's many strange qualities is, of course, its ability to change colour, and its name has passed into our language as indicating a person who keeps changing loyalties. The idea that chameleons try to imitate the colour of their background goes back to Aristotle and led to the popular idea that if you place one on a tartan cloth it will go mad trying to turn itself into a plaid. In fact, chameleons, like people, tend to change colour when they are aggressive, afraid, or sexually aroused. They are better equipped for displaying their emotions than we are, having two distinct layers of colour-producing cells just under their transparent skin. These cells (or chromatophores) contain red or yellow pigments, and they in turn lie above layers which reflect blue or white. To change colour the chameleon sends brown melanin, which is responsible for tanning in humans, up through the layers. The melanin blocks some of the colour cells making the animal darker. At the same time the overlapping chromatophores shrink or expand changing the colour of the skin. If, for example, yellow cells expand over blue cells a green is produced.

Pet chameleons have been observed to turn a mottled charcoal or even dense black when angered, reverting to a soft green when placed in the security of their owner's hands. When a male chameleon in the wild defends his territory, he puts on the brightest display he can manage and turns sideways to an intruder to present the fullest picture. The panther chameleon of Madagascar, as its name might suggest, is one of the most hostile and aggressive of chameleons. When two males meet they inflate to an imposing size and flash angry yellows and reds across their bodies. Should this not deter an opponent they they will charge each other and bite fiercely. So vicious are these contests that the vanquished animal often dies from his injuries – something uncommon among chameleons.

Courtship again is an occasion for dressing up and the diminutive nasutus chameleon abandons his usual dull brown colouration for bright purple streaked with light blue. A patch of light green appears behind each eye and his eyelids turn yellow. The male short-horned chameleon, again a medium brown when calm and unruffled, goes courting with a deep red patch on the back of his head and on his stumpy horn, his eyelids orange and dark patterns on his flanks. The females of the panther chameleon use colour to display their sexual receptiveness. Young females are gray-brown but become a lovely salmon orange when mature. Once mated the females turn black and orange, a signal to males to stay away or else. So chameleons use colour, not as a disguise, but as a way to communicate.

In spite of its nightmarish appearance and popular image as an unearthly monster, the chameleon has to be classified, in human terms, as on the whole benign. It seems unlikely that the myth of the dragon that pervades so many cultures has anything to do with chameleons, but there is a much more likely contender for the original dragon in Indonesia – the Komodo dragon.

The Komodo dragon is really a type of monitor lizard, closely related to the goannas of Australia and the water monitors of Asia. It first became known to the outside world around the beginning of this century, when romantic tales spread of the existence of a lizard over 7 meters long. In reality, dragons, or oras as they are called locally, grow on average to 1.7 meters (5.5 ft) and the largest ever recorded measured just over 3 meters (nearly 10 ft). The Komodo dragon is not the longest lizard in the world – that distinction belongs to the slender Salvadori monitor of Papua New Guinea which can reputedly reach a length of 4.75 meters (15.5 ft).

The chameleon's eyes can swivel. This allows them to look the other way without moving its head and thus giving away where it is

Chameleons can change colour very easily

But, like other monitors, the tail of the Salvadori monitor makes up three quarters of its length. What sets the dragon apart from all other lizards is its bulk – it's by far the heaviest lizard in the world with a sturdy body accounting for half its overall length. An average dragon weighs in at almost 50 kg (110 lbs) and the largest ever recorded weighed 166 kg (365 lbs) – a lot heavier than Mike Tyson and even more formidable.

I had long wanted to see dragons in the wild and jumped at the opportunity of filming. I wanted to make up my own mind about these huge lizards which live at the end of the earth. What was the reality behind the myth?

To start with, Komodo dragons are restricted to an isolated series of islands in the Lesser Sunda chain in the middle of the Indonesian Archipelago. Today the 30 kilometer-long island of Komodo is their main home, but they also live on the neighbouring islands of Rinca and Padar, and the very western tip of the much larger island of Flores. In common with many other island animals, like the famous tortoises of the Galapagos, it seems that the very isolation of the dragons caused their giantism.

The dragon is a meat eater. Young dragons, surprisingly, spend their lives clambering through the trees and bushes hunting for insects, lizards and small birds. Up here they are safe from larger dragons as these lizards are also cannibals. As the dragons grow bigger and heavier they come down out of the trees and hunt the ground for rats, birds and snakes.

Komodo was originally settled as a penal colony in 1915, by the Sultan of Bima, because the inhospitable climate and abundance of poisonous snakes made just staying there a punishment. The survivors soon learnt to build houses on stilts to evade the dragons, and to protect their dead from them by burying the graves under piles of rocks. Like other monitors, dragons seem to be immune to the poison of even the most deadly snakes and avidly kill and eat Russell's vipers and cobras. Adult dragons have no natural enemies and are capable of killing wild boar, deer and even 800 kg (1760 lbs) water buffalo.

It is likely that the ancestors of the Komodo dragon lived on small mammals and insects, just as the smaller dragons do today. There are no other large meat eaters on these islands so the dragons never had any competition from big cats like the tiger and leopard. By growing bigger the dragons were able to feed on a plentiful, otherwise unexploited source of food. They are thought to have caused the extinction of a species of pygmy elephant, found on Komodo until quite recently.

The dragons swim well and are regularly seen crossing the narrow straits between the islands, though it is uncertain whether they colonised the different islands in this way. Instead it is thought that their original home may have been divided by the sea into the smaller islands we see today. The island of Komodo is the home to almost half the population of 5000 wild dragons. They are one of Indonesia's greatest tourist attractions, and are easy to see there, once one has made the journey across the hazardous sea straits. More than 1000 tourists travel there each month by ferry, tourist boat and cruise ship.

The authorities take the danger posed by the dragons seriously and visitors are not allowed to wander the island alone. The dragons are certainly large and powerful enough to seriously injure or even kill a man. Over the last 65 years perhaps as many as 12 people have been killed by the dragons. In 1989 an elderly Swiss-German tourist strayed off into the forest alone. It was the last time he was seen alive. All that was ever found of him were his glasses and his Nikon camera. Today a simple cross is a reminder of the threat that lurks on these islands.

Every day guides take tourists along a nature walk a kilometer or so into the interior, to where the dragons wait. Here you are herded into a corral, a fenced area overlooking a dry riverbed. Twenty feet below the dragons lie motionless, "as elegantly as tree trunks", as the nearby information board states. Safe though we were, this high vantage point was not the best angle for filming and we asked for special permission to take a closer look at our quarry. Accompanied by a guard armed with a large forked stick to fend off inquisitive dragons, we cautiously descended to the river bed. As we rounded the corner, an unforgettable sight presented itself to us. Just twenty feet away and coming purposely towards us were 15 huge dragons. There was no question of simply fending them off with a stick, and we hurriedly backed away and scrambled up the cliff to safety.

What we had not realised was that it was Saturday, and Saturday is the day the dragons are fed a dead goat. It is a controversial arrangement, but it does mean that tourists can see dragons relatively easily. On hearing us approach, the dragons had only one thing on their minds – food. They were not so much after us as after the goat they thought we had brought. That encounter brought home to me the methodical, reptilian behaviour which the dragons exhibit; even eating an egg sandwich near a dragon is asking for trouble.

The tourist spectacle presents a false impression of the lifestyle of the dragon for they are not social. Truly wild dragons are essentially solitary animals, sleeping by night and active by day. The dragons spend the night in burrows in a torpor-like sleep. They literally turn off at sunset. They sleep so deeply that scientists studying them have been able to remove ticks from their skin and take temperature readings of their bodies. In the early morning the dragons come out into the sun and align themselves to soak up as much warmth as possible. The adults spend the

The Komodo dragon's claws can be used to tear a hole in its prey's stomach

day in this way, alternating between sun and shade to regulate their temperature.

Dragons tire quickly in swift pursuit of prey, since they are built for endurance rather than speed. As a result, they usually stalk or ambush animals moving along game trails, or wandering down to rivers to drink. I was surprised to find that, even in short bursts the dragons do not move very quickly. Certainly they are nowhere near as quick as crocodiles and a reasonably fit person could easily outrun them on flat ground. What the dragon relies on in hunting is surprise. Lying motionless for hours on end in the shadows of the forest they easily go unnoticed. It is this ambush technique which is so effective and enables them to catch such fleet-footed animals as deer and wild pigs. As its prey wanders unwittingly close the ora lunges and bites, often knocking the animal to the ground.

Dragons do not kill by suffocation or breaking the neck of an animal. They kill animals by slashing open the body cavity, and the prey dies from loss of blood, and shock. It's a killing technique similar to that employed by hyenas and hunting dogs on the African plains. In accounts of buffalo kills, the dragon may bite the legs of the animal in an attempt to hamstring it. Even if its wounded prey manages to escape, the dragon will follow the scent trail until it discovers the crippled animal. It is thought that the saliva of the Komodo dragon contains anticoagulants which can result in an escaped victim bleeding to death. This fact increases still further the likelihood that a Komodo dragon will eventually capture escaped prey.

Rinca village – site of a few dragon attacks

Dragons have poor eyesight but an incredible sense of smell and constantly flick their forked tongues out to taste the air. Inside their mouths the tongue sweeps across an area especially sensitive to taste, the Jacobson's organ – similar to that of snakes. It is thought that large oras use their sense of smell to track the movements of female ungulates about to give birth, attacking and killing full-term females, or snatching young from between the legs of the mother in labour.

Dragons eat quickly. There is a record of one 45 kg (100 lb) dragon eating a 40 kg (90 lb) pig in 17 minutes – 90% of its own bodyweight. The monitors hold down their prey with their stout legs and massive claws, and tear off huge chunks of flesh which they bolt down. Their enormous gall bladders enable them to digest their large meals.

Even a small bite from a dragon can prove fatal. Their mouths contain a deadly concoction of bacteria, and bitten prey that do manage to escape often die from infection. In 1947 a policeman died on Flores from blood poisoning after being bitten whilst petting a tethered ora. Dragons are the only reptiles besides turtles that cut prey up before feeding – it's something they have to do if they are to consume such large prey. For a big animal they have surprisingly small teeth. Only an inch long, the blade-like teeth are perfectly adapted for cutting, and bear a greater resemblance to shark or dinosaur teeth than to those of reptiles or mammals. Each tooth is serrated and, arranged in rows, they act like scalpel blades, cutting deeper than the ones before them as the ora bites and pulls away. Interestingly the gums normally cover most of the teeth but are pushed back as the dragon bites, riding up again when the dragon releases its hold. This back and forth movement against the serrated edges of the teeth lacerates the gums and turns the saliva pink and viscous. What purpose this serves, no one knows, but perhaps it increases the virulence of the bacterial soup in the dragon's mouth, and the deadliness of its bite. What it does do is give the dragons a rather unpleasant-looking mouth full of dribbling saliva.

Our investigations took us on to the nearby island of Rinca where the danger posed by the dragons was very real indeed. Here, in a raised stilt house on the edge of Rinca village, an Indonesian couple told us the story of their eldest son. The year was 1987 and their son, six years old at the time, had finished his lunch and got up to visit his friends in the village. As he had done hundreds of times before, he climbed down the wooden ladder to the ground. But this time a large dragon was waiting below and attacked him. Hearing his screams his parents rushed to his rescue and a tug of war ensued with the dragon. After a few minutes the dragon let go and rushed off into the forest But it had already severely bitten the boy about the leg, groin and shoulder. Soon after he died in the arms of his mother.

That dragons occasionally injure and kill people is without doubt. Fortunately for us however, they do not normally include humans in their search for prey. Most attacks seem to be isolated incidents – a case of the victim being in the wrong place at the wrong time. Certainly it would not be wise to lie down and go to sleep alone in the forest – that would be asking for trouble. But my encounter with these magnificent creatures had been enlightening and I came away from Komodo wiser, and with a much greater respect for its most famous resident.

Although the Komodo dragon is the largest of the world's lizards, it is not the largest reptile. That distinction is held by the giant constricting snakes. The giant serpents that coil and crush in mythological tales and pursue us in our dreams do exist, though their life styles and habits are far less threatening than our nightmares may lead us to imagine. They are often the leading players in explorers' tales, where the jungles are crammed with giant creatures over 100 feet long which drop from trees onto native bearers and crush the life out of them. Probably because of such misleading information the giant constrictors, though not venomous, are feared almost as much as poisonous snakes.

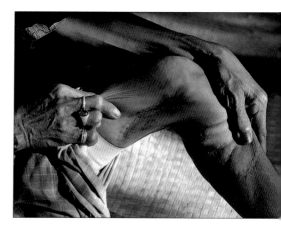

The constrictors – the boas and pythons – are generally bigger than all other living snakes. They are also the most primitive, with recognisable pelvic girdles, and tiny vestigial hind legs just in front of the cloaca, or reproductive opening – a reminder of their lizard ancestry. Contrary to popular opinion, most of these giant snakes do not live in trees – they are simply too heavy – nor do they crush their prey to death. They are ambush predators, lying in wait for their prey to come within range, and then lunging out with lightning speed. So fast is the attack that they can even catch birds in flight. All have a formidable array of large needle sharp backward pointing teeth with which they firmly grip their prey. As they lunge out, they throw coils over their victim in one fluid movement. Each time the victim exhales and its rib cage contracts the snake tightens its coils slightly increasing the pressure until the victim can no longer breathe in. Within minutes it suffocates and dies. The snakes are highly sensitive to movement and monitor the heart beat of their victims. Only when there is no sign of life will they relax their grip, uncoil and, with flickering tongue seek out the head end to start swallowing.

The bite of a dragon contains so many bacteria, saliva and blood that it can take a long time to heal and leaves a very bad scar

The size of the giant snakes has long been a matter of argument, explorers tales sharing with fishermen's bar talk a tendency to improve on a good story. What complicates the issue is that the skin of a dead snake can be stretched to almost twice its original length. In 1907, Colonel Percy Fawcett, on an expedition to the Rio Abuna in the Amazon for the Royal Geographical Society shot an anaconda and reported that: "a length of forty-five feet lay out of the water and seventeen feet in it, making a total length of sixty-two feet". This incredible claim was never confirmed and today few people believe it. As late as 1962 a book was published in which the author describes an anaconda forty-five feet long anchoring its tail to a submerged root and using its "head and neck coils" to drag a grazing cow into the water. Again, there are no independent records of this incident. We may allow ourselves a touch of scepticism of this account because in 1910, Teddy Roosevelt, the former US President and a great hunter, offered a US$1,000 reward for any snake measuring 30 feet or more. This offer was supervised by the New York Zoological Society which, over the years, has increased the amount. It now stands as US$50,000 and is still uncollected.

Constrictors do not ever set out to hunt and eat people, but if a large warm-blooded animal that happens to be human looms into view, they may very well strike as a reflex action. Bill Lamar is a highly respected North American herpetologist, who has spent many years working in the South American forests that are home to the anaconda. He had often heard Indians talk about anacondas lunging at people and ripping their shirts off leaving the victim dishevelled but miraculously unharmed. It made a good story, but Bill did not believe there was any truth behind such tales.

In 1978, Bill was on a field trip studying Orinoco crocodiles in Eastern Colombia. After eight weeks, everyone in the camp had grown weary of a diet of fish and rice, so one afternoon, Bill took his shotgun and set out with two locals to bag something for the pot.

> We were walking across a savanna grassland, working along the edge of a gallery forest that surrounded one of the many creeks in the area. Eventually we crossed into the forest and moved to the edge of a slow moving stream that fed into a large swamp. I decided to cross the stream in order to hunt the area on the other side. We carefully waded into the water but we couldn't cross in a straight line. So it was necessary to wade in the steam itself for a distance while we looked for an exit.

As they walked three abreast, a huge anaconda suddenly lunged out of the water at them.

> We first became aware of its presence when it struck at the lower chest of the fellow on my right. It contacted him fully and attempted to pull him back into constricting coils – a typical way that any constrictor obtains its prey. However, what the snake managed to do instead was jerk his shirt right off his body. I, largely out of surprise and fear, raised the gun immediately and shot the snake. It was sort of a reflexive action.

Bill Lamar and his friends retreated, waiting for the snake to stop thrashing about in its death throes. When they were at last able to approach, he was stunned by the size of the animal.

> It was certainly the largest one I've ever seen, although according to the literature, not by any means the largest one known. It was 24ft 7ins in length. What was really phenomenal was its tremendous girth. It certainly seemed as big around as maybe the waist of an average adult human at its thickest. Unfortunately, I had no means to weigh the snake, but it looked to be well in excess of 300 lbs.

Anacondas can grow large enough to kill quite large prey – some the size of a fully grown man

Although a large anaconda could kill an adult human, there are few verified records of them ever having done so. Why had this anaconda attacked them? Bill Lamar thinks he knows the reason.

> The anaconda had clearly been lying in ambush along a game trail and its feeding response had unwittingly been triggered by us. I am sure in its long life it had never encountered anything but suitable prey items when it was in a hunting mode like that, and it's easy to see how the confusion was caused. Obviously it was a big shock to all three of us, but now in retrospect, I feel great remorse at having killed it.

Having earlier doubted local stories of anaconda attacks, Bill is now a firm, if cautious believer.

> I have subsequently heard more such stories, and I am aware of no fewer than three cases that I consider fully verifiable. That is not to say this is a common occurrence. I think it's an extremely rare occurrence, but I would hazard a guess that every time it has ever happened, it has been a feeding response triggered when someone unwittingly wanders

Bill Lamar with an anaconda, smaller
than the one he met in Colombia

into the ambush site of a waiting anaconda.
Certainly the poor snake had no idea what a
human was, and I guess one would have to
characterise such an encounter as simply
unfortunate.

Dr Lamar skinned the snake and removed various parts
for scientific purposes.

I made every attempt to remove that skin as
carefully as I could, and without stretching it,
and it still measured a full 10ft longer than the
snake had. It would have been consummately
easy to add another 10 ft to that by deliberate
stretching. So it's easy to see how either a
carelessly removed skin or a deliberately
stretched skin would indicate proportions far
off from reality for a snake. The one question
that certainly can be laid to rest is that there are
some truly large anacondas alive. I think it's
important to know, though, that like all large
animals, they're rare.

Of all snakes, the anaconda of South America is the
bulkiest, with a girth of over a meter and a weight of
over 227 kgs (500 lbs) – twice that of Mike Tyson! This
snake's considerable girth suits it to a semi-aquatic lifestyle – it is much easier for
large animals to be aquatic than terrestrial, since the greater density of water
compared to air supports their weight and allows them to move more easily.

The anaconda spends much of its time in swamps and slow-moving rivers.
They often lie in wait for hours, even days, in shallow water only their eyes and
nostrils visible above the surface. Animals coming down to drink or cross these
small creeks are ambushed. Birds, rodents, peccaries and young tapirs are all
taken. Even dogs, sheep and pigs are fair game. Lying in ambush like a coiled
spring the anaconda has to decide, in a split second, whether or not to strike, or
the opportunity may be lost. Any large animal that passes by may trigger a strike.
It is this tendency to strike on instinct that occasionally puts humans in danger.
People are particularly vulnerable if they look small, or if their approach takes the
snake by surprise. A really large anaconda is quite capable of eating a child or
small adult, but is more likely to slip back into the water if approached, where it
can lie completely submerged for up to ten minutes. Fortunately the majority of
large anacondas seem to recognise people as a danger rather than a potential
meal. But just like humans, anacondas can, and do, make the odd mistake.

The Old World is home to many species of python, but only three are any
threat to people. Of these the Indian python is the least dangerous, and it seems
unlikely that it has ever eaten anyone except, perhaps, the occasional small child.
It is the most common python of southern Asia, occurring from West Pakistan
across to south China and down to the Malay Archipelago. This species grows to
6 meters (19.6 ft) and, being much lighter than the anaconda, is a good climber,
sometimes lying in wait for its prey along the branches of a tree. It prefers warm

An emerald tree boa

blooded animals, and like all pythons has a row of heat-sensitive pits along the edge of its mouth, which help it to detect the approach of warm blooded animals. Although its heat sensing abilities are less accurate at a distance than pit vipers, they must be a useful contribution to finding food.

There is an interesting record of an Indian python having killed and eaten a leopard, the python in question being 5.8 meters (19 ft) long and the leopard a quarter of that, excluding tail. Once a snake has gained a good grip on a victim, sharp claws and teeth are rendered useless. In comparison a small child would make a much more manageable meal. Indeed there is a reliable record of a Chinese baby living in Hong Kong being eaten; but for the most part, more Indian pythons are eaten by people than the reverse. They are unfortunately thought excellent meat in some parts of the world, and being rather sluggish in their temperament and movements, rarely try to escape when hunted. Until recently many Indian snakes were collected for the pet trade or for their skins. Pythons and all other snakes are now protected in India, but habitat destruction continues to reduce their numbers.

Africa too has its giant snake: the rock python. Like all constrictors this snake has rows of sharp large teeth which can inflict nasty wounds that can easily become infected and cause blood poisoning. Collectors capturing these snakes are always careful to hold the animals head to prevent it from biting them. In parts of West Africa the python is considered a sacred animal, and in Dahomey it is worshiped by priests and priestesses. In other parts of Africa the python is viewed with superstition and believed to be the harbinger of droughts.

African folklore is rich in stories of children and occasionally adults being eaten by this snake, but as ever with the giant snakes, reliable accounts of man-eating are virtually non-existent. In 1932 a specimen 39.62 meters (130 ft) was allegedly shot in the Semliki valley, but before reliable measurements could be taken the local Bwambwa tribe had eaten it, and it seems certain that the length was grossly exaggerated. In 1961 a reliable report was received from the Ivory Coast of one measuring 9.81 meters (32.18 ft). One of the most promising recent reports describes how two photographs bought in Angola showed a python with the corpse of a man inside it. By comparing the corpse with two other figures in the photograph, the author concluded that the victim was 'a person of average adult Portuguese size' but was unable to say whether the man was killed by the snake, or the python swallowed a corpse.

The largest living snake, and indeed the longest of all reptiles, is the reticulated python of South-east Asia, with a record length of over 10 meters (32 ft). It is the most aggressive of all the giant snakes. This python normally lives near water in wet evergreen forests, but has been seen in the busier waterways of Bangkok where it eats the odd domestic animal and keeps down the rat population. Only occasionally has it attacked humans. In 1972 an 8-year-old boy was swallowed by a 6 meter (19.68 ft) python in lower Burma. The snake was eaten by local villagers in revenge.

In 1927 a group of Burmese hunters took shelter from a thunderstorm and, when it was over found that one of their number, a small man, had disappeared. A search revealed his hat and shoes next to a gorged python some 6 to 9 meters (19-29 ft) in length. The hunters killed the python and inside found their missing friend. Although a large reticulated python is certainly powerful enough to kill an adult human, there may be some small comfort in the knowledge that its jaws probably wouldn't be able to open wide enough to accommodate the man's shoulders.

Giant snakes exist; they are capable of killing people and the larger ones may even be able to swallow an adult. Yet, for the most part, they are shy and unaggressive, living solitary lives in remote places. Only the most painstaking research reveals stories of their having apparently eaten people – stories which are, almost always, impossible to verify.

Of all the cold-blooded creatures, whether poisonous frogs, lizards, or the various types of snake, it is the few poisonous snakes which cause the most human deaths. The highest mortality is not caused by the most venomous of snakes, nor the largest, but the most common, which live near man. They are often called weed species.

By far the most dangerous cold blooded creatures to man are the venomous snakes. Perhaps its surprising, therefore, to discover that less than 400 of the 2700 or so species of snake have fangs sufficient to inject venom into humans, and far fewer could ever threaten human life. Accurate figures of bites and human

The adder – Britain's most venomous snake

fatalities are notoriously difficult to establish, especially for many third world countries – the very places where the incidence of snake bite is most likely to be high. However, snakes are undoubtedly one of the most dangerous groups of animals. The World Health Organisation estimated in 1981 that around 30 to 40,000 people die in the world each year from snake bite. India has by far the most deaths – between 10,000 and 12,000 every year. However, ten to twenty times as many people are actually bitten by snakes in India. Why do they not all die?

Although we normally think of venom as the weapon which a snake uses against an aggressor – and this is its role when humans are bitten – for the snake, it is an aid to feeding. Venom immobilises prey and starts the digestive process. So venom is precious: without it the snake cannot eat. Snakes can control the amount of venom they inject so as not to waste any. A rattlesnake can take up to a month to replenish its supply of venom, during which time it has to fast. So, like many snakes, it may bite in self-defence without injecting any venom. Up to 70% of snakebites are 'dry' bites of this kind. Some snakes even strike first with closed mouths as a warning. The more scared a snake is, the more venom it will inject.

There are more dangerous snakes in Asia than anywhere else in the world. The Americas come second, and Africa and Australia next. By far the safest continent from this point of view is Europe, with a mere seven species of venomous snake. The most northerly of all snakes is the common European viper or adder which is found as far north as the Arctic circle. It is also the most widespread of snakes and the only venomous one throughout much of its range.

The adder is unusual in displaying sexual dimorphism: the male and female are different in appearance, the zigzag down the back of the male being more distinctive than that of the female. Active by day, it eats mainly lizards and voles, and is seldom a threat to humans, though widely feared. Normally it avoids human contact and when a ruined businessman in 1932 attempted suicide through the bite of an adder all he lost was his arm. Snake bite cannot be called a serious threat to life in Europe; in Great Britain there have only been seven deaths in the past 50 years.

Most people are bitten because they have interfered with the snake, either by accidentally stepping on it or by deliberately harassing it. Where snakes are known to be dangerous, people can build up reputations for bravery by tackling them. In America there are still annual festivals in which men try to demonstrate their masculinity by tormenting snakes. They are called 'Rattlesnake Roundups'.

The folk tradition which justifies these unspeakable get-togethers is that local people used to be invited to a friend's ranch and given a banquet in return for reducing the population of rattlers that were supposedly killing off his cattle. Rattlesnakes are very common in parts of the United States, especially in the south of the country from California to Texas. Most ranchers, however, admit that they have no stock losses from snakebite. Another excuse is that these hunts reduce the risk of snakebite to humans. As less than one person in ten million dies from snakebite in America each year this seems less than adequate. In fact they cause more bites than they prevent by encouraging people to hunt out snakes, not to mention the various bizarre acts performed with the snakes before they are slaughtered.

The Rattlesnake Roundups do, however, put an otherwise insignificant town 'on the map', help raise community funds and give the men the chance to show off. This they do with alacrity. They pour petrol and other chemicals into snakes' dens to force them out, pull the rattles off live snakes and sew up the snakes mouths with wire so that they can safely climb into bed with a sack load of them or photograph visitors handling them. All who take part in the search for rattlesnakes in the bush are given certificates of bravery before the hunt starts. Many shows have a 'Miss Rattlesnake Charmer' contest and the curio shops sell articles made from snakeskins and rattles, from snake head buckles to rattlesnakes set into plastic toilet seats.

One of the most infamous of the rattlesnake hunters won a reputation on national television for his skill in picking up a snake by the tail and cracking it like a whip so powerfully that the head broke off. His career as an off-beat celebrity ended when a severed, but still living head, bit him on the thigh. He died from the venom – an appropriate end, perhaps, to someone who should have known better than to 'mess with snakes'.

Venomous snakes bite many people in the West every year, but few people die from them. In the USA about 7,000 people are bitten every year by venomous species, yet only 5-12 people die. In Australia, which has the world's most dangerous snakes, fewer than five people are killed every year. This pattern is typical of the richer countries of the world where comparatively few people work on the land, and those that do are usually well protected with boots. Snakebite victims in these countries are fortunate in being able to reach excellent medical facilities within hours, and having access to the appropriate antivenin and intensive care facilities.

Many of the people who are bitten in the West are either drunk, or snake handlers. Snake keepers, who feed their charges by hand, are sometimes bitten by snakes mistaking their hands for escaping prey. The snake associates the keeper with feeding time and is primed to launch a feeding strike. Such bites are often severe. The hungry snake, eager to start digesting the meal before swallowing it, injects a much larger dose of venom than it would in self defence.

In the third world the incidence of snake bite is high, because of the frequency with which people encounter dangerous species. Often bare-footed, peasant farmers are poorly protected against even the smallest of snakes. Indeed the biggest killer of all is a snake no more than a foot long which normally bites people on the foot. Of equal importance are the conditions under which these people live. Many are desperately poor subsistence farmers living far from proper medical facilities. Not only does visiting a doctor mean time away from work, it is also costly and perhaps unnecessary, especially when the bite appears to be no more than a scratch, and could well have been made by a harmless species. Unfortunately one of Asia's most dangerous snakes, the common krait, is deadly for this very reason. Its small fangs leave only tiny puncture marks that can go almost unnoticed, and symptoms may not appear for a day or two. By then any medical action is too late.

Venoms are complex compounds which vary enormously. The venom of one species of snake may itself vary from area to area, and from individual to individual within one region. This variability probably arose because snakes live in different habitats with different prey species, each particular set of conditions requiring its own special cocktail of poisons. This variability in venom means that an antivenin produced in one area may not work against bites from the same species of snake in another area. To complicate matters further the diets, and hence the venoms, of certain snakes change during their lives. The young of many South American pit vipers, for instance, feed on frogs and centipedes whilst the adults eat small mammals, requiring a different

Rattlesnake roundups are common in the southern states of the USA. The rattle is also seen as a trincket venom to incapacitate and digest them. Nobody yet understands why different venoms are better suited to different prey, but this variation is clearly a problem in the treatment of snakebite. Antivenin is usually made from the venom of adult snakes, so it will not always work well on someone who has been bitten by a young snake.

The history of the production of antivenin goes back to 1887 when it was discovered that animals repeatedly injected with sub-lethal doses of rattlesnake venom gradually built up a resistance and became immune to an ordinary lethal dose. The Pasteur Institute developed this further and found that the blood of an immunised animal would protect another previously untreated animal if injected into it. The antivenin that they produced was such a resounding success that they had to start using horses to produce enough blood to meet the demand around the world for snake bite treatment.

Venom is also required in large quantities. Its extraction is simple and does the snake no harm. Grasping the snake's head firmly, a handler presses down on the venom glands forcing poison out of the fangs into a container. Antivenin is by far the most effective cure for snake bite found, but it is far from perfect. Some people are highly allergic to the horse serum and could die if injected with it. Alan Root, a well-known wildlife film-maker from East Africa nearly died from the effects of antivenin after he was treated for a bite to the finger from a puff adder. Fortunately, all he lost was his index finger.

Because allergic reactions can be a problem, it is vital that antivenin is only administered in hospital where adverse reactions can be treated with adrenalin and other drugs. Much current research is going into reducing the impurities in the antivenin that cause many allergic reactions. Some antivenins are now being made from sheep rather than horse serum because sheep serum seems to provoke fewer

The most dangerous part of producing antivenin is getting the venom

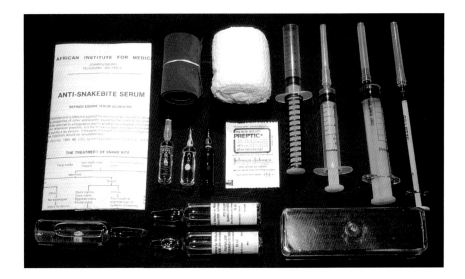

allergies. Research is even being pursued into vaccinating against snake bite, a promising solution in parts of the world where one species of snake bites many people. Perhaps one day a range of safe and easily dispensed vaccines will make the worry of venomous snakes a thing of the past.

A complete anti-snake bite kit for southern Africa

One of the most frustrating things, I think, about snake bite treatment is the widely differing recommendations that are expressed concerning first aid in the field. Most cultures have traditional remedies for snakebite, ranging from the bottle of whisky that cowboys thought would cure a rattler bite, to herbal dressings made from plants with purported medicinal properties. None have yet been shown to have any medical value, although if they calm and reassure the patient they may help to slow the spread of the venom.

The latest craze in North American snake bite remedies is to give the afflicted part of the body a high voltage electric shock. A number of specially modified stun guns have been devised to treat bites from scorpions, insects or snakes. The advocates of this treatment claim amazing success at curing snakebite, but scientists have yet to find any evidence that it does any good. On the contrary it seems to be more dangerous than not treating the bite at all. In one case a 28 year old man, somewhat the worse for alcohol, was bitten on the upper lip by his pet rattlesnake, while trying to kiss it. Because he had, in the past, reacted badly to antivenin, he had worked out an emergency plan of action with his neighbour, based on reading outdoor magazines. He lay down in front of his pick-up whilst the neighbour wired his upper lip to the spark plug with a couple of crocodile clips, started the engine and revved it for five minutes. Not surprisingly the man lost consciousness. He recovered in hospital, but the effects of the electric shock were more serious than the snake bite, and he had to undergo plastic surgery to rebuild his badly burnt lip. There is no firm evidence that electric shock treatment works and the verdict from most scientists is that it should be avoided.

So what should you do if bitten by a snake? There are many differing recommendations, but the following views seem to be generally accepted today. The emphasis should be on early and effective medical treatment, rather than first aid. Firstly, try to identify the snake; however, it is important that you do not endanger yourself by trying to capture the snake if you are not an expert. If a limb is bitten, it should be immobilised as quickly as possible with a splint or sling to discourage the muscular contractions which promote the absorption of venom through the lymphatic channels. Get the patient to hospital quickly, lying on their side to avoid the possibility of asphyxiation from vomiting.

It is important not to apply tourniquets as they intensify the local effects of the venom and can promote gangrene. Surprisingly, the area of the bite should not be washed as the traces of venom on the skin will help the doctors to determine which snake was responsible for the bite and hence which antivenin to use. Being outside the body this venom will do the patient no harm.

A puff adder

The age old treatment of slash and suck has often caused more trauma to the victims than the bite itself. Some venoms stop the clotting of blood and slashing open the wound may actually lead to the victim bleeding to death. In addition, the person sucking could well be poisoned if there are any cuts or ulcers in the mouth.

Hundreds of thousands of people are bitten by venomous snakes every year, but only a small percentage of these people die. If the figures are examined more closely, it becomes clear that only a handful of snakes are responsible for most of the world's snakebite deaths. So which are the most deadly snakes, and what makes them so dangerous?

The species most dangerous to man are those that have learned to live in the environmental conditions that man has created. In Central and South America the lanceheads are one such group of snakes. They are sometimes incorrectly called fer-de-lances: the true fer-de-lance, *Bothrops lanceolatus*, is confined to the island of Martinique in the Caribbean. Lanceheads are large pit vipers, which like areas cleared of forest and turn up wherever man is. Plantations, overgrown fields and gardens all offer the lancehead a perfect home, with a ready food supply of the rats and mice that also thrive alongside humans. Lanceheads have been described as a weed species – they specialise in rapid colonisation of disturbed forest. They achieve this by giving birth to vast numbers of live young: sometimes as many as seventy, all capable of delivering a dangerous bite. The young snakes have a high survival rate, partly because they prey on lizards and frogs and so do not compete with their parents for food. A new plantation can rapidly become infested with lanceheads. They are the most dangerous snakes in the region, accounting for more than half of the thousands of cases of snakebite and most of the fatalities. With an aggressive disposition and a highly toxic venom a large adult lancehead is the most fearsome snake in the New World.

In the Old World it is the cobras which are most feared. Quick to react to a human presence, they hiss and dart out a forked tongue and give the impression of coiled menace. They rear up and spread their ribs to form a hood when roused, and in doing so attract our attention like no other snake. But there can be little doubt that the main reason for their notoriety lies in the two tiny fangs at the front of their mouths, only a few millimeters long, but connected to a supply of poison sufficient to kill an adult person many times their own weight.

Cobras are feared, but they are also respected. They have long been worshiped by Hindus, and in India cobras are now protected by law, because they help to control the rodent populations in rice paddies and farming areas. It has been suggested that cobras indirectly save the lives of more people than they kill with their venom, by controlling the rodents which, if unchecked, would destroy even more crops, bringing starvation and malnutrition to thousands of people. Yet despite this benefit, they still take a heavy toll on rural populations.

There are as many species of cobra across Africa, the Middle East, and Asia, as far Taiwan and the Philippines. One, the forest cobra, lives only in rainforests in Africa, but most species are found in more open areas. The best known of all cobras, and perhaps the most familiar of all venomous snakes, is the Asian cobra, of which there are several races. One of these is the infamous spectacled or Indian cobra, so often used by snake charmers.

Many of the thousands of people who die from snake bites in India every year are bitten by cobras. In India, as in much of the third world, there is great pressure on the land in agricultural areas and many people work every day in the fields without shoes. This brings them into contact with snakes in the most vulnerable of situations. They may be hours or even days away from medical help and even the medical centres in remote areas do not always stock antivenin which loses its effectiveness very quickly. Deep freezing can be a help, but since snake venom varies a lot between regions, it is difficult to maintain a variety of stocks appropriate to the many different regions

Despite their fearsome reputation, monocled cobras are one of the few snakes that look after their eggs

Cobras grow to 2 meters (6.4 ft) long and live in a wide range of habitats from tropical forest to montane grassland, 4,000 meters up in the Himalayas. They are especially dangerous if disturbed in their burrows during the breeding period. Most snakes are not good parents. Once the female has laid her eggs she has nothing more to do with them. But cobras are among the few snakes that not only stay with their eggs during the incubation period, but defend them against intruders. For 60 days the female, and occasionally the male, lies on top of the 15 to 20 leathery white eggs, seldom moving and rarely taking food. If an intruder comes near, the female will rush forward with open hood, hissing and threatening to strike. Should this strategy fail, she will turn her head to show the bold pattern on her hood. Then she will strike.

Unlike the charismatic cobra, you may be forgiven for not recognising the world's most dangerous snake. It is not infamous like the rattlesnake of America, the black mamba of Africa, or the taipan of Australia. It is small and secretive yet widespread and abundant from Africa to India. It is the saw-scaled viper.

Less than 40 cm long and finger-thin the saw scaled viper normally feeds on small rodents, lizards, centipedes and scorpions. The bite is painful but not obviously life-threatening and many deaths result from the victims not realising the danger. The puncture wounds do not always swell or develop blisters. Often the initial pain will subside whilst the internal effects of the injected poison may take up to twelve days to develop. The poison breaks down the walls of blood vessels and the most common causes of death are internal bleeding into the abdomen or the cranium.

Saw scaled viper

The saw-scaled viper was described in 1974 as 'the most dangerous snake in the world to man' and recent research has confirmed this opinion. Surprisingly this snake has by no means the most deadly venom. It is fortunate for people that the saw-scaled viper is small, for the larger the snake the more venom it has to inject into a victim. What makes this snake particularly dangerous is a combination of factors. It has an enormous range in which it is often found in high numbers. The snake has actually benefited from man's activity for, by clearing the land and creating new areas of sandy, dry habitat we have unwittingly provided this snake with new homes. Being small and well camouflaged the snake lies partially hidden in dry soil, invisible to approaching people. Sometimes the snake senses the approaching person, and rubs its rough saw-like scales together to make loud warning hiss, but often it is too late to to take avoiding action. The saw-scaled viper is also one of the most irritable of snakes likely to strike repeatedly if trodden on. Little wonder then that it kills an uncounted number of bare-footed farmers, hunters, herdsmen and villagers every year around the world.

Snakes, both large and small, venomous or harmless, have always held an obsessive fascination for people. Throughout history they have been revered and reviled. In the West many of our attitudes towards snakes have been learned through teachings from the Bible, in which the snake represents evil. In ancient Egypt and Babylon they were revered as Gods, and fertility festivals sprang up in many countries with snakes as part of the sacred ritual. In Asia, snakes are often held in high esteem and in India the cobra – Nag – the second greatest killer of humans, is widely revered. Here women pray to Shesha-nag when they want to conceive male children, local shamans consult Nag Kanni, a serpent goddess, about important village and tribal matters, and in the annual festival of Nagam Panchami, dances and elaborate ceremonials are held in honour of the hooded snake that carries death in its fangs. Here too the ancient craft of snake charming provides a living for the man who can sit unperturbed within striking distance of a those fearsome fangs.

Our relationship with cold blooded creatures is a complex one rooted in our genes and steeped in mystery and legend. As the world crowds into ever larger cities and we become further and further removed from the realities of the wild, it is indeed a pity that our prejudices and misconceptions about such fascinating creatures should be so pervasive. For those people who live a rural life, especially in the third world, snakes are a real threat and do cause numerous injuries and deaths. Even in India, however, which has one of the highest incidences of snake bite in the world, the snake is protected nationwide. Here the snake is seen as a dangerous but essential aid in man's war against the pests that devastate his crops.

In the west we have little to fear from snakes. Most of us will never see one in the wild. We may, indeed, still find it difficult to distinguish one snake from another, a venomous one from a harmless one. But the chances of being bitten by one are remote, and, if you are bitten you are more likely to die of shock than anything else. Surely it is high time we came to view snakes and other cold-blooded creatures with the appreciation they deserve, as fascinating and unique animals?

Squirm

Being a wildlife cameraman sometimes brings me into close contact with potentially dangerous animals. I am frequently asked, "Isn't it risky to get so close to animals?" Often, however, the 'close up' images that one sees in wildlife programmes are taken using long lenses, allowing the cameraman to remain at a respectable and safe distance from his subject.

Few animals frighten me. Why should they? They are never intentionally out to harm me, and on trips into the wilds I feel much more wary of people, knowing there may be someone out there with bad intentions. I love snakes, and am in awe of sharks. But when it comes to spiders my logic and restraint breaks down completely. I can truthfully say that however hard I try, I am petrified of them – not cute small jumping spiders, or frail daddy long legs, but large hairy ones, and any spider webs. It is a phobia which I think harks back to my childhood days, when I stumbled into a huge web whilst running to a swimming pool. I can still vividly remember trying to claw the web from my hair and face, whilst at the same time desperately looking for the spider! Today I can cope with a spider at a distance, but find it impossible to pick one up. No matter how much I try to rationalise this, I still feel afraid. Of all the animals that I am likely to come across whilst filming in remote locations, I know that the creatures most likely to make my life a misery are spiders and those other animals we call creepy crawlies.

Creepy-crawlies are everywhere. Throughout the world there are more than a million known species of insect, living from the tops of mountains to the edges of the oceans. Who knows how many more species are as yet unknown to science. There are so many insects I am told they apparently outweigh the human population of Earth! In terms of survival we are not the dominant species on earth – the long-legged, crunchy bodied, scuttley invertebrates beat us hands down. This is perhaps unfortunate for many people, because the creepy-crawly world is the stuff of nightmares. Their weird morphology, unpredictable movements, and seemingly disgusting habits revolt, and instil fear in many of us. From leeches to water beetles, from bees to scorpions, almost all creepy-crawlies are subjected to pesticides, sprays, electrical bug zappers and rolled up newspapers.

Perhaps the most feared, hated and misunderstood of all is the spider. The bigger, more hairy the spider, the more likely it is to provoke uncontrollable panic among seemingly sane and rational people. In 1967, Geraldine Howard had just such an encounter with a large spider, the huntsman.

I arrived in Australia from England, and like all English people I was

Some people do not fear spiders

The huntsman spider is a large, ferocious looking creepy-crawly. It has caused many accidents in Australia, not by actually biting people, but by simply scaring them

terrified by anything that crawled. One morning I dropped my husband at
work and headed home. I stopped at a red light when suddenly a
huntsman walked across the inside of my windscreen. I screamed and
jumped out and ran onto the pavement. I was standing outside a large
hotel when I realised what I was wearing, a see-through shortie nightie
with nothing underneath. The lights turned green and my car was holding
up the traffic. A man drove it through the lights and parked it. I then had
to run over four lanes of traffic in my nightie to get to my car, which was
by then surrounded by men. I wouldn't get into the car until they had
found the spider which took about 15 minutes during which time I tried
to hide whatever I could, which was difficult with only my hands to use.

To be trapped alone in a small car with a huge black hairy spider is one of the
worst imaginable nightmares for many people. Geraldine Howard's fear was so
great that she could not get back into the car, even though she was in an
excruciatingly embarrassing position. But she was fortunate. Every year many
people have disastrous encounters with huntsmen in cars, as I found out when we
put an advert in a number of Australian newspapers asking for real life huntsman
stories. The response was overwhelming. Many of the stories describe people
panicking and swerving all over the road. People have driven into telephone
boxes, jumped out of their car while it was still moving, driven off the road or
overturned their cars simply because they were trapped inside with this spider.
Some people remember being bitten, but they suffered no ill effects from the bite
itself. Every year a number of people are killed in car accidents, attributed to the
huntsman scares.

I know that I would have reacted in a similar way to Geraldine Howard. But
is it not astonishing that we would rather dodge through high speed traffic than sit
quietly, close to a gently ambling spider? When you compare the damage that half
a ton of motor car can do to you, with a couple of ounces of spider, it isn't logical.
After all the spider problem could be sorted out with a tap from a bedroom
slipper.

As big as your hand, the huntsman certainly looks alarming with its long hairy
legs and eight black beady eyes staring straight at you. So was the lady in the
nightdress right to be terrified? Could that spider, large and hairy as it was, really
hurt her? The answer is a definite no! It may look intimidating – it has huge fangs
and, like many primitive spiders, rears up on its hind legs when threatened. But it
is not at all dangerous to humans. It is a sit-and-wait predator that naturally lives
on trees or in cracks in rocks and ambushes insects that wander past. The
huntsman is sometimes known as the giant crab spider because of its habit of
running quickly sideways. It is flattened in appearance, so that it can easily
squeeze into small spaces for protection, and this often leads it to take refuge
inside cars where sun visors, air vents and numerous other nooks and crannies
seem to be tailor made for it.

My first encounter with the huntsman was on Koolan Island, off the northern
coast of Western Australia. I was staying with some friends while on a filming trip,
and every night two huntsmen would come out onto the kitchen walls to look for
prey. My hosts loved them and tried, in vain, to show me how docile and quite
harmless the spiders were, playfully tapping the spiders legs with their fingers to
try to illicit an attack. They were never bitten. But I refused to go anywhere near

the beasts and always waited for someone else to turn on the light in the kitchen – just in case the spider was sitting on the light switch!

The huntsman's fangs are certainly large enough for it to bite you, but this spider's venom is weak and the bite would be the equivalent of tiny pin pricks. You can get far more painful injuries from handling a kitten. The huntsman is a nocturnal hunter and when it does come into our homes it spends its time quietly getting rid of pests like flies and moths, until an ungrateful and uninformed householder in a panic attacks it with a rolled-up newspaper.

Many of us do shy away from spiders. Of all the tiny creatures that make us squirm by merely crossing our paths, our minds, or our dreams, spiders are the most creepy. Long before the days of Miss Muffet, who sat on a tuffet, they have frightened people away. Miss Patience Muffet, by the way, lived in the late 16th century, She had a father who was a keen spider collector and used to give her the odd one to eat if she fell ill, so its hardly surprising she was not too keen on them. But it seems from the researchers of modern psychology that a fear of spiders may well be something we are born with. It does not depend on our having any experience of them, much less on ever having been hurt by one. It is as if we were pre-wired to be alarmed; that we have evolved an instinctive wariness of spiders that is triggered by their movement and shape. If we have a bad experience with one, or we see our parents or peers reacting strongly against spiders, then the inbuilt wariness can become exaggerated into fear, or even phobia. Other researchers think that our fear of spiders is a disgust response that we learn from our parents, which has been 'handed down' through the generations, since the tenth century, when Europe was first wracked by epidemics. The theory is that since they had no explanation for the outbreaks of disease sweeping the continent, our ancestors blamed spiders, and thus they, and hence we, came to fear them.

Below Miss Patience Muffet was given spiders to eat when she was feeling ill
Right Spectacular *Nephila* spiders produce huge webs

But it is not just spiders themselves that are the subject of nightmares – spiders' webs are horrific to many people. All spiders can produce silk, but only a few spin the large orb webs which are such a familiar sight, strung across plants in gardens. Interestingly, although many of us fear being entangled in spiders webs, few of the spiders that spin the large webs are actually dangerous. Web spinning is a time consuming and energy sapping chore, and many spiders will only make a new one when it is absolutely necessary. Many of the large orb webs have a zig-zag pattern added to the centre of the web. For many years it was assumed that this highly visible feature helped to prevent birds from accidentally flying into and badly damaging the web. But recent research has found that whilst most of the web does not reflect ultra violet light, the central zigzag pattern does. Like flowers which reflect ultra violet to attract insects, it now seems likely that the spiders use the zigzag pattern to attract insects to the web, by mimicking the flower.

The largest webs in the world are made by a group of tropical orb weavers known as Nephila. The female Nephila spins a web which is truly remarkable. The guy lines, which are so strong you can almost twang them like a guitar string, sometimes run from the tops of trees, 30 feet high, right down to the ground. The web itself can have a circumference of almost 20 feet, and the silk is strong enough to catch a bird. Throughout the South Pacific, cobwebs, and in particular those of the Nephila spider are used to make lures, traps and nets for fish. In the

Solomon islands the men collect spider web, winding it around sticks to make large sticky balls. The islanders then paddle out to sea and suspend the sticky ball of silk just above the water surface, hoping to lure fish to it. Needle fish attracted to the lure lunge out of the water and become entangled in the spider silk. Even large barracuda can apparently be caught by this fishing technique.

Nephila are intimidating spiders – or at least the females are, for their large cigar shaped bodies are often gaudily coloured and their legs can span a saucer. The males, however, are tiny, and could easily be mistaken for a completely different species, living apparently parasitically in the periphery of the female's web. At times the Acacia woodlands of the Serengeti are draped in Nephila webs, and I found it most unpleasant driving through them in an Land Rover whose doors were removed for filming. Many a time, huge spiders came swinging in through the open door like trapeze artists to dangle right in front of my face. Luckily, Nephila are harmless to humans and the large females rarely give bites more painful than a scratch.

I have been surprised by many things during the making of this series. Many long held beliefs I had about reputedly dangerous animals have been shown to be based on misunderstood folk tales and myths. Before, I was convinced that the larger, more hairy the spider, the more dangerous it was – hence my dislike of Nephila and huntsmen – but as I discovered, I couldn't have been more wrong. The biggest and hairiest spiders in the world – the spiders commonly referred to as 'Tarantulas' – are far from being the most dangerous. These spiders are more correctly known as 'bird eating' or Theraphosid spiders. The 'bird eating' label was given to them by an arachnologist in South America who claimed that she had seen one up a tree eating a bird. Though they are big enough to kill small birds, nobody has actually seen one do so. Bird eating spiders come from the coastal rain-forests of north eastern South America and Africa. Until recently *Theraphosa leblondi* in South America held the record. But now another has been found in the forests that may prove to be even bigger. It has been called *Pseudo theraphosa*, the false Theraphosid.

The goliath bird eating spiders weigh in at almost a quarter of a pound, with a body four inches long and legs which would span a dinner plate, making it in total about ten inches across. When threatened, it rears up like the huntsman, but these massive spiders only bite in defence, as a last resort. If it feels threatened, the first thing it does is to brush a rear leg rapidly down its abdomen, releasing a

Left The bird eating spiders are found throughout South America, where they prey on small animals. No one has yet seen them eating birds. *Below* They add to their menacing size by rearing up on their hind legs when disturbed.

cloud of fine hairs. Each hair has a sharp penetrating tip and is covered with hundreds of tiny barbs. These work their way into the skin and can trigger an allergic reaction. They can make your hands, nose and throat itch and burn for days. It has been discovered that there are four different types of hair on the New World species, but none on the Old World bird eaters. The effects of the hairs are quite specific and they seem to have been developed against specific aggressors. The bird eating spiders in Arizona, for instance, have hairs that are adapted to inflame the nasal passages of grasshopper mice, which feed on spiders. Although most spiders are hairy, only in the bird eating spiders have the hairs

Top The fearsome jaws of the funnel web spider *Below* The female black widow is more deadlier than the male (which is the smaller of the two)

been modified for defence.

Like huntsmen, bird eating spiders are primitive spiders, with an old design that has been around for nearly 400 million years. Their huge one inch fangs point downwards, and so to get an effective bite they have to rear up and lunge downwards with great force. But despite the widespread fear of bird eaters they are not the most venomous of spiders by a long way. The South American species have very small venom glands and their bite is said to be no more painful than an injection. The reputation of the bird eaters has been built on their huge size and threatening appearance, which goes to show that, with spiders at least, looks are not everything. The size of a spider has nothing to do with how dangerous it is.

The true tarantula is a quite different beast. It too is a 'rear up and strike' spider but that is as far as the similarity goes. For a start it isn't nearly as big, and it lives in Europe, in Italy. The tarantula was blamed for an astonishing outbreak of mass dancing in Italy in the Middle Ages, which lasted for 500 years. Near the town of Taranto, in southern Italy, people began to be bitten by a spider which they called the tarantula. They immediately broke into a violent dance, the tarantella, which was said to flush the venom from their bodies. Nobody is quite sure whether the dance was brought on by the bite or used as a way of getting rid of its effects. People bitten would suffer extreme pain, vomiting, palpitations, muscle spasms and involuntary erections. This practice of dancing went on for centuries and, in the 18th century, a visitor from London recorded that the dances were obscene – possibly because of the erections. His observations only helped make them better known. The dancers, he said, twined themselves with vine leaves, brandished naked swords and red cloths and were suddenly terrified by anything black. The dramatic dance caught peoples' imagination, and spread to southern France, Dalmatia and Spain. Its connection with the bite of the tarantula remained, and so the belief spread that this spider had caused widespread suffering to masses of people.

One sceptic was the writer Oliver Goldsmith, who visited Italy in 1795 and out of scientific interest, magnanimously arranged for one of his servants to be bitten by a tarantula. To his disappointment the fellow suffered no more than intense itching and only slight discolouration at the site of the bite. But throughout Europe the dance continued to be popular, a lively piece in 6/8 time with alternating major and minor sections. Chopin and Liszt, Rossini and Mendelssohn all produced versions. Today the spider's part has been largely forgotten.

To speak of 'venomous spiders' is misleading because all spiders are venomous, with the exception of a couple of insignificant families. The large majority of them are harmless to people because their fangs are too fragile to pierce the skin, or their venom is too innocuous. Although there are spiders the size of dinner plates, many of the 35,000 known species of spider are small, the tiniest, a spider from Western Samoa in the Pacific, being the size of a dot on this page! Spiders do not deserve the exaggerated loathing and fear they inspire, for in all only about 20 to 30 are dangerously venomous to people, and of those there are only about five that regularly come into contact with humans and cause problems.

One of the best known is the infamous Sydney funnel web. It is naturally found in the cool damp vegetation around what is now the beautiful city of Sydney. As the skyscrapers, suburban housing and gardens spread, it simply made the most of the eminently suitable new environment. The suburbs make perfect spider habitat. There were plenty of cool dark places in the foundations of houses, in the rockeries and the compost heaps, for the funnel web to thrive. Here they build their purse-like tubes of silk with surface threads leading down from the entrance to the web-lined burrow. The spider often waits just inside the entrance for a frog, a lizard or an insect to trip the thread, when it rushes out and seizes the prey. In the breeding season the males go on 'walk-about' looking for receptive females, and often enter houses, especially after heavy rains when their burrows are flooded. This is when most bites occur. The spiders are entirely black, the abdomen sometimes being blue-black or purple black, with long slender legs that will span the palm of an adult hand. They can climb well and even run up the matt painted walls of houses.

Another reason why the funnel web is considered so dangerous is that it is not in the least bit afraid of humans. When it is threatened, the 7 mm long fangs often drip with venom, and strike with such force that they can pierce the skulls of smaller prey. When a human is struck, the fangs are often so deeply embedded that the spider has to be torn away. A funnel web has been known to drive its fangs through a fingernail.

In many spiders the female is bigger and more venomous than the male, but the Sydney funnel web is unusual, because both sexes are about the same size, and the venom of the male is far more toxic than that of the female. Only the venom of the male contains a substance called atraxotoxin, which is lethal to monkeys and seriously toxic to man, but not at all harmful to other animals even in large doses. Cats, toads and rabbits have all been injected with this venom without any harmful effect. This cannot be a venom the spider relies on to immobilise prey, otherwise the females, which do not produce it, would be at a disadvantage. And since neither man nor monkey features in the diet of the Sydney funnel web, the production of atraxotoxin by the male is still a puzzle.

Within ten minutes of a bite the venom causes numbness around the tongue and mouth, followed by nausea, sweating, mental confusion and even coma. The last deaths were in January 1979, when a 30 year old woman died, and in January 1980 when the victim was a two year old boy. Fortunately, today there is an effective antivenin available, and few people now die from funnel web bites. If you are bitten by one of these spiders it is recommended that you apply pressure with a bandage over the bitten area – the neurotoxin (nerve poison) is the only one produced by animals which is inactivated by this – and immobilise the bitten limb. It is essential that you get to hospital quickly for treatment with the antivenin.

The presence of the funnel web in the city of the next Olympic games is felt by some to add to the spice of life there. In a recent article on funnel webs, a scientist of the Australian Museum in Sydney wrote "For better and worse, the presence of funnel web spiders lends a certain edge to life in Sydney".

Australia does have the reputation for having more venomous animals than any other continent. Perhaps because they are so dangerous, some spiders have

An Australian redbacked spider

become legendary, the stuff of fables and folk songs. 'The redback under the dunny seat' was one of the terrors of the outback in Australia, to be accepted as one of the hazards of life by the rock-jawed frontiersman and strike terror into the hearts of the whinging poms. The 'dunny' is the outside lavatory; the 'redback' is *Latrodectus hasselti*, the redback spider, which can provide the most agonising experience of a venomous creature likely to be suffered in Australia. It won a place on the pop charts in 1972 when Slim Newton sang:

> There was a redback on the toilet seat
> When I was there last night
> I didn't see him in the dark
> But, boy, I felt his bite!

Redbacks differ from the wandering and funnel web spiders in that they are, evolutionarily speaking, a modern spider, with pincer like jaws that close with a sideways movement rather than the downward pointing fangs of the more ancient species. They also differ because they are timid and unaggressive, and are frightened of humans. When they are disturbed they will often curl up and play dead. They are usually only dangerous when cornered, or when the female is guarding egg sacs. Redbacks like dry, dark places, and tend to come into contact with people because such areas are often unwittingly provided by humans. They seek out spaces under roof eaves, between rafters, under floorboards – or lavatory seats. The male is small and short-lived – he is usually eaten by the female during copulation – and the survivors are too feeble to deliver a bite. But the female, easily recognisable with a red stripe down her dark brown or black body, killed at least a dozen Australians in the first half of this century. Today bites are much less common: as Australia is transformed from frontier continent to westernised suburbia, the outside 'dunny' has become a thing of the past. However, the redback is still there and every year 300 people are bitten by this spider.

Fortunately an antivenin was introduced in 1956. Since then there has been no need to fear the lethal effects which come from slow-acting neurotoxins, as these can be countered by a dose of antivenin even days after the bite. But the immediate effects can be painful. There is an initial pricking pain at the site of the bite, after which the bitten area reddens, swells and sweats. About five minutes later the really intense pain begins and starts to spread throughout the body. The victims are sometimes driven to a frenzy by it. There can be nausea, vomiting, dizziness and palpitations, followed by muscular spasms and fainting. The main indication of a redback bite is swelling at the site. Anyone bitten should be taken as soon as possible to a medical centre for the antivenin.

A close relative of the Australian redback spider, the button spider, lives in South Africa, where I grew up. Another lives in North America and the Caribbean, where it is known as the black widow. Altogether there are 30 or so species living around the warmer parts of the world. They account for about fifty percent of spider bites. They have a fearsome reputation in California where they are most abundant. There is a 19th century tale of a man bitten by a black widow spider while out hunting. He returned home, gave away his watch, said his farewells to his friends and, having put his affairs in order, waited for death. Possibly the bite of the black widow was so often fatal because everybody believed it to be so. At the turn of the century there were many case histories published of the severe,

A wandering spider from Brazil – probably the world's most dangerous spider

often fatal, effects of bites from the black widow. Often these were men bitten on the penis in outdoor privies. The spiders were attracted by the vibrations on their webs caused by splashing and went to the source. The most common symptom was severe spasms in the muscles of the abdomen and in several cases the victims, being convinced that the bite of the black widow was fatal, died.

Like its name – the black widow was so called in the mistaken belief that she always ate her mate after copulation – the spider's poison has been over dramatised. A splendidly eccentric American arachnologist wanted to find out the truth about it so he arranged to be bitten. At first he had some problems in persuading a black widow to oblige but, he wrote:

> The second test resulted in all I could wish. The spider dug into the third finger of the left hand and held on till I removed her about five or six seconds later. The pain at first was faint but very soon began to increase into a sharp, piercing sensation. In less than one hour the pain had reached the shoulder and within two hours the chest was affected; the diaphragm seemed partially paralysed, breathing and speech became spasmodic.

After nine hours of this the good doctor was hauled off to hospital where he spent three sleepless nights. He returned home weakened and nursing a feeling of wretchedness which stayed with him until he finally recovered a few days later.

Tales and stories apart, hard statistics about spider bites are difficult to come by. We do know that between 1950 and 1959, 63 people in the USA died because of black widow bites, but many more were bitten, as only 1% of untreated bites actually prove to be fatal (compared to up to 25% of untreated rattlesnake bites). Now because of the antivenin, deaths are virtually unknown, but it pays to be aware of this spider and to be cautious around its preferred habitats – log piles, outdoor buildings and piles of debris.

But the black widow is not the only spider to cause problems in the United States. There is another spider in the same family as the black widow, the violin spider, that has only recently spread throughout the continent. It is small and brown and totally innocuous looking, but its bite can cause serious ulceration and tissue decay. Its original range is in the warmer southern states but because people move around a lot and have central heating, the violin spider has travelled far and wide in the United States, in packing cases and trunks of clothes. Because it is too cold to live outside, the spiders nestle down in airing cupboards and warm nooks and crannies of houses and are therefore very often found by cleaning ladies! Although it has only killed six people this century, many hundreds get bitten each year. Like the black widow, it is only the female that is dangerous, as the male is too small.

We had to go South America to find the spider that wreaks the most havoc. Ten years ago I was filming in the cerrado of central Brazil and was struck by the number of large black spiders that came wandering around the buildings at night. They were highly aggressive animals, that readily ran towards us and attacked when we tried manoeuvring them with a stick into a better position for filming. At the time I presumed that they were coming to the buildings in search of insects attracted by the lights at night, and I thought nothing more about them. Little did I realise that this was the wandering spider – the worlds most dangerous spider!

As a measure of exactly how dangerous it is, one hospital alone in Sao Paulo treated 1136 spider bites in 1983 – most of them were from the Brazilian wandering spider. A researcher in Britain once kept this spider to study. He only had to open his laboratory door in the morning and the spider would hurl itself against the side of its container, its fangs banging against the glass. The wandering spider is not the most venomous, nor the largest spider, but because they are common in urban areas they encounter people frequently. They do not construct webs, but instead lie in wait for their prey among building rubble, under furniture in houses and even in shoes. There is another, more unsettling reason for their deadly reputation: like funnel webs, but with even more ferocity, they willingly attack humans. Most spiders, if disturbed, will run away or play dead. The wandering spider goes on the offensive. Try to fend it off with a broom and it will run up the handle and bite your hand.

It is one of the curious twists of nature that spider venom is toxic to humans at all. Venom contains such a cocktail of poisons that it just so happens that some damage us and some don't. Spider venom can be either damaging to the nervous system or to the skin tissues – or both. The nerve toxins block the transmission of nerve impulses to the muscles, causing twitching, sweating, salivation and vomiting, which sometimes leads to death through either respiratory failure or cardiac arrest, or a combination of the two. The tissue damage can be local to the bite or very extensive, disfiguring and painful. The venom properties of most spiders have never been investigated, though antivenins have been produced for the deadliest.

The way humans react to certain animals is largely a result of their cultural upbringing. The same animal can therefore have a completely different image in

different parts of the world. Spiders are greatly feared in the western world, even though there are few dangerous species in Europe or North America. However, in parts of West Africa, spiders are far from feared, and are used as a way of divining the future and seeking answers in important matters. This process of divining or 'ngam' is used throughout southern Cameroon, and is a daily event in the lives of the Mambila people who live on either side of the Cameroon-Nigerian border. The Mambila believe that the spider speaks to them through the process of divination.

The Mambila catch large hairy burrowing spiders, *Hysterocrates robustus*. The spiders are poisonous, and the Mambila believe that if they are bitten they could die. The spiders are kept separately in open bottomed ceramic jars close to the village, and live in burrows in the ground beneath the jars. To find the answer to a question the Mambila diviner places a stick and a stone and a set of special cards inside the jar. The cards are made from the leaves of certain trees and palms and have special marks or ideograms cut into them. The ideograms represent different objects and are often paired to depict their good and bad aspects. The jars are then covered over to simulate night and gently tapped. Under cover of darkness the nocturnal spiders emerge from their burrows and forage around on the ground inside the jars searching for the prey that might have made the vibrations caused by the tapping. In the process they move the leaf cards around the arena before eventually retiring into their burrows. In the morning the diviner uncovers the jars and interprets the position of the cards in relation to the stick and the stone, to get the answers to the question asked. If the spider pulls a leaf card back down into its burrow this is interpreted as a very bad sign and a portent of death. Spider divining is purely a male prerogative and its secret techniques help men maintain their authority over women in the Mambila society.

The Mambila people have incorporated the spiders into their lives and beliefs. It is just one response to the problem faced by many people all over the world, the problem of having to live alongside some of the most dangerous animals on Earth.

Left The brown recluse spider
Right A 'Mambila' crab sorcerer examining what a spider says the future holds for him

People now live in all but the most inhospitable areas of the globe. As we have extended human habitats into those of wild creatures, they have moved in with us. We have built theme parks full of shady hidey holes, water and food. In some areas insects, spiders and even scorpions are booming as never before. In Tunisia, the fat tailed scorpion lived for centuries under rocks or in shallow burrows on the hillsides. When the hills were covered with houses the scorpion found shelter with shady places to hide during the day and lots of food at night from the insects that also congregate in our homes. In the summer during the mating season males wander into the kitchens or outbuildings at night looking for females, and rest from the search as day breaks, in shoes, clothing or under cupboards. They are specially fond of wet places because humidity attracts insects, and so will crawl into taps, shower heads, baths and toilet bowls. Many congregate around outdoor water troughs and wells. They are a particular problem in the summer months, when people wander about in the evening without shoes or sleep outside. It is not so much the toxicity of its venom, which is said to be comparable to that of a cobra, that makes this scorpion so dangerous, but its fat tail. The tail of this scorpion is very strong and the point can easily pierce clothes and even shoes. The scorpion also often strikes a number of times, injecting large quantities of venom into its victim. In the wet and humid oases of the otherwise dry semi-deserts, both man and scorpion encounter one another regularly. It is not surprising therefore that there is a very high incidence of scorpion stings throughout north Africa.

To combat the problem, every summer the government launches a bounty scheme which is organised by the Pasteur Institute and pays local people, including school children, for any scorpions they collect. Tens of thousands are brought in each year, and their venom is used to produce antivenin. The first effects on the scorpion population are now being seen, in that the adult scorpions captured are getting smaller – in other words, younger specimens are being collected. But, in spite of that, the fat tailed scorpion in Tunisia is extending its range. Once it was restricted to the southern parts of Tunisia. Today it has been recorded living as far north as the outskirts of Tunis itself.

Scorpions came out of the sea about 440 million years ago, and still look as though they belong there. There are about 600 species of them, and they all look very much the same. They are predators. They eat any insects, spiders, centipedes and crustaceans they can find on the ground. They catch their prey with their pincers, then rip open the bodies with their mouth parts and pump saliva into the wound. The enzymes in the saliva digest the soft parts, reducing it to a nutritive mush which the scorpion sucks up, discarding the outside in small clumps. Only if a scorpion seizes an animal difficult to hold will it use its sting, carefully manoeuvring it into a soft spot, for example a joint, before injecting the lethal venom.

The curved sting is fed by two sacs of venom housed in the end of the tail. The venom is a complex substance containing different poisons which are effective against different prey species. The venom of some scorpions is particularly toxic to insects, others to crustaceans and yet others to mammals. This may be an evolutionary adaptation to environmental pressures but it could also be an accident of chemical composition. Why, for instance, should a scorpion have developed a toxin particularly effective against mammals which are neither a part of its diet nor its predators?

Although the venoms of different scorpions are so chemically varied, there is

a remarkable consistency in the way people react when stung. At first the sting produces a burning pain. After a time this is replaced by a tingling sensation. It is a time when the victim may feel secure in the belief that the effects are wearing off. But, in the case of the fat tailed scorpion, the worst is yet to come. The stricken person becomes agitated and begins to sweat. The pulse becomes fast and irregular. The victim may sneeze spasmodically and their breathing is fast and shallow. Frequently respiratory paralysis follows, and then death. The Algerian Health authorities published figures on the lethality of scorpion stings between 1942 and 1958 which showed that of over twenty thousand people stung almost four hundred died.

A fat tailed scorpion in a typical aggressive pose

But again, as with spiders, looks can be deceptive. Just because an animal has pincers, a long tail and crawls around on the ground does not mean to say it is a dangerous scorpion. There is a common animal that lives in many areas of the southern United States that closely resembles the scorpion and causes alarm when spotted. It is formidable in appearance, with a long tail, similar but thinner than the scorpion's. It is the whip-tailed scorpion. Unlike true scorpions it has no sting to its tail. Its only defence is to squirt a fluid from its abdomen that contains vinegar. Being squirted with vinegar is not exactly nightmarish to us, but for the predators of whipscorpions, like lizards and skunks, it is very unpleasant, and enough to drive them away. Because of its habit of dispensing vinegar, the whip-tailed scorpion is known in the southern states of America as the 'vinegaroon'.

The world of invertebrates is enormously varied. Of all animals they portray the most diverse array of weird features, body types and textures, nearly all of

The tailless whip scorpion (*above*)
does not possess the sting of a true
scorpion (*right*), but can squirt any
assailant with vinegar

them totally unlike anything we can identify with. It seems that it is the look of them that is as offputting as any perceived threat. The actual threat they represent appears to have almost nothing to do with our revulsion, and this is borne out by research done on the psychological basis of our attitude to the invertebrate world.

A particularly good illustration of this happened when I was filming lions in the Serengeti. My colleague Samantha Purdy and I were looking for a place to film a beautiful vista of the plains, and had climbed up a kopje, a rocky outcrop. About half way up we stopped and looked around. Unfortunately, we were not yet high enough, but I did notice an area of flattened grass which had probably been the recent resting spot of a lion. However, we decided to climb a little higher. I had hardly taken a step when a deep and very threatening growl emanated from the bushes a few meters away. Our reactions were instantaneous. We both turned to flee. Samantha, who was about five meters behind me turned and ran headlong into a huge spiders web. "Where's the spider? Get it off me!", she screamed. She had completely forgotten about the angry big cat so close behind her. In the meantime I had spiked my leg on a razor sharp sisal plant and blood spurted everywhere. It probably helped to bring me to my senses. Trying not to hurry, we clambered off the hill and back to the car. From its safety we saw the now unconcerned face of a pregnant lioness looking out over the plains. She had probably been scouting the area for a safe den for her cubs. With hindsight we laughed – how could Samantha have been frightened of an innocuous spider under such circumstances? Our reactions had been instinctive and completely uncontrollable, even though we both knew that by running we could easily have brought the lioness charging after us.

It appears that the long legs and sudden movements of spiders are triggers that we instinctively react against. But recent research suggests that there are two distinctive reactions to creepy-crawlies. The fear reaction which we get from creatures like spiders and scorpions, and a disgust reaction which we have towards slimy animals.

One of the many unsolved mysteries of human beings is why we feel disgusted by certain creatures that can do us no harm. When they reach three years old, children start to react instinctively against slugs, snails, leeches, and spiders without, it seems, having been taught to do so. When we react instinctively against something it is usually something dangerous – like fire or heights. This can be explained as an inbuilt fear – a sort of pre-wired circuit with which we are born to help keep us alive. But primitive man, who may well have fallen from cliffs or burned himself in fires, was never hunted down by packs of ravenous slugs. So why do we humans feel so disgusted by these animals?

It seems to be related to a general capacity for disgust which we may pick up at a very early age through the facial expressions and reactions of our parents to objects we should not put in our mouths. These could be foul-smelling or tasting – or it could be that they are associated with disease. Recent research has suggested that creatures which look like mucus or faeces have this 'squirm factor'. Lizards, slugs and worms are all squirmish creatures, as are those we associate with the spread of disease like rats or cockroaches.

Slugs fill many people with disgust. To protect themselves against drying out they exude a coat of mucus which leaves a slimy trail across our lawns or carpets. Slugs have few real friends although biologists, who are predisposed to be enthusiastic about all living things, have found them charming. One has recently tried to pick up a following for them by issuing the following vignettes under the heading:

Slugettes
- In poor country districts, families that could not afford to buy meat or fish used to get all the protein they needed from eating slugs.
- The great grey slug has more than 28,000 teeth.
- During courtship, the penis of a 15 cm long ash black slug was measured at more than 80 cm.

Leeches too have few friends. There aren't many scenes in the cinema more stomach-turning than the one in *The African Queen* when Humphrey Bogart, after towing the old tub along the river, climbs out of the water to reveal that his naked back and chest are covered with swollen black slimy leeches, all, it seems, pulsating and bloated with his blood. To many, leeches are underwater vampires. And yet they do very little harm and a great deal of good to us.

There are about 650 known species of leeches in the world, and they can be found in African deserts and in polar seas. They are both terrestrial and aquatic and they live from sea level to 12000 feet above it. They range in length from a quarter of an inch to well over a foot. The largest so far discovered is the giant Amazonian leech which stretches to 18 inches long and is now breeding successfully in Welsh laboratories and contributing to medical research.

Leeches are experts at drawing blood painlessly. They have to do this in order to survive. About half the blood-sucking leeches bite their hosts with muscular jaws lined with tiny teeth, and the other half insert a proboscis like a hypodermic needle but with a skill unmatched by the most sensitive of nurses. When the head first makes contact with the skin, the leech releases salivary fluid which contains a local anaesthetic. It then begins to draw off the blood and when it has had its fill it quietly dislodges itself. It can take on board ten times its own body weight and then go for up to a year without food.

The European medical leech has been used for centuries for drawing off blood, and is still occasionally used to alleviate swollen black eyes or to assist the flow of blood following micro-surgery. It is also a popular source of medicines, including an anticoagulant called hirudin, a local anaesthetic, a blood vessel dilator, an anti-inflammatory agent and an antibiotic. Leeches have helped in the treatment of blood clots, eye disorders, rheumatoid arthritis, heart attacks and strokes. They are a living pharmacopoeia for all the ills that flesh is heir to.

It really is strange how the human mind works. Leeches are repulsive to us, yet we tolerate caterpillars, even though they too have a worm-like shape and are often hairy. It came as a surprise to me to find a caterpillar that was really deadly. It is the caterpillar of the saturnid moth, *Lonomia achelous*. A forty-six year old man who crushed one of them with his bare knee in South America had to be admitted to hospital eight days later with

Below Some people are terrified of slugs, but this species only eats algae

Opposite top A feeding leech uses anticoagulant to stop the blood from clotting before it has finished its meal
Opposite bottom A leech's mouth is perfectly designed for biting people

severe headaches, fever, and dark urine thick with blood. He was, otherwise, strong and healthy. Soon, however, he became mentally confused and lost the power of speech. He was given blood transfusions but his condition deteriorated and sixteen days after contact with the caterpillar he lost consciousness. The doctors tried everything to save him – antibiotics, steroids, diuretics and general supportive measures – but four days later he died of a massive cerebral haemorrhage.

This caterpillar occurs throughout South America, and carries powerful, as yet unknown enzymes in its blood and saliva which cause bleeding on the briefest contact. Unfortunately for humans we are most likely to come across the caterpillar when it is at its most dangerous. The caterpillars hatch out from eggs at the top of the trees in dry, savannah forest found in patches throughout South America. The caterpillars form aggregations of up to a hundred individuals and stay together; they 'dance' around in circles, and then the dominant one of the group leads the others in a long troupe away from the area.

As the caterpillars get older they move progressively down the tree, getting bigger and more toxic as they do so. They will eventually leave the bark to bury themselves in the leaf litter and

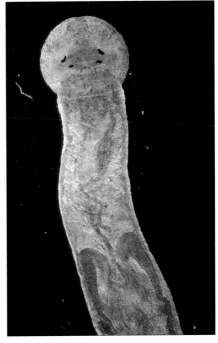

pupate. It is when they are close to the ground and highly venomous that humans come into contact with them most easily. People have been envenomated by leaning against the bark of trees or kneeling down on the leaf litter. In one case a soldier nearly died when he was training in the forest and threw himself on the ground. It is an extreme form of a fairly common defence which caterpillars have developed against predators and in particular birds. Some caterpillars have a poison in their bodies which, if eaten, causes illness in predators, so the animal is more likely to avoid those caterpillars in future. Others have 'urticating', or toxic, hairs which irritate any animal coming into contact with them. Normally their effect is immediate. Why the poison of *Lonomia achelous* takes so long to act is a mystery. If it was designed to put off predators it is a very bad design, because by the time the effects start to show on the unfortunate victim, it very likely would have forgotten what it ate a week ago. However this anomaly may well be to our advantage. Because the poison is so slow acting it suggests that the body doesn't recognise it as a foreign body. These potentially deadly poisons may well prove to be just what is needed in the treatment of blood clots of people suffering from thrombosis.

Many caterpillars use poisons to protect themselves, and some species go to great lengths to make sure they have sufficient quantities of it. The moth *Utetheisa ornatrix*, found in the southern states of the USA and South America, stores a toxic alkaloid from its food plant in its eggs, caterpillars and adults. The poison is essential for its survival and the moth's behaviour is centred on getting as much of it as possible. When selecting a mate, the female moth looks for a male with the most toxins. During mating the male gives her a 'nuptial gift' of poison which she uses to protect her eggs. This sex for poison swap ensures that she gets the best possible protection for her eggs. When the eggs hatch the competition for the poison continues. The caterpillars can get it from the leaves in their diet, but ones which have a low supply of poison sometimes turn cannibal and eat the eggs and pupae of others to bolster their toxin levels. The caterpillars then crawl away from the food plants to pupate to reduce the risk of being eaten themselves.

Our interpretation of the signs in nature is, as we have seen, not always correct – what may look like a friendly little woolly caterpillar may well be far less strokeable than a wet slimy leech.

Killer caterpillars are fortunately not a common occurrence, even in the forests of South America. However, there is one group of animals that one encounters all over the world, and which quite frequently make trips into the wild uncomfortable, to say the least. They are the ants.

Ants have evolved the most complex and highly developed form of colonialism in the insect world and many are feared because of their swarming ability. Many also have painful bites or stings, some of which are extremely unpleasant. I've been stung by the giant ponerine ants of South America – the sting itself made me jump and the excruciating pain and ache burned for days. The fire ants of the Americas are also painful. Their nests, which are small soft mounds of earth, are common in many

Left Great grey slugs are completely harmless yet elicit revolt in humans

Below The hairs on this caterpillar can kill you

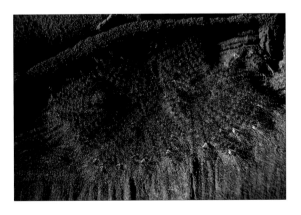

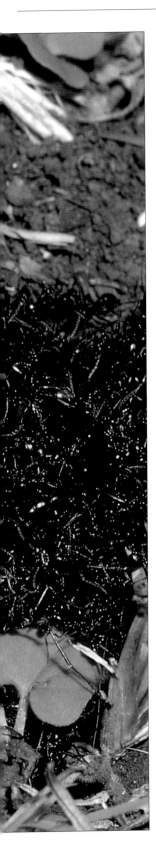

A column of army ants

areas. If you are unlucky enough to accidentally step on a mound it erupts, thousands of tiny red ants swarming all over your legs. Each ant stings enthusiastically. The effect is like being jabbed all over with a hundred needles. In Brazil the ants are known as 'lava pe' which translated literally means "wash your feet" as this is the action you do when trying to brush the blighters from your legs.

Of all the ants the most terrifying are the nomadic species which make no nest but move en masse in their search for prey. In South America they are known as army ants, whilst the ones in Africa are called driver or 'safari ants'. A foraging colony of these ants is one of the most dramatic and awesome sights in the insect world. The ants march in columns, their trails spreading out through the countryside. The columns are protected by blind, massively jawed soldiers which line the sides of the trails. They often stand two or three abreast, their heads straining upwards, and their jaws agape ready to clamp onto any intruder. Beneath this fearsome arsenal march the workers, many carrying larvae in their small jaws. At the head of the columns, other soldiers spread out to scour the area for food. Any animal they come across, living or dead, is attacked, the ants swarming all over it and cutting it into manageable pieces.

I have often come across safari ants on my travels in Africa. Twenty years ago whilst on a university expedition to western Ethiopia we were attacked by a particularly large colony. We were collecting small mammals, butterflies, orchids and other specimens, and had pitched camp in a glade in the forest. One night, in the early hours of the morning, an unearthly scream came from one of the tents, and into my tent rushed Pam our botanist. Apparently she had woken to find her sleeping bag crawling with ants. Her companion, Nigel, a zoologist, woke to find a trail passing right under his neck. No matter how much insect spray we used the ants kept pouring in. Pam, quite understandably, refused to sleep in her tent, but Nigel stoically decided that ants were not going to get the better of him. All night he fought back their advances, building walls of gooey wet talcum powder around his sleeping bag to gum up their bodies. In the morning Nigel emerged exhausted but triumphant. But we soon discovered the ants had made a killing during the night. The previous day local Merle people had brought us two sweet baby mice which we'd put in a canvas bag and hung from the top of the tent. We had, foolishly, thought that there they would be safe. But the ants were not fooled and, snaking a trail up the tent and into the bag they had killed the mice and dismembered them. All that remained in the morning were a few tiny bones picked clean of flesh.

The African driver ants have the largest colonies of any insect, some containing over sixteen million individuals. The driver ants are more fearsome than the army ants because they have sharp cutting edges to their jaws which they use to cut up their prey. They can inflict painful bites, but it is untrue that they represent a serious threat to large animals – only a tethered or injured animal would normally succumb to them. There is a story of a large python being killed by them, presumably because it was too bloated to flee after a meal. On our expedition to Ethiopia we often had problems from ants eating the animals we tried to collect. Throughout the forest we placed small mammal traps – small boxes designed to capture the rodents alive. Every morning we would go on our rounds through the forest to inspect the traps. Sometimes we found the traps completely covered in a writhing ball of ants. The ants were squeezing one by one through the cracks in the container walls and attacking the animal trapped inside. We found some rodents alive, sitting on top of dead and dying ants an inch deep and biting every ant that attacked them. Others were not so lucky – some traps were picked clean by the ants before we arrived to inspect them.

But the ants can bring benefits. There are stories of people who move out of their houses, leaving them for the ants to spring clean. As the ants swarm over the floor they flush out and seize all the scuttling cockroaches that infest the house. Within hours the house is spick and span, the ants leave, and the owners can move back in.

Westerners seem to have a particular hate of cockroaches. Yet the most noxious of them, which lives in Florida, can only spray us with an irritating liquid. The other 3500 species can do no more than burp, wheeze, or hiss. None have the capacity to kill anybody – but scientific research suggests that they may well be able to spread harmful bacteria, which could kill us.

There's much to admire in a cockroach. They've been around for upwards of 320 million years, surviving the dinosaurs and the Ice Ages, which is more than we have so far managed. A cockroach fossil imprint in an Illinois strip mine was dated at 300 million years old and was identical to the living examples still running around the mine works. Cockroaches were so efficient at surviving then they had no need to change. They are resilient and adaptable and can scavenge almost anything, and live almost anywhere. Today's species can live on glue, paper and soap; they can even exist without food for up to three months.

The most unjust accusation hurled at cockroaches is that they are dirty. In reality they spend as much time grooming themselves as cats do. They brush their bodies with spiny legs, combing their antennae and rubbing against solid objects just like ponies rub against trees to scrape dirt from their backs. They have to keep clean to preserve the coat of varnish – a combination of wax and oils – that prevents them from drying out, especially in our centrally heated houses. They do however, inhabit dirty areas of our environment – hospital waste disposal units, garbage dumps, and the nooks and crannies in kitchens where food falls and decays unnoticed.

Because of our hate of them cockroaches are worth millions to the pest exterminators: in America they bring in half a billion dollars a year in a never ending battle to exterminate them. Householders add to the profits of the manufacturers by spending 150 million dollars annually on dusts, sprays and baited traps. Despite our paranoia, and our obsession with dirt and scuttling creatures, cockroaches themselves are harmless – it is the bacteria they carry that we should be afraid of. They are a highly successful group of animals and have taken full advantage of the food and habitats provided by man. They are resilient creatures. You can deep freeze a cockroach and it will survive. But more significantly it can tolerate far higher doses of radiation than we can. One day cockroaches may well inhabit an earth devoid of people.

The largest cockroach is almost 10 cm long, but, as we have seen, size is no indicator of an animals' deadliness. On the east coast of Australia lives a tiny, match-head sized animal that once ranked as a major killer, especially among children. It's the Australian paralysis tick. When the adult female, 3-4 mm long, feeds, she pierces the skin with a barbed tube and draws up the blood. She alternates her periods of feeding with periods of rest and salivation. This is what causes the problem. The secretions of her salivary glands include the usual chemicals to help the flow and digestion of the blood, but they also contain a powerful nerve toxin which causes paralysis. For the first two days feeding, the toxin is only produced in small doses but as the tick's body swells in size so do its salivary glands and their output.

During the first half of this century there were more than 20 known deaths from tick paralysis in New South Wales. One of the last fatal cases in New South Wales was diagnosed as polio and the tick that killed was only discovered at the post mortem; the parasite had been covered by a sticking plaster applied by the doctor. As recently as 1972 a two year old girl was committed to hospital in Brisbane with a paralysis the doctors could not explain. Only when a nurse, sponging her hair, found a suspicious lump was the tick discovered. Today, because of the availability of antitoxins, deaths are now very rare, but non-fatal poisoning is still common, especially among children.

The ticks live in bushland and rain forest along the coastal belt and commonly infest the native wild animals. They also readily infest suburban gardens, especially

An American Cockroach is almost identical to its ancestors that lived 300 million years ago

if they are visited at night by koalas, bandicoots or possums. One or more of the three tick stages (larva, nymph or adult) may be active throughout the year, but need heat and moisture to thrive. Long droughts can so dramatically reduce the population that they may cease to be a problem to humans for years. A wet winter, and a hot wet summer may cause the ticks to suddenly reappear. It is then that they are particularly dangerous because many people have no previous experience of the risks the ticks represent.

For long the paralysis ticks posed a puzzling question. Why, if they are so common, are the native mammals along the east coast not all paralysed or dead? The answer turned out to be fascinating. Some bandicoots, possums, koalas, wallabies and kangaroos in effect may undergo an early vaccination which is tied into the lifecycle of the tick. The adult female tick lays eggs that then hatch into larvae. The larvae are tiny, only one millimetre long, but they too need to feed on blood before they can engorge and moult to nymphs. The tiny young ticks also produce toxin, but in such small amounts that it is relatively harmless to the young animals they infest. But the dose is apparently enough to enable the animal to produce an immunity to the poison. In other words it acts like a vaccination, as long as an immunity develops before exposure to adult forms, which are mainly present in late spring and early autumn. As a result, when the animal is fully grown and has an adult female feeding on it (the adult female is responsible for serious paralysis) it may be naturally immune.

Young children are most at risk from ticks. The effects of a tick bite take three or more days to appear and initially cause a loss of energy and appetite followed by unsteady walking. A day or two later the child may begin to experience muscle weakness in the arms and chest. At this stage, even if the tick is discovered and removed, the paralysis will spread unless an antitoxin is given. Soon the throat and chest muscles are affected and death may follow from respiratory failure, and possible cardiovascular effects.

Even though there is an effective antivenin available today, Australians living along the east coast are advised to watch out for the paralysis tick and to check their children frequently for signs of it. The match head sized ticks favour the scalp, neck, behind the ears, back, and groin. As the tick feeds, it darkens in colour and swells to the size of a pea. If a tick is found it should not be

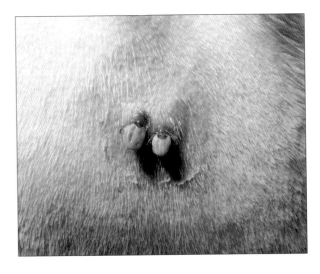

Paralysis ticks attach themselves to a wide variety of animals. In all cases they grow from pin-head sized dots (above; on dog) to engorged ticks almost ten times the size (right; on the back of a human hand)

plucked off with fingers as the act of squeezing it will inject more toxin into the wound, or release toxin already present. Ideally the tick should first be killed by dabbing it with a liquid repellent, head louse cream or scabies cream, containing pyrethrins, pyrethroids or, if these are not available, with kerosene or turpentine carefully applied. The tick will be rapidly paralized, die and fall off within a short time. Strangely enough, the temporary presence of the dead tick is thought to protect the person by preventing or minimising dispersal of toxin from the bite site. The dead tick may be removed after several hours, if it has not fallen off. It is still a mystery as to why the tick injects a toxin at all. It really doesn't make sense for a

parasite to harm its host but as yet no one has come up with a feasible reason.

Often we find that what seems gruesome and nightmarish in nature is harmless and that which looks harmless can be a real threat. The Bot fly does not harm us directly but can cause real damage via its host, the mosquito. Certain bot flys, found throughout South America, lay their eggs on the back of mosquitoes. When the mosquito lands on a human, the increase in heat triggers the hatching of the eggs, which fall into the tiny hole made by the proboscis, and burrow into the skin. A maggot then grows, and eats out a hole in the flesh and it stays there until it is ready to pupate. It will then crawl out of the hole and drop to the floor.

Perhaps this is the worst nightmare of all when it comes to the creepy-crawly world. Animals that invade our bodies, that actually do see us as food or hosts to live on. The bot fly is bad enough, but there is another fly that is far worse. In fact, it causes such problems that it is the subject of a multi-million dollar eradication programme funded by the United States. The screw worm has had a devastating effect on humans and animals all over the world. The maggots of the New World screw wormfly ate their way through more than US$100 million worth of American livestock in the 50s and 60s; the fly was accidentally introduced to Libya in 1988, and in its first year there infested more than 200 people and 2000 domestic animals. By 1990 more than 12,000 animals were killed in one year. The Old World screw worm fly ranges from sub-Saharan Africa to India, South-east Asia, Indonesia, the Philippines to New Guinea – where it is only 110 kilometers away from the vast livestock industry of Australia.

The female fly seeks out wounds and abscesses in humans and other animals in which to lay vast batches of eggs. Within hours the eggs hatch into larvae which burrow their way into the flesh, on which they then feed and mature in less than a week.

The Bot fly larvae (above) will use any animal as a host, including birds such as this palm tanager (right)

If there are no open wounds, then the eggs are laid in body orifices like the ear, nose, and urino-genital passages. The mature maggots are about 15mm long when they leave the host, pupate on the ground, and produce adult screw flies within three days. As the entire life cycle of the screw fly is about three weeks it reproduces swiftly and efficiently. When you add to this the fact that the female can fly up to 200 kilometers in search of suitable animals to attack, you have the threat of a world-wide infestation.

Fortunately scientists have now come up with a solution to the problem. The huge losses to stock in the United States in the 1950s spurred scientists there to look into the possibility of releasing sterile flies to cut down the population. Male flies are exposed to doses of radiation which induce lethal mutations in their sperm, effectively sterilising them: eggs that are fertilised by these sperm fail to hatch. Large numbers of these sterilised males are released into an area in the hope that any females mated by these flies will be unable to reproduce. The first full scale operation was mounted on the island of Curacao in 1954, which was swamped by sterile flies. It worked.

Top The breeding of screw worms is now a very highly organized industry. *Above* The worms are bred in a blood substrate

Within six months all the wild flies had been eradicated. The next step was to move to the mainland and drive the flies southward to the Mexican border. By 1966 the whole of the United States was free of screw worm fly. The effort continued and today the fly has been driven southwards through Mexico and Central America, towards the Darien gap in Panama. The programme of breeding sterile flies has expanded to the point where it employs 1500 people and produces more than 300 million flies every week.

But there have been setbacks. New outbreaks have occurred in Texas where in 1976 the screw worm did damage to livestock to the value of US$300 million before it was again eradicated. There are fears that the sudden release of such massive quantities of irradiated flies may have led to the rapid evolution of a strain of wild flies that will not readily mate with them. So problems remain. To help detect introduced screw worm flies, the quarantine authorities in Miami have trained a German wire haired pointer dog. On the command 'find it' the dog can pick out a screw worm infested animal and on the command 'search' it detects screw worm pupae. There are plans to train other dogs for duties at quarantine stations as an efficient and economical barrier against the screw worm threat.

The scheme is now being adopted around the world and has also proved successful in Libya. More than a billion sterile flies from a factory in Mexico were released there between December 1990 and October 1992 at a cost of $75 million. The screw worm fly there has now been completely eradicated.

Perhaps the largest threat remains in the Pacific, where the flies are within a short flight from Australia. So concerned are the Australians that they have taken the precaution of setting up a unit in New Guinea which can rear as many as 30 million flies a week, should the screw worm find its way across the Torres Straits. All over Australia there are stringent quarantine measures now in operation, but in

1988 nine dead flies were found in a light trap in Darwin. The threat may not come only from cattle ships: in 1984 a 69 year old Indian woman went to a doctor in Kuala Lumpur, Malaysia, with an ulcerated foot. He diagnosed a five to six day old infection from the screw fly. She had arrived on a commercial aircraft from Sri Lanka only two days earlier. People as well as cattle can harbour the parasite and so menace the livestock industry of Australia. The damage can be inflicted without anyone being aware or at fault.

As the screw worms are being pushed further and further down into South America, so called 'killer' bees head north into the US. They were introduced deliberately into Brazil for research, accidentally escaped, sped through central America and are now in Texas. The problems they had caused in Brazil were not of great interest to Americans but, when they crossed the border, the press was quick to see the opportunity for sensational stories. On 18th September 1972 *Time* magazine reported "Like an insect version of Gengis Khan, the fierce Brazilian bees are coming. Millions of them are swarming northward...liquidating passive colonies of native bees in their path." On 15th September 1974 the venerable *New York Times* announced "The African Killer Bee is Headed This Way" and *Apis mellifera scutellata*, the Africanized Honey Bee was launched as an international star. What looked like a note of caution was introduced by the *Philadelphia Inquirer* fifteen years later; but it ends sensationally: "They won't carry off your kids or attack you unprovoked...But don't underestimate their mean streak. They've already KILLED hundreds of people, STINGING some thousands of times. The slightest jostle is enough to send them into a VICIOUS FRENZY. And now, they are heading this way. Not for nothing are they called THE KILLER BEES."

One day in 1986, Inn Siang Ooi, a botany student on a field trip from the University of Miami, was climbing a hill in Costa Rica studying the plants. He came to a bare outcrop and scrambled among the rocks, his attention focused on the flora and not on where he was stepping. He stumbled into a large exposed nest of Africanized bees. They exploded into action and immediately attacked. He tried to get away but the hill was too steep to run either up or down so he squeezed himself into a gap between the rocks and tried to shield his body with them. Rescuers were driven off by the bees and three of them were so badly stung that they collapsed. After darkness fell the bees returned to their nest and Ooi's body was retrieved. On examination he was found to have been stung by eight thousand bees, an average of seven stings for every square centimetre of his body.

That bees should cause death is nothing new – more people die from them every year than from any other animal except the mosquito. But most deaths from bee stings are caused by an allergy rather than the toxic effect of the sting itself. And if we are to include allergic reactions in our calculations we could find that the strawberry ranks high on the list of the world's top assassins. But the honey bee hardly ranks as a global homicidal threat. It rarely inhabits our nightmares.

The case of Ooi was one in which allergy played no part. A healthy young body had been destroyed by massive doses of bee venom. The Africanized bee changed the image of the honey bee in America, and its relationship with people. So what is the truth? How dangerous are they? And what, in fact, are the 'African Killer Bees'? Their story begins in the 1950s when it was realised that the honey bees which had been imported into Brazil from Europe – there are no native species of honey bee in North or South America – were not doing well in the tropical and subtropical temperatures. A Brazilian scientist, Warwick Kerr, was asked to import bees more suited to the climate, and he noticed that the beekeepers of South Africa were reporting massive yields of honey. Kerr knew that the African bees had the reputation of being more aggressive than the European strains but thought that he could cross the two and end up with a hybrid that had the European gentleness and the African productivity. He imported 54 mated queens and introduced them into the Brazilian colonies in 1956. They did well and production increased; but at some point a local beekeeper removed the protective screens that prevented the queens from escaping and 26 of the colonies swarmed in the forest. These formed the nuclei of many swarms which spread at tremendous speed through south and central America. Moving 300 to 500 kilometres a year they reached southern Texas by the end of 1990. The present conservative estimates are that there are between 50 and 100 million nests containing one trillion individual Africanized bees in Latin America.

The sting of an Africanized bee is the same as that of any other honey bee. It is made up of two barbed lancets attached to a sac of venom and driven by powerful muscles. When the bee stings, she drives the lancets deep into the flesh where they are anchored by the barbs. At the same time a specialised gland releases an alarm odour which attracts other bees to the site of the sting so that they too can attack. When the bee pulls away the sting remains anchored in the flesh and continues to throb for thirty to sixty seconds, injecting more venom and giving off the alarm odours. The bee dies shortly afterwards, but usually others have arrived by then to keep up the stinging.

The venom, like that of snakes, is made up of a cocktail of different chemicals, each one possibly being important at warding off a different aggressor. The one that affects humans is called melittin. It affects us in three ways. Firstly it produces local swelling, followed by a tenderness and itchy feeling which may last for some days; secondly a more serious general reaction may develop, which could involve a rash over the whole body, wheezing, nausea, vomiting and abdominal pain; and thirdly, the most serious of all is a reaction which involves difficulty in breathing and falling blood pressure, which can lead to loss of consciousness and death due to circulatory and respiratory collapse. This last reaction is rare in people who are not allergic to bee stings but it can be brought on by large numbers of stings, and this is where the danger of the Africanized bee lies.

These bees are far more sensitive to disturbance than the European bees, and on the slightest provocation will suddenly erupt into a hostile cloud of thousands of bees. What makes them even more dangerous is that they are also particularly sensitive to the alarm odours and produce larger amounts – as much as ten times more – than European bees. So a single colony will attack more readily if disturbed. Their alarm signals may trigger other colonies to join in, so that the total number of bees on the attack may sometimes number tens of thousands. The Africanised bees are also more persistent in their attacks. A European colony will rarely follow a fleeing intruder further than the area immediately around the nest but the Africanized bee will chase a running person for up to a kilometer. The reason for this extreme behaviour may well be linked closely to us!

The bees originally evolved in East Africa and lived alongside people for thousands of years. Humans love honey and bees make honey, a situation which was bound to create tension. The bees had to develop an aggressive strategy to protect their homes, not just from humans but from animals like honey badgers too. It may be that we have unwittingly made the African bee more aggressive by systematically harvesting their food for millennia.

Wildlife film maker Dan Freeman experienced this aggression first hand on a safari in Ruaha National Park, Tanzania, twenty years ago.

> We were camping in the park, and one morning got up very early to try and find sable antelope. On the way we decided to stop for breakfast, and found a suitable place by a Boabab tree, in a clearing. There were about ten of us, and several people got out and started walking around. We had actually checked the tree for bees first, but we didn't see any flying around, so we weren't too worried about them. I suggested making some toast. This was the basic mistake, because the smoke from the fire went up the tree. The angry bees came pouring out, and there must have been thousands of them. We saw them before we heard them – but then the noise became incredible. There were four of us under the tree at the time, and we just got headfuls of bees, and we ran like mad, knowing what they were like. We shouted at the others, who were anything up to 50–60 yards away, to get up onto the track, and they thought that we were calling them because breakfast was ready, so they came back to the tree. As each of them came, they got a headful of bees. Everybody panicked, and ran. I was fortunately one of the youngest and fittest, so I was able to get farthest quickest.

Once he had run about a quarter of a mile, the bees stopped following Dan, and he began to make his way back to the tree, meeting others of the group on the way. Most had been stung about 20 times, but one woman in her sixties had been stung nearly two hundred times. Putting into practice an old bush trick, they collected

Left The African 'killer' bee is a very aggressive bee, but it is kept by bee-keepers in Africa, who have learnt to live with it – *above* bee-hives in Rwanda, Africa. In the Americas, where it has been introduced by man, it is seen as a serious threat (right)

elephant dung, and set light to it – the smoke drove away the bees still crawling on them, and they brushed off the dead and dying bees which had stung them.

We realised that one woman was still missing, and that we had somehow to go and try to find her. At that point someone else came along in a land rover, totally by accident. I got into his land rover, and we went back to the tree, and started driving round in ever increasing circles, until we found her. It was the most amazing sight – she was just standing, in the middle of nowhere, about 20 meters or so from the tree, and she must have had

BEWARE AFRICANIZED BEES IN AREA

well over a thousand bees on her – the whole lot seemed to have just gone to swarm on her head, from shoulder across to shoulder. There was blood coming through the bees – she'd actually, in the panic, perforated both eardrums. She was just standing there, swaying. When she was asked later why, the reason she gave was that she knew we were all in the same situation, and that she was, herself, just waiting to die. We drove up to her and heaved her onto the spare wheel on the bonnet of the land rover, holding onto her legs, and drove back to the others. We shoved her into the fire, clawed all the bees off her, and then we all drove back to the camp.

The group radioed to the Brooke Bond tea estate at Mufindi to send a plane urgently to pick up the critically ill woman, but the message became garbled in transit, and no help came. This was fortunate because her damaged ears would have not permitted her to fly anyway.

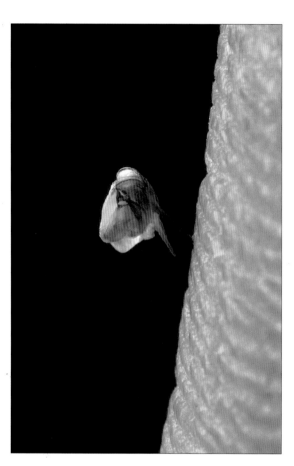

As the end of the sting is barbed and sticks into any aggressor, the venom sacs are torn out of the bee's body. The poison sacs will continue to pump venom into the sting after this has happened, although the bee itself will die shortly after

We sat on our landing strip waiting for them to arrive, and in the mean time it became obvious that she was in danger of dying. That night she got very very low – her heartbeat went right down, she was very sick. The following day it was obvious that something serious was going to happen to her, so two of us made up a bed for her in the back of the land rover, and drove her across country – it was about 80 or 90 miles. We got her to the Brooke Bond Tea estate and they put her into hospital. We stayed the night there, and went to visit her the following morning. It was incredible. She was literally sitting up in bed joking about it all! She had been stung well over a thousand times, just on the head and face.

Her tongue was covered in stings – her head was so swollen it was just grotesque – it was incredible to look at, but it all went down in a couple of days. She couldn't be flown back to Nairobi because of her perforated ear drums, so she was driven back to Nairobi hospital. The doctors were amazed – not only had she survived the whole thing, she wasn't absolutely screaming mad. But one morning, some ten days after the attack, she blew her nose, and she blew out the remains of a bee, which had been stuck somewhere up there, and apparently it just completely triggered the whole thing – the whole nightmare – and she freaked out. She was sedated, calmed down, and it took two or three days for her to get back to normal. She flew back home to the States when her perforated eardrums had finally healed.

Despite this horrific experience, Dan doesn't hold the bees responsible for the attack.

They were just very angry, and I suppose you can't blame them. I met the woman six years later in England, and she, too, had no ill feelings towards the bees, although we both agreed that she had been incredibly fortunate not to die, and probably owed her life to the timely arrival on the scene of a stranger in a land rover!

The United States Government has set up special killer bee hit squads to answer emergency calls from people who find colonies approaching or nesting near their houses. Beekeepers have been advised that they should only approach the Africanized bees wearing a complete protective suit with zippered veil, thick leather gloves and high heavy boots into which their trousers are tucked. They must also wear a thick layer of clothing or two underneath the suit so that the stings cannot penetrate. They must have a large smoker to pacify the bees and are strongly advised to have available a first aid kit containing injectable antihistamine. Kitted out in this way, American beekeepers look as though they are about to face a blazing oil rig or walk on the moon.

Back in East Africa, where the stock of the Africanized bees originally came from, the equipment of the beekeeper is more basic: a goatskin bag for collecting honey, a few torches tied with sisal twine for illumination and to smoke out the bees, and a whistle to scare off wild animals. He (this is men's work) goes out at night, when the bees are inactive, and he tends to go naked – bees can get caught up in clothes. This different approach to the task is not because Africans are more courageous, its just that they have been doing the job for thousands of years and have learned how to live alongside the bees .

In the past, in East Africa, people lived on fruits, honey and wild meat. If the hunting was unsuccessful and the fruit season sparse, they were kept alive by the honey. Traditional beekeepers were

Above African bee-keepers do not use any gloves or other protection when honey collecting.
Right A honey bee

highly valued members of the tribe, learning their skills from their fathers and inheriting the simple tools. They developed a wide knowledge of the forest, of the trees both indigenous and exotic that were useful to them and, of course, of the ways of the bees. The time of honey collection is one of festival for the Babati tribe of Tanzania: they summon the honey parties together by blowing horns and head off as a group into the bush. Usually they choose a moonless night so the bees cannot see them. They expect to be stung a little and the common belief is that you are more likely to be stung if you are afraid. When they return they brew up honey beer and celebrate with ribald honey songs about the pleasures and potency of honey.

In the Americas, a complete protective suit is recommended when working with African bees

So the Africanized bee is a welcome support for human societies in its homeland and a scourge to be feared and eradicated in those countries to which it has been transplanted. But can we learn to live with this bee? Would it be to our advantage if we did? Alfonso Discua of Honduras has a story to tell.

Since the first appearance of the Africanized honey bee in Honduras in the mid 1980s the honey industry there has collapsed, up to 75% of the Honduran beekeepers having burned their hives or simply abandoned them and gone out of business. A great wave of sensational news reports about the killer bees swept the country; the public was panicked; honey production plummeted. Discua decided to try to live with the bees and made himself some protective clothing from old aluminium builders helmets and curtain fabric. One day he was moving ten of his hives to a hillside where cardamom and wildflowers were just coming into bloom. Darkness fell before he could finish the job, so he left the hives behind a fence but close to a neighbour's farm. During the night farm animals broke into the fenced area and jolted the hives. The bees killed the neighbour's geese, chicken and a pig. After being threatened by the neighbour with a gun, Discua paid for the animals and carried on with his bees. Now his production has increased 50% and he has become a great fan of the Africanised bee. He has a message to North American beekeepers:

Don't believe everything you have heard. Don't let what happened to us in Honduras happen to you. With all the sensational news reports we had a mentality of fear regarding the Africanized bee. I've learned from my mistakes. This past year I haven't had one stinging incident, not one. The Africanized bee can be worked with success…Changing the bee is not the solution. What we have to change is the beekeeper.

For many thousands of years before people learned to keep bees, they collected honey in the wild. It was the only form of sweetening available to primitive societies. The gradual transition from honey hunting to beekeeping, that is from going out and collecting honey from wild bees in caves or hollow trees to keeping honeybee colonies close to home in hives was a long drawn out process. It happened at different times and at different rates of progress in many parts of the world, and the different stages can still be seen. But the strange fact is that, although bees have been kept in hives for thousands of years, they are not yet domesticated. The honey bee, whether African or European, is a wild animal.

The African honey bee is perhaps the animal that I fear most. On a number of occasions I have been attacked by bees whilst I quietly went about my own business. My fear is made all the greater by having to deal with not one or two, but many highly aggressive attacking animals. When they do attack, they come at you with their stings appearing to point directly at their target. They get caught in clothing and hair, and buzz irritably and frighteningly. Whilst filming in Trinidad recently, I was attacked by angry bees that I must have accidentally disturbed. They got entangled in my hair and buzzed angrily. I knew I was going to be stung at any moment, and I rushed across to a friend, Nick, to help dislodge them. Fortunately they turned out to be stingless bees, which could only bite in defence. Nick, it transpired, had also once been attacked by these bees. They were one of the few things he too was genuinely scared of.

Even though the honey bee kills more people than any other animal, be it shark, snake or tiger, it does not, generally, have an evil image. The image of the honey bee is, on the whole, that of a creature we admire – almost to the extent of being a role model. It follows the code of behaviour of girl guides (all members of the hive are female, males are only produced at breeding time), being loyal and helpful to its society, sisterly to its fellow workers, obedient to its queen, thrifty in its hoarding of honey, and pure enough in its habits to produce a nutritious sweetener that has gladdened human hearts since the end of the Ice Age. It buzzes happily around the flowers and leaves us alone as it gets on with its own business.

The wasp, on the other hand, has the image of being bad-tempered. 'God made the bee but the devil made the wasp' says the old proverb, reflecting the difference between the ways we react to both of them. The wasp swoops down on our jam pots and fruit and ruins our picnics. It does not have to be provoked to sting. We use its name for characteristics we despise: a 'waspish' person is mean, ill tempered and petulant.

The largest of the social wasps are called hornets, and they are the most feared. They are, in fact, the largest stinging insects in the world, and have the greatest lethal capacity. Hornets have been recognised as a threat to honey bee colonies since Roman times. They can enter a hive and destroy the larvae and pupae. The hornet will usually bite off the head and abdomen of a bee, and then carry the thorax back to its nest to feed its larvae. When a nest is attacked, the guard bees often come out singly against the invader and a hornet has no problem biting them in half as they come. Where there has been a long association with hornets, the bees have developed techniques to defend themselves. Some guards will emerge from the hive, form up in parallel rows and 'shimmer' at the intruder. This involves facing the adversary, raising their abdomens and humming loudly with their heads down. If the hornet does not retreat, they sometimes attack all together and occasionally succeed in killing the hornet.

The Japanese honey bee has developed this technique even further. Within 15 seconds of an attack on a single guard bee, a hornet will be rushed by up to 300 worker bees who do not attempt to sting it. Instead they simply form a ball of bees around the hornet – and bake it to death! Within 20 minutes, the temperature at the centre where the hornet is, has risen to 46 degrees centigrade which is lethal for the hornet but not for the bees.

We have seen how animals which can make us squirm can be quite harmless and others which are beneath our notice can be deadly. But above all it is becoming clear that our attitude is the most important factor in our relationship with the world of the creepie-crawlies. Knowledge brings understanding, which in its turn leads to tolerance and often mutual benefit.

In the panelled Tudor splendour of the Explorers' Club in Manhattan a glittering assembly of the nation's most distinguished bug hunters gathered on the evening of 20th May 1992 for the 100th anniversary dinner of the New York Entomological Society. It was quite a meal.

The action began at 6.30pm, in the cocktail bar which had been set up on a large terrace adjoining the dining room. Here members were served cocktails under a cloudless moonlit sky by tuxedo-clad waiters. They sipped their Martinis and Manhattans, cooled by a gentle breeze and crunched on their crudites served with Peppery Delight Mealworm Dip.

Dinner was served at 8.30 and the 'butlered hors d'oeuvres' arrived to tempt the palates of guests with such delicacies as 'Wax Worm Fritters with Plum Sauce', 'Cricket and Vegetable Tempura', 'Sauteed Thai Water Bugs', 'Roasted Australian Kurrajong Grubs' and 'Mealworm Balls in Zesty Tomato Sauce'. An unscheduled delicacy was a dish of 100 live honey ants ('only one per guest, please'). After a conventional main course of chicken and roast beef, the banquet concluded with 'Assorted Insect Sugar Cookies'. The after dinner speaker, editor of *The Food Insects Newsletter*, said to his wife, "Life doesn't get any better than this. This is as good as it gets".

Which goes to show that its all a question of attitude. In the shimmering haze of the southern African veldt, a mother will comfort her crying baby by plucking a spiny caterpillar from a nearby tree, squeezing out its intestines and popping it into the baby's mouth. It works. In the streets of a Johannesburg suburb, poker-playing men will sip their cans of coca-cola and pass round a packet of dried caterpillars. One of Africa's favourite snacks is the four-inch-long larva of the emperor moth, called the mopane worm, which is eaten fried, dried, stewed or raw. It is even canned in chilli tomato sauce. According to South African Government researchers, these mopane worms are one tenth digestible crude protein. A meal of 20 dried caterpillars fulfils your daily needs for calcium, phosphorus, riboflavin and iron. The appetite for them has lessened since rural people were introduced to western foods, but it is coming back. One company is experimenting with grinding the worms into a protein rich powder for the squeamish. It has surprising powers. A stock farmer in Botswana sang its praises: "Hell, one dose of those worms and my stud bull covered 80 cows and never raised a sweat".

In South-east Asia, insects are popular on the table. The giant water bug of Thailand, which figured on the menu of the New York Bug Banquet, is highly prized, especially the males, which have a unique flavour deriving from their sex pheromone glands. New Guinea tribes have such an appetite for cicadas that they

The European hornet has a powerful sting

have different names for the most tasty species. Australian aborigines are well known for their enthusiasm for 'witchetty grubs' and 'baked bogong moths' while Koreans eat grasshoppers and the silkworm pupae left over from silk making. After a surgical operation, the late Emperor Hirohito of Japan ate little in his last days other than his favourite insect dish: rice garnished with fried wasps.

Insects are popular in city shops and restaurants as well as in more primitive situations. In Mexico City the immature stages of an ant are served in tacos and red agave worms with tortilla. The larvae of a skipper butterfly was eaten with enthusiasm in the USA. until over-consumption affected its numbers. Grasshoppers boiled in soy sauce and cooked wasps are a luxury item in Japanese supermarkets. Insect cookery books are selling well in Europe and the USA.

For most of us, insects hold little appeal as a basic foodstuff, though we may be prepared to try the odd curiosity. But they do offer a wholesome source of protein, fats and other nutrients which are expensive to produce. In dried form they have a high content of protein that is also high in quality: house crickets are a better source of amino acids than soy protein. Today we are all worried by stories of the large areas of forest that have been cleared to make way for cattle ranching, and by the fact that raising large protein animals is an inefficient way to use our planet. In the USA, the weight of insects, spiders and crustaceans is ten times that of traditional livestock per hectare. Insects are widespread and require little husbandry; they use resources that are not touched by conventional agriculture. There are hundreds of thousands of species yet to be tried, offering a tremendous variety of texture and flavour.

Our attitudes to insects are based on the few species we come into contact with, often to our discomfort. We see them as a nuisance, a pest we would be better off without. But if we have only 50 years left of beef eating, insects could well come to our rescue in the not too distant future.

Above Mopane worms are sold in cans in Africa

Left Giant water bugs are eaten by humans, they eat frogs

Below Cockroach vol-au-vents

Below left A selection of giant water bugs

Far left Fresh mopane worms

A Cry in the Dark

One night in July 1991, Ivete Brito's six month old baby started crying. With no electricity in the house, Ivete lit a candle, and hurried across to her daughter. To her horror she found her baby covered in blood. Not knowing what had happened, she frantically searched the room, swinging the candle one way and then another, to light up the darkness. Nothing seemed to be amiss, except that she noticed scores of scuttling creatures on the ground which she took to be mice. Ivete cleaned up the blood and returned to bed, but her baby continued to cry all night long. In the first light of the morning the extent of the baby's injuries became apparent. She had been bitten on the top of her head, on her nose, her legs and her arms. What had caused the wounds? Anxiously her mother took her to the local health office. There they ascertained that she had been attacked by vampire bats and gave her five doses of vaccine as a precaution against rabies. The treatment saved her life.

Marisa dos Santos, a 12 year old girl, was not so lucky. She lived in a nearby house with her parents and five brothers and sisters. Under cover of darkness bats started coming into the house though holes in the roof. Marisa and her fourteen year old sister Marlene were bitten, but Marisa was not treated for the bites. Two months later she started complaining about a terribly sore throat and aching legs. Her condition deteriorated until she was unable to sleep, eat or drink. She was taken to the Couto Maia Hospital in Salvador, five hours drive away, but it was too late. A week later she died of rabies.

The Brito and dos Santos families were among hundreds of people attacked by bats in the middle of 1991. Their small rural town of Apora in the north eastern state of Bahia in Brazil made headline news. It was a tragic but unusual occurrence. Bats were often seen in the area, but had never before attacked in such numbers. Investigations into the incidents revealed that they coincided with the start of logging operations in the neighbouring forests. The bats usual roosting places, caves in the forest, were being exposed to bright sunlight, and this

A colony of vampire bats

disturbance had made the bats look for other roosts. Normally the bats fed on woodland animals around their caves, or on cows and horses. But during their migration from the caves they were forced to feed on whatever food was available, and began attacking people at night.

It seemed a macabre echo of Hollywood films like *The Birds* and *The Swarm*, where animals take revenge on man. The Apora vampire attack became famous, but such a dramatic attack was, in reality, an extremely rare event. Although the freely bleeding wounds inflicted by the bats looked unsightly, it was the rabies virus carried by a few of the bats, and not the bites, which was responsible for all the deaths.

Vampire bats will squeeze through very narrow gaps to get at their prey

Opposite The carnivorous ghost bat from northern Australia is a very skilled flier (*bottom*), picking frogs out of the water before eating them at a perch (*top*)

The Apora incident was a 'nightmare', but it does highlight our vulnerability at night. The power of darkness is woven into cultures around the world. Wherever we live we are affected by it. It is a time when our most important sense, sight, is at its least useful. It is a time when we are most vulnerable.

At nightfall we are all in a strange land. Familiar landmarks fade, and our certainties dissolve. The Book of Common Prayer asks that we "be not afraid of the terror by night, nor the pestilence that walketh in darkness". We may be daylight atheists, but at night our small anxieties become fears, our uncertainties mushroom into nightmares, and we need all the help we can get.

The Eskimos, who spent so much of the year in darkness, believed that the first men came out of the earth and lived in total darkness without knowing death. Then a flood destroyed all except two old women, one of whom desired death. So death came, and with it, the sun, moon, and stars. In both Chinese and Japanese mythology, the origins of the world were in chaos and total darkness. In all these ancient beliefs, darkness was the older, more primitive, more powerfully mysterious than day

In the most ancient religions, Babylonian, Egyptian, Hebrew and Christian, the opposition is made between light and darkness, life and death, good and evil. So prevalent is this across cultures and down the centuries that it is impossible for us not be affected by it, at however subconscious a level.

When I was a child I remember lying in bed terrified by the noises of the night and the shadows on the bedroom walls. For hours I would lie awake trying to make out the images – sometimes they were merely parts of the room, the swaying of the curtains or the shadows of the bed or bookcases. At other times they became monsters of the night – spiders, snakes, bats or big cats prowling the room.

The shadows of the night still play tricks on my mind. Eighteen years ago I was on an expedition to Kenya, to investigate the country's largest river – the Tana. On our journey downstream, we stopped at a place near the area where George Adamson was rehabilitating lions. George's lions were renowned for being unafraid of people, and were often a nuisance to the local Turkana and Somali, and their herds. One morning I awoke before sunrise. I was desperate to go to the toilet. We had dug a "long-drop", as pit latrines are descriptively called, a hundred meters away, and surrounded it with canvas and palm leaves for privacy. In the early morning half-light, I wandered across to relieve myself. Sitting there contemplating the world, I suddenly became aware of a lion, crouched under some bushes a short distance away, watching me. A cold fear swept over my body and I stared back, not knowing what to do next. If I moved, it might attack. I knew I would not be able to get to the nearby car before it caught me, and I was too scared to shout for help. The only thing I could do was wait and watch.

A thought crossed my mind. Was it really a lion I was seeing? In the half light it certainly looked like one, and to complete the picture, every now and then the shape would move slightly – an ear would flick or a leg shift. I certainly was not going to chance walking over and investigating. For over an hour I sat utterly still watching that lion. However hard I stared, I could not make out whether it was real, or a figment of my imagination. Slowly the light in the east grew brighter. Then, all of a sudden, the image of the lion disappeared, and the shadows became the branches and leaves of a bush. There had never been a lion there at all! In the low light, my eyesight had failed me, and with the inadequate human senses of hearing and smell, I had been powerless to determine the real nature of what I saw. That experience brought home

to me just how much we rely on our sense of sight, and just how easily it can deceive and hamper us.

Most of us have at least childhood memories of the terror that accompanied bedtime. Strangely, recent research by a Californian psychologist has shown that girls and boys have different bedtime fears. Girls, it appears, are more frightened of monsters lurking below them, particularly under the bed, whilst boys are scared of danger from higher locations – behind the curtains, or in the cupboard. The psychologist suggested that these different fears are a legacy from millions of years ago, from a time when women slept in trees, and men on the ground. Marauding enemies, whether rival ape-men or big cats were ground dwellers, and so females were genetically programmed to fear attacks from predators below. It seems likely that, in our evolutionary past, the females, who even today have lighter frames and more flexible feet, spent more time in trees, as primates such as gorillas still do. The research showed that in the playground, girls spent more time on climbing frames than boys, and demonstrated greater agility. When shown frightening movies the girls were more likely to pull their feet up onto the chairs – as if to protect dangling limbs from danger. Could we really be motivated by an ancestral memory three million years old, that still shapes our bedtime fears and behaviour? It is an interesting idea, but the research is controversial and the debate continues.

The night is a particularly scary time, not only because we are at a disadvantage because of our senses, but also because many unfamiliar creatures, better adapted for living in the dark, come out of their hiding places to stalk the land.

As darkness descends on north eastern Australia, flocks of budgerigars swirl across the grasslands to roost in the eucalyptus trees. From the depths of nearby caves and disused mine shafts come faint twitterings. With translucent wings half a meter across, carnivorous ghost bats flutter out into the night sky to hunt. The bats prey on lizards, mice...and birds. Homing in on the faint warbling snorings of the budgies, the ghost bats glide silently out of the darkness and fall on their unsuspecting prey, wrapping them in their wings like Dracula, and biting them to death.

Many snakes are nocturnal, though not all. Snakes are cold-blooded creatures, incapable of producing and retaining heat within their bodies. However, they operate most efficiently within a critical temperature range of around 25-3°C. Temperatures just below or above these levels are lethal to the snake. Consequently, in the tropics snakes can operate both during the day or the night. In deserts, though, their activity is largely confined to the night, or the cool of dawn and dusk, and the scorching temperatures of the day send them into cover. In temperate climates, on the other hand, many snakes are more active during the day.

Because night brings threats to animals in the wild, many have developed behaviour which reduces the risks. In the forests of Central and South America, the diurnal anolis lizard always goes to sleep at the far end of a long thin twig, a fern frond, or vine tip, so that any approaching predator will cause vibrations which wake it up. The alerted lizard then drops off and runs away. As darkness falls however, creatures emerge which have themselves developed to exploit its cover. The blunt headed snake spends its day coiled up asleep, often in a bromeliad. Although less than a metre long, this snake is extraordinarily elongated and very slender. Its skeletal system is shaped something like a steel girder, with interlocking vertebrae and scales, that prevent it from sagging. Its neck is particularly thin and the pupils of its large bulging eyes have elliptical pupils like

The bluntheaded snake can support
half its body length in mid-air (*top*),
allowing it to creep up and catch
unsuspecting lizards (*right*)

those of a cat. This is a snake of the night. It forages among the outer branches and thin twigs of trees where the anolis lizard sleeps. It is so light and internally reinforced that it can easily bridge gaps in the vegetation up to half its own length, and project the long thin neck far out to the very tips of the branches without vibrating them. The sleeping lizard has no warning of the impending danger until too late. Its an ingenious method of attack, but one which would be impossible for a snake weighed down by pregnancy. The blunt-headed snake has overcome this by bearing only one to three young at a time, so limiting the extra burden that the adult female has to carry.

A vast array of animals are nocturnal. They are perhaps the least familiar and least scientifically studied of all creatures, save perhaps for the creatures of the deep oceans – the creatures of perpetual darkness. Our misunderstandings of these animals and our fear of darkness have resulted in a wealth of mythology.

It is not surprising that many nocturnal animals cause alarm. Even a harmless moth has become widely feared. The death's head hawkmoth is a resident of Africa, which migrates to Europe each spring. The moth is feared because of the skull or death's head pattern on its thorax. The moths also have the reputation of being able to deliver a painful sting, though no moths are capable of doing so. The death's head hawkmoth possibly got its reputation because it has a broad proboscis which it uses to feed on tree sap, nectar and honey. The proboscis is so strong it is capable of piercing human skin, and it is this which may account for the reputed stings.

At night a wealth of unsettling creatures come out of hiding and invade our homes. The larvae of the carpet beetle chomp through our carpets, and book lice live on the fungi in our books. Silverfish and firebrats on the floor below feed on the minute particles of food that find their way into the dust. In older houses a sinister tapping sound emanates from the walls. In the past the sound of the death watch beetle was often the only noise to be heard by those waiting at night by a sick bed, and so the beetle got the reputation of foretelling death. In fact the sound is, rather astonishingly, a sexual call which this small brown beetle makes to attract a mate, by striking its head repeatedly against the wood on which it stands.

Adaptation to a life in darkness can produce unusual and sometimes frightening physical features. To the people of Madagascar, no nocturnal experience is more terrifying than coming face to face with the aye-aye. It has malevolent and magical powers. If it chooses to point its unnaturally long middle finger at you, you will die – swiftly and horribly. Because of this fear, the aye-aye, which has a curiosity about humans, is often caught and nailed to a stake at the crossing of roads so that a passer-by might absorb its evil.

Yet the aye-aye is not only completely harmless, but of vital interest to scientists. It is the only remaining representative of one family of lemurs – an ancient prosimian or pre-monkey stock – which is a chapter in the story of the evolution of higher primates and man. It is a living fossil. When the island of Madagascar split away from the supercontinent Gondwanaland between 100 and 200 million years ago, to be isolated by the Mozambique Channel and strong westerly trade winds, its primitive populations of

An aye-aye

animals developed independently of the great continents of India, Africa, and South America. In these parts of the world the lemurs were driven to extinction by the more developed monkeys and apes. On Madagascar, the time capsule of isolation allowed these representatives of a first world of animals to survive when their relatives elsewhere were lost in the evolutionary process.

A Philippine tarsier could be classed as a cuddly animal, despite its ghoulish looks

The aye-aye is one of the survivors. It can only be described by comparing it piecemeal with other creatures. It is the size of a domestic cat, has the ears of a bat, the snout and teeth of a rat and the bushy tail of a squirrel. Its eyes bulge out from its skull like a tree frog and when a baby aye-aye cries it sounds like a squeezed rubber duck. But its unique feature is a very long, thin and delicate middle finger – the one the Madagascar people fear.

The aye-aye's chilling appearance is the result of the nocturnal lifestyle it has adopted. Large eyes allow it to gather as much light as possible, and enhance its night vision. Huge ears, which constantly swivel, give them acute hearing enabling them to detect the smallest movements of grubs inside a tree trunk. The aye-aye can detect insect larvae by drumming its fingers on the wood and listening to the echoes that indicate the presence of prey. Once it has located food, the aye-aye can rip through the trunk of the tree with its rodent-like incisors. Now, using its skeletal, elongated middle finger, it probes into the remotest of crannies, and winkles out wood-boring grubs. So flexible is the 'finger of death' it can bend in all directions. It is an all purpose tool, for tapping tree trunks, poking holes in eggs and pumping the liquid out of them, and for getting milk out of coconuts.

Although humans are unable to see well in the dark, many animals have excellent night vision. For optimum clarity at night, the eyes of an animal need to be as large as possible. The eyes of the small nocturnal primate, the tarsier, are so large that they occupy most of the head. The eyes are not spherical, but bulge out backwards into the skull. This means that the eyes can no longer move in their sockets, and so instead, the tarsiers have developed highly mobile heads. This phenomenon is seen in other nocturnal animals, such as owls and bushbabies. Eyes adapted to nocturnal vision are very sensitive to light, and so must be protected during the day. Many nocturnal animals, such as cats, have pupils which close down to small slits during the day.

To further enhance night vision, many nocturnal animals have a reflective layer which causes their eyes to glow eerily when they look into a light at night. This 'eyeshine' is caused by a layer of reflective cells surrounding the rods and cones in the retina called the tapetum lucidum. After light has passed through the sensory cells once, the tapetum reflects it back through the sensory layer, so giving the cells a second chance to respond. This makes the eyes more sensitive at night, but reduces their acuity because the reflection is not perfect, and the image is probably blurred. Despite this, it means that the animal can operate in conditions that we would think of as total darkness. A variety of animals have this extra ability, among them many spiders, crocodiles, old world fruit bats, Cook's tree boa, nocturnal birds such as oil birds and whipporwhills, antelopes, the big cats and sharks. Interestingly owls do not have a tapetum – their eyes are so well adapted to the dark that it is unnecessary. During the day a protective pigment covers the retina, like built-in sunglasses, giving the owl excellent daytime vision.

Vision is by far the best developed of all human senses, and the loss of it at night leaves us relying on our other, rather undeveloped senses. It is at such times that we feel particularly vulnerable. This scenario was brilliantly captured in the feature film *Silence of the Lambs*. Jody Foster, playing a young FBI officer hunting down a serial killer, tracks her quarry to a house. He gives her the slip, and she is led into the depths of the house through a labyrinth of corridors and rooms. Suddenly all the lights go off. She can't see a thing. Even though she has a gun, it is of no use to her if she cannot see where to point it. Aiming one way and then another, she stumbles forward through the darkness. Nearby, the killer, equipped with image intensifying goggles, can see her every movement. Quietly and confidently he watches his prey flounder helplessly around. Unable to see, Jody does not know where to aim, where the danger may came from. Only when the killer cocks his gun does the sound give his position away. Jody fires an instant before he does.

One of the most feared of nocturnal predators has eyes that are specially adapted to see in the dark. It is the most widespread of all the cats, with the exception of the domestic one: it is the leopard – the most successful big cat in the modern world. It can be found throughout Africa, wherever there is cover from which it can ambush its prey, from the Arabian peninsula, through Asia to Manchuria and Korea. Its cult is common in Africa, the skin being the regalia of warriors, and in Buganda it is the symbol of kingship. The tip of the leopard's tail has a special significance in Buganda: it is smoked in a pipe as a magic incantation to call home a straying wife, child or relative. The accompanying prayer asks that, just as the leopard's tail is always restless, so may the heart of the wanderer be restless until it returns home. The leopard's claws were a fetish for making a business stable, and its whiskers were chopped up very finely and used as a poison, apparently causing peritonitis. In former times the leopard's image was

The leopard – king of the night

The spotted hyena has a very bad reputation, but is one of the most highly socialised of all the African plain predators

frequently carved in West Africa as a symbol of wisdom. The priests of Ancient Egypt wore leopard vestments, and a statue of Tutankhamen found in his tomb was seated on the back of a realistic leopard.

The leopard is small among the great cats. The males, which grow much larger than the females, are around 1.5 meters (5 ft) long and 70 kg (155 lbs) in weight – the size of a big dog. The leopard is a solitary hunter, feeding on a wide variety of animals, from dung beetles up to antelopes twice its own weight, including birds, reptiles and invertebrates, hares, baboons, fish and dogs.

Quite often leopards will develop individual tastes within the broad range of their diet. They will then ignore easier prey to go after their preferences. They have been recorded as hunting exclusively for jackals, or ignoring herds of goat while killing and eating the guard dogs. A taste for dogs is common, and a leopard will enter a village at night to take the sleeping dogs from the verandahs of houses. They are particularly adept at creeping up on sleeping animals and will

take roosting chickens and guinea fowl by night from their perches. There are records of dogs and even of humans being killed and dragged away without awakening the other members of the household.

Leopards are the only big cat to regularly live in urban environments under the very noses of people. They live in the suburbs of Nairobi, Madras and many of African and Asian cities. Morphologically they are not highly specialised cats; they are not sleek or built for speed like the cheetah, nor do they have stout limbs like the jaguar, or huge bodies like the lion or tiger. Leopards are in fact medium sized cats, and it is this which gives them the ability to exploit a wide range of prey types and sizes. They are a most adaptable cat, living in rain forests, grasslands, snowy mountains and deserts. In Israel they regularly steal into the kibbutzs to take the odd cat or dog. It is a problem, for the people fear that one day they might take a child.

Man-eating leopards seem to have developed the same individuality of taste that leads others to prefer jackals or dogs. This can begin through scavenging. After an epidemic of smallpox or cholera, which can suddenly kill thousands, it has been noted that man-eating outbreaks sometimes occur, and this has been put down to the leopard having acquired a taste for human flesh after feasting among the corpses. Others first attack humans after being disturbed in a state of excitement, such as after a kill. Colonel Jim Corbett, who became world famous for his one-man expeditions against man-eaters, listed a wave of man-eating in which one victim was claimed in the first year, three in the second, six in the third. By the sixth year, 26 known victims were recorded. Of all the cats, the man-eating leopard develops a high sensitivity to human presence and becomes exceptionally difficult to track down.

What is perhaps most remarkable is that leopards do not become man-eaters more often. They are the big cat most familiar with man. They live in and around African towns like red foxes in Europe, or coyotes in America. So why do they not attack people more often? The reason may lie in the adaptability of this big cat. Leopards seldom take large prey, even though they are quite capable of doing so. And unlike tigers, or lions they are capable of living off very small prey, when their preferred food is not available, so they are less likely to turn to man-eating because of hunger. Man-eating leopards, however, are said to exhibit an almost diabolical cunning and in India have been known to force their way into dwellings at night to prey on sleeping humans.

Perhaps the archetypal creature of the night is the hyena, an animal which has a special place among the nightmares of Africa. Its weird laughing call, its slinking movements, its association with darkness and feeding on the dead have made it widely feared and loathed.

In many parts of Africa the hyena is linked with evil spirits and associated with witchcraft. In northern Tanzania near Lake Manyara, the spotted hyena is associated with the nocturnal activity of witches in Mbugwe folklore. It is said that all witches possess one or two hyenas. The people there say that witches are often seen riding on the sloping backs of hyenas at night, their eerie torches glowing in the dark. Every now and then the witch refuels his torch from hyena butter which he carries over his shoulder. Riding across the plains, the witches visit far off villages, to cast their spells before returning to their homes at dawn to milk the hyenas. As in most tales there is some truth in these beliefs. Witches' butter does exist – it is the oily deposit which the hyena leaves on bushes to mark its territory.

222 A CRY IN THE DARK

In this area hyenas are common and generally regarded as despicable animals, likely to kill calves or goats guarded by small boys. Elsewhere people have been mauled and killed by hyena while riding bicycles, walking in the open, or sleeping in their huts. But to malign all hyenas would be unfair. The brown and the striped hyena are essentially timid loners, unlikely to harm an adult human. It is really only the social spotted hyena which can be considered a danger at night. Weighing the same as a man, it is an extremely powerful animal with colossal neck muscles and bone-crushing jaws.

For all this the spotted hyena is one of my favourite animals. Why, you may ask, do I love such an ugly, cowardly, loathsome creature? I did not always love them. As a teenager in Ethiopia they were one of my pet hates. I knew little about them save what everyone else told me, and theirs was a stereotyped hatred of these animals. I remember, I am ashamed to say, setting out with friends at night in the Rift Valley looking for hyenas to shoot, seeking excitement as youngsters and justifying our actions by believing we were doing the local pastoral Galla peoples a favour by killing off animals that almost certainly molested them and their herds. My opinion of these animals was to change before I left the country two years later. I visited a Polish lady in Addis Ababa who had agreed to look after my yellow fronted amazon parrot which I could not take with me. In her spacious grounds she had a variety of unusual animals. She had many different types of birds, warthogs and other animals. But the one that captivated me most was the spotted hyena. It was simply gorgeous. It had been in captivity since a pup and so had never developed the scars and tattered ears that are so characteristic of wild ones. It was a young animal, perhaps only two years old and its coat was thick and clean, and almost golden in colour. It truly adored the Polish lady and went into a frenzy of squirming and cackling whenever she came near its enclosure. It was so tame that I was able to stroke its coarse fur. For the first time in my life I was looking at a spotted hyena in a different light. This was a magnificent creature capable of affection. It was clean and well groomed. I fell in love with it.

Today I find spotted hyenas one of the most fascinating of all the creatures on the African plains. Because they live in groups, or clans, there is always something going on, something interesting to watch. The pups are jet black and look very much like puppy dogs – and to me they are just as appealing. The mothers are extremely affectionate and spend much time grooming their young. At one year old the mischievous youngsters look like fluffy Paddington bears. But their social life in rival clans inevitably leads to squabbles, scars and tattered ears. As they grow older they become more and more battered looking. Whilst watching them from the confines of a Land Rover in the baking sun, I have often envied their sensible habit of wallowing in cool mud. It may leave them looking shabby and unkempt, but how much more comfortable they appear than the panting lions lying out on the open scorching plains. Yet I still find audiences in the west prejudiced against even the puppy-like hyena youngsters, not being able to see the beauty, for the beast in their imagination. It is sad to see advertisements reinforcing our prejudices by portraying hyenas as thieves, out to steal your car.

What distinguishes the hyena from all other animals is its ability to create a repertoire of incredible sounds, unlike any other I have ever heard. The laughter, whooping, cries and cackling of spotted hyenas is one of the most characteristic noises of the African night. It never ceases to amaze me just how many different calls they can make, and sometimes while out on the plains, I listen intently to some far off sound, unsure whether it is an unfamiliar animal to me or simply a hyena.

It is important for spotted hyenas to have a varied and highly developed means of vocal communication, because they are not only social animals but also highly predatory ones, and so need to understand the intentions of other hyenas. The hyena's familiar melancholy whoo-oop call, which rises in pitch is really a long distance call saying 'I am here'. The giggles and yells come from a fleeing hyena or one in a state of nervous excitement, whilst long moans, lowing and deep staccato grunts indicate aggression. The African night is often filled by a cacophony of sound as hyenas voice their emotions around a kill.

A few years ago whilst filming in the Tanzania, a group of keen birders visited our house at the Serengeti Research Institute. One day we found them diligently searching the ground for the source of a sound which they thought came from an insect. Suddenly we heard the call again. Perplexed they looked around, not knowing where it could be hiding. Fifty feet above them a tiny grass warbler was looping through the air and calling for all it was worth. Our friends hadn't dreamed of looking up at the sky for the origin of the 'zzitt-zzitt' sound. That noise had seemed confusing during the day, but just imagine the wealth of sounds that break the stillness of the night which we are often hopeless at identifying.

For thousands of years nocturnal animals were heard but remained unseen and this unfamiliarity often bred fear. Many of our fears are based on the odd sound of nocturnal animals. For anyone brought up in Kenya the sound of the tree hyrax in suburban gardens is familiar. But for others it's loud harsh screeches could easily be mistaken for the cries of someone being murdered! All over the world animals pepper the night with a cacophony of sounds – screeching petrels, howling wolves, laughing hyenas, oil birds, whirring nightjars, squabbling flying foxes, booming howler monkeys.

Of course, sounds are a vital means of communication. In dense forest or at night, when visual communication is hampered, they are particularly useful. Animals use sounds to communicate over long distances, in order to advertise their presence, attract mates, or delineate territories.

The roar of a male lion can be heard eight kilometres away. In East Africa it is a familiar call, the loudest of any cat, and has been measured at 114 decibels. Contrary to popular opinion they do not roar to intimidate prey. It is really a species-specific call, probably helping to locate other members of the pride, bind individuals together and advertise their presence to rival lions. Frequently the roaring of one individual may elicit others to start roaring. Once, when sleeping at night in the open, on the roof of my Suzuki jeep, in the Serengeti, five male lions started to roar. In the still of night those five lions roaring only meters from me was one of the most impressive sounds I have ever heard. The car shook with the intensity of the noise. It was a sound from the very heart of wild Africa, and it filled the air with nostalgia and bathed me in its exuberance. I loved every minute of it.

Lions can certainly tell the difference between individual calls. Even we can tell them apart; males, for instance, tend to have more 'grunts' after the main roar than females. Five years ago whilst filming lions we decided to repeat an experiment to see how male lions cooperate in defending their territory. We placed a life-sized dummy lion on the plains just out of sight of two resident local male lions. When everything was ready we played back a roar from a foreign male through huge speakers to the lions. Immediately they both stood up and cautiously stalked towards the source of the sound. As they rounded a small rise in the plains they caught sight of the dummy for the first time and stalked towards it. The lion nearest the polystyrene dummy suddenly sprang onto its back and bit a huge hole in it before nervously jumping away. Within minutes, however, they lost interest in the dummy – it couldn't have smelt like a lion and certainly didn't behave like one. They had, however, initially been completely fooled by our unfamiliar roar.

One of the world's most widely distributed species is renowned for piercing the silence of the small hours with a shriek so shattering to the nerves that it was often thought to be a soul in torment. Barn owls have a long association with church towers and graveyards, and are responsible for many a legend of haunting, because of their unearthly screams and ghostly white silent appearance as they swoop and kill in total darkness. As well as screaming, the barn owl hisses, snores and barks – all very unbird-like noises. The 18th century, British naturalist Gilbert White wrote from his country rectory: 'The white owl does indeed snore and hiss in a tremendous manner...I have known a whole village up in arms on such an occasion, imagining the churchyard to be full of goblins and spectres'.

The barn owl has the reputation of often appearing surrounded by an eerie luminous glow. For a long time it was put down to general superstitions that have always surrounded the bird, but recently evidence suggests that the glow may indeed be real, and result from the owls roosting in hollow trees infected with honey fungus, whose spores phosphoresce.

It seems that there is a reason for the startling appearance of the barn owl, with its large facial discs that surround its eyes. The discs are now thought to operate as parabolic reflectors, collecting the faintest sounds and focussing them on the ears, so that the owl can locate and kill the smallest prey in total darkness, using only its keenly developed sense of hearing. If the owl is to hunt by hearing alone it is important that the sound clues it seeks are not disturbed by the noise of its own flapping wings. Its wings and flight feathers are more flexible than those of most birds, allowing it to make very large wing movements which can afford to be slow and therefore more gentle and less disturbing to the air. A special comb-like fringe on the leading edge of the wing surface further helps to muffle the sound of the wing cutting the air.

In the absence of light, many nocturnal animals have come to rely exclusively on sound, to get an

The oil bird's eyes have developed to give it extremely good night vision

accurate impression of their environment. The nocturnal kangaroo rat has evolved an enormous eardrum and large outer ear, allowing it to detect the approach of a rattlesnake from the rustle of its scales, and the swoop of an owl from the wind passing over its feathers.

Hearing can be enhanced by collecting as much sound as possible. Many nocturnal animals do this by evolving huge outer ears, or pinnea, which act as funnels, channelling sound down to the eardrum. Fennec foxes and many bats are good examples of this.

A few birds use sound to find their way in the dark. The cave swiftlet of South-east Asia is a diurnal bird, but nests deep in the recesses of caves far from the reach of light. As the swiflets enter the cave they start emitting a series of high speed clicks, about five a second. The high pitched clicks are of such short duration that they permit the bird to hear the echo from the walls between each click. As the bird approaches the walls it increases the frequency of the clicks to perhaps twenty a second allowing it to quickly and accurately judge just how far away it is from the obstacle and so fly unerringly through the darkness.

Another bird which uses echolocation is the oil bird of South America. It is a nocturnal bird with huge bulbous eyes, but it navigates in the same way as the swiftlet, emitting clicks which in

Above The barn owl flies silently over its unwitting prey, which it locates using highly developed stereo hearing
Below Reports of glowing owls are probably due to luminous spores picked up from their roost sites – in this case the glow is due to being photographed with an infra-red camera

complete darkness allow it to "see" its surroundings, using reflected sound.

One group of animals has developed the art of echolocating to such a degree that they can catch a fast moving insect in flight or detect an obstacle in their path the thickness of a human hair. They are, of course, bats, the source of perhaps our greatest nighttime myths and nightmares.

One of the most commercially successful ghouls ever to inhabit our nightmares is the pale figure with the piercing eyes and unlikely teeth of Count Dracula. He was re-invented by the writer Bram Stoker, but had existed for centuries before in the myths of the Slavonic lands. The earliest tales of vampires told of the souls of the dead which rose from their graves and wandered about in the night to suck the blood of living persons. When the vampire's grave was opened, the corpse was found to be fresh and rosy from all the blood he had drunk. The standard cure was to drive a stake through his heart, cut off his head and pour boiling oil and vinegar onto the grave. Anybody could become a vampire by accident if a cat leapt over his corpse or a bird flew over it. Belief in vampires became specially prevalent in Hungary between 1730 and 1735 and reports of their activities spread all over Europe at this time.

It was then that the bloodsucking bats of South America were first called 'vampires' and the name has stuck. They had been recorded as early as 1526, when *A Natural History of the West Indies* described the bites on humans, the blood loss, and the fact that the bats would return to the same man on successive nights, even when there were plenty of other potential victims available. Modern research has shown that the real vampire bats are even more fascinating than fiction.

Vampires are the pinnacle of specialisation in the bat world. Research has shown that a vampire bat will die if it fails to feed for two nights in a row. To avoid death it must consume as much as half – sometimes even all – of its body weight in blood every night. The remarkable behavioural adaptation, which allows them to survive in spite of this demanding feeding schedule is that these bats feed each other: they regurgitate blood to one another on a regular basis, and so significantly increase their chances of survival. This behaviour is difficult to explain in evolutionary terms, since it looks very much like altruism; and altruism has never been documented in non-human animals. It would seem, at first glance, that the donors, who are losing resources without any repayment, must eventually be outcompeted by the recipients, who give up nothing, and by getting free meals, may live longer, produce more offspring, and pass more of their genes onto the next generation, with less effort than their rivals. This clearly does not make sense, if each individual is pre-programmed to pass on its own genes as successfully as possible, in competition with the rest of the population. But research into the phenomenon of regurgitating blood among vampire bats reveals that most of it is from mothers to children, and that when it takes place between unrelated bats, it is in a situation where something approaching bonding has occurred, and the bat giving up the blood will have the favour returned later.

Only three species of bat live by drinking only blood: the white-winged vampire, the hairy legged vampire and the common vampire. The first two feed mostly on the blood of birds, whilst the common vampire feeds on mammalian blood, including that of humans.

The common vampire is not the huge monster depicted in horror movies, but mouse-sized, only 6-9 cm long with a wing span of 30-35 centimetres. Its fur is

A vampire bat blood-suckling from a sow

usually brown with a whitish grey belly, and its teeth have enlarged triangular shaped incisors with razor sharp cutting edges. It ranges from northern Mexico to South America, on both sides of the Andes, being broadly confined to tropical America from sea level to high mountains over 3000 meters. Vampire bats roost during the day in caves, deep rock fissures or hollow trees, usually in places screened from the light – though, in Mexico, there are colonies of vampire bats in caves which have been illuminated by electric lights so the tourists can see them. Here the bats seem undisturbed by the light or by the curious crowds. Vampire colonies normally only number around a hundred bats, though there can be as many as 2000. They roost in compact groups with the outer bats facing away from the centre, and the colony is a hive of noisy activity, with much twisting and scratching as they groom each other. If there are other bat species in the area, the vampires will occupy the highest point in the roost, the others settling below or to one side.

The common vampire lives for about 17 years, and breeds throughout the year. Strangely for so small an animal, it has a gestation period of seven and a half months, producing a single young which nurses for up to ten months. During this time the mother teaches it how to seek out and feed on prey, and inflict a painless bite. The vampire has a sloping face and underslung lower jaw which make it easier for it to approach and bite its prey. This it does by first removing hair with the scissor-like action of its canines and molars, and then making an incision about 3 mm deep with the self-sharpening incisors. Then it sticks its tongue into the wound and laps up the blood. The lapping of its tongue draws blood up by capillary action through two channels on its undersurface. The incision is so shallow that blood clots would normally form within one to two minutes. But the bat needs to feed longer than this and so it produces an anticoagulant in the saliva which runs into the wound through a channel on the upper surface of the tongue and keeps the blood flowing. So powerful is the bat's anticoagulant that an extract from its saliva has been used to make a new thrombolytic agent which may soon help in the treatment of thrombosis, still a major killer in the Western world.

Within minutes of starting to feed the bat begins to urinate, passing the non-nutritive blood plasma to make room for more food. Despite this, its huge blood meal distends the flexible stomach and often gives it a weight problem which makes it impossible to take off. It can take up to 40 minutes for a bat to finish feeding. A fully fed vampire will often slide off the victim to the ground, and hop about like a bloated toad, urinating all the while to reduce its payload, thus enabling it to fly away. It is now believed that urinating on the victim may serve a specific purpose, for the distinctive smell makes it easier for the bat to relocate the source of food on another night. This explains the strange habit, noted in the 16th century, of their returning to bite the same man, when there were plenty of others available.

Nowadays the common vampire feeds primarily on domestic animals; there is a plentiful supply of them and they are gathered into conveniently large herds. But originally vampires fed on a variety of wild animals including armadillos, porcupines, cave rats and rabbits. More surprisingly, research has recently revealed that they will feed on reptiles such as the giant marine toad, crocodile, ground iguana, turtle, coral snake, vine snake and rat snake. The rat snake is a predator of the vampire bat and, in the laboratory, it lunged repeatedly at the vampire which dodged and manoeuvred itself into a position facing the snake's head, nose to nose. Then it repeatedly licked the rostral scale on the head of the snake with a rasping tongue until the blood flowed and it could feed. The snake lay still, except for a flicking tongue as if mesmerised by the bat. Although it is not yet proven the researchers believe that the bat was at a precise distance in front of the snake's head where it could not be detected – a blind spot from which it could feed in safety. Another surprise for the investigators was that the bats fed on the large marine toad, biting it directly on the parotid gland which secretes a poison lethal to dogs and cats.

When common vampires feed on domestic animals they seem to have preferences, attacking mostly water buffalo then horses, mules, donkeys, goats, pigs, poultry, sheep, dogs and man. The bats try to bite horses and cattle in places where it is difficult to dislodge them: the ears, between the eyes, on the neck, shoulder or back, the flank or the vulva. Water buffalo, which submerge themselves to avoid predation, are often bitten on the inside of their nostrils. Pigs are bitten on the nose, ears and teats; sleeping dogs – usually only the old and deaf ones – on the nose and ears. Humans are bitten on the tips of fingers and toes, nose, ears, just above the eyebrows and on the lips. The vampire is a master of patience and stealth, and the bites are almost always painless and go undetected.

Vampires are most notorious, not for leaving livid corpses drained of their life blood, but less dramatically, for spreading disease. In 1907, a major outbreak of disease killed cattle by the thousands in southern Brazil and subsequently spread to Argentina, Paraguay, Bolivia and northwards. In 1925 the disease spread to cattle in Trinidad and then, in 1929, to humans, when it was proved to be a new form of rabies transmitted by the common vampire bat. There is today a cattle population of more than 7 million head in the area of vampire bat rabies, and more than 100,000 die of rabies every year. In 1987 alone, the losses cost more than US$40 million.

In the past, rabies has not been a serious health hazard for humans, with less than 200 deaths having been reported during the last 60 years. In 1989 alone, however, there were 79 human deaths from rabies in Peru and Brazil. And the problem is growing.

Bites from vampires can be a problem, not just because they can transmit rabies, but also because the anticoagulants in the bats' saliva prevents the wound from healing quickly, and this can lead to serious infection. Although healthy cattle in a mild climate can tolerate quite a severe blood loss without ill effects, a colony of common vampires needs quite a reservoir to maintain it. A single bat will take about 20 ml every day – about two tablespoons full – which means that an average colony of a hundred adults could consume all the blood in 20 horses, 25 cows, 365 goats or 14,600 fowl during a single year.

All three of the true vampire bats are of moderate size, but there are several species of large bat with fearsome teeth that are popularly thought to be blood drinkers. These are called the false vampire bats. The largest of them is the spectral vampire bat, which has a wingspan of one metre. It eats other bats, rodents and birds – including adult parrots, trogons, cuckoos and pigeons – which it catches while roosting. It does not, however, suck the blood of its victims, It catches them whilst they are asleep, falling upon them and shrouding them with its wings before crushing them with powerful jaws. This bat may well be responsible for the belief that the giant vampire, *Desmodus draculae* is still around. This was discovered as a fossil relic in Venezuelan and Brazilian caves in 1988 at the same level as fossils of the three living species of vampire bat, and so some Brazilian zoologists have accepted the possibility that living specimens may yet be found. The spectral vampire is, however, neither spectral nor a vampire.

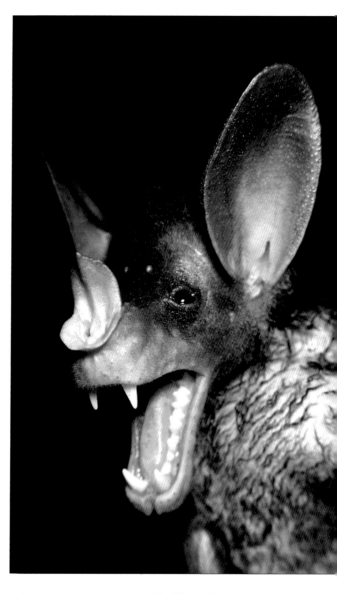

Not all fierce-looking bats are dangerous – the false vampire bat only eats fruit

Because bats shy away from the light and seek out dark inaccessible places to roost during the day, they have always had a reputation for mystery. Bats were long thought to be the familiars of witches, and in mediaeval times women were burned because bats were found flying about their houses. Bats' blood was a common ingredient in witches brews in Europe and across the Atlantic, in the American Midwest and the Caribbean there is an ancient belief that if you bathe your eyes in it you will be able to see in the dark. Bats had other magical properties, even in modern times: it was a Texan lovesick suitor who was advised to place a bat on an anthill until all its flesh was eaten, wear its 'wishbone' round his neck, and pulverise the remaining bones to be served to his loved one in a glass of vodka.

One of the most common themes in folklore about bats and humans is that they will, given a chance, entangle themselves in human hair. This has been particularly terrifying to women. The effects are said to be drastic: some say the bat will cling onto the hair, resisting all attempts to disentangle it until the hair is cut off; others say that the bat will cling there until driven out by thunder and lightning. A bat in your hair means you will turn grey instantly, or the bat will pull it all out in clumps, or the bat droppings will turn you mangy or bald. The French say that a bat in your hair presages a disastrous love affair; the Irish that, if it escapes with a single strand, you are condemned to eternal damnation. All of which gives a peculiar frisson to an experiment which was carried out in a BBC studio some years ago.

During a broadcast of the BBC natural history series *The Living World*, the producer, Dilys Breese, who is of Welsh extraction and has a head of copious, long black Celtic hair, came into the studio and sat bravely and patiently while a bat specialist placed a captive pipistrelle on her head. It stayed there for a while making no attempt to cling on and so, driven by the spirit of scientific curiosity, the team tried to entangle it themselves, parting the hair at the crown of the head and the nape and thrusting the bat inside. Each time it crawled out and sat, either on the shoulder or the top of her head. It refused entanglement. Eventually it flew off and hid behind the studio audio panelling. There it stayed and most of the panelling had to be removed to get the bat out – but the audience was reassured. The myth had been destroyed and the bat had been given a little helping hand on its long road to rehabilitation.

For over 200 years, researchers have known that bats can find their way in the dark without vision, but it was only in the 1940s that the way they do this was discovered. They produce beams of ultrasonic sound waves that bounce off objects in their flight path, and use the returning echoes to 'see' their surroundings at night. We cannot, for the most part, hear these sound waves, because they are in the range of 20 to 60 kHz – and human hearing, even in the young, cuts off at around 20 kHz. Some bats echolocate with their mouths wide open in a terrifying snarl. Other species emit sounds through their nostrils and fly with their mouths closed. One of the most fascinating revelations of recent research has shown that the insects which are the targets of bat attacks can hear the ultrasonic sonar and take measures to avoid it.

As the bat flies out in its search for food, it sends out ultrasonic clicks at the rate of 10 to 20 a second. When it detects a possible meal, the rate increases, to improve the accuracy, to many hundreds of clicks a second, just before it reaches the target. But the hunting bat can only collect information from a fairly short distance – perhaps 5 to 10 meters in front. Beyond that range, the returning echoes are too weak for the bat to pick up. A moth can hear these clicks from a distance of up to 40 meters so the prey knows that the hunt is on long before it is picked up on the bat's sonar screen.

As the moth hears the cruising bat, it need take no action unless the rate of clicks increases, indicating that a target has been located. Then it takes evasive action which is characteristic of the species. A lacewing, which is delicate and slow-flying, will fold its wings into a V shape and nose dive for the shelter of the underbrush; a praying mantis, which has only one ear and so can detect the approach of a bat without being able to locate it, goes into a power dive, flapping its wings to double its original flight speed. There are moths which will execute a wide variety of aerobatics, barrel rolls, loop-the-loops and power dives to escape the attacking bat. But the tiger moth has carried ultrasonic defence to new levels of sophistication.

These insects, known as arctiids, have their own battery of ultrasonic sounds which they can fire back at an approaching bat. They have been observed to change their flight patterns less than other moths in response to ultrasonic pulses, suggesting that they rely more on their ultrasonic defences. These seem to confuse the bat by interfering with the signals which it is receiving, so that it knows there is something out there but cannot work out what it is – a form of jamming. The ultrasonic sounds they emit have another function. They identify the arctiid moth which is transmitting them. It is a nocturnal animal's version of the warning colouration system employed by diurnal animals. The sounds identify the tiger moth, and a bat which has once tried one of these unpleasant tasting meals will avoid them in the future.

Bats are masters of night-time flying. One of the main reasons why bats fly at night is to escape daytime predators, to which they are vulnerable. Their highly developed flying skills and navigational abilities are efficient for feeding in the dark, but not for escaping birds of prey in the light of day. In many places around the world raptors specialise in attacking bats in the twilight as they emerge from their caves.

Around the world, bats are feared, often because they are misunderstood. In South-east Asia, the huge conspicuous fruit bats, with their one meter wingspan, are diurnal and widely adored. In China they are thought to be omens of good luck and in the Pacific Islands they are depicted as heroes in legends. However, in many other countries, where bats are small nocturnal animals difficult to observe and understand, they are feared and persecuted. Myths and legends only help to perpetuate such feelings. There are almost one thousand species of bats, and so varied are they that one could say they have a thousand different faces.

Bats have developed a very precise animal radar, which allows them to catch flying prey at night. Moths have learnt to jam this system, or drop out of the sky when they 'hear' an approaching bat

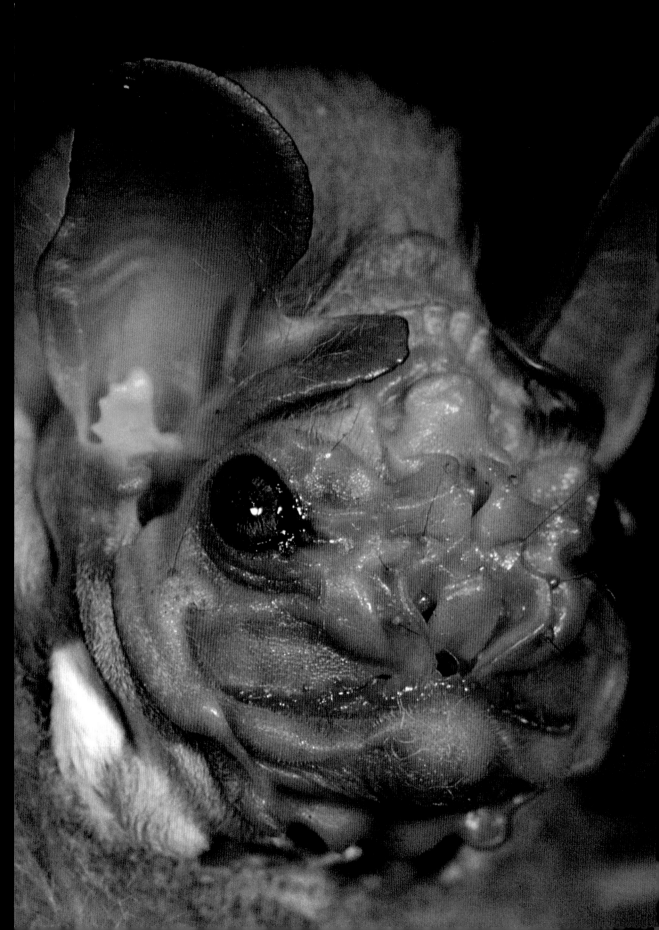

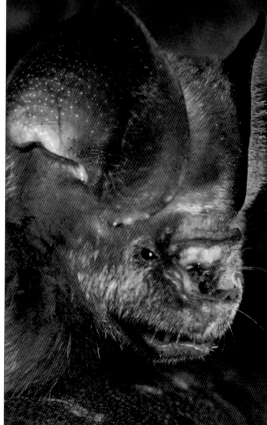

Bat faces have developed a variety of folds and protuberances which help to focus the radar sounds they produce. Bats that do not use sound to identify their prey do not need them, so can appear more attractive.
Clockwise from opposite Wrinkle-faced bat, epauletted fruit bat, tube-nosed bat, leaf-nosed bat, frog-eating bat

The elaborate war games and amazing high speed flight and navigational abilities of bats make them fascinating objects of research, but they do not easily win friends, even when the dark myths about them are destroyed. This is partly because of their looks. The wide variety of faces among bats tends to alarm humans. They have all conceivable sizes and shapes of mouths, ears, nose leaves and tongues. Though many may look terrifying or downright ugly, their facial ornamentations are highly elaborate physical structures, which are often crucial to their way of life, and whose real roles we are only just beginning to discover.

Bats can be divided roughly into three groups. Those that feed on fruit and nectar do not need precise echolocation, since their food is stationary, comparatively large, and can be detected by odour and sight. So these bats have relatively large eyes, small ears and simple noses, giving them a cute, almost human look.

Bats that catch insects in fight, however, require elaborate echolocation technology. Insects fly swiftly and erratically, and many have special ears for detecting incoming bats. The bats and the insects are involved in an evolutionary arms race, each developing more and more sophisticated ways of outwitting the other. The bats often evolved elaborate leaf noses and large ears. The overall effect is to produce a face that looks strange to humans, and so many of these bats have a most frightening appearance. The most bizarre leaf noses are the most proficient echolocators – the horseshoe, the long leaf-nosed and Tome's long eared bats. The leaf nose is important in the transmission of echolocating calls. Experiments which have temporarily altered the shape of the leaf nose of a bat have shown that the pattern of sound radiation is also altered, so affecting the bats perception of its surroundings. It is ironic that the leaf nosed bats are often thought to be the most frightening of bats, since they are technologically the most advanced and the most deserving of admiration.

The last group of bats have responded to the moth-bat arms race by giving up the echolocation business altogether. Instead of emitting ultrasounds which tip off the moths of their presence, they reserve echolocation mainly for navigating around obstacles. These navigational signals are specially designed to be hard for insects to detect – they are of short duration, low intensity, and high frequency; in other words they are brief, quiet squeaks. These bats find their prey by listening for the tell tale flutter of a moth or scuttle of a beetle. Since this 'gleaning' requires very sensitive hearing, these bats often have very long ears. Although their faces look bizarre, people tend to react with amusement and curiosity, for long ears are more acceptable to humans than the long nose leaves of the echolocators.

Perhaps the most bizarre looking mammal is the wrinkle-faced bat which, surprisingly, feeds on fruit. The face of this bat is flattened and naked and, although it does have a small leaf nose, its face is also covered with an array of folds, flaps and wart like growths. And to cap it all it has a deep chin fold, a flap of skin which they sometimes pull over their faces when roosting – no one yet knows why they have this unusual feature.

Whilst researching this television series I contacted Merlyn Tuttle, one of the world's leading experts on bats. He is also a first class bat photographer, and for years has been promoting the good aspects of bats. One of the dilemmas we had in producing the series was how to show unsightly or loathsome animals in a fair, unbiased way. We wanted to tell the truth about the animals, be it good or bad. One of the animals we wanted to film was the vampire bat. Dr Tuttle was very helpful but rather sceptical about our goals, and he described the reaction he had from a picture he had taken of a pallid bat catching a scorpion . He had been delighted with the picture, and thought that it would enhance the bat's image, as here it was killing a creature reviled by man. But his picture produced an unexpected response. People were repulsed by it, and it merely reinforced their stereotyped impression of the bats – here was further photographic proof that bats were indeed loathsome creatures. Today, Merlyn Tuttle is careful to only take pictures of bats with their mouths closed so as not to alarm people further.

Echolocating is not the only way of seeing in the dark. A number of nocturnal creatures have developed other means of detecting prey, even in the dead of night. Common vampire bats may home in on their prey using echolocation and vision, but they then have to decide just where the best place is to bite their victim. For this they use heat sensors on their leaf noses to help them locate blood vessels lying close to the surface of the skin.

Infra red is used by a variety of creatures of the night. All snakes are sensitive to changes in temperature and to infra-red radiation. Some snakes, however, such as the bushmaster and rattlesnake, have developed this sensitivity into a powerful means of detecting prey, even in pitch darkness. On each side of the head, between the eye and the nostril, pit vipers have a cavity which is heat sensitive and allows them to locate prey in the dark. Until recently it was thought that this did not operate very accurately, and that it was only sensitive at close range, but recent research has shown that these pit receptors are represented spatially in the brain and the snake not only sees the image from its eyes but, superimposed on

A rat in infra-red – as it would appear to a hunting snake

that, an infra red image from the pits which allows it to strike with great precision. A pit viper such as a rattlesnake can register a change of temperature of a few thousandths of a degree centigrade allowing it to detect a mouse 30 cms away using body heat alone, or a larger object such as a person several metres away. Most pythons and boa constrictors also have heat sensitive pits, in fact they have a row of small pits along the edge of their mouths, but theirs have less than half the range of the pit vipers' pits.

In the absence of light, touch, and sensitivity to vibrations in the air or on surfaces have also become important means of finding one's way, capturing prey or escaping predators. Snakes are sensitive to vibrations of the ground, which they can feel through their scales. Tarantulas have hairs on their abdomens which are sensitive to vibration and which help them locate the movements of insects.

Some creatures have developed long antennae or appendages to help them feel their way around their environment in pitch darkness. Perhaps one of the most bizarre is the tailless whip scorpion, or amblypygid. Occurring in South America, and related to spiders and scorpions, amblypygids, or scorpion spiders as they are sometimes called, are flattened in shape so that they can creep into crevices in rocks, or underneath tree bark to escape predators. They have three pairs of long legs, but the fourth pair, the forelegs, are extensively elongated to act as antennae. The animal uses these to feel its way around and to locate prey such as crickets or cockroaches, which it then pounces upon and crushes with its huge spiny palps. For all its frightening appearance, amblypygids are not venomous and are harmless to man.

In extreme circumstances a cat can depend on its whiskers to tell it where it is

The whiskers on a cat's face are similarly of great importance to an animal that spends much of its life prowling around at night. A friend of mine once had a kitten that had been bitten in the head by their pet dog, when it had come between the dog and its dinner. The bite was serious, and the kitten lost the immediate use of one of its eyes. Over the next few weeks, it gradually lost the sight in its other eye, and became totally blind. By then the owner had become too attached to the cat, and the thought of having it put down was too much to bear, so the cat was allowed to live. When I visited my friend a few months later I was immediately struck by the very short whiskers the cat had – they were broken off and ragged. Then I watched spell bound as the cat walked around the room. Dee had been careful to leave all the furniture in exactly the same place. The cat walked across the room, gently brushed up against a table leg and came to the bottom of the sofa. It turned its head and looked up towards me with its blind eyes. Then with a spring it jumped onto the sofa – a perfect jump. It carried on across the sofa and up onto the mantle shelf where it weaved in and out of the vases and porcelain ornaments before coming to the edge of the shelf. Again it paused, looked down, wiggled its haunches in preparation to jump and leaped off the ledge, landing perfectly on the floor. I was stunned. How did the cat do this amazing feat? I just could not imagine doing the same thing were I blind!

Without its eyesight the cat relied a lot on its powers of hearing, often following behind someone, listening intently to their footsteps to gauge where they were going. However, the loss of its eyesight was made apparent when it tried to hunt. Out on the open lawn it would creep quietly forward, intent on a blackbird it could hear foraging on the ground somewhere in front of it. Here, in the open, the cat's whiskers were of no use to it, and its hearing not precise enough to locate the exact position of the bird. Still twenty five meters from the bird the cat crouched, ran and pounced. Still a long way ahead, the bird looked up quizzically at the cat, flew a short distance and carried on searching the lawn for worms. So nonchalant was the bird that it seems that from past experience it had become familiar with the strange behaviour of this particular cat!

Whiskers give an animal a sort of 'vision of touch'. Experiments at the University of Lausanne in Switzerland have shown that blindfolded house cats can walk around a cage littered with toys just as easily as cats that could see. The reason is that cats whiskers are so sensitive that they can detect minor changes in air currents moving around objects, allowing 'sightless' cats to avoid obstacles without even touching them.

Whiskers are very important to a cat hunting at night. When stalking they hold their whiskers straight out on either side of the face. As it pounces the cat brings its whiskers forward so that in the split second before catching its prey the whiskers come into contact with it and tell the cat the exact position of the animal. Once the prey has been caught the cat wraps its whiskers further forward around the prey so that it can detect the slightest twitch of the animal and warn it of it squirming free.

Cockroaches, who like cats, have a nocturnal lifestyle, also rely on specially adapted hairs to 'see' their environment. They have a barrage of minute hairs on their abdomens, which are sensitive to the smallest vibration in the air. At the least disturbance, they scuttle at great speed to the nearest hiding place, forcing themselves into cracks in walls, or any other small gap. This is the reason that one rarely sees cockroaches, even if they are present in the house in large numbers – they can sense your approach long before you reach the kitchen, so by the time you turn the light on, they are no where to be seen.

When I first visited India I was astounded by the cockroaches that teemed at Bombay airport. They flew in through the open window as big as 747s, and, immediately on landing, scuttled off. It was not just their size that astonished me, but the fact that they flew, something which I would have never seen before.

The cockroach is so common that it lives almost everywhere that we do – except for the polar regions. And it lives on just about anything – shoe polish, glue, wallpaper, ink, soap and plastics. If these are not available it can exist for up to three months on water alone. Perhaps the most remarkable thing about cockroaches is that they have been on earth, almost unchanged, for over 300 million years.

There are, altogether, probably about 3500 species of cockroach on earth, ranging in size from 5 mm to 9 cm. Only about 50 species have acquired the habit of living alongside human beings and, of these, only three are serious pests – the German, the Oriental and the American.

The German cockroach, which is called Russian by the Germans, and Prussian by the Russians, originated in North Africa, and came to England from Asia Minor and the Black Sea region in laundry baskets brought back during the Crimean War in the mid 19th century. It soon spread from there to North America. It is now common throughout South-east Asia and Australia. It prefers the warm, moist environments of kitchens and restaurants, and is the most common cockroach found in ships and aircraft. It is also the most prolific: one egg case has the potential of giving rise to up to 7 million adult cockroaches in 12 months.

The Oriental, or common cockroach prefers things cooler and tends to live in cellars. It followed the route of the German from North Africa. It spread to Spain and from there to Central and South America, but does not thrive in the tropics.

An American entomologist has written of the American cockroach: "Appropriately the American cockroach is altogether superior to the Oriental and German roaches in size, appearance and the ability to use its wings in flight". This is true but reflects no credit on America since the insect, like the other two, has a name which bears no relation to its origins. It came, in fact, from Central Africa and has spread throughout the humid tropics around the world.

We might admire the cockroaches for their tenacity, we might be disgusted by them for their appearance, but should we fear them? This – the degree to which they are responsible for disease – is a question on which much research is based, but the evidence against the cockroach is mounting. For many years we have come to accept them as an inevitable part of the catering industry – cockroaches will invade kitchens, and the attitude has developed that, so long as they are not actually served up to the diners, there is little that can, or needs to be done about them. Colonial housewives used to be reassured that their presence in the kitchen was not a sign of dirt – quite the reverse as cockroaches, according to the colonial old wives tales, prefer to live where the hygiene is good.

But that cockroaches can carry, and therefore transmit, pathogens, has now been proved beyond doubt. In hospitals they have access to a wide range of pathogens carried by humans, and pick them up from soiled dressings and eating sputum. The fact that a cockroach has these organisms in its gut and faeces does not mean, of course, that they have infected humans – quite the reverse. But since they tend to defecate as they eat, and produce copious amounts of saliva to soften their food, it is obvious that they must spread around the pathogens they have picked up. They can also pick up and transport bacteria on their legs and bodies which makes it possible to spread these to humans through contact with items of food. Practically all the bacteria involved in food poisoning has been found occurring naturally in cockroaches, and as these bacteria can often survive for ten days in the gut of a dead cockroach, the extermination of a population will not immediately stop the spread of infection.

All in all, cockroaches ought not to be welcome guests in our homes, hospitals or restaurants. They have survived electrocuting traps, insecticidal lacquers which they avoid, insecticidal sprays, to which they are resistant, and the whole armoury of an industry dedicated to the elimination of pests. They have 300 million years of adaptation behind them and are far more resistant than we are to radiation. They will, almost certainly, outlast us.

Although the 'guilt' or 'innocence' of the cockroach has yet to be fully established, there is one nocturnal creepy crawly which can certainly harm us, as many people have had the misfortune to discover. These creatures have modified legs just behind the head, which are claw-like, and equipped with venom. All centipedes are nocturnal, and live in damp places. Some live in perpetual darkness in caves. One group, the Scutigerids, are remarkable for having very long legs, and are extremely agile, the fastest being able to outpace a swiftly walking man. They are medium sized centipedes, and are found in all tropical countries, though the largest, which grow to about three inches long, occur in India and southern China.

The largest of all centipedes are the gigantic Scolopendra from the rain forests of Central and South America, which can measure almost a foot long. Centipedes are primarily carnivorous, feeding on flies, spiders, cockroaches and other invertebrates. The very largest Scolopendra will take small mice, toads, geckos and small birds.

All centipedes have poison glands for paralysing and killing prey. The bite is inflicted not by the jaws, but by the curved, horny claws of the front pair of legs which act as fangs. Although they are feared in many tropical regions, most centipedes are relatively harmless, and only a few can give a painful bite. The most dangerous are the large Scolopendras of the tropics, which can inject a large amount of venom.

The bite of the Scolopendra of Brazil produces intense pain, blistering, swelling and subcutaneous haemorrhage in humans. One species found in the Solomon Islands is said to have a bite so painful that it defies description, and in Malaysia bites produce symptoms more severe than those from indigenous viper bites. Although there have been a number of reported human fatalities by centipedes, most have not been verified. The only authentic case was a seven year old child in the Phillipines, who died 29 hours after being bitten in the head by a centipede. Fortunately, all centipedes will usually try to escape rather than fight,

A bite from some giant centipedes can easily kill a mouse

One of the last things you would want
to find in your bed

and even the large Scolopendra do not normally bite unless molested.

There are some animals, however, which actively seek out humans to attack. Around the world there are a group of flies whose maggots feed on flesh. They are the blow flies, which include the well known green bottles and blue bottles. In Africa, south of the Sahara, lives one of the most infamous of all – a blow fly whose larva is known as the Congo floor maggot. The adult, a yellowish-brown and black fly, is often associated with humans. The adult females lay their eggs on the sandy floors of native huts, and when the larvae hatch they bury themselves in the crevices and cracks in the ground. After dark, the maggots creep out of their hiding places and crawl over to people sleeping on the ground. They search for soft parts of their victims, especially the mucous membranes found around the mouth and the nose perhaps because the blood vessels here are very near the surface. The maggot then drives its sharp mouth parts and hooks into the victim, and begins to suck up blood. The bite is normally felt as a slight prick, and the maggot continues to feed for about twenty minutes. The maggot feeds once or twice a week, though it can survive many weeks without a blood meal. The mature maggot pupates in cracks on the surface of the soil and the adult fly appears two weeks later.

In some areas, like the Chaillu mountains of the Congo, large concentrations of blood filled larvae have been found under the matting where the Pygmies slept. Such large concentrations would cause considerable discomfort, though like bed bugs, their effects vary considerably depending upon the level of the infestation. Once thought to feed solely on human blood, the larvae have now been found to be common in antbear and warthog burrows in the Serengeti in the complete absence of man. At the beginning of the 20th century the Congo floor maggot was found throughout the French Congo, but today it is seldom encountered. It seems that improvements in the standard of living, such as cementing floors, and sleeping on beds rather than mats on the floor has helped reduce the problem, as the larvae are unable to climb vertical surfaces. The maggot may be an annoying pest, but it is slowly becoming less important to the lives of people living in the African interior.

Houses in Europe and America often provide an ideal home for unwanted occupants, too. If we suddenly return to a darkened kitchen in the dead of night, there is always the possibility of a sudden scuttling behind the furniture, and the vanishing view of the rear end of a house mouse. They have learned to live with – and off – humans so efficiently that, like cockroaches, they have spread all over the inhabited world, wherever food is available. Strangely, they are not completely dependent on us: they were found thriving in deserted houses on islands off the coast of Scotland over 80 years after the last islanders had left.

The house mouse is supremely adaptable. It can eat almost anything, and can even live without water if there is some moisture in the food. House mice have been found in bags of grain or flour, and many have spent their whole lives there. Others colonise the deep freeze units of meat wholesalers and live at constant temperatures below -9°C (15°F). Here they make nests from the cloth used for wrapping the meat, and often gnaw out holes in the frozen carcasses in which to build their nests. These mice tend to grow larger than others on a rich diet of fat and liver.

Mice are aggressive and territorial animals and have strong social hierarchies. The dominant ones can afford to stay in the holes by day and only emerge at dusk. The weaker ones are chased away from the feeding sites at night and so have to risk feeding before it is completely dark. They communicate with each other through a series of high pitched squeaks and whistles, which are mostly beyond the range of our ears. Although they have large eyes, house mice do not rely on them, but find their way about the house by following fixed and familiar routes marked by known objects. If you put a new piece of furniture along one of these routes, the mouse will explore it carefully, using its keen sense of smell and sensitive whiskers, before incorporating it into the mental map of its nightly journeys.

House mice are a nuisance rather than a threat to health, and the damage they inflict on sensitive householders is mainly emotional and psychological, although there is a risk to humans from bacteria in mice urine and faeces. They have a larger, far more deleterious cousin.

The rat eats a fifth of the world's crops each year; it carries a score of diseases which can infect and kill humans; yet as a laboratory animal, it has contributed

House mice eating cat food

more than any other to the progress of medical research.

Rats are the most destructive four-legged creatures on earth. For centuries humanity has waged a constant war against them. They have been trapped, set upon by trained dogs, caught in snares, sterilised, electrocuted, their burrows flooded, fired and fumigated – even assaulted by germ warfare. But they are still the most numerous and successful mammal on earth, with the possible exception of humans. Their resilience is astonishing. In response to our constant barrage of anticoagulant poisoning they have produced a population with an inherited genetic resistance. These so-called 'super rats' can withstand one hundred times the dosage that would kill a normal rat. After the testing of America's atomic arsenal on Engebi island, in the Eniwetok atoll of the western Pacific, the place was left deserted for years. Then a party of biologists made a research trip and found the reef fishes, the plant life and even the soil to be still radioactive. The island, which had been blasted with intense and lethal radiation was heavily populated with rats. Not maimed or genetically deformed, reported one member of the team, but robust rodents so in tune with their environment that their life spans were longer than average. These too are 'super rats'.

The most common species of rat throughout Europe and North America is the brown or Norwegian rat, rather unfairly so called because it spread from an area east of the Caspian sea on sailing ships in the 18th century, some of which came from Norway. They replaced the black rat which had been established in Europe for about 500 years, having arrived on the ships of the homecoming crusaders. The brown rat is larger and more aggressive than the black, and has largely taken over the land based territory, leaving to the black rat the holds of ships and the areas of docks and coastal towns. There is still a large population of black rats in the southern United States but, even there, they are steadily being replaced by the more prolific and destructive brown rats.

This is not, as it may seem, wholly a bad thing, because the black rat lives in close contact with people and is therefore a more efficient spreader of diseases. It has been held responsible for the Black Death outbreak of the plague in 17th century Europe which lasted for three years and left over 25 million dead. The plague bacillus is still with us and outbreaks can still occur in Africa, Asia and both Americas. There is a Federal Plague Centre at Fort Collins, Colorado, which monitors outbreaks and tests the fleas found on rats for the bacillus. Infected fleas have been detected in San Francisco, Denver and Tacoma, Washington and although prompt measures saved the day, it is still theoretically possible for other outbreaks to occur in western cities today.

The brown rat can make its home wherever food is available, and many cities contain as many rats as people. Often they go unnoticed because they are nocturnal animals and avoid people. They have a wide range of diet – meat, fish, fruit, grain, nuts, green plants, flower bulbs, eggs, cloth, even soap. Because the rat's incisors keep on growing throughout its life it needs to gnaw hard abrasive food to sharpen and wear them down. So rats will chew on lead pipes, sheet metal and concrete blocks and have caused outbreaks of fire through gnawing on the insulation of high voltage electric cables.

City rats have learned to keep off the streets where they may be picked off by dogs, cats, or the traffic. Adjacent high rise blocks of flats may contain populations of hundreds of rats, but there is usually little traffic between them. In lean times the weaker rats in a colony may be forced to migrate to another, but they are almost always rebuffed and die. The population of rats seems to rise to the level which the environment will support and then stabilise. Attempts at eradication have only a temporary effect on this. For example, a poisoning campaign will deplete a rat population for a time, but the reproductive powers are so great – a single pair can have 15,000 descendants in a year – that the numbers are quickly restored as soon as the poisoning ends. As one scientist put it: "Poisons or traps merely make space for more rats to grow".

The most sensible approach to reducing rat populations in our cities seems to be to cut back on the available food, water and shelter available to them. This 'environmental manipulation' offers the best hope of working out a system in which we can live alongside rats with the smallest degree of friction and the greatest understanding on our part.

In contrast to the urban West rat problem, the rural Asian problem is quite different. Each year they consume at least 48 million tons of rice – enough to feed 250 million people. In India they eat about a quarter of the total grain produced, and mass poisoning campaigns have not been effective. When shiploads of grain were landed from America, the rats ate them too, leading to complaints from US Senators that America's grain was being exported simply to feed India's rats. Part of the problem here is a reluctance to kill them based on a religious respect for life – most Hindus are vegetarians. If illness strikes a Hindu family, the wife will sometimes complain that her husband has been killing rats. And rats traditionally

bear the golden shrine of the elephant god, Ganesha, the symbol of prosperity. There is even a temple in Deshnoke, Rajasthan, where sculptured rats flank the image of the goddess Bhagwati Karniji and live rats are fed on the sanctuary floor with little bowls of sweets, grain and milk.

So the pest eradication officers have problems with tradition, but there are also traditional ways of helping them. The Irula tribe, which years ago had a great reputation as snake catchers and earned a living selling king cobras, rat snakes and other large serpents to the snakeskin industry, had to find other employment when the government banned the trade in the 1970s. So a few of them formed a Rat and Termite Squad (RATS) and they use their traditional skills to keep down the population of rats in the rice fields of Madras. They catch the rats by hand, reaching into the holes and hauling them out by the scruff of the neck. Then they hook the tails around the lower incisors and snap them off so the rats can't either bite or chew their way to freedom. Bags of live rats are then taken back to the villages to be barbecued or curried with rice. They even bring back their own rice, taken from the storage chambers of the rat burrows. The Irula rat catchers have impressed India's Department of Science and Technology with their skills and there is hope that, with their sponsorship, other villagers might take up this ecologically sound method of rat catching without the use of poisons, which destroys the community's pests at the same time as adding to its food supply.

Where the rat population booms in the rural parts of Asia, nights can be disturbed by their swarming over the rubbish tips, squeaking down the village streets and even crawling over sleeping people in their search for food. The darkness holds other, more immediate and more deadly perils. There is a lustrous black snake with paired white bands crossing its back, which grows to a little over

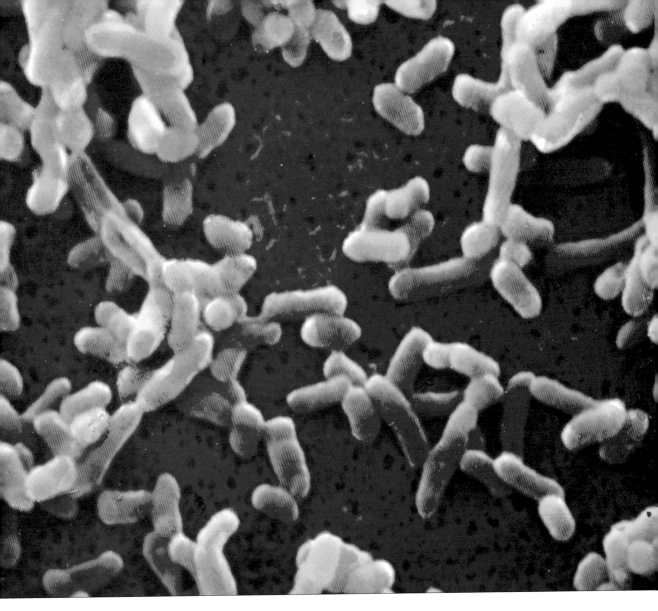

The bacteria that are carried by rats are far more dangerous than the rats themselves – the bacteria that causes Black Death (magnified 2,400 times)

a meter in length and is often found where humans live. It settles quietly and unnoticed in houses and, being nocturnal and of a placid temperament, can stay there for some time without being seen. This snake lives largely on a diet of other snakes and goes in search of them at night, investigating small spaces and burrows, and sometimes crawling into bedding. Any moving object which touches the snake's head as it is foraging triggers an automatic strike. A hand, arm, or leg that stirs as a person sleeps will be bitten.

The common krait is one of the most poisonous snakes in the world. Its venom is 15 times more virulent than the cobra's. The lethal dose for a man is the secretion equivalent of only 1 mg of dried poison. It operates on the blood and the nervous system. The symptoms are a fiery pain at the site of the bite which disappears after a time. Severe abdominal pain, probably due to internal haemorrhage, sets in later, followed by slow paralysis. The eyelids and lower lip droop, the victim cannot walk and eventually cannot breathe. Death follows from 5 to 12 hours after the bite. Often, there are no immediate symptoms, and the bite is ignored, with fatal consequences.

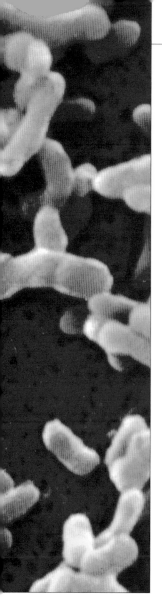

It is a strange fact that the most deadly of the terrors of the night may often disturb our sleep, but never enters our nightmares. A puff of breath will blow it away; a flick of the finger will put an end to it. Only the females can do us harm and yet they have been responsible for the deaths of half the people who have ever lived. Meet the mosquito. Its life history has a greater impact on mankind than that of any other living creature – and it is a fascinating story.

The high pitched whine that keeps us awake works as a mating call. Different species send out different tones. The males rarely fly unless a sound at the right frequency makes the fine hairs on its antennae vibrate in unison. Then a nervous impulse is sent to its brain, flying mechanisms are triggered, and it takes off and heads for the source of the sound. The females mate only once – usually on the wing and then they can lay batches of 100 or more eggs every week for several weeks. After each feed of blood they rest until the eggs develop and then find a laying site, usually on water.

The eggs are spindle-shaped and about two-thirds of a millimetre long. They can hatch only in water. The incubation period depends on the temperature, but in summer is usually only a few days. The larva is an odd-looking specimen: a swollen thorax and a cylindrical abdomen composed of nine distinct segments. Its head is equipped with two pigmented simple eyes and a mouth topped by a heavy moustache. This vibrates in the water and causes currents to flow past the mouth so that small organic particles such as protozoa, bacteria, algae, fungal spores, pollen become entangled in the bristles. From time to time a bolus of these small particles is passed into the mouth and swallowed. The larva breathes atmospheric air through a pair of spiracles or tiny openings in the eighth segment of its abdomen.

The larvae go through four moults of their outer skin as they increase in size. After the fourth moult they stop feeding. Then they enter the pupal stage when they are shaped rather like large commas. At this stage they have a flexible tail which allows them to dive with a series of spasmodic jerks as they somersault down to escape danger. They are eaten in their millions by fish, frogs, waterfowl and rival insects. The survivors, after only two days, swallow a huge gulp of air which enables it to swell and burst the pupal skin. A soft bodied and totally helpless adult emerges to rest in the sun until the cuticle is hardened, the wings expand and it can fly away.

The common krait is very dangerous

At this stage, of course, the mosquito is completely harmless. It is not born with virus or parasites in its body. It must first take a meal from an infected host animal and then live long enough for the organisms it has picked up to develop into an infective form which can be passed on to another host. This generally takes ten to fourteen days.

When the female is searching for a meal she has a battery of highly developed senses to help. She can detect carbon dioxide from a breathing mammal, as well as the warmer currents of air that flow from its body; she can pick up the faintest chemical traces of mouth and body odours – and it may well be the minute variations in the chemistry of skin secretions that cause some people to be bitten more than others. Recent research suggests that the anopheles mosquito – the species which transmits malaria – actively seeks out malaria carriers because the disease organisms make their blood easier to draw up.

The female mosquito can land on most parts of the body without a person becoming aware of it. Then it points a long proboscis down to the skin. The proboscis itself never pierces the skin but acts as a sheath for a set of finely pointed probes called stylets which sink through the skin. Then muscles in the mosquito's throat start a pumping action which draws up the blood; at the same time a tiny amount of saliva goes into the wound. This contains agents which delay clotting and make the blood flow more freely. It also often contains agents of disease.

The itching and swelling that follow a mosquito bite are not indications of disease, just a response to the saliva. Some people react strongly to this, and need antihistamine drugs as lotions,

The animal that indirectly kills the most people is the mosquito. The bite of some species transmits malaria. Many schemes have been tried to kill the adult or the larvae (*left*), but few have eradicated the problem

creams, or by mouth. The real danger is from a single cell which is called Plasmodium – the malarial parasite.

These protozoa pass into the blood of the victim, and then into the liver. They infect the liver cells in which they develop further for the next six to eleven days without causing symptoms. At this stage they are called schizonts.

When mature, the schizonts burst, releasing numerous tiny parasites called merozoites into the bloodstream. These penetrate the red blood cells and it is now that the first symptoms appear. The merozoites develop into ring shaped trophozoites which are the forms of the parasites that doctors can see through their microscopes and which confirm the disease.

The trophozoites grow inside the red blood cells until they burst, and release large numbers of tiny parasites into the bloodstream, each able to infect a new red blood cell. This release of parasites coincides with the fever. It takes two to three days for the newly infected blood cells to release yet more parasites, and this explains the intermittent character of malarial fever.

Some of the trophozoites develop into forms called gametocytes, which are capable of infecting mosquitoes. These are sucked up during a blood meal, and then develop inside the mosquito's stomach. Between seven and twenty days later, the infective forms of the parasite are present in the mosquito's salivary glands, and are ready to infect a new victim.

The incubation period of malaria, following a bite from an infected mosquito, is at least five to ten days. But it may be as much as a year before symptoms appear, especially if antimalarial drugs have been used. The main symptoms are fever, chills with sweating and headache, abdominal pains sometimes rapidly followed by jaundice, and coma. The severity of the symptoms depends on the number of parasites in the blood. Long term residents in malarial areas can develop a sort of immunity but visitors, and particularly children, often develop a severe and even fatal disease. About one million infants and children die from malaria each year in Africa alone.

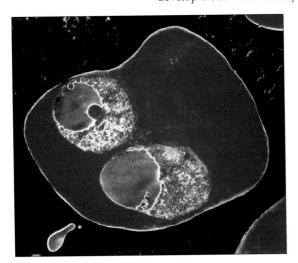

A human red blood cell harbouring two blue malarial cells

You do not have to travel to a tropical country these days to pick up malaria. Occasionally mosquitoes hitch a ride in a plane, jump off in Rome, Paris, Gatwick or New York and bite someone there. If the victim develops a fever, the local doctors do not, understandably, consider malaria as a possibility. People have developed malaria after transfusions from infected donors who may not be aware that they are carrying the disease. An elderly American died from malarial fever after surgery. His blood transfusion had included a unit from an African student who had lived in the USA for three years and was free of symptoms.

The battle against mosquitoes continues, but it is far from clear who is winning. Malaria is no longer a serious problem in Europe but, although it was socially and economically acceptable to drain the pontine marshes around Rome to keep down the mosquito population, similar measures cannot be taken in the Far East. Rice is the staple diet of most tropical countries and mosquitoes breed in the rice fields. More rice means more mosquitoes. The spraying of houses with residual insecticides seemed to be working for a time, but mosquito resistance to these insecticides is growing. The arms race continues.

As we have seen, our fears are not always based upon animals that are dangerous or that cause us any harm. Distanced as we are in the West from the land and a rural way of life, the truths about the animals that inhabit the planet are conveyed to us by the media and seldom by first hand experience. Often what we see and read is what we are fed, simply to sell publications, or increase audiences for the cinema or televisions. From everywhere catchy headlines scream out at us, often imparting misinformation, reinforcing misconceptions, and masking the facts.

Many of the worst of our nightmares of nature are due to our ignorance; conversely, there are dangers in the natural world that we need to inform ourselves about when we venture into areas where we do not have total control.

My attitude towards animals certainly changes the more I have to do with them. The more I know the less I fear and I am sure that that is something that affects most people. On her first trip to the Masai Mara to film lions, my colleague, Samantha Purdy, was extremely anxious about lions. On that trip three lionesses stalked directly towards our car. Having removed the car door and replaced it with a mount for the camera, I was filming them from what must have looked like a very open and vulnerable position. It was something I would have experienced many times before, but Samantha, sitting behind me was terrified. As the lions got to within a few meters of the car she suddenly shifted position, wobbling the car and ruining the shot. At the time I was livid, but I soon realised that it was only natural she should be scared. She knew very little about lions, their behaviour and what to expect on a filming trip. Within weeks, however, she had learned a lot about lions and had had her worst fears allayed. Today, because of her experience and knowledge of lions, she is the first person I would choose to go filming big cats with.

The fears that have become instinctive to us over the long period of human evolution have served us well as protective devices in the past. If controlled they will serve us well in the future. All too often we fail to appreciate the very real danger that the environment itself can present. We are frail creatures with little capacity for survival without artificial aids. Exposure from the cold or heat, dehydration and drowning are dangers all too often ignored, with dire consequences. Our fears of unknown or unfamiliar creatures need to be put in perspective, and tempered today by an awareness of man's biggest killers which are all products of our own way of life: motor cars and heart disease. So recent are these killers that we have had no time to evolve to fear them. Since the advances in medical science mean that we may well be able to combat heart disease in the near future, and since the world's oil reserves are finite, we may not have time to develop an innate fear to these threats, before they disappear from our world for ever.

Picture Credits

Key: t - top; b - bottom; l - left; r - right; tl - top left; tr - top right; bl - bottom left; br - bottom right

Page 4 Wild Images (Tim Martin); **5**(1) NHPA (Patrick Fagot); **5**(2) Auscape (Ferrero-Labat); **5**(3) Bruce Coleman (Carl Roessler); **5**(4) NHPA (Daniel Heuclin); **5**(5) NHPA (Karl Switak); **5**(6) M. Brock Fenton; **8** Bruce Coleman (Norman Tomalin); **9** Reflections (Jennie Woodcock); **10-11** Michael and Patricia Fogden; **12-13** Allstock (Art Wolfe); **14** Bruce Coleman (Jane Burton); **15** Nature Photographers (E. A. Janes); **16** Planet Earth (Jonathan Scott); **17** Wild Images (Richard Matthews); **18** Mary Evans Picture Library; **19** DRK Photo (Stephen Krasemann); **20-21** Bruce Coleman (Erwin and Peggy Bauer); **21**(l) Planet Earth (Thomas Dressler), (r) Planet Earth (Purdy and Matthews); **22-23** Auscape (Jean-Michel Labat); **24** DRK Photo (Stephen Krasemann); **25** FLPA (Mark Newman); **26** DRK Photo (Stanley Breeden); **29**(t) Wild Images (Tim Martin), (bl, br) Dr P. Kumar; **31** Dr. P. Kumar; **32** Allstock (Tim Davis); **33**(t) Werner Forman Archive (Museum of Anthropology, University of British Columbia, Vancouver), (b) Hulton-Deutsch Collection; **34-35, 36-37** Bruce Coleman (Erwin and Peggy Bauer); **37**(l) Oxford Scientific Films (Michael Leach), (r) DRK Photo (Wayne Lynch); **39** Oxford Scientific Films (Daniel J. Cox); **41** Mary Evans Picture Library; **43** Allstock (René Lynn); **44-45**(t) Wild Images (Richard Matthews), (b) Planet Earth (K. and K. Amman); **45** Ardea (Joanna van Gruisen); **47** Wild Images (Richard Matthews); **49** Bruce Coleman (Mark Boulton); **50-51** Planet Earth (Jonathan Scott); **53** Allstock (Tim Davis); **54** NHPA (Peter Johnson); **55** Wild Images (Richard Matthews); **56-57** Oxford Scientific Films (Belinda Wright); **58** Oxford Scientific Films (James Robinson); **61** Auscape (Ferrero-Labat); **62-63** Auscape (Labat-Ferrero); **63**(b) NHPA (Eric Soder); **64** Auscape (Kevin Deacon); **65** Mary Evans Picture Library; **66**(t) Range/UPI/Bettmann, (b) Ardea (Ron and Valerie Taylor); **67** Planet Earth (Doug Perrine); **68** Oxford Scientific Films (G. I. Bernard); **70** Science Photo Library (Tom van Sant/Geosphere Project, Santa Monica); **71** Planet Earth (Norbert Wu); **72**(t) Planet Earth (Gary Bell), (b) Norbert Wu; **73** Planet Earth (Doug Perrine); **74** Bruce Coleman (Charles and Sandra Hood); **75** Norbert Wu; **76-77** Planet Earth (Marty Snyderman); **79**(t) Wild Images (Adrian Warren), (b) Bruce Coleman (Dieter and Mary Plage); **81** Ardea (Ron and Valerie Taylor); **84**(t, bl) Ardea (Ron and Valerie Taylor), (br) Pacific Stock (Dave Fleetham); **86** Planet Earth (F. J. Jackson); **87** Wild Images (Richard Matthews); **89** Range Pictures; **90**(l) Norbert Wu, (r) Oxford Scientific Films (Howard Hall); **91** Scott Polar Research Institute; **92** Norbert Wu; **93**(t, b) NHPA (Norbert Wu); **94-95** Auscape (D. Parer and E. Parer-Cook); **96** Wild Images (Tim Martin); **97** Planet Earth (Gary Bell); **98**(l) Norbert Wu, (r) Bruce Coleman (Charles and Sandra Hood); **99** Auscape (Alby Ziebell); **100** Bruce Coleman (Michael Glover); **101**(t) Planet Earth (Mark Conlin), (b) NHPA (Peter Parks); **102**(l) Auscape (Ben Cropp), (r) Norbert Wu Photography (Ben Cropp); **103** NHPA (Anthony Bannister); **104**(t) Natural Science Photos (Hal Beral), (b) Ardea (Valerie Taylor); **105** Oxford Scientific Films (Peter Parks); **106**(t) Peter Scoones, (b) Oxford Scientific Films (Fredrik Ehrenstrom); **106-107** Georgette Douwma; **108-109** Planet Earth (Christian Petron); **110-111** Natural Science Photos (Ken Hoppen); **114**(t) Michael and Patricia Fogden, (b) Georgette Douwma; **116** NHPA (G. I. Bernard); **118-119** Robert Harding; **120** Wild Images (Adrian Warren); **122-123** NHPA (James Carmichael Jr); **124-125** Michael and Patricia Fogden; **125** Wild Images (Tim Martin); **126** Allstock (Tom McHugh); **127** Bruce Coleman (Austin James Steven); **129, 131** NHPA (Anthony Bannister); **132-133** NHPA (Daniel Heuclin); **134** NHPA (J. Weigel); **137** Wild Images (Adrian Warren); **138, 139** Wild Images (Tim Martin); **140-141** Auscape (Kathie Atkinson); **141** Robert Harding (Adam Woolfitt); **143** NHPA (Daniel Heuclin); **144, 146** Wild Images (Tim Martin); **147** FLPA (Chris Mattison); **148-149** Wild Images (Richard Matthews); **150** Wild Images (Adrian Warren); **151** Wild Images (Richard Matthews); **153** NHPA (Martin Wendler); **154** Wild Images (Adrian Warren); **155** Allstock (Clayton A. Fogle); **157** Planet Earth (Paul Stevens); **159**(l, r) Oxford Scientific Films (Jeff Foott, Survival Anglia); **160** Oxford Scientific Films (Joaquin Gutierrez Acha); **161** Bruce Coleman (Austin James Steven); **162, 163** Wild Images (Tim Martin); **164** Wild Images (Adrian Warren); **166** NHPA (Karl Switak); **168**(t) Mantis Wildlife Films (Jim Frazier), (b) Wild Images (Richard Matthews); **170** Mary Evans Picture Library; **171** Mantis Wildlife Films (Jim Frazier); **172** Wild Images (Tim Martin); **173** Planet Earth (Mary Clay); **174**(t) Planet Earth (David P. Maitland), (b) Oxford Scientific Films (James H. Robinson); **176** Natural Science Photos (J. A. Grant); **178** Michael and Patricia Fogden; **180** Oxford Scientific Films (J. A. L. Cooke); **181** Robert Harding (Julia Bayne); **183** Bruce Coleman (Waina Cheng Ward); **184**(t) Ardea (P. Morris), (b) Planet Earth (Hans Christian Heap); **186** Oxford Scientific Films (Kathie Atkinson); **187**(t) Bruce Coleman (C. B. and D. W. Frith), (b) Bruce Coleman (Kim Taylor); **188** Oxford Scientific Films (G. I. Bernard); **189** Neil Bromhall; **190-191** Bruce Coleman (Peter Ward); **193** Bruce Coleman (Kim Taylor); **194, 195** Bernard Stone; **196**(l) Michael and Patricia Fogden, (r) Oxford Scientific Films (Raymond A. Mendez, Animals Animals); **197** Wild Images (Tim Martin); **200** DRK Photo (Stephen Krasemann); **200-201** Bruce Coleman (Peter Davey); **201**(b) Ardea (Douglas W. Napier); **202** NHPA (G. I. Bernard); **203**(t, b) Wild Images (Tim Martin); **204** Oxford Scientific Films (Scott Camazine); **206-207** Bruce Coleman (Kim Taylor); **208** Ardea (Peter Steyn); **208-209** Oxford Scientific Films (John Mitchell, Photo Researchers); **209**(t) NHPA (Anthony Bannister), (bl) Bruce Coleman (C. B. Frith), (br) Tim Martin; **210** Bruce Coleman (Gunter Ziesler); **212** Wild Images (Tim Martin); **213**(t) Ardea (Jean-Paul Ferrero), (b) NHPA (ANT); **215**(t) Wild Images (Tim Martin), (b) Michael and Patricia Fogden; **216** NHPA (Silvestris Fotoservice); **217** Oxford Scientific Films (Ron Austing, Photo Researchers); **219** FLPA (F. Pölking); **220-221** DRK Photo (Jeremy Woodhouse); **224** Ardea (Adrian Warren); **224-225** FLPA (E. and D. Hosking); **225**(b) Bruce Coleman (Kim Taylor); **227** Oxford Scientific Films (Stephen Dalton); **229** Ardea (Pat Morris); **231** NHPA (Stephen Dalton); **232** M. Brock Fenton; **233**(tl) M. Brock Fenton, (tr) Ardea (Eric Lindgren), (bl) Planet Earth (Norbert Wu), (br) Ardea (Pat Morris); **235** Planet Earth (John Downer); **236** Ardea (Jean-Paul Ferrero); **239, 240** Wild Images (Tim Martin); **242** Bruce Coleman (Jane Burton); **244** Oxford Scientific Films (Tony and Liz Bomford, Survival Anglia); **245** Planet Earth (John Downer); **246-247** Science Photo Library (CNRI); **247** Ardea (Jean-Paul Ferrero); **248**(l) Ardea (Pat Morris), (r) Auscape (Kathie Atkinson); **248-249** Oxford Scientific Films (G. I. Bernard); **250** Science Photo Library (CNRI).

Television Production Team

SERIES PRODUCER
Richard Matthews

PRODUCERS
Mary Colwell
Martin Hughes-Games
Adrian Warren

RESEARCHERS
Jan Castle
Tim Martin
Honor Peters

PRODUCTION TEAM
Corinna Gallop
Sophie Cole
Mandy Gittings
Sarah Payne
Jo Stocker

PRODUCTION SUPERVISOR
Peter Jones

POST PRODUCTION CO-ORDINATOR
Nigel Ashcroft

GRAPHIC DESIGNERS
4:2:2. Videographic Design

DUBBING MIXER
Graham Wild

DUBBING EDITOR
James Mather

MAIN CAMERAMEN
Richard Ganniclifft
Richard Matthews
Mark Payne-Gill

ADDITIONAL CAMERAMEN
Neil Bromhall
Rolf Czabayski
Mike DeGruy
Martin Dohrn
Steve Downer
Geoff Gartside
Mike Herd
Rodger Jackman
Martin Phillips
Mike Pitts
Bruce Reitherman
Peter Scoones
Philip Sharpe
Keith Taylor
Keith Turner
Simon Wagen
John Waters

SOUND RECORDISTS
Lyndon Bird
John Storrer
Dennis Towns
Mark van der Willingen

FILM EDITORS
Will Ennals
Jill Garrett
David McCormick
Sue Outlaw

ASSISTANT EDITORS
Stuart Davies
Darren Flaxstone
Susanne Parker
Dan Rees

MUSIC
The Insects

Index